Shopping List

A Horror Anthology

HellBound Books Publishing LLC

A HellBound Books LLC
Publication

Printed in the United States of America

Shopping List

Compiled and Edited by Mitch Workman

A HellBound Books Publishing LLC Book
Houston TX

Dedicated to each and every one of the phenomenal authors, the nightmares of whom are captured within these very pages, creative talents who have entrusted us with the product of their blood, sweat and tears – we hope we have done you proud.

Foreword

A massive, monster *thanks,* Dear Reader, from everyone here at HellBound Books Publishing for choosing our superlative anthology for your delectation – we are all incredibly proud of 'Shopping List', and hope that you love our baby as much as we do!

We decided upon the shopping list theme for this particular volume as an antithesis to those wildly successful writers (they know who they are) of whom it is often said *'we would read their damned shopping list if they published it!'.*

Well, we have given twenty-one of the hottest authors in the independent horror scene the opportunity to have their shopping lists read by you, our Dear Reader!

And what a fascinating exercise in voyeurism it is, an absolute *must* for those of us who love to peer over at the conveyor belt in the grocery store to see what our fellow shoppers have bought, and gain a candid insight into their everyday lives when they are at their most vulnerable.

So, here you have it, a sneaky glimpse into the 'day lives of the creators of wonderfully dark and tales, along with the hope that they are simply people and not terrifying monsters like the slithering and murderous things that they vividly in prose.

also note, as you dare yourself to venture ward into the darkness and terror within some of our tales are writing in 'British is, we make no apologies, we have the Brit' syntax and spelling because zed those stories would have been to spoil their wonderful uniqueness – and the Brits did *invent* the language, after all.

Now, it's on to the main event, those twenty-one gut-wrenching, heart-stopping yarns that you have parted with your hard-earned to enjoy – and enjoy them you will….

HellBound Books Publishing LLC

Contents

Shopping List

Robert Over's Shopping List

1 lb Ground beef
Celery
Peppers
Vidalia Onion
Cilantro
Black beans
Chili Powder
Wasabi
Laundry detergent
Bleach
Beer
Cookie dough ice cream

Coach Augustine: Smoke and Claws

Robert Over

I flung myself over a fallen log as something howled behind me. The beast was near. The hairs on the back of my neck prickled and I sped up, weaving around trees and ducking under low hanging branches. I heard hot breath at my heels and smelled the fetid stench of decaying meat that came with it. I slid down an embankment, wet leaves clinging to my feverish skin. At the bottom, I jumped to my feet and started scrambling up the other side, but something had changed. The sound of heavy eager breathing and the rusty scent of dried blood was gone. Had the beast vanished? I pulled myself up the last few feet and turned around, searching for yellow eyes in the night. The forest was empty and the only sound was my frantic heart hammering in my chest. I turned around, ready to continue my break for freedom when an immense black shadow leapt at me. I stood there, my heart stopping as yellow eyes and sharp teeth sailed towards me, death reaching out to swallow me whole.

A blaring angry beeping sound filled my head and I nearly fell out of my bed and onto the floor as I came back to reality. Instinctively, I reached out and hit the clock on the side table a with a free hand. The beeping continued, echoing through my small bedroom like some confused song bird. A dream, just a dream.

I looked up at the window across from my bed and saw the sky outside was still dark. The night sky in Worcester is never fully black due to the massive amounts of light pollution, but there was no way it was dawn yet.

I grabbed my offending phone, slid a finger across the cover to still the incessant beeping and lifted it to my ear, "Hello?" I said.

"Coach, you gotta help me. I feel like my head's splitting open."

"What? Wait a minute." I shook my head trying to clear my sleep fuzzed thoughts. "Is that you Brady?"

Brady is a student of mine. I'm a soccer coach for Garret Hawthorne High School Just north of Boylston in Greene. Brady however, doesn't play soccer, he's strictly a football man. I don't tutor him in either of those activities. Instead I teach him how to hunt, how to fight the powers of darkness and how to cope with being a werewolf.

"Coach, do you know how to stop it? Can you, I dunno, make it go away?" Brady said.

"Tell me what's happening, Brady," I said. "Nothing's gonna happen to you, I promise."

I looked at the screen on the phone again, checking the time: 2:43 am, and then the date, two weeks until the full moon. He couldn't be turning, it was way too early. Sometimes in early adolescence, werewolves morph uncontrollably, shifting from human to wolf back and forth, usually in dreams. Brady was beyond those days, though.

"What's up, Brady? Are you turning what's going on?" I asked.

"Can you help me or not?" Brady said, slamming his fist against something. "I just, I can't think and ... Oh crap." I heard the sound of glass shattering.

"Hold on Brady," I said. "Hold it together for a little while longer and I'll come find you, ok?"

Brady muttered something unintelligible.

With one hand, I pulled my jeans on while the other hand pressed the phone to my ear. "Where are you?" I asked.

"Franny's house," said Brady. "Oh man. Her parents don't even know I'm here. Oh shit oh shit oh shit."

I tried to buckle my belt as I waddled across my pitch-black room, but it kept slipping out of my fingers. "Where does Franny live, Brady?" I asked. "I need to know where you are."

"On Flagg Street, number 95," said Brady. "Oh god it hurts, Tom. IT FUCKING HURTS!" Brady let out a yelp of pain and then I heard a cracking sound before the line went dead.

"Hurts, Brady what do you mean it hurts? Are you ok?" asked, knowing I was talking into a dead line but unable to stop myself. After what people in my line of business call growing pains, a werewolf's turn shouldn't cause him a lot of pain. Brady himself referred to it as the equivalent of doing thirty dead lifts in about ten seconds. It's pain of a kind, but more like exercise.

I hit the bedroom light and immediately regretted it as light dove into my skull and played merry hell with my brain. This wasn't the first time I had been rousted out of bed before daybreak to deal with supernatural insanity, but it never got any easier. I pulled a shirt over my sweaty skin and tried not to smell the fear sweat that permeated the room. That had been one hell of a dream.

I grabbed my gym bag from under the bed and redialed Brady's phone number. Predictably, he didn't pick up. Either his phone had died as the magic around him stirred to life, or he decided to stop answering just to increase the drama. I opened the front door to my apartment with a free finger and ran out to my car, laces flapping in the breeze.

My gym bag might seem like an odd choice of gear to bring with me when planning to tangle with a moody teenage werewolf, but it holds a couple of items not normally found with your average coach gear. In addition to a change of clothes, running shoes, and a few devices of torture marketed as muscle tension relievers, I kept a tackle box way at the bottom of the bag filled with wonders no one from the normal world would believe or understand.

I slid into my dented, scratched, and well-loved Honda, smelling the familiar scent of the cracked leather seats, ancient fried food smells and the Fresh Mint air freshener. I dropped the bag on the passenger seat and burned rubber as I swerved onto the street. Sometimes I wonder if the designers who built Worcester's streets hated people, because they seem to have exclusively made planning decisions that cause accidents, destroy bumpers, and confuse newcomers. As I pulled out, my rear bumper hit the raised sidewalk and made a screeching sound as it did the bump and grind with a patch of cracked asphalt. I cursed, praying the damned thing wouldn't fall off and held my breath as I pulled onto the road.

I redialed Brady's phone again and again as I drove, but he didn't respond. Unfortunately, complex electronics tend to malfunction around magical phenomena. I am not a werewolf or a wizard or any other supremely magical being so whatever magic I possess deals little to no damage to my personal electronics, which is good because being a high school coach doesn't pay well enough for me to replace an iPhone as often as Brady goes through his.

When I finally pulled onto Flagg street I slowed down and began sliding down the road searching for Brady's bright yellow Mustang. I found it parked behind a grungy looking pickup in the driveway of a crumbling Victorian. All the windows were dark and no one was screaming so that was a good sign. I drove down the road a little further and parked in front of a nearly identical building. With any luck, I would be able to figure out what was going on, fix it and be on my way before someone called the police about a mysterious car parked outside their house.

I slunk back to Franny's house and nearly ran into a slim dark figure wearing a grey sweatshirt and checkered pyjama pants.

"Who the fuck are you?" said the newcomer.

I squinted into the startled face and saw a latino girl about the same age as Brady. She had a heart shaped face, bloodshot eyes and her clothes stank of burnt compost.

"Are you Franny?" I asked.

"Franchesca, You the coach?" asked Franny.

"Yup," I said. "Where's Brady?"

"I dunno, he ran out of here about twenty minutes ago," Said Franny. "Why would he call you anyway, aren't you just his coach?" Her lips were pressed into a thin line and I could sense that her jaw was clenched under the shadow of what had to be Brady's sweater.

"Yea, I'm his coach," I said, not quite sure where to go with this. Franny didn't seem like she wanted me here even though Brady was obviously in trouble. "Do you … know about Brady?"

Franny gave me a scornful look. "The fuck is that supposed to mean?"

Oh boy, it looked like I was skating on thin ice with this woman already. "Oh boy," I said. "Look this is gonna sound crazy, but Brady is a …" I paused. How was I supposed to just say it?

"A WHAT?" she asked, glaring at me with eyes that could cut through steel.

"A werewolf," I snapped. Didn't she realize he was in danger? My own voice echoed back from the quiet buildings around us. I really shouldn't have said it that loud.

Franny's attitude changed, she had looked like she was standing up to authority, ready to hold back anyone who fucked with her, but when I told her about Brady, the defiance went out of her in an instant. Her arms came up from where she had crossed them in front of her and she put her face in them. "Oh god," she muttered, and I could hear quiet sobbing sounds coming from her.

She believed. The moment I met this girl, I thought I would have to deal with her disbelief on top of Brady's situation. Thank god I didn't have to try and persuade her that her boyfriend had stepped out of a horror movie before she was willing to help me. "What happened Franny? Where did Brady go?" I asked.

"He ran off down the street," said Franny in a small voice. I had pegged her at 16 or 17 when I met her but her voice made her sound about 10 when she said that. I tear track ran down her cheek and she angrily brushed it away.

"Alright. Do your folks know what happened tonight?" I asked.

Franny looked at me like I had asked her if you had to wear pants in public. "You kidding? God no. They're away tonight," she said.

I sighed in relief and unzipped my bag. I began to rummage through the rickrack in there until I found the tackle box. I popped the latch and pulled out a tiny vial about the length of my thumbnail. This was not going to be fun. I squared my shoulders and snorted the green murky liquid in the vial all at once. Fire raced up my nostril and bloomed in my sinuses. With it came the stench of burning rubber, the scent of old banana peels and then the rest of the scents from the world, heightened to unbelievable levels.

I turned to see Franny looking at me as if I had totally lost it.

"It's—" I paused to sneeze, "A tracking potion. Don't look at me like that. You can't tell me you accept werewolves and not magic." I shook my head and tried to fight my way through the pain. There had to be a better way to make this shit than using wasabi as one of the base ingredients. "I'll be able to follow Brady's scent with this, it gives me the scent tracking abilities of a dog. But damn does it sting." I sneezed two more times.

"Maybe I was wrong," said Franny. "Maybe I should call the police."

I looked over at her, smelling the thick clawing odor of her fear under the mixed scents of burnt marijuana and lilac from her perfume. "What are you crazy?" I asked. "Do you want Brady to get shot tonight?"

She stood there for a second, her face going from resentful to confused and then to worried. That was probably a better state to be in I judged. Franny shook her head. "I can't believe I'm doing this," she said.

"C'mon then, he headed this way. Do you know if there's a park or something near by?" I asked as I strode off down the street following a heady scent of mingled man and wolf. I looked back at her, my eyebrows raised.

She rolled her eyes and said. "There's empty land behind those houses," indicating a row of dark houses to our right.

Brady's trail veered sharply to the right a few hundred feet down the street, right in the direction Franny had indicated. I followed it and found a line of disgruntled flowers down the side of a dark house. I pushed aside a hydrangea that was missing number of leaves and found a footprint in the soft mulch underneath. I let my breath out and strode in after Brady.

At the edge of the woods, Franny stepped on a dry twig. The sound of snapping wood was like a gunshot in the calm night air. I froze. If the werewolf found us sneaking up behind him, he would probably tear out our intestines and ask questions later.

"Move very slowly and don't make a noise," I whispered.

Franny sneered at me and mouthed my own words back at me.

I closed my eyes, gritted my teeth, and strode into the woods, letting my nose guide me. The potion made my sense of smell like a second sight. I knew where the trees, bushes and hidden pitfalls were all around me even with my eyes closed. Each of them had their own unique odor, everything from the dew lining the grass to the elephant ear mushrooms growing out of a fallen log off to my left.

I could hear Franny behind me, sounding like an elephant charging joyously across a mountain of light bulbs. Worse than that, I could smell her. I knew I smelled of sweat, fear, and bad dreams, but Franny was terrified and on top of her fear was the marijuana. If Brady smelled her, he would do one of two things. Either charge deeper into the forest to keep from hurting her or, worse, start hunting her.

The deeper we went into the woods, the stronger the wet dog smell got. After a few minutes, it was almost a physical presence that got into my mouth and nose and hung in the back of my mouth on every breath. I stopped and stood still taking in a giant breath of air, trying to smell more than Brady's scent. I smelled pollen coating the leaves and branches of almost every tree around me, wood smoke clinging to the air a few blocks down, and the unmistakable odor of blood. The creature had made a kill.

Franny stopped right behind me and shot furtive glances around us. "Is he here?" she asked in a whisper.

"Close," I said and put my forefinger to my lips.

I stopped when the odor of blood was so strong I could actually taste it. I looked down and found a splash of maroon dappling a patch of grass near the base of a birch tree. Franny and I crouched down to look at it. There were little strands of hair caught on the grass and I peered close to get a better look.

"Brady? Is that you?"

I stood up quickly my head snapping to the same direction Franny was looking. Brady was sitting with his back to a tree a few feet away from us, his head bowed over his naked torso. Franny started forwards but I grabbed her shoulder and held her back.

"Let go of me, pendejo," she said, trying to tug her arm free.

Brady turned his head to look up at us. His eyes were wide and shocked and something dark was smeared across his mouth in thick strokes. Cutting through what must be blood, were tear tracks making clean lines down his face. It looked like he was wearing inverted war paint.

When his eyes met mine, they turned yellow and my heart started pounding like an engine in my chest. I dropped my eyes to his mouth and started making calming noises. It is never a good idea to look directly into a werewolf's eyes, they view it as a challenge.

"Brady I'm here to help you," I said.

"What the hell are you doing here?" said Brady.

"You called me, Brady," I said. This was going to be more difficult that I thought.

"NOT YOU." Bellowed Brady. "Franny, go home. It's not safe."

"You just ran off. Why'd you do that to me?" Asked Franny. "And what the fuck happened to you? Are you okay?" Franny tried to shake her arm out of my grasp again. "Get offa me."

"Franny, I'm not safe. Don't you get it?" Said Brady putting his hands to his head. He looked at me again, his upper lip pulling back to reveal teeth that seemed a little too sharp. Before I could react, he launched towards us, grabbed both of my shoulders and shoved me up against a tree. "GET RID OF IT," he said. "Get this monster out of me."

"I… I can't do that Brady." I said, trying to break his grip. His hands were quickly cutting off the circulation to my forearms.

He bared his teeth and I could see his canines were much longer than those of a normal human. A patch of hair popped out on his right cheekbone and in a couple of seconds became rich and dark. I could smell saliva and fresh blood on his breath along with the ghost of the pot he smoked with Franny.

"WHAT FUCKING GOOD ARE YOU?" Yelled Brady.

"Take it easy Brady," I said. "You need to get control of your emotions before they take over."

"All of those practice sessions, all of those lessons drilling it into me over and over again to never hurt anyone, and you never did what I really wanted." His words were getting less and less intelligible as his voice got more guttural.

"No one can cure you," I shouted. "Why can't you get that through your thick skull kid? This is who you are. You can't ignore it and expect it to just go away."

His fingers dug trenches in my skin and veins popped out on his forehead. Almost as an afterthought, he threw me to the ground and turned away. I hit the earth with enough force to knock the wind out of me.

The moment Brady let go of me, he turned. I watched as he fell to his hands and knees and black fur raced across his skin like a black rash. In a couple of seconds an enormous black wolf stood where brady had been. I could see the same abnormally shiny yellow eyes partially hidden by folds of dark fur.

Brady pulled back his lips and began growling at me. The sound paired with those prehistoric looking teeth made my stomach drop a few feet. He hunched down, his back legs tightening as he readied to spring at me.

All the while Franny was standing a few feet away, her mouth wide open and her eyes as big as saucers.

I glanced from Brady to a large branch a foot or so away from me and, in that moment, he struck. I grabbed hold of the branch and brought it back across my chest in a sweeping arc. It was about three feet long and as wide as my forearm. Someone must have been doing some wood cutting out here recently because it was still heavy with water.

The branch smacked hard against Brady's muzzle and his head turned to the side as the rest of his body kept going. I sprang to my knees and went into a baseball batter's stance.

"Wanna play tag? Is that it, boy?" I asked him.

Brady started padding a circle around me and I responded by keeping my pace in the opposite direction.

"Oh, wait a minute. You want the stick, don't you? You wanna play fetch?" I asked.

Brady let out another burbling growl and pulled his lips back even further, giving me a better view of his fangs.

"Who's a good little puppy?" I asked. Normally, provoking a werewolf in the middle of his turn is a good way to end up dinner, but this was his second turn tonight. He had to run out of energy soon.

Brady leaped at me but I dodged to the side, missing his snapping jaws by a couple of inches. I wound up, keeping myself between Brady and Franny, and swung the tree limb to knock his hind legs out from under him. Brady hit the ground, rolled, and stood again.

He growled, his fangs pure white in the dark woods, and launched at me a third time. Now I had my rhythm going and I twisted to the side again, dealing the werewolf another hard smack to his midsection. I held back, not wanting to seriously injure him, but Brady landed in the bushes. We kept at it, Brady charging at me as he got angrier and angrier and me dodging him and brushing him off with the tree limb. After about five minutes of taunting and abuse, Brady was panting hard as he got back up.

This time when he jumped at me, I took a step back and my leg caught on a branch. I fell to the ground with Brady on top of me, wedging the branch between his teeth. At the same time, I brought my knee up into

Brady's nuts, always the best way to immobilize any guy.

The wolf let out a high-pitched yelp and collapsed on top of me. I pulled his face up to mine so that I could look directly into one yellow eye.

"Enough Brady," I shouted. "You need to regain control or you really will kill someone."

Brady's eye narrowed and I could see fury building in that sullen gaze again.

"STOP IT!" I commanded, filling my voice with all the anger I felt for being put through this at 3am before a work day. "Do you want to hurt Franny?"

Brady's eyes widened and I felt his grip on the branch loosen a little.

I pressed my advantage. "Do you care about her? Do you? What if I wasn't here? Would you have killed her by now? Do you think you'd be snacking on her corpse?"

Brady drew away from me.

"If you don't gain some control over yourself, you'll end up dead, or worse hurting the people you care about," I said.

The wolf shivered and a naked boy was lying on the ground next to me, all of his fury and anger gone, replaced with fear and self-loathing. Brady sat on the ground, his knees pulled up to his head. He put his hands over his eyes and I could hear deep wracking sobs coming from between his fingers.

I got on my knees and put an arm around his shoulders. Franny came over to us slowly, her arms outstretched. I couldn't tell if she was warding off a potential attack or trying to comfort him.

"Hey Brady. It's ok," said Franny, taking Brady's hand.

"No, it's not," said Brady through his fingers. "I'm a monster. Look what I did to Mr. Fullerton's cat."

I looked down at the bloody mess at my feet. A few feet away I could see a swatch of orange fur and a paw. Brady had really gone to town on that poor cat.

"Brady those are just …" I swallowed. "Instincts. You have desires that your wolf wants to fulfill. I mean it would better if you found something wild, but …" My words were not having a calming effect on Brady. Franny glared at me with even more intensity and I stopped talking.

Franny grabbed hold of Brady's hands and pulled them away from his face. He shied away from her, unwilling to meet her eyes. Gently, but firmly, she grasped hold of his stubbled chin and turned his face to meet hers. "Brady, you killed a cat. That's all it was." she said.

"Well yea, but it could have been anything. It could have been you," he said, his voice turning into a whine.

I rolled my eyes and got to my feet. "Don't be stupid Brady. That would never have happened."

"What?" said Brady. "But you said …"

"Yea, I did. I needed you to feel something uniquely human or you might have kept trying to kill me." I said.

Franny looked between Brady and me, cautious relief etched in her expression. "Don't be such a pussy. You kill animals every day, every time you eat meat. Remember when I took you to my gramma's farm and she served us chicken. This is no different. She had to kill those chickens to serve them to us," she said, words harsh but her tone soft.

"She did?" asked Brady, his lip curling in disgust.

"What, you think chicken grows on trees like apples?" asked Franny, punching Brady in the shoulder.

"You're no killer Brady, even with a shaggy winter coat on."

The side of Brady's mouth twitched up in a little smile. That was a good sign.

"If you can shout your dad down after he demanded you break up with 'that back street tramp' you can deal with a little killing now and then," she said, making little quote marks in the air when she said back street tramp.

Brady looked up at me. "But you said I could have killed you," he said.

"Well yea, but I kind of provoked you," I said. "Besides, you can kill someone any time you get behind the wheel of a car. It's just a matter of risk."

"So, everything you said …?" Said Brady.

"Yea, I lied to you," I said brushing the dirt off my hands. "I wanted you to come face to face with your wolf and decide to stop the turn."

"I can control it?" said Brady.

"Of course, you can." I said. "You're still you when you're a werewolf. You might be a little less squeamish when it comes to dinner." I glanced meaningfully towards the remains of the cat. "But you're still Brady under the fur. That's why you wouldn't have hurt Franny. C'mon, can you tell me you don't remember what you were thinking during the turn?"

Brady swallowed. "Yeah. Kinda." He said. "But it's all fuzzy and overwhelming. I want to run and hunt and… and kill."

"Yup," I said. "Your emotions are simpler and stronger when you're a wolf, but it's not like you turn into Freddy Krueger or something."

Brady looked down at the ground, a look of dejection on his face.

"Hey." I said. "This is normal for you. C'mon, let's get you home."

"Uhh, coach?" said Brady. He looked from me and then down at his naked body.

"Ah," I said. "Let me get you a towel from the back of my truck."

Several minutes later Franny and a properly clothed Brady were sitting in Franny's sitting room side by side on a loveseat.

"Ok," I said. "Now I need to know what happened tonight."

Brady and Franny looked at each other and then at me. Brady looked guilty while Franny still held her defiant glare. Apparently, I would have to do a bit more than wrestle a werewolf to earn her trust.

"I don't want to know about the sex," I said, raising my hands into the air. "Whatever you two do between the sheets is your own business. I want to know what triggered your change, Brady."

Brady blushed and looked down at the ground while Franny rolled her eyes at him. After a minute he spoke, "It's been a rough night Coach."

"Tom, call me Tom, Brady. I think we can dispense with the formalities," I said.

"Well, my folks threw me out," said Brady.

"What?" I said. From what I knew, Brady's relationship with his folks was good for the most part.

"We had a fight," said Brady. "Dad was acting completely irrational. He pulled some strings and got me accepted to Yale for college, but I told him I wanted to stay here. He said that Yale was the best chance I had to make something of myself, you know dad stuff and I told him I still wanted to stay in Worcester. I mean he knows why. I don't know why he thought he could just drop that on me like a bombshell and expect me to be happy and all. I mean come on."

"Why don't you want to go to Yale?" I asked, pretty sure I knew the answer already.

"It's like a two-hour drive between here and Yale," he said. "I don't wanna make that commute. And it's not like Franny can get the governor to pull strings on her behalf like my dad did."

"I see," I said.

"And then dad was all, 'this is because of that girl you're seeing, isn't it? You need to realize that this is just a phase son.' More bullshit on top of that and you know, I got kinda angry. I said some stuff I shouldn't have and stormed out," he said.

Franny put an arm around his shoulders. "You know, Brady, I'm still gonna be here if you do go to Yale. We can see each other on the weekends."

"Well yea, but he just wants me to end it with you," said Brady, he slumped his face into his hands again. "And then we had some weed and…"

Franny slapped a hand to his mouth and whipped her head around to look at me.

I put my hands up in the air again. "Whoa, Franny. I'm not the cops. I'm not gonna bust you two for smoking pot."

Brady took Franny's hands in his. "It's okay, Fran. Coach, I mean Tom, is cool. Hell, he ran out here at three in the morning to save my scrawny ass. I'm not sure who else would do that for me."

"What happened after you started smoking?" I asked.

Franny continued to stare at me, her mouth pursed and her hands clenched in her lap.

"Well," Brady chuckled a little, "I guess I had a bad trip or something because I woke up about an hour ago feeling like the walls were closing in on me. Usually it's calming you know. I can just let go of things for a while, but this stuff made me paranoid as hell. I felt an itch running down my back and I thought I was turning you know. I started thinking what if I turned and attacked Franny, I could hurt her. I got more and more twitchy and then I locked myself in the bathroom."

Franny licked her lips. "You scared the crap out of me Brady, you know that?"

"I'm sorry, hon," said Brady pulling her towards him. With Brady's arms around her Franny started to relax a little. "I don't know what got into me."

"I think I do," I said. "The weed. You don't need the full moon to turn Brady, that's more of an urban legend. Once you have control of yourself, it's voluntary. You can do it whenever you want, but it's a lot easier around the full moon. Don't ask me why. Magic rarely follows conventional laws of reason. Anyway, when you smoked, you must have gotten paranoid enough to trigger a flight or fight response. That can cause you to turn, but it usually doesn't happen until you're a bit older. My recommendation is to stop smoking, or at least don't do it while you're stressed out. I'm sure the emotions surrounding your fight with your father had something to do with what happened tonight."

I stood up. "I am going to go back home and turn in. If anything else happens, either tonight or over the next couple days, don't hesitate to call me immediately," I said. "Brady, I'm not going to lecture you about what to do with your life, but your parents care about you. I'm sure your dad will have calmed down now and the two of you may be able to compromise." Brady looked at me sullenly and nodded. I nodded back and opened the front door.

The cold air hit my skin and I could feel the dampness at my temples turning cold. Brady had really put me through my paces tonight. Any longer and he might have had me. I got my gym bag from the bushes where I had hidden it, got back into my car, and turned around, heading for home.

When I got back to my apartment, I shoved my gym bag back under my bed, turned off the lights and slumped into my bed. At that precise moment, the alarm clock started beeping at me. I let out a groan and picked it up. The little screen read 6:00, it was time to get up for work.

Christopher O'Halloran's Shopping List

Dog Food
Cat Litter
Junk food for the girlfriend that I'll inevitably end up eating too
Veggies that'll rot in the crisper
Video games I don't have time to play
Eggs

Speed of Shadow

Christopher O'Halloran

Miss Green had told Tracy's 2nd grade class that nothing could travel faster than light, but she silently disagreed in the self-assured way only a seven-year-old can. Her own experiments proved that one thing was faster, if only by fractions. When she went home that day she had shone a flashlight in her dad's dark dining room in an attempt to witness the speed of light. The shadows of the chairs climbed the wall seemingly at the same time the surrounding light hit it, a forest of wooden legs and high backs. Tracy discovered that the shadows were there before the light, though. When all was dark, the shadows remained; the light only revealed their hiding spots.

They drove down a slush covered road surrounded by forest on both sides and Tracy stared out the window as the headlights on her dad's old sedan lit up trees. The light sent their shadows stretching up through the forest. They were strange woods to them, a new road her dad had never taken them down. He had taken an unusual exit when the radio began squawking about a pile up a couple miles down the freeway but the detour didn't bother Tracy. A scenic route was better than the fast pace of the freeway, the winding roads better than the monotonous stretch where time became infinity.

She imagined cougars prowling through the woods beside them and bunnies hopping over branches, nibbling on wild lettuce. She saw bears that weren't there, hiding in the shadows, ready to jump out and snatch anyone who stopped on the side of the road to change a flat tire. A quick meal to fuel the hibernation they would be taking part in when winter came. Hibernation was another subject covered by Miss Green. Tracy learned that if bears didn't get enough food before winter, they would die of cold.

***

She was aware that she would die one day. Probably not soon, but some day distant in the future, preferably after a long life of climbing trees and playing ponies. Her dad had had The Talk with her when her gerbil died last month. Tracy's frustration got the best of her that day and she had cried her eyes out when Nibbles wouldn't wake. She tried her best to get him up but no amount of shaking or poking got his little eyes open. He just lay on his side with his mouth open as if he was stuck in the middle of drawing a deep breath. Her dad had found her sitting cross legged on the floor of her bedroom with the rodent in her little palms. He got down on one knee, not an easy task for a man as rotund as he.

"Oh sweetie," he said, wiping the tears away as they cut streaks down her cheeks. "What's wrong?"

Tracy sniffled and held her pet up to him like an offering. "Nibbles won't wake up. I found him lying in his cage and he wouldn't wake up. I tried everything!"

Her dad took the gerbil in his own hands and looked him over. "I'm sorry honey, but I think he's gone."

"Gone where?" she asked him. Her dad had the answers to any question she asked in subjects ranging from geography to biology, but at this he remained silent. She was going to repeat her question when he began to talk.

"He's died, Trace."

When she asked him why, he explained to her that every living thing died at some point. Sometimes they got too old, sometimes they had an accident. And sometimes it just happened for no good reason but, at some point, everything died.

"Will I die?" she asked him, eyes wide and mouth agape.

She heard a click in his throat as he opened his mouth and stumbled over his words. He closed his mouth then before opening it to start anew. "Yeah, but not for a very, very long time. As time goes on, people live for longer and longer. You'll probably get bored of all the things on Earth before you go."

"Oh," she said, taking in the new information. She worked it around in her head for a bit, trying to count how many years she would have, but losing track. A disturbing thought stopped her while she was contemplating her mortality. "Will mommy die? Will you die?"

"Yeah, we all will at our own time. When we're ready."

"Okay," she said and looked him dead in the eye. "Just don't die before me, okay? You need to stay with me so I can ask you things."

He rolled back onto his bum and put one arm around his daughter. "You got it bubs." Sitting like that beside her, Todd realized that he still had the lifeless rodent in his hand and he placed it on the ground before wiping his hands off on the side of his jeans.

***

As their car bounced up and down on the back road, Tracy began to grow bored. "How much longer?" She asked her dad. He glanced up at her in the rearview mirror.

"It'll be a while honey. Just go to sleep. I'll carry you inside when we get home."

"Okay." She went back to looking out the window in the backseat and closed her eyes. She tried to sleep but no matter how hard she thought of sheep frolicking over fences (a trick her mommy had taught her to fall asleep quickly) she kept getting bounced awake by the bumpy road.

Rubbing her eyes, she poked her older brother in the shoulder. He was in the front seat with earbuds crammed in, running down to an iPad he held in his lap. He ignored her.

"Robbie," she said, reaching through the gap between his seat and door to poke him again. "Can I have the iPad now?"

With a sigh of frustration, he pulled his right earbud out. "What?" he asked.

"Can I have the iPad?"

"Piss off," he said, placing the earbud back in. Their dad reached over and yanked out the left earbud.

"Don't talk to your sister like that," he told him.

"Whatever," Robbie said and put the earbud back in. He had turned fifteen that year and was under the impression that he didn't have to listen to his parents anymore. Todd and Marissa had talked about his attitude with him endlessly, but it got them nowhere. Todd thought that the divorce had left his son feeling lost and confused, but every time he tried to broach the subject the boy had turned him away, jamming his headphones on or simply storming off. He reassured Marissa that until Robbie started acting suspicious or his grades started declining, they had nothing to worry about. While Todd had learned not to bug him, figuring that he would come to him when he was ready, Tracy never stopped trying to reach out to her big brother.

"It's okay daddy," she said, "I can wait."

He looked back at her in the mirror. "I appreciate your patience." He reached over and shook his son. "I'm sure Robbie does too." The teenager rolled his eyes and Tracy turned her attention out the window again. She watched the raindrops roll down the glass and pretended they were racing, each drop in a mad dash to reach the rubber at the bottom of the window. It wasn't as exciting as Angry Birds or Fruit Ninja, but Tracy imbued the drops with backstories and characters, letting her imagination run wild.

She pitted two fat drops against each other, arch rivals from neighboring countries as different from each other as black and white. They started down the window, gravity pulling them down and the wind pulling them towards the trunk of the car. The drops were named after boys at school who sometimes made jokes at her and pulled her hair and sometimes brought her flowers or shared snacks with her. She had her money on the right drop, Michael, but her heart lurched as it paused halfway down and the left drop, LeBron, gained the lead. Tapping the window, she urged Michael on. "C'mon," she whispered under her breath and her heart gave another lurch as she noticed the shadow of a man gaining on their car.

He was a black shape almost blending in with the night and his legs were spinning madly like the wheel of a bicycle, just a blur under his torso. Tracy craned her body and looked at him out of the rear window. He was far behind them on the road and falling further back every second, but his speed made her jaw drop. She had never seen a man go that fast. He faded into the darkness, a shadow merging once more with the surrounding black and she sat back forward in her seat, wondering if what she saw was real.

"Daddy," she said, getting her father's attention, "How fast are we going?"

"About a hundred," he said, looking back at her. "Why do you ask?"

"Can a person run that fast?"

He laughed his big belly laugh, a sound that always brought a sense of pride to the girl when she caused it and she began to smile. "Of course not," he told her. "Usain Bolt couldn't keep up with us. We're practically flying!"

Tracy didn't know who Usain Bolt was, but she was still smiling as she returned her attention to the window in search of another pairing of raindrops she could imagine racing. As hard as she tried to focus on the water though, she couldn't help but keep looking back at the darkness the car left behind at 100 kilometers per hour.

***

A couple minutes later, Tracy heard her dad's phone start to ring. It buzzed away next to his McDonald's cup in its holder with the irritating sound of plastic on plastic. Her dad took one look at it and sighed.

"Mom," he told the kids before accepting the call and putting it on speaker. "Hey Marissa, we'll probably be another 40 minutes. There's an accident on the freeway so I took a different exit. We'll get back on at the next one. Shouldn't slow us down too much"

"You better not be holding the phone. The fines have doubled this year." Tracy's mom sounded mildly irritated, a tone not uncommon whenever she had to speak with her ex-husband.

"I'm not, you're on speaker."

"Okay. Hi kids!" When addressing her children, Marissa had a cheery tone as if her words were thick and coated in fruit syrup. "Did you have fun at Nan's?"

Tracy leaned forward against the seat belt. "Yeah, mom! She made those marshmallow squares again!"

"Yummy! Where's Robbie?"

"He's watching a movie on the iPad," Todd explained.

"You shouldn't let him play on that thing all the time. It's all he does, either that or his XBox. Always with his eyes glued to a screen." The note of irritation was back in her voice and Todd took a pull from his McDonald's cup to restrain himself from shouting at her. Few things got on his nerves, but Marissa's complete lack of trust in him was top of the list. It happened every time he had the kids on his own. She frequently voiced her suspicions to him, claiming that he wasn't taking care of her babies properly and it had been a major contributing force to their divorce.

"There isn't a whole lot to do on this drive," he said, placing the cup back in the holder. "It's not a big deal."

"It is a big deal!" No longer mildly irritated, Tracy's mother was downright angry. Tracy turned her head away as her parents started to fight. "I bet you're smoking in there with them too," she said and out of the corner of her eye Tracy saw her dad fingering the pack he kept in his jacket pocket. He left them there, though; Todd kept his children's lungs smoke free at all times.

They went on like that, back and forth, while Tracy went back to looking out the window. She watched the trees flash by, big Christmas trees too big to fit in anything but a giant's house. Picturing her dad trying to drag one of those gargantuan trees up the stairs to his apartment made her giggle. The laugh caught in her throat when she saw sudden movement in the trees. With an explosion of broken branches, the dark figure broke out from the forest to the road and began chasing them again.

She turned around and stared open-mouthed out the back window as it followed their car, its legs pin-wheeling with the same rapid movement as before. It was far enough away that Tracy couldn't make out the details of its face, but even her near-blind Nan would've been able to see the maniacal grin stretching from ear to ear. Tracy couldn't be sure, but the man looked to be gaining on the car.

Turning back forward, she noticed that they were stuck behind a big semi-truck. They were going way slower than before. The man would catch up to them soon. What he would do when he got to them, she didn't know. But her seven-year old mind felt the terror of a weak animal cornered by a predator.

"Robbie," she croaked and was surprised at her voice. It felt like small vibrations on a tight wire and came out puffy and weak. Her brother continued watching his movie, unaware she had said anything. In the driver's seat, her dad went on arguing with their mom about something he had let the kids eat. They had once again fallen into their old habit of talking about them as if they weren't even there, but Tracy didn't care about their tone. There was a bigger problem and it was gaining on them.

When she turned back around she saw him, now only a car's length away. The sight filled her with a dread that welled up in her, black and paralyzing. She whimpered but was heard by neither of the men in her life. His smile was inhuman, wider than she had ever seen. His lips were pulled back showing huge teeth as big as the notebooks she had gotten at school. He was panting like a dog, but had a look of joy she had never seen on any animal. His limbs and torso looked as if they had been pulled by horses and stretched with so much force that he became long and slim all over. He was reaching his arms out towards the car, opening and closing his hands like a child grabbing for a candy bar he desperately wanted. Spit dribbled from the corners of his mouth and flew off in streams behind him.

The man -if she could call it a man- had a head, round like a basketball, but black as the rest of his body. He wore no clothes but could not be called naked as he had no genitals or even a semblance of skin. He was an absence of light, a speeding shadow in pursuit of her family. Just yellow, bloodshot eyes and blindingly white teeth held within a nightmare.

Tracy turned around and poked Robbie. He brushed her off and continued watching his movie. "Dad," she said trying to get his attention.

"I'm on the phone, honey." She usually hated when he brushed her off like that, but now she only felt panic.

"Look behind-"

"Don't interrupt Tracy, you know better than that," her mom told her from the cup holder, the syrup in her voice dried up, a common result of talking to her ex-husband.

"I should let you go, anyway. We've still got a while to go."

"Whatever. Just don't let them drink any soda. There's no helping you, but I will not let them balloon up like you did."

"Thanks, Marissa."

"Love you, kids!" The tender motherly voice was back but Tracy didn't hear it. She was looking back at the man. He met her eyes and looked jubilant as he held her in his gaze, his breath billowing out from between his big clenched teeth in white puffs. He was almost within arm's reach. Tracy had the feeling that if she rolled her window down she would smell his breath and it would smell like the box she had placed in the ground after Nibbles passed away.

He was alongside the rear corner panel of Todd's sedan when his arm reached out towards Tracy's door handle. She frantically fumbled the lock, confirming the door secure but knew he would get in anyway. Closing her eyes and covering her head, Tracy waited for the sound of ripping metal and speeding wind. Instead, she heard her dad's phone beep as he hung up. She felt the car increase its speed. When she opened her eyes, they were passing the semi and leaving the shadow creature in their dust.

***

"Henry is taking your mom on a surprise trip to Bellingham so you kids get to spend the week with your old man." Todd put his turn signal on after the semi-truck flashed its lights indicating that it was safe to get back into the lane. He turned the wheel and gently crossed over the broken line separating eastbound traffic from westbound. Tracy had twisted back around to look out of the back window and the truck driver saw her pale face. He gave her a casual wave and she turned back around.

"What?" In her come down from her panic she had forgotten her manners and felt stupid for it. "Sorry, I mean pardon me." Her dad wasn't as strict on the pleases and thank-yous but mom had an ear for it and would chastise her for any indiscretion so she tried to keep in the habit. She didn't understand the importance of it all, but her mom had claimed that the kind of rough and childish behavior she got away with around her dad would not fly if they ever sat down to tea with the queen. I don't know if that would be such a party anyway, Tracy thought. Who would bother with a stuffy old queen in the first place?

"You're gonna be staying with me this week!"

She brightened up at this and brushed away thoughts of the slender shadow man. At any rate, they were getting further and further away with every mile and she no longer considered him a threat. Not for them anyway. She felt bad for the truck driver, who he would undoubtedly target next. Maybe not, though. Maybe he's just after little girls. Tracy knew there were people always after little girls; her mother had drilled stranger danger into her head since she could understand spoken word.

"Yay!" She clapped her hands together and Todd looked back at her in the rearview mirror with a smile.

"Good," Robbie said, wrapping up the earbuds that were connected to the iPad, "Henry's a dildo."

Todd slapped his son lightly on the thigh in just a token gesture of punishment. "Don't talk like that about him. Your mom loves him and you should respect him." The words were hard but his tone was full of humor and the slightest trace of sarcasm.

Tracy giggled. "What's a dildo?" she asked her father.

He blushed and cleared his throat as Robbie started to laugh. "It's just a silly person. Somebody whose only purpose is to stand there and maybe twirl around a bit." This sent Robbie into a coughing fit as he tried to stifle the guffaws coming from his belly.

"I see..." Tracy made a mental note of the word 'dildo.' The next time Michael and LeBron started calling her names, Tracy hoped to impress them with her brand-new insult.

Robbie passed her the iPad from between the two front seats and she thanked him before unlocking it and opening the Candy Crush app. "Are we going to go straight to your place?" He asked his dad, pulling his phone out and checking the time.

"Well, you'll probably need some more clothes so we'll go to your mom's first. Pack a couple bags and send the two newlyweds off with some well wishes."

"Ugh," he said, "Do we have to? Why can't we just wear what we're wearing now?"

"I don't want to smell your ass for the next week," Todd replied.

"Come on, I can turn my underwear inside out, backwards, backwards and inside out. That's like four days of use! I can go commando the last couple days, no problem."

"Never go commando in jeans, kid. If I only teach you one thing as your father it should be that." He looked over at his son with a serious expression. "You really don't like Henry, do you?"

Robbie rolled his eyes. "It's not just him. It's mom too, the way she is around him. She looks at him with these stupid eyes and they have these stupid in-jokes. You try to talk to her and she just treats you like a kid.

Like anything we say is just 'cute' or whatever. It's annoying."

"Ah," his dad replied. He drove in silence, chewing over the idea of Marissa falling in love all over again like an overcooked steak. The thought should have brought him joy. Someone he cared about was happy, happier than she had been in a long time. Instead it tasted of gristle. "She hasn't looked at me with those stupid eyes in a long, long time."

"Gross, I don't want to hear about it!" Robbie cringed, but there was an air of over exaggeration in it.

Todd shared a laugh with his son and it felt good. He looked forward to the boy's older years. With any luck, he would be able to teach his son how to be a man instead of Henry. Tall, well-built Henry with the good job and better waistline. Todd looked down at his own protruding gut and felt a twinge of guilt. The soda and cigarette combination would be a one-two punch that took down greater men than him. He made a resolution to quit in the coming New Year. He would be around for his children. He wouldn't let them be raised by a dildo.

"At least he doesn't beat you."

"You don't beat me."

"I beat you in Madden."

Robbie laughed again. "Yeah right. We'll see about that old man. I'm packing the XBox when we get home. To mom's, I mean."

"You're on, bubs." He was looking at his son and smiling when the tire blew. It stunned Tracy and pulled her out of her game. She dropped the iPad and it slid onto the floor as the car began to shake and pull to the left.

"Shit," her dad exclaimed and pulled off onto the shoulder. Tracy sat in horror, the image of the shadow appearing in her mind. The desire in his eyes, the lust in his grin.

"Why are we stopping, daddy?" she asked him. She turned around in her seat and looked out the back again. The road stretched out far behind them and she couldn't see anyone there. Moonlight gleamed off the wet asphalt and the trees stood on either side of them, trapping them and making Tracy feel like she was in the bottom of a canyon as rain started filling it up. If they stood still the shadow would reach them and they would drown.

"Just a flat tire, hon. We'll have it changed in a jiff. Robbie, give me a hand and grab the spare from the trunk." The men opened their respective doors and got out, her dad bending over to pull the latch that popped the trunk. "Sit tight. We'll be rolling real soon."

"No daddy, we need to go!" Her words were only halfway out when her father closed the door and walked back to the trunk. She watched him pull a black bag from within it and heard his muffled voice ask if Robbie could handle the tire. Through the glass, she thought she heard Robbie say "piece of cake" but couldn't be sure. Her heart was beating so fast she could hear it, dull in her ear. Her mouth tasted like metal and she double checked the locking mechanism in the back seat.

When the car started to lift from the driver's side she let out a small squeal, but got herself under control. He's gone, she thought, we've been past him for a long time now. He probably went after the truck driver, anyway. The thought brought a feeling of guilt but she shook it off. If he had to go after someone, she was glad to be spared.

She heard the sound of metal scraping on metal and thought that it was the sound of her dad taking the popped tire off the car. It wouldn't be like changing a bike tire, it would be slower. She shook that thought off too. It wouldn't be. Yes, a car was bigger and more complicated than the Raleigh she had at home, but it didn't have a chain to fuss with. Tracy twisted in her seat as her dad got to his feet. She watched Robbie take the spare out of the trunk and begin to roll it to the front of the car. She twisted back to watch her dad as he put his hands in his lower back and stretched his belly out. The tiny pops in his spine could be heard even through the rolled-up windows.

"Got it?" He asked his son, but before he got an answer the shadow tore through his body and sent it rolling down into the middle of the road. Tracy screamed and fumbled at her seatbelt as the shadow continued off in the direction they were heading. As she got it off, she heard Robbie shout for his dad and saw him run off into the road. Tracy was bounding out her door and after him in no time.

"Dad!" he shouted as he fell to his knees at the body of his father. The big man was sprawled on his back with his arms and legs stuck out like a starfish. His face and arms were rubbed raw from the road and he stared up at the stars, blinking with confusion. When he tried to talk, blood wept from the corners of his mouth.

"Wa fuh-" he said before coughing. Dark flecks of blood flew out and speckled Robbie's face.

"We need to get back in the car, Robbie!" Tracy was tugging on his sleeve, trying to pull him away from their father but he was too heavy. "It's going to come back!"

"What was it? A motorcycle? Where were its fucking lights?!" He was hysterical.

"It's not, Robbie, it's a monster! Please!" She was crying now and runners of snot ran down her face. She didn't care, they needed to go. They needed to get back to the car.

"I need to get dad out of the road, it's not safe here." He was crying too, but he wiped at his eyes with his arm and grabbed his dad by the hand. When he began to pull, a large gash opened, running along his torso and Todd's children were treated to the sight of his organs desperately trying to keep him alive. Their father let out a bloodcurdling scream and Robbie let go of the arm. He sat down hard and began to sob in between his knees.

"Please!" Tracy screamed. Her head was hurting like there was some sort of balloon inside it, slowly expanding and pushing on her skull. She looked in the direction the shadow had run off in and saw it far away where the road climbed to a hill. He was at the top and his legs had stopped pin-wheeling. They were splayed wide and he was silhouetted in the moonlight. He was way too long, and he seemed to stretch even longer before her eyes. She watched him as he lifted one arm high into the air and began to wave like a childhood friend greeting another from across the street. They were jerky movements, full of clumsy energy. He lowered his body and his legs began to move, slow at first but increasing to that same blur she had seen from in the car.

"It's coming back, Robbie," she told him, "We need to get off the road."

Her brother had seen the shadow with its mocking wave. Robbie wiped at his nose and got shakily to his feet. "No. That asshole killed our dad. He killed our dad!"

Tracy looked at where the man who lifted her onto his shoulders for every parade rested and saw that he was no longer breathing. He just kept looking up at the sky as if he was waiting for the hand of God to reach down and pull him up to heaven. She fell to her knees and began to wail as her teenaged brother staggered so that he was standing in front of his dad in a protective stance. "Get in the car, Trace."

She looked up but couldn't find the strength to stand. "Robbie," she whispered and the shadow sprinted on, gaining on the boy with inhuman speed. A whine came up from his direction, high and full of tension. It sounded like a dog being held back from a big meaty bone. There was no leash on the shadow though, and it came.

"EEEEEEEEEEEEEEE!" It whined and Robbie roared at it. It was primal and full of a strength Tracy had never seen in him.

Over the sounds the two were making, an enormous horn blared. It sounded like a fog horn, but they were not near any oceans. The truck, Tracy thought, and got to her feet. "Robbie!" she shouted but her little voice was drowned out by the truck's loud warning. Fortunately, the lights from the cab washed over the boy and he understood what was happening. He juked towards the car and sprinted away from their dad's body. Robbie wasn't as fast as the shadow that had followed them from God knows where, but he was fast enough.

He cleared the path of the truck and Tracy heard the squeal of its brakes. The wheels locked up, but the weight of the semi pushed it forward and she saw it flatten the shadow as it turned towards her and her brother. As the last wheel rolled over the figure, it caught it and dragged the shadow along the road.

***

They sat by the car and looked at their dad in the brake lights of the truck. The red of the lights washed over the blood and Tracy thought the puddle pooling

49

around her father could've just been rainwater. She realized however, that the rain had stopped.

The man who had waved at Tracy from the cab of the truck opened the door and almost fell out. He was a small bald man and he tripped as he rushed forward to the body of their dad. "Oh God," he was saying, over and over. Tracy realized that he thought he had hit their dad. He hit something, she thought and got to her feet as the truck driver called 911. In his haste to get the clearly dead man help, he had forgotten that there were two kids in the car with him. Tracy didn't mind. She didn't want to deal with him just then. She started to walk towards the back of the semi-truck.

"Where are you going?" Robbie asked, scrambling to his feet.

"It needs to be dead."

He followed her to the truck and they both looked down at what was pinned under the back tire.

The figure looked up at Tracy from beneath the tire. It was rubbed raw with bits of black, smoldering pieces ripped off and strewn along the road. When she looked at it, she understood at once that it knew what it had done. It knew that she would spend the next month, maybe year, crying over the loss of her father. She would no longer be able to go to him with one of her many curiosities about the world, would receive no comfort from any hurts and hear no corny dad jokes. The shadow showed tremendous joy at tearing apart her father. From under the semi-truck's big wheel, his smile stretched even wider. It reached grotesquely around the back of his round head and Tracey heard a creaking come from within its thin throat.

"What's it doing?" Her brother asked her, sounding like a small child instead of a teenager on the brink of manhood.

"I don't know," she replied, "It sounds like laughing." The shadow's arms stretched out towards her and opened and closed its long fingers like a child trying to grasp something it felt it deserved. Tracy took a step back, repulsed by the creature. It oozed dark wet liquid from where bits of its flesh were worn away by the asphalt. It looked like oil, like some natural slime a snake would secrete. Are snakes slimy? She didn't know. She couldn't ask her dad. "Robbie, are snakes slimy?" When she looked to him for an answer, he was gone. "Robbie?" She spun in a circle, searching for him.

Robbie had hopped over a smashed concrete divider. When he came back over it, he was holding a large, heavy slab of stone. He hefted it high as he came closer to the thing trapped under the semi truck's wheel. The shadow stopped laughing.

Eric W. Burgin's Shopping List

Sliced Pickles
Ketchup
Jasmine Rice
Curry Powder
Tahini
Fish Oil
Fruit
Eggs

Cold Cuts

Eric W. Burgin

Pickles, that's what this needs. Hugh opened the refrigerator and pulled out a jar of sliced dill pickles. He laid several slices on top of the cheese. Now the mustard. Hugh smiled and licked his lips.

"Don't worry," he said as he spread the Gulden's Spicy Brown on the top slice of Wonderbread, "this will be ready in two shakes."

A moment later, Hugh turned around and set a plate in front of his guest, Freddy McAyer, the heavy porcelain clinking against the worn wood tabletop. A miniature American flag on a toothpick pierced the center of the ham and cheese sandwich (don't forget the Gulden's!). "Ready to eat? Sandwiches are the best."

Freddy looked at Hugh and nodded.

"I'm so glad you're here," Hugh said, "there is nothing like sharing a sandwich with your best friend."

"Yeah, Hugh," Freddy said and smiled before taking a bite.

***

"I'll be there in a minute; I just need to make a call." Jared hoped the floor boss heard him over the forklifts that sped across the warehouse; all he needed was Seth to yell at him again.

He hurried to the office, his boots thudding on the concrete and echoing in the lofty heights of the ceiling. His break was only ten minutes, and if he didn't find another player for Friday's poker game, the guys would murder him. They were down to three players now because he had driven John and Jeff away. Not my fault they couldn't take a joke, the cock suckers. When he closed the door, a hush enveloped him, the sounds of his coworkers audible but muffled and the forklift engines reduced to a dull hum. He picked up the phone and dialed.

"Fuck," he said when he heard Hugh's voicemail greeting. He hung up and dialed again. He knew Hugh was leaving work in an hour and Jared didn't have his home number or cell. He had, in fact, thought it was odd when Hugh refused to give them to him. This time, Hugh answered.

"Rosemont Office Supply, this is Hugh Barber."

"Hugh. Jared over at the warehouse."

"Hey, what's up?"

"Not much, I was wondering if you were free Friday, a couple of guys are coming over to play poker, and we need some fresh meat."

"I'd love to, but I have plans."

"More important than poker?"

"Freddy and I are hanging out."

"Again? Geez pal, you two some kinda homos now?"

Jared heard Hugh's forced laugh. "Hardly, you're the cock sucker. Seriously, though, his wife just left him, and he needs a distraction."

"Why don't you bring him along, I am sure we can fleece the both of you."

A heartbeat of a pause. "Sorry man, we have plans."

"Oh come on, what's a better distraction than beer and poker?"

A longer pause now. Are you even listening to me? "Hugh?"

"Not this time."

"Seriously? Shit. Okay, I'll ask around work. Later."

Jared heard Hugh grunt something and the phone click. He stared at the mouthpiece for a moment, then set down the receiver. "What the fuck is his problem?" He shook his head and wondered who the hell he could bring to the game.

***

"How was the poker game?" Hugh asked as he looked across the plastic booth at Jared, and reached for the salt. He was happy to have something to take his mind off the weekend.

Jared swallowed his fries. "It was okay. Never did find anyone else, so there was just the three of us. God, they gave me shit. Not only did I not bring anyone, but I took them for a hundred bucks. If it wasn't for that, I'd be passing that shit right on to you." He smiled as he dipped another fry in ketchup. "You ought to slow down on that stuff; it'll kill you." He pointed the fry at Hugh before popping it in his mouth.

Hugh smirked and rolled his eyes, then proceeded to shower his fries with salt.

Hugh set his burger down. "Sorry, I blew you off. Glad you won some money, though." He took a sip of pop.

"No worries man, just wish you'd come join us sometime. Beer, music, poker. What's not to like?"

That did sound good to Hugh, especially since Freddy wasn't around anymore, and he could use a friend. He looked at Jared. Nah, he's not the right kinda guy. "Maybe. When do you play next?"

"Labor Day weekend."

"Okay, cool. I'll see what I have going on."

Jared finished his meal and let out a belch. "Man, next time we ought to hit Stan's; I'm dying for a hoagie."

Hugh looked up at him and grinned. "Sounds like a plan, my man."

Jared laughed and cleared the table. Hugh sat smiling and watching him.

***

"Thomas!"

Jared looked up at the sound of his last name and brought the forklift to a stop.

"You gotta call," his supervisor said around the unlit cigarette dangling from his mouth.

"Who is it?"

"How the fuck should I know, but make it quick or it'll come outta your lunch hour." Seth spun on his heel and stomped away.

Who the hell would call me at work? he thought as he climbed down from the forklift. Ma? Jared's pulse quickened, and he trotted across the warehouse floor. His mother was healthy as far as he knew, but after her flu scare last winter... He sprinted to the office.

Jared snatched the receiver from the desk, fumbled it but caught the cord. The receiver swung back and hit the desk before he could secure it. "Hello? Ma?" He huffed into the phone.

"No, it's me. How are ya, buddy?"

Jared was silent; his face screwed up in thought. The voice on the other end of the phone was a man, and not a concerned one, no policeman or doctor. This man was bright, almost jovial.

"Are ya there, buddy?"

Jared stammered, searching his catalog of familiar voices. "Hugh? Why are you calling me at work?"

"Thought about your invite and I'm in! I think the poker game will be loads of fun. What should I bring?"

"I..." Jared's breathing was returning to normal, but he could not get his mind off his mother. "Just whatever you want to drink I guess."

"Fantastic! Pick you up from work on Friday?"

"Sure," Jared said at the same time he heard a click and the line went dead. He set the receiver on the cradle, missing on the first attempt, then shuffled back to the main warehouse, shoulders slumped. What the hell was that?

***

At the poker game, Hugh was charming and talkative, and he lost enough money to make Jared's friends happy and invite him back for next time.

"That was fun. God, am I tired, though." Jared stretched in the passenger's seat, little grunts escaping his lips as he did. "Ah, that's nice."

"I'm all jazzed up," Hugh said, "do you wanna come over for a nightcap? I don't think I can sleep right away."

"I dunno, Hugh, it's after midnight."

"Come on, one beer, and then I'll take you home. I have a few options in the fridge. Are you hungry?"

"Nah, I had my fill of chips. I had so much salt my lips are burning."

Hugh laughed. "All right then, just a beer."

"No way, I'm nearly dead, and I have to run into work in the morning."

"Okay. How about football tomorrow at my place? It's opening weekend!"

"Yeah, that's cool, what time?"

"Just before lunch? I'll throw something together, and we can eat while we watch."

"That should work, I'll be off by ten at the latest, we just have some pallets to rearrange. God, I love overtime. I'll need your address, though." Jared laughed. "Shit, three years working together and I don't even know where you live."

"I'm out in the sticks, kinda hard to find. I have to come into town tomorrow; I can meet you at your work and go from there. Ten?"

"Are you sure it's not out of your way? I can just print a map."

"Like I said, I gotta be over there in the morning anyway. You can follow from there or ride with me."

Jared smiled. "Let's make it eleven, and I'll wring them outta another hour of O.T."

Hugh laughed. "Sounds like a plan my man."

***

Hugh sat at his kitchen table staring at the empty chair across from him, its chrome still gleaming even after all these years, though the plastic had chipped and faded in places. It started life as an office chair but had been re-purposed, as had all of Hugh's furniture, and did not match anything else in the cramped kitchen.

"Why'd you have to move away?" Hugh still stared at the chair, chewing on a Twix bar he couldn't taste.

He stood up, eyes flashing with anger, his own chair crashing to the floor. "Why?" He leaned over the table, slimy chocolate bits flying and pattering down on the empty chair. He straightened, picked his ancient school chair up off the floor and set it upright. He looked at the table, toeing the floor like an embarrassed child. "We had so much fun." He collapsed into his chair, deflated like a used balloon.

The clock ticked over to 2:00 am and Hugh's watch beeped. He looked at it for a long moment as if it were a foreign object. "I guess you never liked me after all. But I'll show you. I have a new best friend, better than you, and he'll love my sandwiches." He paused, and his eyebrows lifted. He already likes hoagies, he thought.

***

Jared stepped out of Hugh's old Nissan onto the gravel drive with a crunch under his work boots and shut the door, taking in his surroundings. "You weren't kidding; this is the sticks. Any neighbors?"

"Nope, nearest one's a mile or so that way." He pointed behind Jared as the hot engine ticked and popped as it cooled.

"Man, I'd love that. I got people yelling, kids playing, that kinda shit all the time in my building. This silence is great."

Hugh's smile faded. "It can get to you, but that's why I invite my friends over so much. I'm glad you're here." He smiled again.

"Glad to be here, and thanks for driving, it means I can finish these off." He raised the six pack to his chest and patted it."

"And if that's not enough, I have more in the fridge." Hugh waggled his eyebrows up and down. He strode toward the house. "Come on, let's have a beer and get some grub. I hope sandwiches are okay; they're kinda my favorite."

"Sounds good." Jared followed up the walk.

Hugh mounted the porch steps, and the wood squealed in protest, as did the rusty storm door. He unlocked three deadbolts.

"Worried about getting robbed?" Jared asked.

"You never know what can happen, man," Hugh said and opened the door. He stood aside for Jared to enter. "Castle Barber," he made an exaggerated "voila" motion with one hand and flipped the light on with the other.

Jared stepped inside what was decidedly not a castle. Orange plush carpet covered the floor in the front room which contained a banana shaped couch that must have been 11 feet long and covered with a patterned flower sheet, a coffee table covered in newspapers and magazines, and a La-Z-Boy that looked older than Hugh. The TV, all glorious 32 inches of it, stood in the corner trying not to be seen. The smell, however, did not fit with the decor. "My God what smells so good?"

Hugh smiled. "Pulled pork's been simmering in the crock pot all night. Kitchen's this way."

Jared made his own "voila" motion. "Lead me to that succulent meat."

They paused a second, and both burst out laughing.

The adjoining kitchenette was not much better than the living room, with faded yellow linoleum coming up in spots, and a motley collection of chairs around a stout oak table, but it was clean. Jared set his beer down on the counter with a clink. "What can I do?"

"Not a thing, you're the guest. Take a seat, and I'll get the food out."

"You're the boss." Jared pulled a beer out of the pack and twisted the top off. "Ah the breakfast of champions," he said after his first drink. He sat down in an old office chair and set his beer on the table. His wrist stuck to the arm of the chair, and he noticed both arms were covered in a gluey film. "What's with the sticky chair?"

Hugh was bent over, head in the refrigerator, and froze. "Huh?" He looked back over his shoulder at Jared. "Oh, I was um." He stood and turned toward Jared, never taking his gaze from the arm of the chair. "Had to tape it together while the glue dried. Stupid thing keeps breaking."

"Ah. Maybe you should get a new chair; this thing's seen better days."

Hugh was silent for a few seconds. "Yeah," he smiled, "I hate buying new furniture when there is so much out there that's serviceable. Ready to eat?"

"You bet."

Hugh tossed a package of buns on the table and followed them with paper plates. He put the rest of Jared's beer in the fridge and emerged with lettuce and tomato already cut into bun size slices.

After the sandwiches, they moved into the living room, watched football, and drank. Jared finished all six of his beers and five more of Hugh's before passing out on the couch.

Hugh stood over him, his second beer in his hand, and watched him sleep for a few minutes before setting his beer on the table. "If you're going to spend the night, we need to make you more comfortable."

***

The smell of coffee was the first thing Jared recognized when he woke up. The jackhammer headache was the second. How much did I drink? He tried to wipe the sleep from his eyes, but he couldn't move his arm. What the hell? His eyes popped open, but the light sent searing pain lancing across his temples, and he squinted against it as he looked down. He was sitting in Hugh's kitchen on the old office chair, but his hands were attached to the arms with silver bracelets from wrist to elbow. Fuck bracelets, that's duct tape! He pulled against it and tried to yell but only muffled sounds came out. His mouth was taped shut. He closed his eyes and let out a slow, easy breath.

Jared looked around for Hugh. Did he? No, that was impossible. The thought of the sticky chair arms tickled the back of his mind, but it couldn't get past his immediate concerns. The kitchen looked much like it did last night: beer bottles on the counter next to Hugh's keys and a bottle opener, the usual appliances, although the toaster looked straight out of a 50's Sears catalog. A loaf of bread, jar of mustard, sliced pickles, cheese, and sliced meat lay on the counter like a mini assembly line. He looked at the bottle opener again. No good, nothing sharp. He pulled at his bonds, the cords in his neck standing out, his teeth grinding together. He relaxed with a grunt. In addition to the tape, there were straps around his chest and waist: He could hardly move. His nose was plugged, a victim of his lifelong allergies, and it was becoming hard to breathe. Calm down Jared; it won't do you any good to pass out. After a few easy breaths, he scanned the room again.

Idiot! I'm in a kitchen; I could just get a knife. He tried to push his chair away from the table but realized his legs were taped to the chair and up off the ground. Fuck, fuck, fuck! He shook his body from side to side trying to loosen the tape, to move, but a tug on his leg made him look down: Hugh had taped him to the table. His face got hot as panic's nails clawed up his spine. He closed his eyes and took a long, slow breath: in, out. When he opened them, he looked through the door into the living room but could see nothing except the edge of the couch. He looked to his arms again searching for any tear or weakness in the tape. I'm stuck. His eyes widened as he connected the dots between the sticky residue on the chair and his current situation. Hugh! He began to shake. No, this isn't happening, it's got to be a joke. He thrashed again but with his whole body this time, every muscle. He screamed as he did and squeezed his eyes shut to stop the tears. He collapsed back into the chair, straining to breathe through his stuffed nose, the years of beer and fast food had his heart hammering in his chest.

A shadow fell across the floor from the doorway.

"Good morning sleepy head," Hugh said, "I'm glad you're up, I'm starving!"

"Hugh, what's going on? Let me out of this," Jared said, but of course, all that came out was muffled nonsense.

"Well, what else could I do? You're the one who slept so late, and I certainly wasn't gonna wake you." A grin spread across Hugh's face that reminded Jared of Batman's Joker. "But I skipped breakfast so we could eat together."

Jared tried to respond again, but his head swam with the lack of oxygen.

Hugh leaned down and glanced sideways, the back of his hand along side his mouth as if he didn't want the kitchen to hear. "I know it's a little early for sandwiches, but we'll call it brunch okay?" Hugh tittered. "I'm so glad you're here."

He turned away from Jared and opened the bread. "I hope you like roast, I make it myself, no deli meat here!"

Jared's vision blurred, and tears rolled down his cheeks. This can't be happening; it's got to be a joke.

"Here you are," Hugh set a plate in front of Jared with a clink, "roast, cheese, tomato, lettuce, and mustard. Mmmm Gulden's."

Jared looked down at the sandwich, its tiny American flag garnishment standing at attention on the toothpick.

Hugh set a matching plate in front of his chair and lowered into it. "The bread is fresh and soft; I bought it new yesterday just for you." He picked up his sandwich and raised it in the air. "To best friends," he said, waggled his eyebrows and took a bite. "Oh, I'm sorry," bits of bread flew from his mouth, "how rude of me." He set his sandwich down and peeled the tape off Jared's mouth. "There you go, dig in."

Jared drew in a soul-sucking breath. "God man, what are you doing? Why am I tied up?"

"We're having brunch Jared, just like best buddies do. Now let's have a bite of sandwich."

"I don't want a sandwich; I want out of here." Jared strained against his bonds again to emphasize his point.

Hugh's face went blank as if someone had flipped his emotion switch off. "Don't be rude Jared. I made this for you; you should eat it. That's what friends do."

The flatness of his voice woke up the survival instinct in Jared's head, and he realized he was truly in trouble. Pain and lights flashed as Hugh's fist slammed into Jared's nose, and he heard the crack as it broke.

"Let's eat, okay? I made this special for you, and I want it to be nice."

Jared thought he sounded like a toddler. Blood dripped from his nose, down his face, and pitter-patted on his shirt. "Yeah, all right," he said, "can you free my hands so I can eat?"

The Joker grin came back. "Ha, no need for that! I'll help you; that's what friends do." He pulled the flag out, dropped it on the table, and held the sandwich out. Jared took a bite. It tasted... off. The bread was soft and warm, but the meat was gamey, like venison. He chewed as he fought back the rising gorge in his throat, and swallowed. "Thank you."

"You bet, buddy." He presented the sandwich again, and Jared took a bite. "We're going to have so much fun," Hugh said and took a bite of his own sandwich.

After brunch, Hugh cut him loose from the table and wheeled him into the living room. They spent the day watching TV and eating more sandwiches: another roast beef, burgers for dinner, and a pulled pork hoagie as a late night snack. When Jared pleaded with Hugh to release him, his captor ignored him, and when he tried to bargain, Hugh taped his mouth and acted like nothing was out of the ordinary. The last thing Hugh made him eat were a few pills.

* * *

"Wake up sleepy head."

Jared opened his eyes and through the haze of drug induced sleep, saw Hugh bent over looking at him. His nose felt like a pulsing melon of pain.

"There you are. Happy Labor Day! I love three day weekends, don't you?" Hugh set a plate in front of him. A bagel sat on it, melted cheese sliding down the sides. "Sausage bagels! I thought something different was in order, so I fixed up some of my homemade sausage." He smacked his lips. "You chose a great time to come over, I have lots of meat in the freezer, so you're going to get the best food, none of that store-bought stuff. I have steaks and roasts, and I made a lot of sausage."

Jared winced when Hugh pulled the tape from his mouth. It felt like his face was raw, and he imagined a pink rectangle centered on his mouth. "I have to go to the bathroom, Hugh." He didn't, but he hoped it would convince his captor to let him out of the chair.

"No you don't. You went in the night, but don't worry, I won't tell anybody about your little indiscretion." He tittered again, and Jared flinched. "Besides, good ol' Hugh took care of it."

Jared just stared at him. What the hell is he saying? "But I really do need to go; I can't eat until I do."

Hugh's eyes died, they flattened, and they reminded Jared of Shark Week. "No, you don't Jared. During the night, you pissed and shit in your pants like a fucking baby. I cleaned you up because that's what best friends do, now eat your sandwich." Hugh's eyes came alive. "I made it special."

Oh God, Jared's skin crawled, and sweat popped out all over him as he looked down and could see the bulk in his pants, the white top of the adult diaper peeking out from his belt. "What did you do? God, Hugh, I'm not eating anymore. You gotta let me go. I swear I'll never tell anyone about this."

Hugh slapped him, and his head rocked back. "You're gonna eat, you shit," he paused for a moment, and a new grin slid in place. Not the Joker grin, this one was the demented clown grin. "Yeah, you're gonna eat shit." He stormed from the room, and Jared could hear him rummaging through something.

"Hugh? I'm sorry! I'll eat, I promise!" The tears started again.

Only the rummaging answered him.

He thrashed, but he was stuck as fast as he had been the day before. "Hugh," he was blubbering in a pool of his own terror, "I'll eat, I swear, just come back and feed me please."

He turned ashen when Hugh loomed into the doorway. "No," Jared said, but the word oozed from his throat and fell unnoticed to the floor.

Hugh grinned his Joker grin. In his left hand was a white U of plastic and fabric, the weight of Jared's "indiscretion" evident. "Open up, buttercup," Hugh said and stepped forward as Jared began to thrash and scream.

***

Two days. Two days and what, six sandwiches? Eight? Jared couldn't remember, the drugs were fogging his thoughts. Sandwiches and— his mind scurried away from the thought of the diaper. That was the last time he had refused to eat, and although he had cooperated with Hugh about everything, he knew he was going to die here. It had been a long weekend and, although he was supposed to work today, they probably wouldn't miss him until tomorrow, maybe even Thursday. They'll call, but when will they worry? Will anybody worry? Yesterday had been the same as Sunday: Sandwiches, TV until lunch, then back into the kitchen for another God damn sandwich, then more TV. After dinner, a beer and the pills.

Something was different today, though. It was morning, he was still in the chair, but Hugh was not here, there was no sandwich for him. Floorboards creaked somewhere in the house. So, he is here. Maybe he slept in.

"I have to go to work today," Hugh said a few minutes later as he came into the kitchen. "I'm sorry, I don't have any sick hours left." He proceeded to make a sandwich and set it in front of Jared. "This will have to hold you until I get home, but I promise I'll make it up to you with something special." He grinned as he removed Jared's tape.

"I need to get to work too; they'll miss me."

Hugh shrugged and fed Jared the sandwich.

***

Tears fell from Jared's eyes as he sat in front of the TV fighting the urge to piss. He had watched a local fluff news show, an aging minister hawking eternal salvation (only $29.99), some older, but still beautiful, model hawking an age defying cream (only $49.99, but wait there's more!), and now Judge Judy was yelling at some couple about their daughter.

He let go, and the warmth of urine spread out in his crotch. Fuck you, Hugh, he thought. He supposed he should be thankful that he hadn't been raped or tortured, but the humiliation was just as complete. There has got to be a way out of this. Every time he was alone he looked for something that could get him out, some way to contact the outside world, but there were no phones, no sharp edges peeking out from the shadows for him to rub against and cut his tape. Hugh had prisoner proofed his home. He couldn't even scoot his way around the room because there was some kind of lock on the chair's wheels. He strained at the tape regularly, but it did nothing.

The doorbell rang. Oh God! Jared strained against his bonds, he screamed, he rocked back and forth. The doorbell rang again. He screamed again, rocked again, and felt himself go off balance. Shit! Jared crashed to the ground and pain coursed through his shoulder, neck, and temple. Judge Judy rambled on, but the doorbell fell silent. He tried to kick, tried to wriggle across the floor, but he became winded after only a few seconds and had only managed to turn in a circle. He repeated this every few minutes for the better part of an hour until he realized he was accomplishing nothing. His tears dried and all the fear went with them. Anger seeped into the spaces where the fear had been.

If I get out of this, Hugh, I'm going to kill you.

***

"Well, it looks like you had some fun," Hugh said when he set his keys down and came in to check on his captive, a FedEx package under his arm and a plastic bag dangling from his hand. He bent and peeled the tape from Jared's mouth.

"Yeah," Jared said, "Judge Judy pissed me off." On the TV, the local weather girl flashed her too white teeth from her too tan face which floated above a too tight dress.

Hugh threw his head back and laughed. "I can see that," Hugh grunted as he lifted Jared to an upright position, then wheeled him into the kitchen.

He had been laying on his arm, and it was a cold, dead piece of meat. Jared rotated his shoulder, trying to encourage the blood of life back into his dormant extremities, realizing that his only accomplishment was an arm that flopped like a fish. What? He looked down at his numb arm as the pinpricks of feeling needled him and his eyes bulged. The arm of his chair had broken. He had been laying on the way out of this mess for hours, watching TV and feeling sorry for himself. He flashed a look at Hugh, but his captor was turned away. He did his best to pull his arm closer and hold it steady as if nothing had changed. He hoped his face remained that way as well. "What's for dinner?"

Hugh looked at him over his shoulder; the Joker grin firmly planted on his face. "Hungry, huh? I got something special for you, just like I said I would, but it's a surprise." He patted the FedEx package. "And something for later." He tittered as he turned back to the counter.

Jared heard the rustle of plastic bags as he wiggled his left hand, testing to see if the arm of the chair had come completely loose.

"I cooked some steak last night while you were sleeping and stopped at the store for this." He pulled a paper bag from the plastic grocery bag. "Fresh hoagie rolls and provolone cheese. I thought Philly cheesesteaks would just make your mouth water."

Jared forced a smile. "Yum."

Hugh heated the steak, onions, green peppers, and cheese in a pan then brought the pan, hoagie rolls, and bread knife to the table on a wooden cutting board. "You've been so good I thought you needed something special." He sliced the rolls open and laid the pieces open faced. He scooped the steak mixture onto each sandwich. "I don't eat a lot of steak, but, the freezer is full." He closed up the sandwiches and held one out to Jared. "There you go, dig in."

"Thanks," Jared said as the sounds of his stomach cheered at the smell of food. He took a bite and savored the taste, closing his eyes and chewing slowly. The meat was unlike anything he had eaten before, but tender and good. The peppers crunched, and the onions were caramelized and delicious. What are you doing? You need to get out of here!

Jared swallowed, wondering how he could get his captor to drop his guard. "Hugh."

The man looked up, mouth full and smile plastered on his face. "Yeah, buddy?"

"I really appreciate this, I do, but." He hesitated, thoughts of the diaper crawling over his mind. "Do you think I'll ever be able to walk around again? To go outside?" He braced for that change, the flatness to drop over Hugh's face, but it didn't come.

"Oh maybe someday. I like our time together, just you and me, but I have to make sure you don't get any ideas like Freddy did." He raised his sandwich when he said this, tipping it slightly toward Jared.

Jared looked at the sandwich in Hugh's hand, then down to his partially eaten one in front of him. The freezer is full, Hugh had said, and that gamey taste. His mouth watered and bile bubbled up from his stomach. No, it can't be, I must be going mad.

"Something wrong, buddy?" Hugh offered another bite to him.

"No, just wondering." He swallowed audibly. "Where did you say Freddy moved to?"

Hugh's eyes flattened again, his face drained of emotion. "That's none of your business Jared. You should eat your dinner, so we don't have another incident like the other day."

Jared's heart hammered in his chest, and a cold sweat had popped out over his entire body. "I'm sorry Hugh, I just want to... know more about you."

"Oh!" Life flowed back into Hugh's face, and he lifted the sandwich back up to Jared's mouth.

Jared nibbled at it, taking only bread. Saliva filled his mouth, and his stomach clenched.

"I've had a few close friends over the years like Freddy, but they all seem to move away. Unlucky I guess."

Jared swallowed. God how many people has he done this to? "And was Freddy as good a friend as I am?" Please don't offer me another bite, please.

"Never!" Hugh's eyes widened, and his head snapped up. "You're the best friend I could ever have!"

Jared watched the sandwich in Hugh's hand wave about, the meat peeking out, the cheese clinging to the bread. He belched hot bile and swallowed it back down.

Jared didn't want to believe he was eating human flesh, but he had to know. "Hugh, what really happened to Freddy."

Hugh's eyes slid to the sandwich. "I told you, he moved away. Who cares about him, let's finish dinner."

It was as much confirmation as Jared needed. He gagged, forcing back a dry heave and the horror of what he had done. "Drink," was all he could say.

Hugh flinched. "Oh lord, I'm sorry, I hope there is nothing wrong with the sandwich." He scrambled up and to the refrigerator.

Jared tugged with all his might at the broken chair. He yanked, and yanked but it wouldn't budge.

Hugh came back to the table with a beer.

"No beer," Jared said, thinking his stomach would complete its revolt, "do you have 7-Up or Sprite?"

"Yeah, in the garage, I'll be right back." Hugh hurried from the room.

Jared pulled, he jerked, he thrashed his arm back and forth. Hours seemed to go by when finally, the arm came free. Jared held it aloft in a triumphant moment, but the realization he still had three limbs bound crushed his jubilation. How is this going to help? Then he saw the knife next to Hugh's sandwich. He heard Hugh's footsteps and put his hand back down to his side.

"Here you go," Hugh came around the table to give Jared a drink.

With all his might, Jared whipped his fist and the chair's arm at Hugh's head. He heard a crunch when it connected with Hugh's temple, and the man wheeled backward, arms flailing, and he crashed to the ground. Hugh lay there motionless as Jared reached for the knife, but the strap around his chest stopped him. Fuck! He reached around the back of the chair as best he could, straining a shoulder that refused to bend that far. He groped until he found the buckle and pulled as Hugh moaned. The strap popped off, and Jared lunged for the knife again. His fingertips brushed it, he strained, never taking his eyes off Hugh for more than a few seconds at a time. His index finger pressed down on the blade, and he curled it, but the knife wouldn't move. He wiggled it back and forth until finally, it inched closer, and he could pick it up. Hugh groaned again and shifted. The knife was dull, but it did the job, and in moments his arms were free. The strap around his waist came next.

"You bastard," Hugh said as he rolled to his side. Blood cascaded down his face.

Jared looked Hugh in the eyes but never stopped cutting the tape from his ankle. Finally, his right foot came free, but Hugh was up on his feet.

He swayed a little, his eyes unfocused. "I thought we were friends, but you're just like all the others. Now you have to move away too." The words were flat; the emotional switch was off again.

Jared shoved the table up and over into Hugh's lap and jerked toward the door. Hugh stumbled and fell back to the floor.

Jared sprinted toward the door, but the chair was still attached to his left leg, and it crashed into the back of his thigh. He glanced back and when he saw Hugh on the ground, bent over and freed his other leg. Jared heard an animal roar just before Hugh slammed into him and the two of them crashed to the floor. "Motherfucker!" Jared screamed and tried to stab Hugh with the knife, but the man grabbed hold of Jared's arm and stopped the blow. They writhed on the ground, shouting and grunting like beasts. Jared twisted and rained down blow after blow to Hugh's back with his good fist, all the while the other man held Jared's arm with one hand and tried to wrest the knife out from his grip with the other.

"Let." Punch. "Me." Punch. "Go!" Punch.

"Never." Hugh bit Jared at the base of the thumb.

Jared screamed and released the knife. He bucked, kicked, and slid away from Hugh who scooped up the knife and spun to face him.

"Come on Jared; I promise things will be different. We can still be friends; you don't have to move."

Jared got to his feet and backed away. "You're insane."

Hugh followed. "And you're just like the others." He pointed the knife like the accusing finger of God. "You said you were my friend."

Jared turned and sprinted to the door. Two locks and a chain stood between him and freedom. He undid the chain and the first lock with ease, but fumbled at the second, unable to turn the bolt. He heard Hugh running at him and turned with every ounce of strength he could muster and swung the back of his fist at the approaching man's head. The blow sent Hugh sprawling and the knife flying toward the hallway. He turned back to the door and tried the lock again.

"I'm going to gut you, Jared. I'm going to gut you, skin you, and cut you up just like the others."

Jared looked over his shoulder and saw Hugh standing down the hall, the recovered knife in his hand and murder in his eyes. He slapped at the lock in frustration. Come on you motherfucker.

"Okay, Jared, time to move away." He swayed again, one knee buckling for a second.

Jared blanched and gagged. My God! He sprang at Hugh while the man was off

balance, and brought his foot down hard on his ankle with a gut-wrenching snap.

Hugh screamed, and Jared practically jumped back to the door. The lock clicked, and he wrenched the door open and sprinted to the road.

***

From the Greenfield County Gazette, September 17th, 2015

Local Man Wanted for Kidnapping and Murder

In the strangest ordeal to hit Greenfield County in memory, local resident Jared Thomas was kidnapped by fellow resident Hugh Barber after the two watched football at the suspect's home on Saturday, September 5th. It is unknown at this time why Barber abducted Thomas, as they had been friends for a number of years.

According to the sheriff's office, Mr. Thomas was allegedly abducted and imprisoned by Barber and repeatedly assaulted over the course of three days. On Tuesday, September 8th, 2015, the victim fought off Mr. Barber and escaped to a nearby residence where the sheriff was called. Mr. Thomas was rushed to the Greenfield County hospital for treatment of his wounds. At this time, he has been unavailable for comment.

Sources close to the Sheriff's office have told The Gazette that officers were dispatched to Mr. Barber's home, located at 1468 Rural Rt #3, where the scene was examined and secured. There was no sign of Mr. Barber or his vehicle, a black 1987 Nissan Maxima. Based on the statement of Mr. Thomas, the contents of a chest freezer at the property are being tested for the presence of human DNA. As of this writing, the remains of 19 people have been located and transferred to the coroner's office for examination. If you have information regarding the whereabouts of Hugh Barber, or a man fitting his description, please contact the Greenfield County Sheriff Office information line at 1-800-555-9932.

Russ Gartz's Shopping List

Toilet paper
Dark chocolate cocoa powder
Canned tomatoes (the kind with diced onions and green bell peppers)
Rigatoni
Coffee (Columbian)
Protein powder (chocolate flavor)
Dental floss
Parmesan cheese (grated)
Cranberry juice
Milk (2% fat)
Butter
Coleslaw
Bagels (blueberry and raisin-cinnamon)

Deathlust

Russ Gartz

1480, Spain, Night

"I hope you enjoyed yourself, Your Emi-" Miquel Gusbalm's head was suddenly jerked to the right. The salty taste of blood filled his mouth.

"You should be more careful," hissed a thin, reedy, voice that came from beneath the hood of a cape. "You make a lot of money with this inn. It would be a shame if the wrong people became… interested in what goes on here. Hmm?"

"Of course… Señor Gomez."

A smile of succulent victory appeared in the shadows of the hood; bright, satanic blue eyes almost glowed in the dim light.

Miquel suppressed his anger as the caped figure gently slapped his bruised cheek, like an overbearing father would a son, "Good. I'm glad we understand each other."

The muffled whimpering of a woman caused both men to turn and look towards a closed door that was at the top of the staircase.

Miquel and the caped figure locked eyes. Miquel suppressed the anger of a cheated man who knew he could do nothing about it. If Don Juan Ramirez were here, you would feel the sting of his steel… pig! thought Miquel.

"For your trouble," the caped figure chuckled and flung a few silver coins onto the bar.

As the caped figure turned to leave, Miguel smiled; he couldn't resist, "Oh, Señor Gomez, I pray you will be cautious going home. A madman is killing members of the Holy Inquisition; it seems they are only safe in the Citadel."

The caped figure stopped and shuddered.

Miquel smiled as he wiped blood from his lip, "But, there are some who say, it is a vampire who is killing these … servants of God."

Outside the tavern the caped figure stumbled into a coach, "Back to the citadel," He pounded on the roof of the carriage. The caped figure fumed, "One day, Miquel, you will pay for your insolence. The Citadel always has room for one …"

He felt the coach slightly rock from side to side, as if a man had leapt off the from the driver's seat. Then nothing, except the hoot of an owl in the distance.

The hood went back over his head and he bolted from the carriage, "Are you deaf as well as dumb!" he roared as he shock the coachman.

The coachman responded with his head falling unnaturally onto one shoulder.

"Oh my God!"

The coachman's body landed with a thud as the carriage roared off like the devil was chasing it. A dog cautiously approached the dead coachman, sniffed, and gently lapped at the blood that had dribbled from two punctures in the coachman's neck.

***

"Go in peace; sin no more."

"Bless you, Father," replied a young man as he exited the confessional; his sword rattled against his armor as he left.

Father Jose Maladod, known for his dedication to God and the holy church, sighed and massaged the back of his neck. Through the lattice of the confessional, he could tell the sun had gone down. "Ummph. Time for bed," he said to no one. He grasped the knob of the confessional door… and couldn't budge it.

"Don't you have time for one more confession, Father?"

Father Jose swallowed as he recognized the voice; a rich baritone with a slight bit of base. The image that came to his mind was that of a nobleman, tall, aristocratic, handsome, dark hair, a thin mustache, and goatee. A man who had worked his muscles to perfection and who seemed to dance rather than fence with a sword.

Father Jose grew cold as the memory passed and he heard the door to the opposite confessional close. Through the lattice, he could see a pair of red glowing eyes. To do God's work, you sometimes dance with the devil, he thought.

Father Jose swallowed hard, "How you get into this house of God—"

"Is not in any way amazing. If you can't keep the Devil out, you can't keep me out." The owner of the red eyes leaned back and steepled his fingers in front of his face, as if daydreaming, and gently laughed, "Your ignorance of my kind, and your own kind, fascinates me."

"Killing that coachman last night was unnecessary! He wasn't a member of the Inquisition!" exploded Father Jose, "every soul you take—"

"I only take blood; souls I leave to God.

"And besides, while slacking my thirst I thought I would get our dear Bishop's attention." Fangs gleamed as the vampire smiled, his red lips made his teeth menacing, "And I succeeded."

Father Jose steeled himself, "We agreed to do this my way! Bishop Bectano and his devils must pay for their crimes against God. But this is more than satisfying your bloodlust!"

"Ha!" replied the vampire, "My bloodlust is nothing compared to a man's deathlust."

"What?"

"My kind only lust for blood … for food. And never more than one can drink in a night. After all, blood is the holiest of wines. One must be grateful for such a gift from God.

"But a man's deathlust is like a fox in a hen house. The fox kills far more chickens that he can eat. Why? The fox lusts for killing.

"And as with foxes, so it is with men. Like an onion, peel away the layers of delusion, and you find deathlust in a man's heart."

Father Jose twisted in his seat, desperate to change the subject, "If Bectano is brought to justice, Holy Spain will be rid of this curse! Too many innocent lives are taken in the name of God!"

"Ah yes, the Inquisition wastes SOOO much blood."

"This is more than about blood!"

"I agree," snarled the vampire as he ran a finger along an ornate brooch; a pained expression creased his handsome face.

"May God forgive you, Juan. I am after justice, not revenge," said Father Jose.

"Forgiveness, my old confessor?" said Juan as he got up to leave. "What makes you think God will forgive you? What makes you think your deathlust is less than Julio Bectano's?"

***

"She is a witch. Tomorrow, we save her soul," calmly said Bishop Julio Bectano from his seat where he dispensed holy justice in the name of the king.

"NO! NO!" screamed the young Jewish woman as citadel guards dragged her away.

What a shame, to burn something so lovely, but what can one do with the uncooperative, thought Bectano, who smiled. But Jews have lost their souls anyway.

"Will there be anything else, Your Eminence?" asked a guard.

"Where is my valet? I sent you to find him an hour ago! I need my garlic!"

"I-I-I don't, Your Eminence--"

The guard felt his cheek explode in pain as he fell to the stone floor.

"I am surrounded by fools! By idiots!"

Guards outside of Bectano's private apartment quickly plastered themselves to the wall as they heard the sinister swishing of his robes and the out of place angelic tinkling of his ornate crucifix. With the reflexes of a chicken scrambling for its life, a guard flung the door to Bectano's apartment open.

Bectano's rage suddenly turned to fear. "Oh my god!"

Pablo, Bectano's valet, was laying on the floor. His normal brown complexion was a ghastly white. A small pool of blood formed a red halo around Pablo's head, his eyes frozen in horror.

***

Juan perched beside a gargoyle on one of the citadel's towers; delighting in the screams coming from Bectano's apartment. With his middle finger, he gently cleaned the blood from the corner of his mouth and gently, passionately, sucked it. "Your screams, Bectano, are almost as sweet and succulent as dear Pablo's blood," he whispered to himself. Juan smiled, it had been worth the effort to carefully and silently drag Pablo's body up the Citadel walls and toss it through the open window.

What a shame, the poor Jew. She was almost as lovely as my… Juan leaned back and smiled. He knew it was stupid to reminisce like an old fool. But like a man who has too much wine, well… just one more…

It was a fine spring day in the market square. A slight breeze gently blew her dark hair that reached to the middle of her back. Any woman with her cheekbones, dark eyes, and vivid lips would have been called beautiful. A face and figure Aphrodite would kill for, thought Juan as he approached her. But when Rosa saw him, it was her smile that let Juan know that God had sent angels to live among mere mortals.

He chided her for dressing like a peasant and that the servants could go to the market for her. She playfully shot back that her clothes were comfortable and she liked to pick out her own food as she chomped on an apple. Besides, it was a beautiful day, much too beautiful to sit in the hacienda. He laughed; he could never argue with his Rosa, especially when she was right.

The angelic setting was smashed by the Guards of the Inquisition. They demanded Rosa surrender to them. Before his ornate sword was out of its scabbard, Juan's head exploded in pain.

Blackness … silence.

The blackness became torch light. Muffled sounds became screams for mercy. He looked down and saw crude leather bindings that strapped his wrists to a chair. Rage tore through him as he saw his sword in the scabbard of an Inquisition guard. Pain shot through his body as he jerked himself up. Blood spurted from his wrists.

"Ah, Don Juan Ramirez, you are awake," leered Bishop Bectano, "you must be wondering where your dear wife is. It would be uncivilized to keep you in suspense."

Bectano grabbed hold of a tarp and jerked downward.

Like the Christ, Rosa had been nailed to a cross. Her simple clothes had been replaced by dirty, bloody loin cloth. Blood ran from her mouth.

"A pity she did not confess to her crimes," hissed Bectano, as he held out his hand, "and I couldn't stand her lies anymore." Bectano undid the wrappings of a blood soaked bundle … that held a human tongue.

Splinters of wood exploded into the air as Juan broke free; anger flooded through him. His only thought was to get his hands around Bectano's throat. Just as he reached the horrified Bectano, Juan felt his own sword thrust through his heart.

Finally, darkness covered Bectano's sneering, laughing face.

Juan snapped back into reality, his head pounding. His instincts had survived his death. Lashing out with one hand, Juan grabbed one of the gargoyle's ears, preventing him from falling into the Citadel's courtyard. His body hung like a rabbit caught in a hunter's snare.

With his free hand, Juan wiped away the tears of blood from his face.

An image of another vampire came to his mind, "You are no longer human. Let her go, let yourself find peace. The longer you stay drunk, the more you deny like a man, the more it hurts."

"Forgive me, my dear guru" said Juan under his breath, as the pounding in his head subsided, "I'm enjoying being drunk."

***

"Please, my old teacher, you must help me! A vampire is killing the members of the Holy Inquisition… and soon he will kill me!" Bectano was on his knees clutching Father Jose's simple robes; sweat had started to drop on the floor. Sunlight filtered into Father Jose's church in long shafts, one of which fell on both of them, as if Heaven had singled them out. In the shadows, the image of Jesus on the cross looked down.

Jose grabbed Bectano's hair, "This is payment for your sins. And, oh, how you've sinned."

He roughly released Bectano's head and turned to face the cross, "Do you really think I don't know what goes on in the Citadel, hmm? You think torture will make a man embrace the church… embrace the Savior's teachings?!"

"It is my duty to root out heresy in the kingdom! I must--"

Bectano's head suddenly swung to the right. The echoing of the slap heightened his loneliness and terror.

"And does that 'duty' include, false arrest, whoring, rape, and murder?!"

Father Jose held Bectano's head with both his hands, "You—are—condemned."

"Please… PLEASE! My old teacher, did you not say that God could forgive any sin? That his love embraces the vilest sinner?"

Father Jose turned away, faced the cross again and sighed, "Yes, I believe that," and turned to face Bectano, "but only if one is truly repentant. One can say anything in the confessional, but God will know if you are sincere… or not."

The old priest closed his eyes. Victory!

"This not well known, but a man who let's God truly into his heart - will have no fear of a vampire," Father Jose raised his finger to make the point, "in fact, a vampire is repelled by such a display. The undead find such displays of faith and love abhorrent to their foul natures."

Father Jose walked to the altar, "There are rituals to demonstrate this faith and love."

A huge grin broke out on Bectano's face, "Oh Father, I knew you would-"

"But …"

The grin turned into a frown.

Father Jose walked back to the kneeling Bectano, "You must confess, before the town, when the powers of darkness are at their peak… tonight."

The silence was broken by urine streaming on to the church floor. Bectano's face was frozen in terror, "The crowd will tear me to pieces!"

Father Jose gently took Bectano's head in his hands, "I will be there tonight, to hear your confession. You will not face the crowd alone."

A smile graced the old priest's lips, "Be at peace, Julio. When the sun rises tomorrow, the Gates of Heaven will be open to you again."

"How, how will you make sure the vampire will not come?"

"I know the way to keep safe from him."

Father Jose smiled as he heard a lamb gently bleating from the yard.

***

"We should be inside, Your Eminence. The vampire will be hunting for us," said the Captain of the Guard. He tried to reassure himself by grasping grip of the ornate sword in its scabbard. The thunder and lightning from the approaching storm further furrowed the captain's brow.

"We must wait for Father Jose. Then we go to the market place," nervously replied Bectano as he turned away from the Captain. In the moonlight, he could see what looked like a giant needle, on a board, that pointed to Heaven. He gulped. It was the raised platform that held the stake where he had sentenced so many. The light from the moon bounced off his crucifix as he nervously toyed with it.

Already, Bectano could hear the crowd gathering, Oh get here you old fool!

From behind, Bectano heard the rustling of leaves... then a thud. Bectano whirled around; the Captain was gone. "Where are you?!" demanded Bectano.

From nowhere it came; the rich baritone voice with a slight hint of base, "The dear captain will not be joining us. I have sent him to his… reward."

Cold sweat drenched Bectano, "No! It can't be!"

Bectano felt a sharp sting across the back of his hand. He instinctively clutched his bleeding hand to his chest; the crucifix tumbling into the mud at his feet. The pain in Bectano's hand quickly vanished as he felt the point of a sword at his throat, "Juan Ramirez!"

Juan smiled; blood ran down from the corners of his mouth. "Ah, I am so glad you remember me. Of course, I have never forgotten you …"

"You're dead! I saw you die!"

"To rise as a vampire. As God saw fit."

Juan lovingly caressed his sword, "Ah, my old friend, it has been far too long since I held you. Do you remember all our dances, all our victories … how we celebrated? Now, just one more dance, one more victory, one more celebration."

Bectano found his head turning in the direction of the crowd, whose dull cries were now muffled shouts. A sting at his throat brought his head around to face Juan's glowing red eyes.

"Oh, don't worry about them. By the time they come looking for you, we will be at dinner," said Juan, "but, I won't be dining. You see, I would never soil my pallet with your filthy blood. My friends, well … they aren't so fussy. Ah! They accepted my invitation. Look."

Bectano gasped. The ground behind Juan was moving, like the waves on the ocean. There were bright spots on the waves … moonlight reflected on hundreds of pairs of eyes.

"You disappoint me, Bectano. I thought you would find rats charming company," sneered Juan; the moonlight bouncing off his fangs.

The smile faded from Juan's face. A pained expression appeared, "But first, I will cut out your tongue."

The smooth baritone became a growl, "So I can hear how well you scream without it!"

"I knew you would break our agreement!" scowled Father Jose as he stepped out of an alley.

"It would be rude not to thank you for getting Bectano out of the Citadel. The stench of all that innocent blood being spilled! No vampire could not enter that foul place.

"Go back to your church and concentrate on saving souls, my old friend," sneered Juan as he pressed the tip of his sword into the folds of Bectano's chin, "this soul is far beyond redemption."

"The Inquisition must end!"

"Your desire for justice is nothing more than deathlust. I told you, go back to your church!"

"Please, Juan, don't force me!"

Juan painfully growled, "You think I don't smell that lamb's blood in that bucket behind you, hmm? I see you can read between the lines of Exodus. But before you can splash it on him or me, I will skewer this pig."

"God, forgive me." Father Jose upended the bucket on his head and rushed between Juan and Bectano. Juan recoiled as a hand burned by a flame, "AHHHHH! FOOL!"

"Come!" screamed Father Jose as he dragged the stunned Bectano along with him towards the stake in the market square. As they approached the crowd, Father Jose began to feel it. A warm, cozy feeling in the belly. Heat began to radiate through his body, powering him on. It felt good, strong … righteous.

Bectano tried to run away but Father Jose's hand had become an iron shackle. The small priest jerked Bectano off his feet as if he were a small boy. Looking up, Bectano froze as he saw the leering smile on Father Jose's face.

It was then that Bectano heard it. Softly at first, then louder, more menacing… terrifying…

"Death to Bectano! Death to Bectano! Death to Bectano!"

Father Jose felt the chanting vibrate through him… and something else. The delicious sensation of his own blood pounding through his body. It felt powerful, majestic… divine.

"Death to Bectano! Death to Bectano! Death to Bectano!"

"Out of the way! Out—of—the—way!" screamed Father Jose. His fist swung left and right, right and left, like a scythe, sweeping the crowd out of his way as he dragged Bectano behind him.

"Death to Bectano! Death to Bectano! Death to Bectano!"

Bectano suddenly felt himself crash into the base of the stake. Shaking his head, he looked out, "God in Heaven, please help me!" As far as he could see, torches waving like wheat in the spring. Pair upon pair upon pair of wild eyes. Hands clawed for him.

"Death to Bectano! Death to Bectano! Death to Bectano!"

Power that was a divine symphony flowed through Father Jose like the tide; subtle, pure… unstoppable. He reveled in it. The capillaries in his face burst from the fierce smile. He grabbed Bectano's robes and with one hand held him up over the crowd, "Confess … NOW!"

"Death to Bectano! Death to Bectano! Death to Bectano!"

Bectano could feel fingers grabbing at his feet, "I-I-I confess! I CONFESS! The Inquisition is false! I have tortured and murdered for my own gain!"

"Is that ALL?!" sneered Father Jose as he grabbed Bectano's head with both hands.

"Death to Bectano! Death to Bectano! Death to Bectano!"

"No! No! No! Rosa Ramirez caught me coming out of the brothel! I had to silence her and Don Juan -- Ahhhhhhhh!!!"

Father Jose drove his thumbs into Bectano's eye sockets. He could not hear the roar of the crowd; only the symphony of lust and power that poured through him; unstoppable like rolling thunder. The gentle tug he felt was the crowd ripping Bectano out of his grip. The music in his ears was Bectano's screams as his arms are legs were torn from his body.

Covered with Bectano's blood, the crowd began to attack itself; there was no innocent blood left to spill. No one could feel pain as bones were broken, skulls were split, bodies stabbed; only an ecstasy of death.

The large bat above the crowd power dived for the platform. Just before the bat crashed into the platform the wings became arms and the diminutive legs became the strong instruments of the fencer. But the red eyes remained.

Juan, resplendent in black, his cape blowing gently in the breeze, stood toe-to-toe with Father Jose. He grabbed Father Jose by his robes and shock him, "Jose! I was wrong! We were wrong! Snap out of this … now! For the love of God, NOW!"

Juan felt a tug on his cape and instinctively kicked out with his foot. An enraged Miquel was sent flying backwards into the crowd. The torch that had been in his hand went flying into kindling at the bottom of the platform.

"No ... no ... NO!" sneered Father Jose as he started to choke the vampire; insane laughter came from his mouth.

"God, please forgive me." Juan tightly closed his eyes.

Father Jose felt a shock as he was pushed against the stake. He tried to get away, but couldn't. He looked down to see the hilt of Juan's sword sticking out of his chest. "Juan?" asked Father Jose. Tears of blood ran down Juan's face as the flames began to consume the platform. For what seemed an eternity, Father Jose's eyes finally closed.

***

From the hillside, Juan could see the fire in the Market Square was still burning. As when he was a boy, Juan knelt down and bowed his head, "Most merciful Father, I humbly beseech you. As you have with my beloved Rosa, clasp to your bosom the soul of my teacher, my friend, Jose. For many years, he was one of your most dedicated servants. Please forgive his transgressions. His greatest sin was that he forgot why he was here. Amen."

"And what about you?" asked a familiar voice.

Juan turned to face a Mongol dressed in black with glowing red vampire eyes; his guru. Juan smiled back, "I thought I was merely drunk. But the pain is finally gone."

Juan's guru knelt beside him and Juan once again bowed his head, "Most Merciful Father, I humbly beseech one more thing of you," both vampires raised their faces to the stars, "Remove my humanity, remove my deathlust."

Mark Slade's Shopping List

Marble bread
Thousand island
Dijon mustard
Cheese
Meats
Banana peppers
Tomatoes
Lettuce
Drinks
Sun chips
Baked chips
Root beer
Avocado
Crackers

Touch Me, I'm Sick

Mark Slade

It was never about love for Mike and Carrie. It was always about sex.

Wherever they found themselves, the attraction was so strong that they couldn't keep their hands off of each other. Dropping their kids off to school, Carrie would climb into Mike's Classic '66 Dart and they would pull around the school—behind the chain link fence where the baseball diamond was empty and have their way with each other. On a weekend picnic at the park with Wade and Denny, Carrie would see Mike with Jen and Francine. They would chat a few minutes, then go off with their respective spouses and children to eat their lunches. Carrie would excuse herself as Mike did. They would search each other out, go into a Porta-potty on the opposite of the park where their families were and go at each other like horny, rabid animals.

The funny thing was, up until a week ago, they were complete strangers.

Only Wade and Jen knew each other from work, and had brought—actually, dragged—Mike and Carrie to an office party. Wade and Jen were in advertising. They worked closely on an ad program for the Church of

Latter-Day Saints that had become something of a pop-culture phenomenon. A child that is bullied at school, bullied at home, grows into an adult, comes back home to help the bully who is now homeless and bring his father home to live with his family. Neither the message, nor the way the commercial was shot, was the reason the ad was such a big hit. It was the great CGI effects used to morph the child into an adult as he offered his hand to the bully sitting on the sidewalk. For some reason, the campaign had gotten into the American public's consciousness and sparked debate on social media, for good or bad. The agency was so proud of Wade and Jen, they threw a party to honor them. Wade was a banker. He found advertising more boring than banking. Carrie felt the same way. Her interest in real estate was waning to the point she was thinking of going back to teaching high school.

"Hey," Jen said to her husband. "I'd like you to meet Wade's wife, Carrie."

"Oh," Mike changed hands with his drink. "Hi. Nice to meet you."

"Nice to meet you," Carrie flashed her big brown eyes at him in her usual shy, little girl way. Mike exuded all the arrogant charm of a jock.

Mike smiled, shook Carrie's hand.

Carrie looked at Mike, Mike looked at Carrie, eyes wild, body full of electricity. Both of them had this unholy urge and desire to strip each other's clothes off and screw each other silly, right in front of everyone. It was all they thought of the whole evening. For most of the evening they stayed away from each other. Sometimes trading meaningful glances, or nervously brushing past each other as one of them worked the room.

Finally, neither one could take it anymore. Carrie sat her drink down, made sure her purse was on her shoulder and headed out the door for some fresh air. She stood in the parking lot, partly hoping Mike wouldn't follow, but mostly needing him to. She heard footsteps on the gravel behind her and there he was, hands in his pocket, glaring at her. Carrie trotted to him, grabbed him by the arm and off into the bushes they went. Her dress went up, his zipper went down. Her pantyhose rolled down, his penis came out, driving hard inside her. She pushed her face into the bushes, gripped the tiny limbs in her hands and took it.

Intense as it was, satisfying somewhat, both were disappointed it ended in a few minutes.

Carrie rolled up her pantyhose, fixed her dress. Mike placed his penis back into his trousers and zipped up. Without words, they beheld each other guiltily. Mike sighed, nodded, and walked away. Carrie waited until Mike was out of sight before she started back. She retrieved her phone out of her purse and pretended to speak with the baby sitter.

"No, Tina," Carrie gave out a fake laugh as she came upon Wade. "Denny cannot have the rest of that chocolate pie. Yes, tell him I said that! Goodbye!"

Wade had a strange look on his face. Carrie stopped smiling until Jen strode over like she was on a cat walk and handed Carrie another drink.

"Uggg! Kids!" Their glasses touched in a toast. "But we need them to validate our existence in this world."

Carrie giggle, took a sip of her wine. "Ain't that a fact!" Carrie stepped backwards and bumped into Charlie Dixon, one of the other ad people. Carrie nearly fell over backwards, spilling her wine on the office carpet.

"I'm sorry," Charlie said as he caught Carrie.

"Oh!" Carrie giggled.

"Are you alright?" He asked, showing a bit of concern, but was mostly annoyed.

"Yes," Carrie said, steadied herself on Charlie's arm. "I guess I'm tipsier than I thought."

Charlie smiled, nodded, and headed for the bathroom.

"Hey," Wade approached her. "Who is Tina? Your Aunt Delia is taking care of Denny tonight."

Carrie gave Wade a cold gaze. "It was a joke, alright? Just relax. I won't embarrass you anymore." She said and rolled her eyes.

***

When Carrie finished her shower, she noticed a bruise on her midsection. She ran her fingers across it. It didn't feel like a bruise. It didn't even hurt. It almost looked like a tattoo.

"That's weird," Carrie said examining the mark in the mirror. "Maybe I did it in my sleep… scratching… hmmm… I don't know… I wasn't wearing anything tight past few days….."

"Honey?" Wade called out before entering the bathroom.

"Yes?" carried called back.

"I got an odd phone call from Jen," He looked distressed, in a daze, almost walked into the bathroom cabinet.

Carrie finished drying off and pulled Wade to her, wrapped her arms around him. She kissed his ear. "Oh, honey, what's wrong?"

"Remember Charlie Dixon? You met him at last night's party?"

"Yeah?"

"He died," Wade's voice broke slightly. "In his sleep. He was only thirty-five."

"What caused his death?" Carrie led Wade to the bedroom, sat him on a footstool in front of the bed.

"Apparently… a heart attack. He was… only thirty-five." Wade looked confused.

"Maybe he just didn't take good care of himself." Carrie rubbed Wade's shoulders.

Wade scoffed. "No," he raised his eyebrows at her. "Charlie was a health nut."

***

They finished inside the porta-potty, again, having almost nothing to say.

Mike shrugged, gave Carrie an embarrassed smile.

Carrie sighed. "This is crazy," she said, fixed her bra and shirt.

"Yeah," Mike nodded. "I don't even know you." He laughed nervously.

"We can't keep doing this," Carrie closed her eyes, reopened them, trying to compose herself.

"I've never done this before," Mike said.

"Well, I'm not a cheater, either!" Carrie said, her nostrils flared.

"Whoa lady… I didn't say you were.…"

"Is….is it… just me? Or… is this… something hard to control? I mean… I don't even have to see you… ever since the party a few days ago…"

"No," Mike fastened the button on his shorts. "I've… been driving down your street, hoping Wade wasn't home."

"He wasn't home yesterday." Carrie breathed uneasily, fixed her honey-blonde hair back into a pony tail. "You should've come inside." Carrie touched Mike's chest.

"Yeah," he sighed, flinched slightly at her touch.

They heard footsteps outside the porta-potty. Carrie withdrew her hand quickly. Mike placed a finger on his lips, Carrie held her breath the best she could.

A man in light brown khaki shorts and a shirt appeared at the porta-potty door. Mike rushed out, closed the door quickly. The park worker stood with his hands on his hips, cutting his eyes at Mike. Beads of sweat rolled down the man's unkempt beard.

"Hi," mike said.

"Sir? Was there another person in there with you?" The park worker said with all the authority given to him by NATO.

Mike laughed nervously. "No. Of course not."

"Well I'll just have a look myself…"

"Look," Mike touched the man on his elbow, and he instinctively pulled away. "Okay," Mike whispered. "Hey… yeah… I have someone in there. I made a mistake…"

"You bet you did!" The park worker growled.

"I've got fifty bucks here that says you didn't see anything," Mike took the bill out of his wallet and offered it to the man. The park worker eyed the money and Mike, not sure what to do. "C'mon, man," Mike cleared his throat. "This is a better situation for all involved. I'm sure you're the only one that has seen anything. Just give us ten minutes and we'll disappear. As a matter of fact, it looks like rain… we'll both leave immediately."

The park worker took the fifty dollar bill, rolled it up, and dispatched it into his front pocket. "Ten minutes," he pushed a finger in Mike's face and walked toward the edge of the lake.

"Ten minutes," Mike echoed the park worker and watched him disappear around a cluster of trees. Mike opened the door to the porta-potty and shooed Carrie out.

"Thank you for not getting me involved." Carrie kissed Mike.

He tried to dodge the kiss, which was more a brush on the lips. "Yeah, well. We better get back to our families. I'm sure they're wondering about us."

By the time Carrie and Mike reached the picnic area, there was a crowd gathered at the edge of the lake. Carrie went left to Wade's side and Mike went to the right, fought to separate the middle of the crowd, where Jen was front and center. Jen glanced over her shoulder and saw Mike. She ran to him.

"Oh geez, honey. I was getting worried." She said, her hand cupping her mouth.

"I know, I went to find a bathroom and got lost," Mike said.

"You wouldn't believe what has happened."

"Why? What happened, Jen?"

"This," Jen led Mike to the edge of the lake.

The park worker that Mike had just bribed was floating face down, his body motionless.

***

They finished in the backseat of Mike's Dart. Mike laid on top of Carrie, her skirt up around her waist, her sweater top and bra on the floorboard. Mike rested his head on Carrie's breasts. She hugged him close and, feeling a tender moment, kissed his ears and neck. She admitted to herself, seeing him without his shirt, she liked the way he was cut. Nice and lean, more muscle than Wade.

100

"This is crazy," Mike said, his voice muffled from kissing Carrie's erect nipples. "We're having sex in a parked car behind the school that our children go to."

"Yeah," Carrie said, moving her hand across Mike's back. "Very crazy. Even crazier is that we don't know why we started this. Obviously both of us have more to lose if our spouses find out."

"Do you feel guilty?" Mike looked up at her, his started water a bit.

Carrie sighed. "Sometimes." She answered.

"Sometimes?"

"I guess that wasn't the answer you wanted," Carrie said. Her fingers brushed something, like a cut drying up. She pulled her hand away, saw a dark brownish red liquid covering her fingers.

"I don't know what to say. I feel guilty, but…" Mike let the words trail off. "At the same time my body yearns for you."

"Mike?" There was panic in Carrie's voice.

"What?"

"You're bleeding!"

"No—how?" Mike slid away from Carrie, touched the left door window. He felt a stinging sensation, the liquid—blood or ink—or whatever it was, caused his skin to be glued to the window.

"You're bleeding on your back!" Carrie sat, her bare feet smacked Mike in the chest. That's when she noticed the cuts scabbing over Mike's body were moving, covering his body; and had started to look like a tattoo was forming. "Oh my God!" Carrie cried out. "The wounds are moving—Mike!"

Mike was frantically searching his body, began to remove his trousers from his legs when he saw the same thing happening to Carrie. Mike gasped. "It's on—it's you too!" He screamed. "Look! Look!"

The wounds were moving across Carrie's breasts down to midsection and even across her neck. She felt the liquid burn slightly on her skin, especially her legs and pelvis. She had to take her skirt off, just for a few minutes until this thing passed, this warm burning that hurt, and was simultaneously orgasmic.

Soon, both of them sat there completely naked and let the process play out. Once in a while, one or both would moan and sigh.

"I don't know what's going on," Carrie said, breathless. "I can say that I kind of like this feeling. I know that sounds weird. From the look of things, you like it too,"

"I think it over," Mike said. Breathing heavy, he touched Carrie's newly tattooed shoulder, eased his fingers to her right breast and tweaked her nipple with his thumb. Carrie quivered, leaned in, and kissed him.

"How do we explain this?" Carrie looked wantonly into Mike's eyes.

"I haven't had sex with Jen since we started, let alone let her see me without clothes on."

Carrie. Nodded. "Same here,' she told Mike. "Wade hasn't asked to have sex, nor made any advances. We just lie in the bed, far apart from each other."

Mike scoffed. "Yeah. Listen to each other breathe. We barely say anything to each other unless it's about work… or bills…" Mike began to dress when he saw Carrie place her bra overtop of her breasts.

"Or about the kid." Carrie added.

***

Things got worse for Mike and Carrie.

They found there was stiffness in the joints, walking was like walking in quicksand.

The last people they'd touched after they had sex was their parents. For Mike, it was his Father, who had died in a car accident on I-45. A semi jackknifed, and a nine-car pileup ensued. For Carrie, her Mother passed away. A brain aneurism while working in the gift shop she owned. It was tough for both Mike and Carrie mentally, but also physically. Getting to those funerals was tough. Mike had to use a cane to walk to his father's funeral, which was held on top of a hill in Cedar high cemetery. His father always bought the cheapest products, whether that was car insurance or cemetery plots. Carrie fared better. Her mother's funeral was held at a private church gathering. Still, family had to help her in and out of the church, and she couldn't stay long at the wake, the pain was too much for her.

Wade didn't attend the funeral, nor did Jen attend Mike's funeral for his father. They had to attend the funerals for their own parents. Yes, Mike and Carrie were not the only ones affected by their choices, so too were their spouses. Jen's father committed suicide. He went upstairs to the attic and hung himself with an extension cord. No note or explanation was given. Wade's mother and father died in their sleep. Carbon monoxide poisoning.

Mike and Carrie stayed away from each other for a month. Those urges were strong. Very strong. Mike found himself driving around Carrie's neighborhood at midnight, hoping Wade was gone. He so badly wanted that booty call. But Carrie was doing the same thing. She showed up at Mike's bank. Hoping he was in his office. She even pretended to want a loan. She told the secretary she had to see mike specifically. Mike was at a meeting, a long lunch.

Carrie called Mike. She didn't care if Wade found out. They had to do something. Whether it was to screw first then talk… no. They wouldn't even touch each other. Not only that, she really could not move well enough for sex. They spoke briefly, decided to meet at one of the houses she was trying to sell.

Mike hobbled into the house, bent forward, he couldn't stand straight at all. Very strange for a man in his thirties. Carrie steadied herself on the walls as she entered the ranch-style house.

"We need to talk about this," Carrie finally broke the wall of silence.

"I agree," Mike sat down on the couch beside her. He so badly wanted to touch her, even though she was dressed like a bag lady. The desire was at an all-time high, and when his penis became erect, he cringed in pain. Carrie inched her hand closer to Mike, thought of the consequences, and withdrew quickly.

"What we've been doing," Carrie continued. "Has had an adverse effect on our lives."

"I know," Mike nodded. "We've been causing all the deaths lately. Somehow, someway. I don't understand it."

"I might. You're going to think I'm crazy."

"No… nothing can be crazier than the last two months."

"Okay," Carrie struggled to take her blouse off. "Take your clothes off."

"Uh, I don't think we should do this…" Mike cleared his voice.

"No, Mike. We aren't going to have sex… even though….right now, I want to more than life itself… but we are not going to. We're going to fight it." Carrie stood, let her baggie sweat pants fall to the floor, then her oversized panties.

Mike kicked off his trousers. He wore no underwear because they irritated his genitalia, not only chafing, but large red splotches appeared before the skin thickened and turned a golden brown.

They stood naked in front of each other. Painful to stand, they held on to the couch or end table.

"See?" Carrie pointed to her tattooed body.

Mike gasped. "Oh my God. You too? This is one giant body tattoo of a man and woman naked, kissing."

True. From the neck to their toes, Mike and Carrie had the same tattoo. A man and woman caressing each other, kissing. Their clothing, nothing more than white wraps, lay at their feet. The green skinned man with wings, held a bow and arrow in one hand, the other on the red skinned woman's breast. Both had piercings up and down their bodies. The woman had her hand around the winged man's erect penis. The background consisted of brownish red, and five different flowers at their feet: Ashoka tree flowers, white and blue lotus flowers, Jasmine, and Mango tree flowers.

"I researched this," Carrie said. "The people in our tattoo are Sanskrit Deities. Kama is the God of desire and longing. Basically, their version of Cupid. Rati is the Goddess of passion and lust. They offended the higher deities with multiple crimes, including murder. All said to be done because of their self-obsession with sexual gratification. Their punishment was an unbelievable desire to fornicate several times a day, and afterwards, their worshipers and followers would die in various ways, some horrendous, some benign, based on the amount of evil in their souls. Eventually, Kama and Rati were turned to stone, a statue, for all to see them in an unholy sexual pose. There have been different paintings and pictures of the two in different poses. I found ours in my search on Google images. I nearly fell out of my chair."

"So…" Mike tried to form his words. "This is a curse?"

"Looks that way." Carrie answered nonchalantly. "You're a banker, giving out loans."

"Right." Mike chimed in.

"I sell property. Did you have a client by the name of Ajay Kapur?"

Mike thought about it, his eyes lit up. "Yeah," he said excitedly. "His restaurant failed six months ago"

Anger crossed Carrie's face. "We need to confront him, before this gets worse!"

***

Mike had looked up Kapur's address from the banks files on his phone. Kapur owed a lot of money to the bank and was reduced to living in a trailer park on lower east side of town, where the gangs and other criminal element frequented.

He was staying in a house that should have been condemned. One side of the house was falling into a sink hole, where the other part was being held up by center blocks. The grass had grown up waist high, and the chain link fence around the house had several holes cut into it, obviously as escape routes for those on the run or for thieves.

The door was cracked open. A thin, white haired Indian man sat in a chair that was badly in need of reupholstering. He was wearing a tattered tank top and unclean underwear. His toenails had grown out extravagantly, as well as his fingernails, to the point that they curled around his toes and fingers. Sitar music was playing on a record, a slow, stirring female voice rang out over top of it.

Two figures stood in front of him, not moving at all. They stood there like statues in a park. They were naked, the woman's hand clutching the man's genitalia, the man's hands holding on to the woman's erect nipples.

Mike and Carrie painfully pushed on, still naked, made their way into Kapur's house.

"I knew you come," Kapur said, in a sing-song accent. "Just like the other two."

Carrie gasped, then screamed out. She buried her face in Mike's chest.

"Jen and Wade!" Mike stated. "They did an advertising campaign for your restaurant."

"If that is what you want to call it," Kapur said. "Terrible commercials. Bigoted. Racist. Made me look a fool. My family told me so. I didn't listen. I told them I was a performer. I lied to myself. I was okay with it, as long as it made me money, kept the business going. Stupid me."

"Why us, then?" Mike asked.

"Why?" Kapur was surprised by the question. "You gave me a loan that you knew was too unreasonable. That I would never be able to pay off. And little miss flirt there sold me property in a dying area. That shopping center was bankrupt. You people withheld that information."

Mike felt his bones and joints stiffen, harden like concrete. Carrie had already become stone, probably the second she hid her face into Mike, her arms wrapped around his neck. Mike wanted to speak on everyone's behalf. His jaw was stuck, his mouth left open. He had become stone as well.

"I will stay here in my chair," Kapur said, depressed.

"I will die, watching my four oppressors caught in embarrassing, compromising positions."

Mike blinked one last time, his face contorted, trying to convey the horror he was experiencing.

Jeff Baker's Shopping List

Hamburger buns
Portabella Mushrooms
Silk Milk (Unsweetened)
Bottled Water
Cheddar Cheese (Block, not shredded)
Sliced Bread
Lottery Tickets

The House of the Skinwalker

Jeff Baker

The room literally turned inside-out when I stepped in it, which was pretty much the way my Spring Break had been going.

It was my Junior year and we'd taken off for Mexico that morning. My car was a much-used piece of crud, but my buddy Drew had been given his, a year-old Chevy four-door, by his Great-Aunt when she'd stopped driving. The plan was simple: Cruise down to Mexico, driving all night in shifts, get a motel before we hit the border, sleep, hit Mexico, party for a couple of days, head back to Wichita, Kansas and be bright-eyed-and-bushy-tailed the next day of class. And we got to start the vacation a day early because I had no classes on Tuesday and Thursday that semester and Drew had managed to get out of his classes for that Thursday, by virtue of being ahead in all the work and his ability to win over just about anybody. Bags were packed, cash carefully stowed away, car tuned up, alarm clocks set for 5:00a.m. That was the plan.

5:20, I show up in the dorm parking lot with my overnight bag full of last-minute stuff and a bottle of orange juice, my vision fuzzing in the way it does when you aren't used to getting up that early and find Drew leaning up against the car, talking to not one but two girls dressed in near-identical outfits but carrying only one suitcase.

"Hey, Billy!" Drew called out, waving me over. "These are the Stoltz Sisters. They've never been to Mexico before, so I invited them along!"

At least he'd invited the one who was hanging all over him along, I thought as I walked up, wondering if Drew was serious and how cramped the car was going to be. "Clarice, Cheryl, this is Billy Gonzalez," Drew said. He wasn't specific about which girl was which. They could have been twins, they both had long hair that looked light brown, they were skinny and wearing identical jeans and sneakers, but different t-shirts. The one sister said "hi," but she was still hanging on to Drew and grinning right in his face, not looking at me.

The other sister looked at me for a moment and then looked down at her feet. Shy, I thought. Nothing wrong with that. At least it wasn't a date. The only girl Drew had ever fixed me up with had spent the evening talking about how exciting my major (Business Administration) sounded and how I didn't really look like anybody named Gonzalez.

We drove to the convenience store on South Meridian and got a couple of cans of pop and a box of donuts. Then we hit the highway. Drew driving for the first leg of the trip, he and Cheryl Stoltz talking and laughing in the front seat. I was in the back with Clarice and their suitcase. She sat silently, barely saying a word. I pulled my jacket around me and curled up in the seat and dozed, only waking up when Drew and Cheryl broke into cheers when we hit the Oklahoma State Line about 7:00a.m. I looked over the suitcase I was leaning on. Clarice was staring out the window, a half-eaten donut in her hand. I saw the reddish ground rushing past and glanced back at the "Welcome To Kansas" sign vanishing in the distance. I managed to sleep for a few more hours. I remember half-dozing and seeing Oklahoma City zip by seemingly at a million miles per hour. Drew and Cheryl were chatting nonstop, all but sitting in the same seat.

We had lunch at a roadside cafe on the Texas-Oklahoma border that had seen better days, but was clean and had working restrooms and an adjoining gas station. All of which made up for the place's lack of prestige. I checked out the gift shop—well, actually, the gift table—when we were paying the bill. I thought about buying a self-described "Texas-Sized" map of Texas refrigerator magnet for fifty cents to give to my folks. But then I thought about whether I wanted them to even know about this trip. We did pose for a couple of pictures leaning up against the car, arm-in-arm with the girls at the gas station, courtesy of a couple of bucks slipped to the guy at the gas station who took the picture and got to use the retro instant camera I'd gotten for Christmas before I did. We laughed at the pictures, Drew was flipping me off in one, and then got back on the road.

The Okay Texas Cafe and Gas was where Drew and I swapped places. I could only imagine that he'd been waiting for the opportunity as he and Cheryl slid in the backseat and stuck the suitcase to one side. I was busy adjusting the rearview mirror in the driver's seat as Clarice stepped into the front passenger seat beside me. I'd barely heard her speak during lunch, except when she'd ordered a grilled cheese sandwich and a cup of coffee. I'd had a ham and cheese sandwich and a couple of coffees. She closed the passenger side door and sat there staring out the window, just like she'd done in the backseat. Me, I was staring at the roadmap. I'd never been in Texas before, but Drew had marked our route from Wichita through Oklahoma, Texas and New Mexico with a green felt tip pen.

"Hey, Drew, I thought we were going to take the highway down to Juarez, you've got all these side roads marked up." I said

"Yeah, it's a more direct route than the highway." Drew said. "Cuts off a few miles."

I stared at the greenish line on the map. It looked like a lightning bolt with hiccups. And a more direct route would have been to cut through the Oklahoma Panhandle. But, hey, it was Spring Break. I looked in the back seat, Drew and Cheryl were snuggling together. I checked the road signs against the map, Drew's green line was pretty darned accurate. I shrugged to myself with a "What the hell," and headed off down the road, which was at least paved.

I wasn't expecting Clarice to be much of a conversationalist, and she wasn't, so I drove through the next few hours paying attention to the route marked on Drew's map as well as listening to the radio stations fading in and out. We'd crossed the border into New Mexico when we switched places again. I was trying to doze in the backseat when Drew about ran us off the road. He braked like crazy on the shoulder, raising a fog of dust and bringing me wide awake. Cheryl was screaming in the back seat, Clarice actually looked up with some concern, the first real emotion she'd shown since I'd met her nearly ten hours ago. Drew and I got into a shouting match—the precursor to a great Spring Break Experience—outside the car during which he finally admitted that he really hadn't slept much when I was driving. Cheryl started giggling during this. And that he hadn't slept a lot the night before we took off.

Cheryl kept on giggling and looking at Drew when I pulled out our map and pointed to a spot just to the side of Drew's green line.

"Five miles off our route. I'm driving. We find out if they've got a motel and a burger place. If not, we sack out there in the car and eat candy bars and drive to Mexico when we're awake, okay, man?"

Drew nodded, he was as pooped as I was. We drove north as the sun was setting making it all look like a collage of black, orange and red when I saw the sign pointing to Fire Hills, and, more welcome, a billboard advertising "Gassy-Mart! Your place for Fuel-Food-Fun!" The Gassy-Mart was just before a rise in the road and the sign announcing "Fire Hills, Unincorporated. Pop. 100." We were more grateful that Gassy Mart had a small sit-down restaurant, and even though the sodas were flat and the chili, soup, and sandwiches we were ordered lukewarm, it felt like arriving in Valhalla. After dinner, I bummed around the rest of the Mart while Drew topped off the tank of the car, Cheryl hanging on him, Drew laughing and almost knocking the nozzle out of the gas tank, getting some gas sloshed on her skintight jeans. I turned away from the window and checked out the compasses, rubber dashboard figures and automotive supplies. I bought a map of New Mexico, I figured it'd come in handy. I was at the register when I wondered where Clarice was. She was over by the display of tires, staring out the window.

It was dusk when we pulled into Fire Hills, a couple of houses on the left and another ridge, a smaller one, off to the right in the reddish distance. And a neon sign "Motel" on the road right in front of us. We drove down the curving road about a half-mile and came to the sign declaring "Fire Hills Motel" with a bunch of small dark wooden houses in a fake resort-cabin style, and the larger cabin with the neon "vacancy" sign being about the only light around. The ridge to the right was a dark brown. The sky was a deepening blue-black with a reddish line on the horizon. The cabins were blackish lumps. It looked like a velvet painting my Dad had brought back from a business trip to Mexico when I was a kid.

The inside of the cabin reminded me of all the motel offices I'd been in on vacation. Magazine rack, tall front counter that served as a desk, half-opened doorway behind the desk, pen chained to the desk by a wire, florescent lights with one of the two bulbs burned out. The room was a rough dark wood, the desk was made of the same wood. I could see a calendar on the wall by the desk and a poster of some girl half-visible in the back room behind the partly closed door.

The guy behind the counter was definitely Native American, his dark hair pulled behind his head, wearing some sort of tribal necklace and a t-shirt with a picture of a lizard drinking a can of beer on it. He wasn't much older than I was, I guessed. He looked up and grinned at us as we walked in. When he saw Cheryl and Clarice his grin got bigger.

"Hey, folks! Here to rent out a couple of cabins for a while?"

"Naah," Drew said. "We just need one. For tonight."

"The four of you together?" the guy asked.

"Yes!" Cheryl said suddenly, making a point of grabbing Drew's hand.

"Too bad," the guy said. He pulled out a faded notebook with several signatures on it, the most recent dated last week. "Cost is seventy-five bucks per night, you can pay now or pay half now and settle up when you check out tomorrow morning."

"Great." Drew said, grabbing the pen and signing in. "We're here for Spring Break. From Wichita. Kansas," he added.

"No better place to spend Spring Break than right here in Fire Hills," the guy said.

"We're on our way to Mexico," I said.

"Are those the Fire hills over there?" Cheryl asked, pointing at the wall.

"Yeah," the guy said as Drew pulled out his wallet and I fished for mine inside my jacket pocket. "Those hills have been sacred to my ancestors for thousands of years. We were holding sacred rituals up there before any white man had seen this country. We still do sometimes."

"Oh, can we go see?" Cheryl asked.

"No. Those hills are sacred," he said counting the money Drew and I had handed him. "I've never even seen one. And we don't go up there at any other time because of," he paused as he put the money in a drawer, "Yenaldlooshi." he said grimly.

Clarice looked up and stared. Drew looked around a little nervously. The guy went on in a quiet voice, one that matched the shadows in the room.

"They call it the Skinwalker. It's an evil spirit. It haunts places that are sacred in order to turn them evil. It eats human flesh, and that's just for starters."

I was feeling uncomfortable. I thought I heard a soft noise somewhere. I glanced out the window and wished I could see a light in the dark other than from the vacancy sign. The guy went on.

"We didn't want to build all of these tourist cabins years ago, but we had to because the tribe needed the money," he said fumbling through a desk drawer. "We had to put some of them on some property we wouldn't have touched for any other reason." He pulled out a key on a ring and held it out to Drew.

"The cabin you're staying in was built on land sacred," he jingled the keys a couple of times, "to the Skinwalker."

Drew swallowed as he reached for the keys. That was when the voice burst out of the darkening room.

"Skinwalker, my butt!"

I jumped, Drew wheeled around and nearly fell over. There was a fiftyish man in a sweatshirt, jeans and a greasy ball cap standing in the darkened doorway to one side of the desk.

"You trying to scare away customers again?" The guy behind the desk shrugged and smiled. The man went on. "This is Gerald. Don't pay a word of attention to anything he says. His name ought to be Running Mouth."

Cheryl and Drew and I laughed. Even Clarice cracked a smile. Gerald smiled, not as broadly as before.

"I'm John," the man said and shook our hands. "I've lived here all my life and the only spirits I've seen around here came from the liquor store." I was starting to feel a little better, the laugh had done it, I guessed.

"If you really want to go up Fire Hill, you can when it's daylight," John said. "Not much to recommend it though. You know what you'll find up there?"

"No," I said.

"Brush. Beer cans. Maybe stub your toe on a rock." He looked over at Gerald. "Only rituals performed on those hills have to do with Gerald, a six-pack and a girlfriend."

Gerald winced.

"You guys make sure you get the blankets out in your cabin. It gets cold here in the desert at night." John said.

"We'll do that," Drew said, starting to head for the door.

"Hey," John said. "If you want a good breakfast go into town to Mamma Carrie's. Can't miss it. It's the only place still open."

"Thanks," I said.

"And mention my name," he said. "She'll treat you good. Tell her you know John Nightwalker."

Something in the name brought back the uneasy feeling I'd had moments ago. All that stuff about the Skinwalker.

John had been right, it was getting chilly. First thing we looked for in the cabin after we found the light switch were the blankets. We found a stack of them in the closet, fuzzy wool with some kind of native pattern.

"My Mom used to call this a Navaho blanket." Drew said, grabbing one for himself and Cheryl and tossing me one. I grabbed another blanket and handed it to Clarice. The cabin wasn't that big, there was a back bedroom which Drew and Cheryl claimed immediately, and a front room with a window that looked out onto the road through a thin curtain. A short hallway joined the two rooms together passing the closet where we found the blankets, a small kitchen and a smaller bathroom. There was a couch in the front room and a small table between the couch and the front door. The back bedroom had a double bed and a nightstand.

We didn't really unpack. We just brought our suitcases and bags in and grabbed the necessities, then stuck them out of the way in a corner. After the long day we'd had, as late as it was, we were ready to crash. But we sat out on the small front porch for an hour watching the stars. It was so quiet I imagined we could hear the stars moving across the sky. When we finally all went to bed, I told Clarice to take the couch and I wrapped myself in one of the blankets on the floor in the hallway.

"Yeah, I'm the perfect gentleman," I muttered to myself after a backward glance at Clarice. But it was better than sleeping in the car.

I didn't know what time it was when I woke up, but it was still dark. I blinked a few times to clear my vision and stared down the hall. I could barely make out the dark shape of the couch with Clarice doubtless asleep under the blanket, the dirty rectangle of front window dimly illuminated by the starlight. It looked a lot like Mom and Dad's front window when I was growing up. Maybe because I was laying down, looking at it at an odd angle in the middle of the night the window looked more like a diamond than a rectangle.

I froze, the window was moving.

Solid glass, no panes, puttied into the wall but it was moving, shifting, changing shape as I watched. I jumped up, the window was still moving. Even though it was getting bigger the room was getting darker. I could barely make out a darker smudge in the darkness where I knew the couch was. I looked towards the back bedroom where Drew and Cheryl were. I knew the hallway was just a few feet but it looked like half a mile. The bedroom door looked far away and tiny but I felt that if I reached out my hand I could touch the door from where I was standing. And if I did I would find it the size of my thumbnail.

My knees were wobbly. I remembered the kid at the office had said the land was sacred to the Skinwalker. What if he was right? What if it was real and was outside, surrounding the house? What if it was inside?

What if it somehow was the house?

I turned around again, the front room was a tiny black square in the huge rectangle of dim light that was swelling, moving towards me like a manta ray.

I was facing a dark wall, something hard was pressed against the side of my head. I was lying on the floor wrapped in the blanket, facing the wall in the hallway. I pulled off the blanket and stared around. Dark room, ordinary window, nothing but quiet.

I pulled off my shirt, it was soaked, I'd been sweating in my sleep. The cabin felt a little cold. I made my way to the bathroom and drank a glass of water. I turned off the light and felt for the door handle. In the hallway, I could barely see the walls and where my blanket was. I stared. In the dark the walls seemed angled somehow. I closed my eyes, remembering the dream I'd just had. I got down to pull the blanket over me and stuck my hand towards the darkened wall. The shadow swallowed my arm, it felt like I'd stuck my hand into tall, cool grass. I jerked back, rolled into the middle of the hallway and, lying on my back saw the darkness on the ceiling swelling like a balloon. The wall opposite me looked like it was covered in black mold.

I scrambled to my feet just in time to see Drew's suitcase slipping towards me, pushed by the darkness. I slapped my face. I had to still be dreaming.

"Clarice!" I yelled. I was startled, if I was still dreaming my voice would have come out like a thin squeak or not at all, but it was loud and I could hear it reverberate through the hall. But there was no response.

"Drew!" I yelled again. "Cheryl! Clarice! Hey!" I took a step towards the couch and the dark floor was suddenly sloped at a steep angle. I slid, reached, and grabbed and at the same time I saw the ballooning darkness swell and engulf me. I screamed. For an instant I could see the stars and the top of the cabin with our car parked on the road in front of it. I turned and saw Drew and Cheryl huddled together in bed. I tried to move but the darkness rushed over me like a wind.

My head hurt, something was wrapped around it. I opened my eyes. I was lying on the floor in the hall, my own arms wrapped around my head. I could see the blanket opposite me. I lay there a moment, the dizziness like a mild hangover going away. The cabin had soft orange light streaming into it, meaning morning. I heard distant sounds of cars on roads from outside. No dream, I realized, not this time. I sat up, and shivered. I'd slept for I don't know how long on the bare cabin floor in just my jeans and socks. I stood up and stretched, what time was it? My cell phone was in the car and I hadn't noticed a clock in the cabin.

"Probably so we miss check-out time and pay for another day," I said aloud. I cleared my throat, I was a little hoarse from sleeping on the cold floor all night.

I pulled a shirt out of my overnight bag and put it on standing on the front porch, just noticing that the car was gone when the car pulled up. Drew stepped out, clutching a paper bag. Cheryl walked up beside him, snuggling under his arm. They looked, in my opinion, way too well-rested.

"Good morning, sleepyhead!" Drew said, tossing me the bag. "Microwave burritos from in town. We had ours already." Cheryl grinned up at him as I opened the sack and unwrapped the burrito. I was famished.

"We should be in Juarez by this afternoon," Drew said once we were back in the cabin.

"You drive," I said finishing the burrito. "I had a rough night."

"So we gathered. That's why we didn't wake you. How come you didn't sleep on the couch?"

"I didn't want to disturb her," I said. Drew was like that sometimes, imagining that everyone wanted to hop in the sack with everyone else.

"Who?" Drew asked.

"Clarice," I said. "I was fine on the floor. I had the blanket."

"Who's Clarice?" Drew asked. I sighed, Drew could be that way sometimes, too.

"Some girl we picked up back in the parking lot. Came with us, remember?" I said.

"No," he said. The expression on Drew's face was genuinely puzzled.

"Shy? Didn't talk much? Her sister?" I asked, pointing at Cheryl.

Cheryl stared, open mouthed.

"I don't have a sister," she said.

"Twin sister," I said, getting a little impatient. "Clarice." They were both still staring at me blankly. I shook my head, I was definitely awake. I was remembering the nightmares of the night before and starting to feel a little shaky.

"Did you get any sleep out here last night?" Drew asked.

"Yeah," I said. "Well, some," I admitted after a moment.

"Are you sure you didn't," Drew began, but I cut him off.

"Wait," I said, rummaging in my overnight bag. I know I've got…yeah!"

I pulled out the photo that had been taken of the four of us at the gas station just before we'd reached Texas.

"That's us with Clarice," I said, handing it to Drew. Drew stared at it a moment and handed it back to me.

"It's just the three of us," he said.

The photo showed Drew and Cheryl and me leaning up against the passenger side door of the car, grinning like idiots. No Clarice. I turned the picture over, remembering I'd scrawled our names on the back: Drew A., Cheryl S. and Billy G., Spring Break 2007.

I was starting to shake. I wasn't crazy, at least I didn't think so. And I knew I was wide awake.

"Maybe you'd better sit down," Cheryl said.

"Yeah, maybe I'd better," I said sitting down on the couch, next to the neatly-folded blanket. I knew what I'd seen; there had been a second girl with us. And now there wasn't. I studied the back of the picture. My handwriting, no doubt about that. I turned the picture over and stared at our smiling faces and rumpled clothes. There was a definite person-sized space between Cheryl and me. And my arm wasn't just leaning against the car at an odd angle, it looked like my arm was around someone's shoulder except the someone wasn't there anymore.

Clarice.

Spring Break went downhill from there. We made it down to Mexico, but I wasn't in a partying mood. We drove back to Wichita in one long all-day, all-night session. It was only when Drew was dropping me off in the dorm parking lot that I recognized the necklace Cheryl was wearing was the one Clarice had on when we all met days earlier.

I didn't see a lot of Drew after that and when I did he was always with Cheryl. I buried myself in studying and when I wasn't doing work for classes I was on the internet or in the school library looking up everything I could find about Skinwalkers. That's what I was doing one Sunday evening right before the library closed for the night. I had a bunch of books and a couple of magazines spread out on a table and I was just leafing casually through a dusty old copy of something called "The Encyclopedia Of Folklore and Superstition" when I came on an entry that totally grabbed my attention.

"Doppelganger: Literally, Double-goer; a malevolent spirit-being in Germanic myth which appears in the form of a living human to drain that human of all its vitality until it becomes docile enough for the Doppelganger spirit to completely remove and replace, taking over the human's life and becoming real."

My head felt light. I remembered how I'd felt when I'd suddenly found myself above the cabin that night. I read on.

"The Doppelganger purportedly can distort reality and perception so the sudden presence of an exact duplicate of its intended victim goes unnoticed."

There was more, but I didn't read it. I leaned back in my chair, stared up at the ceiling and whistled softly.

"Good luck, Drew," I said.

Tim Miller's Shopping List

Duck Tape
Hacksaw (+ spare blades)
Nylon rope (12ft should do)
Shovel
Refuse sacks (heavy duty)
Muriatic Acid (6 Gal)
Bleach
Swedish Fish (2 packets)

Lottery Tickets

<u>Backne</u>

Tim Miller

Jerry hated working in a factory. He'd been a material handler for almost three years and it sucked. Some guys loved it. He would admit any day of the week he liked driving the forklift. Well, most of the time. Sometimes unloading trucks and having to place loads into super high places was the worst. You couldn't see where the fuck shit was. One time a skid got caught on something, as he pulled the forks out, the skid came with it and two fifty-five gallon drums of cleaning solution came crashing to the floor.

Fortunately, no one was standing nearby or they'd have been killed. Since that incident, he was much more careful. Half the time he didn't even know what was in most of the barrels. They all had hazmat labels on them. That was all he needed to know. Not to mention they always smelled something awful. Even when they were sealed his eyes watered just from the odor.

When possible he wore a respirator when hauling the things around, but that wasn't always an option. They took too long to put on, and usually didn't help. Sometimes they made it all worse, trapping the odor inside. Totally nasty. It always felt like fire was going up his nose. At least what he figured fire going up his nose would feel like, as actual fire had never physically gone up his nose.

One day, they received a shipment of some especially strange looking barrels. These were green drums stacked onto a skid, but didn't have any hazmat labels. Not that it mattered to Jerry. These would go onto another loft on the far side of the warehouse. Unfortunately, they would have to go to on the very top. Jerry's least favorite, as he wouldn't be able to see what he was doing. Had to play it by feel.

He lifted the skid and elevated the forks as he backed away from the truck. He drove to the loft and raised the forks as high as they would go. Once it was raised up, he tilted the forks backward slightly to get a good angle, when something dripped onto him. First it got onto his helmet, then it came down faster until it was pouring down in a steady pour.

"Motherfucker!" Jerry yelled as he undid his seatbelt and jumped out of the seat. He made it out, but not before a bunch of the ooze hit the back of his collar and ran down his back. It was warm and gooey whatever it was.

"Jerry! What the hell are you doing?" Carl called out as he ran over. Carl was the plant supervisor.

"Those fucking barrels are leaking. That shit got all over me. Look!" Jerry turned around. He hadn't seen what the actual substance was but could hear Carl gasping.

"Jesus fuck. What is that shit?" Carl asked.

"I don't know. The driver had the MSDS for it. There were no hazmat stickers on it."

"Shit. Does it hurt?"

"No. What's wrong?"

"Nothing man. If it doesn't hurt. Just go home. Maybe get it checked out if it bothers you. That shit is all green and sticky looking."

"What about the forklift?"

"Just leave it. I'll have someone take care of it. Get out of here."

Jerry nodded and headed home. He could feel the sticky substance along his back but still hadn't seen it. When he got home, he stripped out of his work clothes and held up his shirt where he saw the green sludge for the first time. The entire back side of his shirt was covered in it.

"What the fuck?"

He climbed into the shower and began to rinse off. Whatever the substance on his back was hadn't bothered him at all until the water hit it. The second the water touched his back, his whole body burned. He screamed and jumped away as white hot pain shot through his entire back side.

"Holy shit! Fuck! Shit! Fuck! Shit!" He jumped up and down, almost slipping and falling, but keeping his balance after grabbing the rail. He stepped out of the shower and toweled off. The burning in his back continued, but subsided slowly. Looking at himself in the mirror, he cranked his head around to see what his back looked like.

The green goo was gone, but his back was bright red as if it were badly sunburned. The pain was gone by the time he'd toweled off and dressed. However, he did suddenly feel exhausted. Jerry climbed into bed and pulled up the covers. Before he knew it, he was sound asleep.

When he awoke, his back was throbbing. Climbing out of bed, he headed into the bathroom to look at his back again. This time, he almost threw up at the sight.

His back was covered in bright red pimples. Hundreds of them clustered together. Some of them had whiteheads already. Others were just red and puffy.

"What the fuck?" he said to his reflection. He needed to go have it checked out, but also needed to get to work. He was already running late. He couldn't let something as simple as a breakout cost him his job. His plant only allowed three sick days a year and all were unpaid. Carefully he pulled on his shirt before he finished dressing. Once his boots were laced up he headed out to work.

Most of the day had been uneventful. Typical loading and unloading of various trucks. No one mentioned the strange barrels and leak the day before. He'd wanted to ask his boss just what was in there, but Carl had been tied up in meetings all morning. Jerry was relieved when the lunch bell sounded. He climbed out of the forklift and headed to the break area when someone from behind startled him.

"Holy shit!" the guy yelled.

Jerry turned around to find his co-worker, Mike standing behind him looking horrified.

"What's wrong?"

"Dude, your back is all wet. What the fuck." Mike took a step closer. "God and it stinks."

Jerry reached over his shoulder, feeling along the back of his shirt, and sure enough, it was completely saturated. But with what?

"Jesus Christ," Jerry said. Out of panic, he began to remove his shirt right there. His co-workers in the break area looked on horrified and confused as he pulled his shirt all the way off.

"What the fuck?" Another co-worker yelled. A female worker screamed as people started backing away from him. Jerry felt something running down his back.

He ran into the bathroom to look in the mirror. When he saw it, he screamed himself. His entire back was covered in huge, yellow zits. Many of which had burst. Greenish/yellow pus oozed all down his back. Some falling off in large clumps.

Sirens sounded as Jerry stepped out of the bathroom. There was an ambulance pulling up outside. Two paramedics came in, a guy and a girl, both carrying medical bags and wearing rubber gloves.

"Are you the one with the fluid discharge?" the male medic asked.

"I guess so. I'm not sure what's going on." Jerry turned around.

"Oh my God!" the female medic said. "Any idea what caused this?"

"Some shit spilled on me yesterday from a barrel I was unloading. I have no idea what it was, and no one will tell me. I woke up today all broke out. Now it's like this."

The male medic stuck his finger into one of the holes in his back. More greenish syrup oozed from the opening. The medic held the finger up to his nose and took a sniff.

"Smells like acid," he said. "Does it hurt?"

"Not really. Did you just stick your finger in there?"

"No. Let's get you on the ambulance," the woman said before grabbing a blanket and throwing it over his shoulders. He hoped once they got to the hospital they could figure out what it was. Except as they were walking out, Jerry noticed several of his coworker's faces were covered in red and yellow zits. Some didn't notice, but others were looking at each other and freaking out.

The medics looked at each other as the girl finally spoke up.

"I think we need to quarantine the whole plant," she said. "Including us."

"Are you serious?" the guy asked.

"Yes, I'm serious. Look at this. Everyone is getting whatever this guy has."

Jerry's face and arms began to itch. He reached up and felt thick bumps all over his cheeks and forehead. Looking at the medics, their faces were breaking out as well. None of the current breakouts were as bad as his back. Except he was about to be in worse condition than everyone else. The other employees began screaming at him as the paramedics looked on.

"What did you do to us?"

"What the fuck is wrong with you? You infected all of us!"

"Are we turning into zombies?"

Jerry tried to back away as they closed in on him.

"I didn't do anything to you. One of the barrels spilled shit on me! Seriously! I woke up all broken out. I just thought it was a rash. Then at lunch my back looks like this. I had no idea! I didn't know!"

Some of them were holding various tools in their hands. One man he didn't know approached. His face had gone from red and puffy to yellow and greasy looking. It was covered with whiteheads that were throbbing and ready to burst. He stood inches from Jerry.

"You did this to me," he said. "Now I'm gonna kill you!" The man lifted a hammer and reared back. Before he could swing, Jerry punched him in the face. As his fist connected, dozens of zits on the man's face popped at once. Yellow pus and fluid splattered onto Jerry's face and into his mouth. It tasted salty as he gagged, trying to keep from throwing up. The man fell to the ground and looked up. He looked as if his face was melting off.

The entire right side of his face was covered in yellow clumps of pus and sludge. The others' faces began turning yellow as well. When the man's face began oozing yellow slime, they all attacked Jerry at once. He swung in every direction as many jumped onto his back. One person grabbed him in a chokehold, but he was able to slip free as greasy pus lubricated his face and neck.

The entire mob fought like mad as their zits continued popping and squirting. They rolled and tussled around in a huge pool of greenish yellow sludge. One man shoved another man's face into a puddle of pus, holding him down until the man drowned. Jerry felt someone thrust their entire hand in an opening in his back. The person's hand fished around as if it were looking for something as more slime oozed from the opening. Jerry broke away to see it was the female medic. He couldn't even make out her face under all the pus which caked her hair to the side of her head as huge clumps fell from her face. Her eyes were wild-eyed as she screamed and jumped at Jerry, digging her nails into his face, ripping his flesh and zits free. Bloody pus dripped down his face and nose as he tumbled backward, hitting his head on the floor, and knocking him unconscious.

When he awoke, he was lying in a hospital bed. Looking around, he saw the room was dark and there was plastic lining the walls. Someone stood over him wearing a fully encapsulated hazmat suit.

"Jerry. Glad you finally woke up," the robotic voice from the suit said.

"What's going on? Where am I?"

"I'm Dr. Cole. You're at the CDC in our special quarantine unit. You had quite an ordeal."

"I guess. I thought it was just a nightmare. I had this really bad acne on my back and everyone at work got it too and attacked me. It was so gross and freaky."

"I'm afraid that was no dream. It all happened. You were exposed to some rare bacteria that caused the breakout. It also causes temporary dementia and paranoia."

"Yeah, I noticed. What was in that barrel? That stuff that fell on me?"

"That barrel contained the actual pus from another set of victims. I'm not sure why it wasn't marked. The fluid itself contains some valuable properties."

"What does that mean? Do you have a cure for it?"

"Cure? No. I think you're mistaken. We are harvesting it. This stuff can be easily weaponized. It is very potent and you of all the victims seem to have an endless supply."

"What?"

"Yes. That's what all the tubes hooked to you are."

Jerry looked at himself and for the first time he noticed dozens of tubes connected to his back, arms, and legs.

"What is all this?" Jerry asked.

"Think of it like this. You are one giant Slurpy. So we have several people with straws hooked up to you to make sure we don't miss or lose a single drop. Just a few ounces of that stuff is worth a fortune."

"You can't do this!"

"I'm not. The Pentagon is. I just work here. Sorry, kid. Don't worry, though. I left you some DVDs to keep you company during your stay." The doctor held up a box containing a bunch of movies that looked like they just came from the Wal-Mart bargain bin. "I think they have Piranha Shark vs. Bugnado in there. That's a good one. Anyway. Here you go. I'll be back in a few hours to check on you."

As the doctor turned and walked way, he knocked on a steel door that made a hissing sound as it was unsealed. The doc stepped through and the steel door slammed shut. Jerry looked around and flung the box of DVDs across the room. He tried to climb out of bed, but the tubes kept him in place. They had been surgically embedded into his skin. Panic began to set in as the reality of his situation hit. He'd spend the rest of his life in this place as a one-man pus factory for the government.

"You can't do this!" he screamed. "Let me go! You can't do this!" Tears ran down his face as he looked at the ground. He caught sight of one of the DVDs. It was called Attack of the Pus Monster. He threw his head back and laughed. Once the laughter started, he couldn't stop it. He laughed hysterically at the irony of the whole thing. Attack of the Pus Monster? He was the Pus Monster. But that gave him an idea. He reached back and began tugging at the tubes, despite the pain he'd ripped one free. Chunks of skin and pus dripped from it as he pulled on the next one. When the doctor came back, he was in for a big surprise. A surprise from the real-life pus monster.

Nick Swain's Shopping List

Vanilla Coke
Peanut Butter
Bubble Gum
Cinnamon Bakery Muffins
Steak
Breakfast Blend Coffee
Paper (for the typewriter)
Duck-tail Grease
Zippo fluid
Vinyl Records (mostly Rock 'n Roll)
Horror Films (varying from classic monster flicks of the
thirties to psychological thrillers of the eighties – and plenty in-
between)
Anything by Stephen King that I don't already own.

The House on the Back Road

Nick Swain

Roger Witworth's wife's unfiltered cigarette smoke stifled the inside of their '88 Lincoln Town Car. Her window was less than a third of the way down, and the wind seemed to push the noxious fumes purposefully into his face. He hated her smoking. It wasn't so bad in the house, where he could retreat into the next room, but here in the car it was ineludible. "Sandra, do you mind? You know I can't stand the smoke." She did, but all the same she looked at him sharply. Like it was inconceivable that he would ask that of her. "Damnit Rog! You know I get cranky if I don't have my caffeine and my nicotine, and I don't have my caffeine because you decided to stay clear of any gas station or diner by taking this country bumpkin road. So just suck it up will ya?!" He gripped the steering wheel tighter in frustration, but said nothing. He knew no matter how cattish her reaction was, it could be so much worse. Better to have watery eyes and an itchy nose.

His right hand went to the radio and scanned through the stations. Mostly static. He stopped on the channel playing Jim Reeves, who was singing about his four walls closing in on him. Roger thought about his own four walls in that airless Lincoln. How it trapped that toxic fog all around him. How Sandra had been so caustic and disagreeable since they'd left Virginia. How impossibly stuffy it was in that car for being such a cool November day. Roger Witworth's walls were closing in on him too, but for different reasons than Jim Reeves.

They were on a long, desolate, and seemingly ceaseless backroad in rural North Carolina, that they'd been driving on for the better half of an hour. They'd gone this way to avoid a traffic jam they heard about at their last gas station interlude. Roger had wanted to keep going until making a stop was necessary, otherwise they'd never make it to her sister's before dark. But Sandra had pissed and moaned about stopping for coffee since they'd started their trip.

While filling up his tank, he got into a friendly conversation with a local man at the pump next to him. The man, who said his name was Robert, was wearing a Colts hat, and Roger was from Indiana originally. And after talking about the Colts latest loss to the Giants, Roger mentioned that he and his wife were on their way to Durham to see her sister; whom he didn't care for. The local man told him that he'd heard on the radio about an ugly three car pile-up ahead on the highway, and how traffic was supposed to backed up for miles. After a quick and dreadful premonition of his wife and sister-in-law blaming him for their delayed arrival, and then scolding him to the point of a migraine, Roger listened to the local man who told him about a secluded backroad just a few blocks around the corner that would save them about two or three hours of daylight. And Roger was more than grateful to hear about this wonder road.

But what stuck out most in his mind was what the man said, after that.

"Don't stop. Just keep going through," the man had told him.

When Roger asked what he meant by that, the man replied with a modest grin that seemed disingenuous, "Oh you know, everywhere is spooky when no one else's around."

For a moment after he said this, Roger was turned off at the idea. What put him right back on it was the prospect of his wife shrieking in his ear about what was taking so long to get there. Just about that time, Sandra walked back out of the gas station, a scowl on her face. Apparently, the coffee machine inside was broken, and the young counter man didn't seem to have any real ambition about getting it fixed.

"I'm sure your sister will have some, and we'll be there soon thanks to this fella," said Roger.

The man nodded and smiled, "Hello Ma'am".

Sandra kept the frown and furrowed brow on her face and walked to the passenger's side.

"Whatever, hurry up Rog." She said, and then slammed the door. Roger looked over and saw the man had something of a sympathetic look on his face. Roger thanked him, got in the car with his wife, and they made their way down the street in the direction the man had instructed.

And here they were.

Sandra flicked her cigarette out the window and turned to Roger, exhaling the last bit of cancerous vapor into his face.

"So, Selina met someone. His name is Johnathan. Apparently, he's a bank teller. Maybe we'll get to meet him while we're there."

"Oh?" asked Roger, not bothering to use a tone that could have made him seemed somewhat interested. Which Sandra noticed.

"Oh? That's it? That's all you've got to say?"

"Well, what do you expect me to say? Okay. I'm glad your sister met someone, else. I hope this one sticks."

"Oh shut up, Rog! You don't know what you're talking about. And I can't believe you took directions from some small town redneck and drove us down this weird, creepy road!" She bawled into his ear, quickly changing the subject before he had a chance to explain that he did know what he was talking about.

He cringed a little as her warm, smoke ridden breath met his face. The sound of her voice embittered him. He hated her.

And he found it baffling, how the woman that once meant more to him than life itself, he now loathed with every inch of him. The same woman he once considered to be his 'Brown-eyed Liz Taylor' now seemed to resemble someone more like Joan Crawford in that movie with Bette Davis.

Things hadn't always been like this. They were in love once, when they were both ten years younger and before Sandra got pregnant. That was the only reason Roger had proposed to her. That's what you were supposed to do, right? Marry the woman who was to be the mother of your child and live happily ever after. At least, until the wife loses the child before it's ever even brought into the world. That changes things. The doctor said no one was to blame, that unfortunately those things happened sometimes, and that fate could be cruel, and blah blah blah…

Though neither of them actually said it, they each felt that the other was responsible. Roger decided that it was Sandra's chain smoking and her poor self-care (she'd been quite depressed those six months) that had done in their unborn baby. And in turn, Sandra felt that if Roger had been a more attentive husband and soon-to-be father around the house instead of spending all his time working to be promoted at the car depot, that things would have turned out differently. Much differently. Since then, a vindictive decade-long verbal war had gone on, and no matter what they argued over, it was always really about whose fault it was. And neither of them felt like they were winning.

"We should've just stayed on the interstate. The accident that hick told you 'supposedly' jammed up the road would be clear by now."

"Why don't you just take a nap or something," Roger proposed jadedly.

"Don't you talk to me that way, you no good son of a bitch!" She barked back at him.

"Look, you've been insufferable since we left Richmond, and I'm tired of hearing it. I can't control the weather, I can't control the flow of traffic, it wasn't my fault the coffee machine was busted, and it isn't my fault that the radio doesn't play more Phil Collins. So quit fucking railing me about it!"

For a moment, Sandra said nothing. She couldn't. Her eyes and mouth remained open in incredulity. But then, "You bastard!" She bellowed, spitting and hurling herself on top of him,

clawing at his face with her long, 'love red' colored finger nails. It was a long time coming.

"Sandra, stop it!" Roger shouted, trying his best to keep his eyes on the road ahead and to hold his pissed off wife back in her seat with his free hand. But she was unrelenting in her attempts to scratch at his face - which she finally did.

Sandra stopped her attack, taken back by the wound she'd left on her husband's face. Then she looked at her nails to see if there was blood on them.

There were two parallel cuts, one longer than the other, bleeding moderately from Roger's right cheek. He felt his injury and looked down at his hand, and as he stared at the small, inane amount of blood that seemed to peer back at him, he felt all the animosity and disgust he had towards his other half overflow. He let go of the wheel and burst towards her, both hands out front, adjacent to one another. He was going to strangle her. He had reached the peak of his forbearance, and tumbled over it. He was going to strangle her. Strangle her and shut her big, fat mouth up forever. No more repetitive bitching, no more cigarette smoke in his face, no more impassive introductions to his skank of a sister-in-law's latest, brainless fling. At that moment, the venom they'd use on him in the gas chamber after charging him with murder, seemed enchanting compared to that witch's cigarette fumes. Sandra's bulging eyes jutted out of their sockets in horror as her husband's firm hands began to clasp around her smooth, frail neck.

Then all at once, the car sheared off of the road, slashing both of its right tires on the rough, corroded edges of the asphalt. They plunged off of the shoulder and down a shallow hill into a tall grass field, and before the muddy ground could slow it to a stop, the car rolled a good ten feet more into the tough thicket. The impact of the car hitting the untrimmed grass sent Roger forward, pounding his head into the windshield and leaving a tiny chip across the durable glass. Sandra's forehead slammed with such force against the glove compartment that it popped open, and left a blood spot where her face had struck.

Roger was able to push himself off the steering wheel, that he felt had cracked one or two of his ribs, and sunk back into his seat. It was all quiet again on the back road, except for the radio which was still playing

Patsy Cline sang about "Walkin' After Midnight", while Roger's head sunk into his palms. He was still awake and coherent, but fuck his head hurt. All he could think of at that point in time was how much his head hurt, how sturdy that grass was, and what the hell he was going to do about the car. He didn't have to look, he knew from the racket it made when it happened, that both tires were blown and not only did they not have a second spare tire, they didn't even have one spare. Even in the excruciating pain he was in, Roger realized the irony of someone in his line of work not having a spare tire. And neither of them had a cell phone; though Roger wanted one. Sandra said they were too big, and too costly. "A waste of money", were her exact words. Yea. My money, he thought. But that unpleasant memory was quickly subsided by a more recent, unsettling one. The recollection of what he had been doing to his wife just before the car crashed itself into this jungle field.

Jesus. What if we hadn't crashed.

He slowly opened his eyes, and reluctantly, turned his head. Sandra was face down on the glove compartment where her head had struck so violently. But as far as he could tell, she was still breathing.

After musing over what had happened, and the current situation that it had led to, Roger shoved the car door open and lugged his legs out. He could see the top of a tall, leafless tree that they'd been fortunate enough to miss while flying blind, closer to the road. On one of the bottom branches, a crow cawed. CAW CAW CAW! The tree itself was nightmarish. Something that would have been an amenity in one of those old scary stories he heard around the campfire as a boy. He knew what the man at the gas station meant by 'spooky,' even before observing the rest of his surroundings. There was something off about the whole atmosphere of the place.

He could smell the air, like someone near a beach would be able to smell the salt from the sea in the wind all around. But the scent was all wrong, more bitter. CAW CAW!

"Shut up." Roger murmured, heaving himself out of the car.

He feebly guided his way to the other side of the sedan, and managed to lift Sandra out, and lay her somewhat gingerly on the shallow grass at the bottom of the hill. But not before rummaging through her purse and tossing back several aspirin.

Roger got out one of the 'just in case' water bottles from the trunk of the Lincoln, and splashed it in Sandra's face. Her eyes shot open, and she immediately sat up and buried her face into the palms of her hands, smearing the makeup around her eyes. Roger thought it made her look like a scared, wet raccoon. Her shaken eyes shifted to his and became hostile. She slapped him across his unscathed left cheek and then went for a second on his right, but he grabbed ahold of her arms before she was able to.

"How could you, you son of a bitch! How could you?" she blubbered, trying to jerk herself free of his possession.

"Sandra, I'm sorry. Please, I'm sorry." He pleaded. "I don't know what happened. I just… I mean Jesus, Sandra, you cut me! Look at my face, you-"

She cut him off with one forceful shove, and after losing what little balance he had bending down on his knees, Roger fell to the dirt. "Oh that's right, Rog! It's my fault. My fault you crashed the car, just like it's my fault you're a loser car salesman!" The snarling face she made while saying this, repulsed him as much as what she was saying infuriated him. Of course it was her fault! He thought. That stupid bitch tried to mangle my face while I was doing sixty! He pushed himself up and towered over her.

"You're damn right it's your fault!" He roared at her. "What the hell did you think was gonna' happen when you jumped on me like that? I wanna' know how you thought that was going to end!"

"That's no excuse for what you did to me, you pig! I wish I'd died in that crash, so that you'd have to live with it on your conscience!"

So did he.

But he didn't respond. He backed away, and turned his resentful eyes towards the small hill they had rolled down on. He ascended it, and stopped when his feet met the road. The same road he and his vexatious wife had just been driving and fighting on. There was nothing. Nothing but the forest, filled with naked trees, and ungroomed fields for as far as he could see. The border of the woods looked haunting, with the red and brown leaves sailing slowly through the air in front of it, instead of hanging on staunchly to the now leafless branches. He knew they were in trouble. They hadn't passed a single car, or even a house since turning onto this so-called miracle road. They would have to walk the way they had been heading and hope for the best. Surely the road ended somewhere. There would have to be a phone or a service station farther up the road, closer to society. They'd need to leave now to take advantage of all the daylight they had left. As spooky as the place was now, he couldn't imagine what it was like in the dark. The hardest part would have to come first. Telling Sandra.

"This idea is just as stupid as your last one, Rog! And look where that got us." Sandra Witworth complained as her husband gathered some supplies from the car, including another water bottle, a Swiss army pocket knife, a pack of matches, and a large, steel EverReady flashlight. He remembered purchasing the flashlight about a year ago, when they were anticipating an ice storm that had the potential to knock out the power throughout the state.

"Rog! ROG! Are you even listening to me?"

"We can't just sit here and wait Sandra. There's no telling when, or even if someone will come by. Besides, do you really want to be out here when the sun goes down?"

That was something Sandra hadn't considered. She analyzed both directions of the long, forsaken road and turned back with an uneager look on her face. Her eyes fixed on the road ahead as she took a slow, deep drag of her cigarette. Then she dropped the butt to the pavement, and crushed it beneath the heel of her expensive blue, snake skin shoe (that Roger paid for). She blew the last bit of smoke in Rogers direction, then trooped on past him while he stood still, waiting for her next objection. "FINE. I can't wait to find someone and tell them all about what you did to me." She said pompously, not bothering to look back at him.

Roger looked up at the grey, gloomy sky and thought, Yea. Well keep it up and I'll finish what I started. You, repulsive bitch. Then he jogged ahead, to catch up to his once, significant other.

The old, decrepit Victorian house gave them both an unspoken visceral of fear. It was surrounded by the same lifeless trees and wild grass that had been there since the beginning of their venture. A couple of the dark, wooden shudders hung crooked from the dusty windows they were attached to. The paint on the outside of the house that may have once been a dark brown, was now a rotting grey, slowly chipping away. On the second level of the house the balcony's middle balusters were missing, and the ones left on each side pointed out jaggedly towards them. It looked like a truck had plowed through it, but somehow without damaging the rest of the structure. Several crows perched on the roof were staring down at them, their beady black eyes filled with indifference. This was a murky afternoon, but it seemed darker here. Shadowy. It was like the sun refused to shine any of its nurturing light on this ominous patch of land.

They'd been walking for just under two hours when they came across the place. Before that, the closest they came to civilization was when they passed the remains of what looked like a ramshackle tool shed, that somehow seemed misplaced in a field all by itself. By then, Sandra had already topped off the last of the water, and was berating him for not packing more. After that it was about how sore her feet were, then after that it was right back to how there was nothing to drink. Roger could feel his head throbbing. The slight relief from the aspirin he took earlier was gone, replaced with an even more merciless headache. He popped the last two pills in the bottle (thinking about how there were a few more before Sandra had taken some herself) and spent the rest of their hike trying his best to tune out her squawking.

When they finally came across the house, there was no mailbox and no driveway. Only a gap in the line of sinister trees, exposing the house. They almost kept going. In fact, they were about to, because aside from the daunting appearance and disconcerting vibe of the place, it seemed utterly vacant, with no sign that anyone had been there in years. No sign except for the glimmering of what they determined to be candlelight, barely shimmering through the window on the turret of the house. And here they were.

"I'm not gonna do it Rog! I don't like it." Sandra exclaimed. She was standing in the opening of trees by the road now, backing up a little every time Roger drew near, urging her to go back towards the eerie house.

"I don't like it either. But the sun's gonna go down in less than an hour, and I'd rather not walk around out there in the dark," Roger told her, knowing it was futile to expect Sandra to grasp the actuality of their predicament.

"There's no FREAKIN way Rog! Look at that place. Turn around and look at it. I'm not gonna go knock on The Munster's door and ask to use the telephone!"

Roger didn't turn around. He knew what the place looked like. Besides, he was too busy rubbing the temples of his head, with his eyes shut. He wished he was somewhere else. ANY where else, with anyone else. "Look. Sandra, would you rather wait inside a house for a tow truck, or spend God only knows how much of the night wondering down that, never-ending road?"

"I didn't wanna do any of this Rog! It's your-"

"OK." He interrupted sternly. "I'm gonna try the house, you do what you want."

And without hesitation, he turned away and headed towards the rickety front steps. She made the same dumbfounded, open mouthed look she did in the car the first time he snapped back at her. He heard her mutter an array of obscenities at him, and then about him. Then she walked across the lawn, up the stairs, and joined him on the porch. Like he knew she would.

He smiled smugly to himself as Sandra stood behind him.

"Well? Go on, knock on the damn door!" She said.

The smile vanished. Roger suddenly noticed the door-knocker for the first time, even though he was standing right in front of it. It made him feel, uneasy. It was a rusty, silver expressionless face, and Roger wasn't sure if it was supposed to be a man or a woman. The eyes were the same color as the rest of the face, and it seemed to illuminate in comparison to the dark, eroded paint on the rotting door it was bolted to. He didn't want to touch it. He closed his right hand into a fist and gave three commanding knocks just beneath the vacant, genderless face that he felt was staring at him. Just like all the crows were.

No answer. He gave three more forceful knocks. Nothing. Three more and nothing. Then the knocking turned into a perpetual pounding. "Hello! Hello! Hello!" he chanted like a broken record, while practically beating at the door.

"Oh Jesus Christ, Roger, just stop it! There's nobody here..." "Shh." He ordered with a whisper, and index finger to his lips. "Did you hear that?"

"What're you talking about? I didn't hear anything."

"Hello!" He shouted, giving the door three more knocks; this time tentatively. What seemed like an infinite amount of time passed, though it was only a few seconds, and then it came. "Come in!" Said the voice of what sounded like an affable, young woman from inside the house. This time Sandra heard it too. Her eyes opened as wide as they could and that familiar look of angst and disbelief was there again. Rogers eyes were back on the door-knocker. He didn't know what else to look at. He was beginning to sweat, and he felt sick to his stomach with apprehension. But just the same, he reached out and clutched onto the cold, worn, brass doorknob. "Rog..." He didn't wait for her to finish. He twisted the knob and unhurriedly, eased the door open.

The troubled feeling Roger Witworth had since he arrived on this unpleasant property, was only exacerbated when he opened that front door and stepped inside. The interior of the house, was a cliché of every other house like it. It might have been laughable, if it wasn't so damn frightening. How could anybody live here? An old, wooden staircase with metal railing was to the right of them. It led to the upstairs hallway, and there were no doors visible from where they stood. To the left of the staircase, and directly in front of them, was a short hallway that led to what looked like the kitchen. To the left of that was the den. There were no chairs, couches, coffee tables, or any other kind of furniture. Only a small foot stool, facing the fireplace. There were picture frames with gold rims and floral patterns engraved in them, here and there on every wall. But there were no photographs in them. In any of them. The shattered shards of glass from the frames, remained on the floor below. Behind Roger, and to the left of the door next to his quivering wife, was a mahogany hall table. On top of it was an expensive looking crystal bowl filled with rotting fruit, that emitted a putrid stink that lingered throughout the wide antechamber.

"Hello?" Roger's voice echoed. There was no response.

"Rog, let's get out of here" Sandra whispered, with a shaky voice.

"Hello!" shouted Roger.

"ROG!" No whisper this time.

"You heard her too, Sandra," Roger said, turning to his wife. Who he just noticed, looked truly afraid. That amused him a little. It was dim in there, but enough light from the outside shown in through the dust ridden windows to be able to see. All the same, Roger took the heavy steel flashlight from his windbreaker and pressed the on switch. The luminous light it produced showed that the air was thick with dust, and the way that it was powdering down continuously reminded Roger of snowfall.

"Nobody could possibly be here. Look at this place."

"Then how do you explain the voice?" Roger protested.

"I... I..." she couldn't. She wished that she could, but she couldn't. She had heard the voice. And it gave her a chill to hear that someone could be inside this grotesque structure.

"She must be upstairs, where the light was," Roger suggested.

"I don't want to go up there."

"Then wait here." He said plainly, without looking at her. He didn't know it, but she was giving him an unsavory look and a rather vulgar hand gesture. Roger climbed the stairs, holding onto the railing like it was guiding him. His light fixed on the start of the hallway, at the top of the stairs. The heavy mass of dust he was breathing in, only amplified his headache. But he couldn't stop now. He didn't know why, but something inside him wouldn't allow it. Sandra was following him up the stairs now - reluctantly. Roger made it to the top and turned left to look down the hallway. It was much darker up here, and the light from the EverReady moved at the same pace as his eyes. What he saw disturbed him. It was a long, shadowy corridor. The walls weren't any different than the ones downstairs, lined with the same empty, broken picture frames. But what disturbed Roger, and made Sandra grab onto him in horror, was that the doors to all the rooms, had been sealed off by layers of bricks. All of them, but the last door on the left at the end of the hall, where a dim light could be seen flickering. Dried mortar hung crudely from every brick, on every sealed door. Whoever did this, was certainly no a brick layer.

"Roger, no. Please...." Sandra whispered to her husband, as they made their way down the hall, costively. He didn't say anything back to her, he didn't have it in him. All the stamina he had left, went into getting down that hall to see what was in that room. As they passed the first doorway of bricks, Roger thought he heard something on the other side, scratching. He knew that it was just his imagination, it had to be. Or maybe rats. Yea, it must be rats in there clawing at the bricks, trying to create another exit for themselves. Roger and Sandra, eased their way into the barely lite room and saw that there was no one there. Only a cherry wood desk with a matching chair centered in front of the only window in the room. On top of the desk was the lit candle they had seen from outside. It was a plain white pillar candle, that looked like it had been burning for quite some time. Short, and surrounded by melted wax. Roger shined the light around the room as they inched closer to the desk. It was a filthy, white room. Cobwebs occupied every squalid corner of the walls, and the aged wooden floor creaked more and more with every step they took. When they got to the other side of the room, they saw an envelope in the middle of the desk, melted wax covered the top. Roger aimed the light and saw that it read,

To whomever, is infelicitous enough to come across this dwelling.

Roger felt his heart stop for a moment, then started up again at full throttle. If Sandra saw this and was upset, he didn't notice. He was too busy trying to keep himself composed. He wasn't really sure what infelicitous meant, but he had the feeling that it was, well, negating. With great trepidation, he reached down and freed the envelope from the wax holding it.

"Rog." Sandra said, faintly behind him. Again, he didn't respond. Instead he opened the envelope, and pulled out a cream-colored piece of paper. He unfolded it, and saw that there was a letter.

"Rog..."

The letter read,

*May the world forgive me, because
God will not. May the world forgive
Me, for what I have brought upon it,
and for what I do not have the
courage to do, to appease it. If you
choose to placate it, my pitiful friend,
just know that its appetite is quite
rapacious. Therefore, it would be
unwise of you to make this your
permanent residence. I wish you
nothing but, serendipity.*

*Yours Forever,
Elizabeth Clauson*

The letter slid from Roger's moist palms, and he rushed to lean against the wall closest to him. He felt as though he might faint. He needed water, a shot of whiskey, and something more effective than aspirin.

It's a joke. That's all. Some bored teenagers are watching from somewhere, laughing at us. Those sick little shits, whatever happened to TPing houses? But from where? I don't see any peep holes.

Suddenly, there were footsteps. He whipped his head around and saw that it was Sandra, running out the door, a cream-colored piece of paper glided to floor behind her. She had read the letter. Roger pushed himself off the wall and went after her. She had already made it to the bottom of the stairs, by the time he got to the top. He lost sight of her for only a second when she made it back to the door they came in from. He finally caught up, and found her pulling wildly at the door.

"No! No! No!" She cried out.

He took ahold of her shoulder, but she pushed off of him.

"It's locked!" She wailed.

"What the hell do you mean it's locked?" He asked doubtfully, reaching for the door knob. It was locked. He pulled and pulled. Then he kicked and kicked, but it was pointless.

"This doesn't make any sense. We're the only ones here!" He argued, still pulling at the door.

"I told you, Rog! I told you we shouldn't have come in here! You stupid, stupid man!"

"Shut up!" He hollered. He was starting to panic. He was pulling desperately at the door, but it barely even shook. How is this possible? He thought. How is this happening?

"You stupid, stupid, stupid, stupid man!"

"Sandra, shut the fuck up!" He roared in her face. He had let go of the door knob and clung onto both her arms, and was jerking her back and forth, screaming in her face for her to, "Shut up! Just shut up! Don't you know how to do that?"

The hateful sensation he felt back on that road in that suffocating car, was back. Sandra was sobbing like a frightened child as he rocked her vigorously where they stood.

"Can't you just... Can't you..." he broke off into a coughing fit. He released her, and raised his jacket sleeve over his face, in an attempt at some relief from the odor. The odor, that came all at once and out of nowhere, overwhelmed and exceeded the revolting smell of rancid fruit. The stench was unarguably that of human hair, burning human hair. Its smell was so prevalent; it was like someone was throwing handfuls of chopped off ponytails into a lit fireplace. But the only fireplace in sight was as empty now as it had been when they first walked in. There was no smoke, or any other sign of where it was coming from.

"Come on! Maybe there's a backdoor." Came Roger's muffled voice through his sleeve, grabbing his wife's hand. She was choking on the aroma and wiping away her tears when he pulled her down the corridor that lead to the kitchen, flashlight in hand. The broken glass from the picture frames on the walls cracked beneath his loafers. He noticed, but thought nothing of the two identical doors on each side of the hall, facing one another. They got into the kitchen, and noticed it was even duller in there than in the front of the house. The only window, was above the sink that was jam-packed with broken dishes, and had been sealed off by bricks. The only source of light (besides Roger's flashlight) was a poorly lit warehouse style bulb on the ceiling, that buzzed noisily like an insect zapper above them. The oven, which door was open and had a small, busted television set inside of it, looked like it was from the fifties. The tiled floor was covered in dirt and odd trash, like beer bottles and fast food wrappers. Roger turned his attention to the right side of the room and saw what he assumed was the backdoor, had not so surprisingly been sealed off by mortar covered bricks, fulfilling the great sense of foreboding he had while hauling his wife in there. This was disheartening enough, but what made Roger freeze in place (and almost piss his pants) and Sandra squeak a little, was the man-sized hole in the wall. It looked like some sort of malicious predator's cave in the wild. Roger stared into this break in the wall with a kind of jittery expectation, like at any moment, a black bear would emerge from the depths of it. There was no bear.

"You see, Rog? You see what I mean when I say you're stupid? What're we going to do? We're stuck here!" When Sandra spoke first, Roger felt the slightest peace of mind. Especially when the bear didn't appear.

"Look Sandra, It'll be ok. I'll find something to smash the lock on the door. I'll-"

"You can't do anything right!" she screamed. "We'll rot in here before you find a way out! My sister told me! She told me, but I just wouldn't listen! She said, don't marry some dumb car salesmen! She..." Roger was rubbing his temples again. A now-common feeling was reaching its boiling point inside of him, and holding it in was influencing his headache. "... She was right! You're a stupid, poor example of a..."

HUMPHHH.

The echoing noise cut Sandra off. They both heard it. It sounded like a gigantic bull, exhaling with all its might through its wide nostrils into a microphone and out of an amplifier somewhere in the kitchen. It was so loud it was as though the air around them shook. And it was clear where it came from. Sandra stopped raving, and Roger's eyes flew open as he turned from her. They both quietly stood still, and stared off into the cave-like hole in the wall.

It sounded like steel horseshoes, pounding the floor as something moved closer, and closer, and closer. They couldn't run, not yet. They were petrified by something greater than fear. Something that makes you comprehend how someone could actually be scared to death. With every step, that horrible noise grew louder, and every time they thought it was about to revel its self from the darkness, it didn't. Roger's feet were glued to the kitchen floor by the terror that had draped over him, waiting for that bear. Something finally did appear, but it wasn't the wild animal Roger thought it would be. What appeared were the faint features of a tall, slim figure just beginning to surpass the shadowy border of the hollow cavern and the grubby kitchen. They saw the pallid, boney face of a grey-haired man who had to be at least six feet tall, and wearing a dark grey, disintegrating suit. A skinny black tie hung loosely around the unbuttoned collar of its shirt. It stopped once it reached the light, and stared at them. It stared at them, like it was seeing through them. Through them, through the filthy wall behind them, through the wicked woods outside, and straight into the real world they had come from. It's eyes… Roger looked into it's deep, empty eyes and saw they were no different than the crows perched on the roof. He knew that it wasn't a man, even before anything happened. Its eyes had the surrounding whites of a man, but its irises. They should've had some kind of color in them; they only had black. Sandra hid behind Roger and squeezed onto his arm. He hardly noticed.

It began to vibrate. No… Tremble, with a kind of hatred and repugnance in its eyes that may never be understood. Then they changed. The black circles shrunk to pin-sized dots, surrounded by bloodshot scleras. It lifted its lips and introduced a set of gunky yellow teeth, that started to slowly and unevenly protrude towards one another. They became sharp and acicular, like one of those angler fish in the dark nethermost of the deep sea. Its wrists snapped inward as it raised them to its chest, producing a sickly crunch that sounded more like twigs cracking while being stepped on; Roger would remember that sound for the rest of his life. Its fingers extended - at least six inches - and formed hideous claws that were as sharp as the fangs. Its face…… The skin on its face began to melt. It began to melt, but in a thick, gruesome, and nauseating way. Chunks of hot, steaming flesh dropped from its skinny face and onto its ragged clothes, leaving blood stains behind as it met the floor by its feet. It was still shaking. Shaking like an angry man who had just spent an hour trudging through a heartless blizzard. Its eyes remained on them through the entire transformation.

This was enough to snap Roger out of his cowardly spell. He didn't think about what was happening; how unbelievable it was, or what he was going to do about it. He just knew he didn't want that thing staring at him anymore. He turned and started into the hall, Sandra still fixed to his arm. Half way through he was struck-dumb by what was in front of him. There was a thick fog that filled the room they'd just been in. It was so dense; they couldn't even see the front door, that should've visibly been a few feet in front of them. And the smell of burning hair was stronger than ever. Perplexed, they began backing away, but then Roger remembered the sludgy ghoul with the malevolent eyes in the kitchen. When he whipped around he was horrified to see that the thing was in the entry way, moving in their direction. Thunderous footsteps echoed in the narrow hallway. It wore the black, unpolished dress shoes of a man, but there must've been hundred pound hooves inside each shoe. It was moving slowly. Slowly, but surely.

"Ro…RRRoger…" Sandra stuttered through chattering teeth.

In that moment of inescapable doom, Roger and Sandra held each other in a way they might have years ago, without having to be in an impossible kind of danger. But there was no love in their embrace; only the convenience of having another human being to cling to. Someone to share the terror and hopelessness with.

Then Roger noticed the door behind her. Shifting Sandra aside, he twisted the door knob. Locked. "Shit!" He turned back, and saw the twin door on the other wall, and flung it open. He found a wooden staircase leading down to another door, and without contemplation, jumped in, pulling Sandra along. Well, yanking her along really.

He shut the door and saw the bolt lock was broken, and hanging lavishly from the frame. They flew down the stairs and seized for the knob. It was locked. The same second Roger tried to twist it again, there was a tremendous thump from the door above. They both froze and looked up at it. The door wasn't locked, but this thing wasn't bothering to open it. It was trying to break through it. With the second thump the door jutted out in an almost cartoonish way. But the third time, a slim hunk of wood shot off down the stairway, striking the wall next to them. Roger pulled at the knob, and Sandra pulled at his hands. They pulled for their lives, because every time that thing slammed into the door another piece of wood would come shooting down at them, and each piece would be bigger than the last.

"Come on! Come on, you piece of shit!" Roger demanded, while Sandra cried out in fear. She had stopped pulling, and was watching the unknown monster above force its way inside. The hole in the door it had created was wide enough to see its face, and it stopped its attack when Roger turned to look at it. Its soulless, black dotted eyes seemed to gleam as it peered down at them, and its jaw shifted from left to right, as though it had been punched in it.

"Holy Jesus!" Roger blurted out, as he went back to tugging at the door.

The thing above also went back to work, ripping apart the first door.

"Oh God, Roger, hurry! Hurry!"

"Come on! Come on, please!" Roger begged, pulling, and pulling, and pulling. Then, just as the entrance that thing was creating seemed large enough for it to take its first heavy footed step through, there was a click and the locked door flung outward. And there they were.

When Roger slammed this door shut, he locked it (not that it would matter to that thing), and heard the same click that he had when the door opened, apparently on its own.

This can't be real. It can't be.

They were in a dank, tenebrous basement and the only bit of light was coming from a filthy, rectangular window on the far wall near the ceiling. In a matter of minutes (if Roger didn't have his flashlight) it would be pitch black in there. He shined the light around and saw the awful things that hoarded the room that they'd sheltered themselves in. There were used, but unlit, white pillar candles, everywhere. Dozens and dozens of them, maybe hundreds, maybe more. They were all over the floor, the bookshelves, and the few tables around them. They filled the window seal, and they circled in an organized fashion around the wooden folding chairs that had been put out in neat rows. Like someone with a projector watching a home film with friends would set up. That wasn't all. There were bizarre, foreign markings written in what looked like chalk, all over the walls in straight, meticulous lines. There was something else. Inside a large circle in the middle of the floor, in the same white chalk, there was a pentagram. It was instantly recognizable. And so were the blood stains inside of it. Within it, there were more strange symbols; that Roger thought looked Egyptian.

"What in the name of..."

Bang!

That thing had made it past the first door and was going at this one now. Bang! Splintery bits of the door came at Roger, causing him to stumble backwards. A third bang. Sandra let out a quick, ear-ringing shriek that any scream queen from a B-movie horror flick would've approved of. A fourth bang. Another piece of wood shot towards them. Another bang.

"Do you see, Rog? Do you see what happens when someone as stupid and useless as you, goes out into the world? This is all your fault!"

"Sandra… I… I…"

"What, Rog? You what?" Another bang. "You're a dumb, broke, sad, drunk, impotent man, and this is ALL YOUR FAULT!"

Bang.

"Shut up!" That recent, and suddenly reoccurring feeling was boiling over inside of Roger, again.

"I should have married David Rowski! He's a lawyer, a lawyer wouldn't have gotten me into something like this! He wouldn't have taken directions from some dumb hillbilly!"

"Sandra, shut the fuck up before I feed you to that damn thing!" Another bang. The largest bit of wood yet hit the floor.

"You don't have the balls, Rog! You can't do anything right!"

Roger's headache had become unbearable, and it felt like sweat was pouring down from his forehead. It had become noticeably darker in that basement.

Bang! Bang! Bang!

"I hope that disgusting thing gets you first, so I can die with some satisfaction!"

Roger's hands began to tremble, much like that thing outside the doors entire body had done just minutes ago.

"I HATE YOU, ROGER! I HATE YOU! AND THIS IS ALL YOUR FAULT, JUST LIKE WHEN YOU KILLED OUR BABY!"

That was it. Roger swung his right arm backward, then brought it back up. The large steel flashlight, that had escorted them from their broken down car and into the tombs of this godless house, met Sandra's jaw with such force she was actually lifted off her feet. She landed on her back, in the blood stained, chalk-full circle.

Bang!

"I don't have the balls? I can't do anything right? Looks like I did this right, you fucking cow! I hate you too!" He bellowed at her. She was sprawled out on the circle in a position you'd get into if you wanted to make a snow angel. "AHHHHHHH!" Roger cried out, freeing years of aversion and spite all at once, while striking Sandra's face with the hefty flashlight. Again, and then again, and then again.

"Stupid! Stupid! Stupid!"

Blood spilled from Sandra Witworth's pulverized face and onto the chalk symbols transcribed into the stone floor. He didn't notice, because he was busy bashing in his already dead wife's head, but the pounding at the door had ceased.

"Stupid bitch!" He hollered his last bit of slander and eased back, breathing deeply. The bloody flashlight slid from his hand, and sent a wild stream of light around the room as it rolled to a halt. He caught his breath, and glared down at his wife; who was now unrecognizable.

Roger sat on the floor, legs crisscross like he was in grade school. He'd realized that that thing out there had stopped tearing apart the door and now he was watching it, waiting for it to start up again. He sat there in the dark for what might as well have been an eternity. Then stood up, went over, and very cautiously opened the door. There was nothing. He saw nothing, and heard nothing. Whatever had come after them, was gone.

He left the room without looking back, leaving Sandra and his flashlight behind in the basement. There was nothing above in the house either. The foul stench Roger thought he'd never escape, was gone. Nor was there any sign of that monstrous being; not even the flesh that it had left on the floor of the kitchen it inhabited.

Roger Witworth, didn't stick around to look for it. He rushed over to the front door, and found that it opened without trouble; he had an uncanny feeling that there wouldn't be any. When he paced across the porch, and down the stairs, he saw that the sun had just about finished setting. It would be night anytime now. He cut through the lawn, passed the gap of dead trees, and was back on the road.

He glanced over at the house for only a second, and then headed down the road in the direction he and Sandra had been headed. Never knowing that those markings on the wall, in that dark basement where he left his wife, spoke of blood sacrifice as a means to propitiate a nameless entity that lurked in the walls of that cursed abode. As Roger made his way down that eternal road and into the onset of the night, there was no smile on his face, but he felt exultant.

JC Raye's Shopping List

Piñata
Ketchup
Gauze
Hot glue
Blinking hair wear or glow sticks
Acne cream
Mousse
3 large bags coconut-sweetened
Thank you cards
Party baggies
Black hair dye
D&D gift cards - 9

The Kick

JC Raye

I do have to confess, when Reverend Tatman grabbed Lucy Finn by the back of her bustle, natched off her hat, and tossed it into the street, for a moment I think everyone in front of the mercantile chuckled a bit. Lucy, 32, and a widow, had a kind heart and a sweet singing voice, but a damn near horrible taste in ladies' hats. It was when the preacher pushed her to her knees on that rough plank porch, screaming about "the scales of justice" and yanking out a sizeable handful of her shiny black curls, that everyone stopped laughing and started running. Toward or away, depending on your sense of gallantry, I suppose. Maybe some folks were running for help, I don't know. Wash and I (Wash Phineas, town of Bodie's best barber and my friend since childhood) ran toward. A few other men followed suit. Now Wash has about fifty pounds and a few hundred peach pies on me, so I got to the porch steps just a second or two before he did. But that was one second too late to stop the enraged Reverend from throwing Lucy through the picture window of Mudge's General Store.

"Erving!" I screamed at the Reverend, grabbing his right arm, my mind still trying to register what I was seeing. Lucy's legs were now hanging, half-out of a shattered eight-foot-square window pane. Like a giant rag doll that had been flung by a petulant child. One side of her shirred up green skirt was torn straight to the hip, as was too, the exposed black petticoat beneath it. Inside the tear, a naked white thigh that likely never saw the sun, now bore a jagged, bloody slash, 'bout five inches or so in length. One black lace glove looked flayed in Lucy's upturned palm. A small strip of it was waiving in the warm breeze like a little flag of surrender. Now the upper part of her torso was laying atop a silver tray of shattered teacups and saucers. And if that weren't trial enough, right while I was standing there, the ladies form for dressing gowns, which also had been in the window, fell over too. It splayed Lucy's arms to either side, mirroring a bizarre crucifixion. She was struggling to get up, and squealing like a newborn. Arson Mudge, the store owner and his wife Millie were in a panic trying to assist her. But, each pull and tug caused the woman pain as shards of glass and china cut further into her arms and legs.

The other fellas were up on the porch directly, and swarming the Reverend from all sides, while he did his best to try and reach Lucy's head again for another swipe. We all lost our grip on him for a moment. He was kickin' like a branded mule. My hands slide from his bicep to his wrist. It was then I realized the mighty Reverend had taken much more of a hair donation then I thought from my original viewpoint across the street. The clump of hair was larger than a full-grown fox's tail. I closed my eyes involuntarily as the thing brushed over my cheek during the scuffle. When I opened my eyes, Erving Tatman's face was right up to mine, and he was screaming and sputtering and looked like he might bite my nose clean off. "August!" he screeched at me, his receding white hair standing straight up on his head, "There must be retribution for that poor bird's suffering! I know you understand!" As you can imagine, I had no response.

Suddenly the sheriff was on the porch, and thank god for it. "I think Miss Lucy's had quite enough retribution for today Reverend if you don't mind." The lawman gently placed his hand on the preacher's shoulder and it seemed to calm him a bit. "Why don't we get you somewhere where you can calm down and tell us all about it."

Charles Dalton Seers. The 12th lawman I've ever come to know, and by far the smartest man I ever met in Bodie. A retired gunslinger gone constable, as is common these days, he was just shy of six feet, made of granite, and had the hand grip of a steel trap. If his bulk didn't put pause in your action, his piercing eyes, the color of pitch, would do the job. It only took Seers a second or two to assess the mayhem and give out some quick instruction to the lot of us holding Erving, as well as to the small crowd of people in Mudge's store desperately trying to help poor little Lucy Finn.

We had us a good sheriff. But we always had pretty decent lawmen on down through the years. The county newspaper loved to paint a picture of our town as some sort of lawless land. But that's city writers who'll just never understand the workings of mining town. I'll give ya that we had a lot of homicides in Bodie. That's true enough. But you have to remember, most of those killings included willing participants. Men who offended, or were offended, and decided a gunfight to be the only fittin' solution. If there are still town records to check, you'd see that in all the time I lived there, robberies and rapes were very few. Well, except for the stage which got bothered from time to time. But that's outside the city limits. And it was on more than one occasion I ran into a passenger who said they had been treated downright courteously by the highwaymen who robbed them.

Sadly, there wasn't a day go by in Bodie though without two sapheads heads getting into a skirmish about women, property, politics or maybe just who was the better man between'em. Oftentimes an argument would ensue from some imagined insult or when some young man jumped the pecking order at the bar. But a smart man, like Seers, looking for a place to retire as a constable, knew that in a town like Bodie the death of a local, whether by gun, knife, or fist, was bred from an agreed-upon tussle. There wasn't much to do but pull the body out of the street and notify next of kin, if there was any.

Now if you can get past all that, you'd also know that Bodie is beautiful place to hang your hat. Set right on the eastern slope of the Sierra Nevada's. Why in our county we got granite peaks and mountain streams and rollin' sagebush hills. There are meadows filled with wildflowers of every color, and we even got a few of those bubblin' hot springs. Course the winters can get rough. Was a winter storm that killed W.M. Bodie, our first prospector and town founder.

So later that day, seven men and one woman, Addie Gallagher, the school teacher, were gathered around Sherriff Seers' desk at the Bodie Jail. Seers said it was the best place to take Tatman as it wouldn't draw a crowd and it was where we could have a private meeting so as he could do his best to sort out the facts. The jailhouse was on King Street next to Kirkwood Livery. Just off North Main. And the Reverend, who was up in his 60's, near as I could figure, had expended just about every drop of energy he had back at the store. Getting him onto the back of Hent Seever's wagon, driving him the 300 yards to the jail, and dumping him in one of the open cells was easier than expected.

The jailhouse was a small building, about 25 feet square, with two rooms. The larger front room had the two cells and his desk. The cells had full open bar fronts, floor to ceiling. The small room in the back was a bunk. Seers did own a home on the south side of town, but the bed I reckon was for longer nights, or where guests might need to sleep one off. Though the structure was never built well, and from the outside seemed to look more like a nine-foot pile of kindling rather than an official town building, Seers kept the interior washed down, neat and organized. The inside of his office made you feel much the same way the man did, like everything was in apple pie order. The small black corner stovetop was clear of its ash, and 4 tin coffee cups, all facing the same direction hung on a board above it, all a'shinin. Books, maps and papers were smartly stacked in one place on the side of his desk by the wall. The farthest part of the room from where I was standing had a white wash basin and pitcher on a spindly legged table. They too, were unchipped and spotless.

"So, what happened Addie?" Seers asked her, "Wash here says you were leavin' Mudge's right when all hell broke loose. Sorry Ma'am. I mean, when the trouble first began."

"That's alright, Sherriff," Addie soothed, "I expect we all might still be in shock. Nothing like this has ever happened in this town. Well, with a woman, that is."

"Ma'am." His tone was soft and agreeable, but clearly urging her to get to it.

"Well it was her hat." Addie said, "It had something to do with Lucy's hat." One of the men, can't remember who, remarked that Lucy's hats were some of the ugliest he'd ever seen. The men murmured some general agreement on that. Not put off by the interruption, Addie continued. She had dealt with miner's children far too long to let a little disruption distract her. "No, it wasn't that. It's what was on the hat that was clearly bothering him. You see that hat was decorated with what's called a bird of paradise. A stuffed bird with exotic coloring? She was lookin' at the men for some sort of confirmation or hint of comprehension. She didn't get it. "Well, it's a very expensive embellishment, and Lucy had it shipped all the way from Virginia City. I know this, because she told me she waited three months for it to arrive.

"Excuse me Addie," Wash gently interrupted, "but why would a stuffed bird make the man take leave of his senses that way?"

The pretty young school teacher smiled softly. She put a hand to collarbone and softly patted it, lookin' around at all of us like she was still decidin' if she was going to tell us the rest at all. "He said…this may not be the exact words he used mind you, or the exact order of the conversation…"

"That's ok Addie." Seers said, "Just tell us as straight as you remember it."

Encouraged, Addie continued. "The Reverend said it wasn't fair. It wasn't fair that such a beautiful one of God's creatures should have its feathers plucked to adorn some rich woman's head. He asked her if she would like to have her feathers plucked. He asked her… if she believed in the scales of justice.

The front door to the jailhouse burst open, and our resident sawbones, Emry Beale, hurried in. I think he gave us all a start. Arson Mudge was right on his heels.

"Lucy okay, doc?" I asked.

"She's going to be." Beale said, "She's cut, cut in a lot of places, and frightened for sure. Lord knows it could have been much worse. She's very lucky. "

"She out of the window?" Seers asked. "You need any help over there?"

"Millie and her sister Haddie are helping her over to my office now. She'll need plenty of stitches." Beale paused and straightened out his tie a bit, "To be honest with you sheriff, I never treated a scalp wound like that before. It might be a little rough going. I just came over quick to see if the Reverend will also be needing any medical attention."

Arson Mudge, interrupted the good doctor. "And I am going need someone to shore up my window. It's gonna take weeks to order some new glass. I don't wanna be spending my nights sleeping in the store window with my rifle tucked between my legs." Good ol' Mudge, always had his priorities straight. Some of the men standing near me bit their tongues and shook their heads.

"Hows' that Reverend?" Mason Num, local pain-the-rump, called out to the preacher. Tatman, was wide awake and listening to all of us, but still sitting on the cell floor where we dumped him. "Need anythin' from the doc?" Num said. "A prayer book maybe? A store catalog so you can circle the hats you don't like?" A few of the men chuckled.

"Num," Seers said, "Now you know that's not helping one bit."

"August," Seers nodded to me, can you maybe get at Mudge's window today?"

"Sure Seers" I said, purposely not making eye contact with Arson Mudge. "I got the time and spare boards from the porch I built last week fronta Joe Rowley's Saloon." You see I was carpenter, and the son of one. And I was lucky enough to have made my living as one of the few good chips in town. Well, not luck. I had rightly had earned my reputation as a hard worker, and, as a man who could be trusted to do a thing without needin' supervision or liquid motivation to do it.

"And whose gonna pay for that?" Mudge whined to the group. "Probably only fair that the church should make good on that, don't you think Sheriff?"

The Reverend Tatman, who was now standing upright in his cell, added, "We need to be fair to both man and beast alike." Tatman raised his arm with a torn up sleeve outside the bars as if he was givin' some fire and brimstone sermon to us. This time a few men, including myself and Wash, laughed out loud.

Num could not just let it pass. "Well that's fine Reverend. I 'll let my pooch know. He'll be glad to hear you're lookin' out for him."

This time when the men laughed, Sheriff Seers' face colored, his patience fading quickly. "Alright that's enough. Num, you better shut your big bazoo or you and the Reverend will be neighbors here by end of day. You got that? Now gentlemen, I'll need two volunteers to stand guard here in the office for a few hours, not you Num, and one to come with me and Arson back to the store. Aug Chodt's on the window and Doc, thanks for the update, but you better see to Lucy. The rest of you, I'm sure you got work or family obligations at home on this lovely Saturday morning to keep you well occupied. And don't let me hear you been spreading rumors till we know how the cat jumps.

Now I was listenin' to Seers' voice, but I wasn't lookin' at him. I was too busy lookin' at Fielding. Fielding Reiser, Bodie's banker. He was standing off to the left of the group nearer the two holding cells. Something was happening to Fielding. And I guess I might have been the only one who saw it happening. Now the next part is kinda hard to describe. One moment, Fielding was himself, hands in pockets, listening, commenting. He seemed concerned about the Reverend, and about Lucy Finn, and probably even more so about the fact that he had torn the armpit out of his little brown stripe suit while helping the men tackle Tatman and carry him off to the jail. Someone who didn't know Fielding mighta glanced at our town's squirrely little banker and seen nothing out of ordinary. Twitchy hands, hair combed to the side, finished with a greasy fish tail swoop. Fluffy eyebrows reaching up his forehead like the fingers of piano player. But I saw different. He was suddenly standing in an e-rect a posture as I guess is humanly possible. Like he got a jolt of lighting in his tailbone. He looked like a man who had taken a hard swallow of Forty Rod and it had just kicked in. Now my pa pulled me out of school to work when I was no taller than a whiskey barrel, so I don't have a fancy mouth as some. But saying it looked like something kicked in on Fielding Reiser was sure near as I can relay it. He stood like that for maybe 15 seconds. Still as that. Then, he unbelted his trousers, squatted down where he stood, and took a shit on the jailhouse floor.

Then everything seemed to happen real fast.

"Fielding, what in the Sam Hill…!" Wash shouted, pointing. Several of the men shifted their position in the small room to see why Wash was yelling and hopping about. Miss Addie moaned in disgust and thrust her kerchief to her nose. Seers cussed and hopped off his desk where he had been seated.

Fielding, still in a crouch, looking confused by all the attention said, "Well you didn't all expect me to stand in this room and hold it all day, did you? I had to do it."

Just then Millie Boone, burst in the office so fast, the door clipped Mudge in the back and made him howl. Sherriff! You gotta come. It's my sister Haddie.

"Millie now you can see I've got my hands full here." Seers said.

Millie's eyes were wide and scary-like. "No Sheriff," she said. "You HAVE to come. She's eatin' all the preserves in the store."

Seers face was now the color of sunset and this was the only time I ever heard him shout. "Woman, are you telling me that I have to come over there because your sister is eating a jar of raspberry preserves?

"NO!" Millie screamed, "She also eating the glass!"

The mayhem that ensued in the days followin' reminded me of a flash dust storm I experienced once as child. Things got out of hand real fast. Now again, this ain't in no particular order, and remember, I am digging up memories that for a long time I was trying to forget. Maybe some of this will sound even normal to folks from the outside, or from the north. Hell, I only know from my own. I never was one to keep a journal, or a calendar. And in a town like mine, most of the population is usually a mix of drifters, miners, and mill workers. Temporary people. When the mines were producing at full tilt, we could have as many as three thousand of those. So I can't account for any of them. I am mostly telling you about what happened with the eight hundred or so folks who laid down roots in Bodie. People I knew first hand.

In the days and months that followed, our town funeral director, Dillard Tulley took an axe and cut down half the hitching posts on Main Street. The street is a mile long, and you'd think someone would have stopped him sooner, as it was occurring in plain view of about 25 places of business. But hell, you can't just run up to man wielding an axe. It needed some serious figuring first and it took a whole lot bodies and one wood table to get the job done. When we finally got the jump on him, Tulley told us he done it 'cause it wasn't fair that he had to tend to so many bodies as of late. And if new people arrived, they wouldn't decide to stay in town if there was no place for them to tie up their horse.

Caldonia Burnham, 16, daughter of Merrill and Vera, and her little sister, Annie, 7 years old, were said to be just hanging laundry in back of their home one day when, according to Annie, her sister "ran away." Annie told her parents, and later the sheriff, that they were hanging a sheet and her sister starts to mention how their mother never made dessert anymore, and how she hadn't collected berries for a pie in ever so long. Annie says Caldonia just drops the sheet and starts walking up the hill that abutted their yard. Feeling like something was wrong, Annie says she called after her sister, and then chased after her. Annie followed Caldonia for about 50 yards. Pulling on her big sister's arm slowed her, but did not stop her, so the poor little thing just ran back home screaming for her mother. A search party turned up a shoe before nightfall, but that was all of Caldonia anybody ever found.

People went missing too. Not packed up and left, just missing. Millie Mudge was keeping the count for a time. That made as good a sense as any, seeing as most folks visited her store pretty regular. Wasn't families missing either. And it wasn't runaway husbands hitching up with a cattle drive to take time away from family responsibilities. The Mayor's wife, Eloisa was missing too, for only half a day. Because at four o'clock that afternoon, when everyone was looking for her, one of

Gailey Roight's children found the lady in their family chicken coop. Eloisa had succeeded in carefully pluckin' the feather off every single bird and explained to her husband and the searchers that it was because he was too cheap to order her a feather pillow so she could get her beauty rest.

Businesses closed. The restaurant closed. I ran into the owner, Alonzo, the day he was nailing the sign to the front door. He said folks was just outright stealing the china. Saying it was due to the fact they fancied it themselves. And one of his best waitresses was getting in the habit of taking off work any old time she felt a hankerin' to do so. She told the manager that she been on time for five years, and now he owed her some.

"Can you believe that Aug?" Alonzo said, "A gal taking a notion like that in her head?" Why it got so bad that customers were walking right into his back kitchen and just helping themselves, accusing him of making them wait too long for their food. Now I've been thoroughly accused of stretching the blanket a bit in my day, but every one of these accounts is true. There were all manner of things going on in Bodie, of people getting "the kick." Thievings and poisonings, beatings and horse killings. There's a tale about a newly married young couple and branding iron which would chill your blood, and I ain't going to visit that here.

I got outta Bodie in 1931.Exactly one year from the time Lucy Finn was picking glass shards out of her thigh, I was drawing up my money from the Bank of Bodie, packing up my clothes and the few precious items I owned, and planning to hop the next stage, or the ore train if need be. Tail between my legs? Yes sir. In the prior months, I'd seen more disturbin' acts than a circus ringmaster sees in a lifetime of travel. And they weren't even comin' close to slowing up.

That day I left, had been the worst for sure. Millie Mudge came by to drop off some sundries for me. I lived in small homestead which I built and I bought, just about 50 yards behind the Miller Rooming House on Green Street, the more central part of town. Probably another reason I was always getting side work. I was just on hand in that location. Close to the school, stores, the engine house. I could throw a stone in any direction and hit any one of five saloons. But most anyone could say that about the saloons in Bodie. Hell we had thirty of 'em.

Millie told me Sheriff Seers was missing. Office was open, and the back bunk quarters was also unlocked. Bed was made, cold cup of coffee on his desk. She was very worried and very scared. Clearly, looking for some stability in talking to me. As she was telling me about the perfectly made up bed, and jail keys just sitting on their hooks for anyone and their brother to make off with, I was her watching her close. You have to watch everyone close now. Watch for the kick, and be ready to run, or defend yourself on the spot, or maybe stop them from hurting themselves. Funny thing, I think the kick actually made better listeners out of all of us.

As I listened, I never noticed before what a beautiful woman she was. Even with her bottom lip quivering, and strands of sandy hair falling out of their pins, there was no denying she was striking. And not in a painted lady kinda way, just a natural beauty as some have. Her eyes seemed a mix of green and gray swirls, and they were large, very much like china doll I saw a little girl holding once, when her daddy lifted her down from the stage. Millie' full figure was neatly and tightly tucked into a plain apricot-colored dress. The apron over it was plain too, except for a long ruffle across the bottom. Just a hint of something fancy, something wild. I found I could not stop staring at that ruffle.

When I grabbed her, she seemed surprised. And when I cupped one of her breasts in my hand and made her kiss me, I felt it was the least she could do, since I had never been lucky enough to find me a good woman like her. I am not sure why she pulled the Colt on me that had been neatly tucked into her ruffled apron, or why she shot that hole right thru the palm of my hand. I wanted to ask her to stay and explain herself, but she seemed to want to leave very badly. So I let her.

Now, the town doctor had left over a month ago, and as much as I did not want to leave the safety of my home, I figured I'd head up to Wash's barber shop. He'd been known to lay stitches on a man in times of emergency, and I guess I had I had me one of those. I didn't walk on Main Street up to the shop. Didn't really know how I would explain to anyone about my bloody hand wrapped in tablecloth. Didn't really know if I'd run into Arson Mudge and his shotgun neither. Instead, I skinned along the creek behind my house that runs the length of Main. Bushes and trees would hide me well enough till I got to the Walsh's.

Pushing open the front door of Wash's shop shoulda brought me some relief, to be both out of public view and also to see my friend. It didn't. Cause there he was. Sittin' on a stool in his empty shop, holding a knife and fork and chowing down on his own cat. His wife's cat. Cooked a'course. But even charred, you could see plain as day what it was. It was Bonfire alright, the large orange tabby I'd let sit in my lap on many occasions in that very damn stool. And Wash was enjoying every bite.

And somewhere in the back of the shop, in the living area, in the darkness, I heard his wife making a very strange sound.

Now I am an old man. Been an old man for near on 20 years, and let me tell you, I have heard frightening sounds in my day. I've heard the growl of bear in a bluff charge not ten feet from me, and I have heard the howl of wolves too close for comfort. I have heard the sinister buzz of a diamond back rattler, threatening to drain every drop of his venom right into me if I ventured out just beyond the safety of my fire. But never in my fool existence have I heard a sound as terrifyin' as I heard in the back room of Wash's shop that day, while he was picking cat out of his teeth.

His wife was moanin' back there. Wash was chewing, and cutting, and chewing and smiling at me. And she was moanin'. Suddenly, my mind was all in a stew, putting two and two together as they say. His wife wasn't making that sound 'cause she was just sad about her cat somewhere in the darkness of that back room. Something else was wrong. I looked at Wash's plate. It wasn't just cat. There was something else. Something… that looked like a tongue. Without realizing it, I was biting my upper lip, hard, and I felt a thin ribbon of sweetness slide down the inside of my lower teeth.

"Your wife ok, Wash?" I asked.

"Well she could be better." he replied, without stopping to swallow. I could hear the slush of the meat in his wide yellow choppers.

"Really friend?" I nudged, "'Cause it sounds like she might be in a little bit of pain back there."

He paused, mid-chew, and looked at me directly this time. "Well, friend, as you can see here, I am right in the middle of my lunch. But you'd be more than welcome to step on back there and check on her if you've a mind to.

Wash lifted an edge of the soiled white towel wrapped around his neck, up to his mouth and blotted his greasy lips. "'Cause it wouldn't be quite fair for me to have to stop in the middle of my meal now would it? I already told Maye how important eating on time is to me.

I backed out of the shop and nearly feel down the two steps. Thankfully and almost mercifully, the wind took the door and slammed it closed right in front of me. God forgive me I could not go back in. I knew she was hurt, but I just could, not, go.

Well, that was the final straw. I walked home at quite a clip. Didn't even care who saw me then. My whole body was shaking as if with a fever. I can remember my jaw rattling and a feelin' of rot in my stomach. I didn't tell a soul I was leavin' town either. Don't recall any part of leavin' really. I just got out.

Been here in Grant Grove ever since. It's a nice little rooming house. Price is fair. Chow's more than decent. Keep to myself mostly. That modern library just up the street there has got a book on Mono County. Course that book says that folks left Bodie because of the great fire in '32. Wiped out nearly ninety-percent of the buildings. There's before and after pictures and such. I saw it once. That sage hen who runs the place damn near bent my ear for the better part of an hour, goin' on and on, telling me about my own town and showin' me the pictures in that historical book. Hell, I hear tell my town might be on record as having the shortest life in the history of the western towns. But that's just what people say.

Now I'd love to jaw on this with you a might longer, but I am afraid we'll have to cut our conversation short. Got me some plans. You know how that is.

You see that saloon there at the end of the street? No. Not that one. The one all lit up? Right. Well some fella told me the bartender there cuts his whiskey with turpentine and sells it to out-of-towners that way. Now, that's not right. I thought maybe I would head on over and show him exactly what turpentine can do to a body when you drink enough of it. It's very dangerous. And it's only fair...

You're certainly welcome to join me.

Jovan Jones' Shopping List

Coffee Flour
Paprika Eggs
CelerySugar
Pecans Rice
Garlic powder Miller High Life
Seasoned salt KC Masterpiece BBQ Sauce
Chili powder Bread
Italian seasoningSteak Sauce
Bananas Louisiana Hot Sauce
Cantaloupe Margarine
Strawberries
Honeydew
Avocados
Tomatoes
Lettuce
Onion
Mushrooms
Cilantro
Tony Chachere Creole Seasoning
Parsley
Garlic
Pepper jack Cheese
Ground turkey
Lamb chops
Pork chops
Pork ribs
Sirloin/chuck steak
Oysters
Mussels
Whiting canned salmon

A Nightcap with Selena

Jovan Jones

A large crowd gathered at the bar that night. Droves of people showed up to watch the championship boxing match. Women in tight T-shirts and Daisy Duke Shorts dashed from one table to another taking order after order. Attractive waitresses batted eyelashes and put an extra hitch in their hips as they flirted with the guys, tolerating the excessive machismo for the chance at a decent tip. Heavily tattooed young men with Yancy's Bar and Grill T-shirts clanged dishes in bus tubs. The commentary of an ex-fighter blended with the vociferous crowd noise over several big screen TVs hanging about. The patrons were accompanied by friends, spouses, co-workers, but one woman sat alone at the edge of the bar stirring the ice in her glass. Men stared, but hesitated to approach her.

"Don't you fellas see this lady stirring ice in an empty glass," the salt and pepper haired bartender said to the men in the vicinity; playing wingman. The guy was old school. He hailed from a time when bartenders were better than psychologist and life coaches.

"Oh, no that's alright," she said. "I'll get my own drink. Thanks."

The bartender waved her off. "Relax lady, a woman as pretty as you don't have to pay for nothing. Have a drink on one of these guys." He pointed to the handful of men whose courage grew with every sip of their brew.

"What are you having?" A heavily muscled dark haired Italian man said through a slick Clark Gable-like smile.

"Triple shot of Jack." She nodded to the bartender.

"You got it, sweetheart."

The Italian man offered his hand. "Donovan Letto."

"Selena Mariposa."

Donovan paused and stepped back to refocus his eyes on the beauty in front of him. She wore a tantalizing ocean blue dress that exposed one side of her curvaceous honey hued hips, and allowed her buxom bosom to breathe. Her full lips were soft caramel shaped into a permanent sensuous pucker. Her almond shaped eyes were dark tornado cloud grey and filled with intrigue. Looking into those peepers triggered salacious imaginings Donovan desperately attempted to conceal.

"Are you involved with anyone, Selena?" he asked.

She chuckled, and took a sip of her whiskey.

"What?" Donovan released a nervous laugh.

"Who do you think will win tonight?" Selena asked looking up at the T.V.

"Rodriguez," he answered. "Definitely Rodriguez."

"Yeah?"

"Yeah, sure. Why? Who do you think?"

"Kilpatrick, all day."

"I don't know, but . . ."

Selena threw a hand in the air cutting him off. She said, "Let's make a bet."

"What's the bet?"

"Kilpatrick wins you owe me ten bucks. Rodriguez wins I owe you a drink at my place."

It took a while for Donovan to respond. She'd taken him by surprise. "Okay, yeah."

"Okay." Selena shot him a sly grin.

They got acquainted over a basket of Buffalo wings and fried pickles. They watched as Fitzpatrick danced and hit a sloth footed Rodriguez with combination after combination, until he landed a devastating body blow that curled him like a roly-poly bug and dropped him to the campus. Selena called for the bartender to close out her tab. Donovan pulled a ten from his pants pocket. She took it and slid it between her breasts.

"I'm in the black GT500," she said, "follow me if you can keep up."

Donovan smiled, slapped a twenty on the bar, and pirouetted toward the exit.

***

"You have a nice place here, Selena. I'm surprised you don't share it with someone special."

She gave him an "oh please" smirk and said, "Look, Donovan there's no need for adolescent charm."

"Wait a minute. I…"

Selena tossed a finger out in front of her to silence his explanation. "I've many a courter. You're just a spur of the moment thing."

Donovan took offense, inwardly. He wanted to control his emotions in hope that their encounter would lead to a sexual one. He watched Selena with her legs crossed sitting at the table uncorking a bottle of red wine. Her fingers slid up and down the neck of the bottle slowly as she looked into Donovan's eyes.

Those eyes of hers, he thought. His manhood prickled. She poured him a glass.

"Thank you."

"Don't mention it."

Selena stood from the table to grab a bottle of whiskey from the cabinet.

"Aren't you going to drink some of this wine with me?"

"Nah. I have enough of that stuff in my system to last an eternity." She smiled coyly.

Donovan grabbed the glass and lifted it to his lips. He swished the dark red wine and gave it a sniff. It was pungent, vinegary, but wasn't all expensive wine? "What year is this?"

Selena chuckled. "You're a wine enthusiast?"

"Sure. I know a little bit."

"Sure you do. Just drink it."

Donovan set the glass down and stood. He gleamed at Selena. He said, "I don't know who you think I am, but I'm no dummy here to amuse you." He extended his palms outward to convey that he had enough of her ribbing. "I figured you were a tease, anyway. See you around." He motioned toward the door. Selena stopped him.

"Relax, will ya?" She placed her spread fingers on his chest and gave him an enticing grin. "Look, Donovan I get a lot of guys with big talk trying to impress me. It just gets old. I simply want to enjoy a handsome man without all the bull. I know you understand." She massaged his inner thighs, letting her hand nudge his member in the process. He went in for a kiss.

"Slow down, let's drink first." She handed him the glass of wine, pressed her body to his and whispered in his ear. "Enjoy your wine and I'll be right back." Selena turned and started down the hall. "I'll put on some music. Go on, drink. Relax. I want to show you something beautiful." Selena's words danced off her tongue with erotic intonations spurring his heart's rhythm into flurried palpitations. She pointed her cell phone to the stereo and clicked it on. A sultry songstress bellowed about her lustful longing of a misplaced lover over the blare of horns, and the two cents of a piano. He watched her saunter down the hall; her backside shimming to the beat of the drum in the song. He downed the glass of wine, and immediately poured himself another.

Donovan fell to his knees and gripped his chest. Am I having a heart attack? His heart beat like a madman on the walls of an asylum. He stretched out on the floor hoping to find relief, but pain shot throughout his body. Despite the pain his eyelids grew heavy. He wanted to sit up, but realized he couldn't move. In the distance, he heard the whine of a door opening. The hardwood floor creaked under Selena's steps. He strained to look up, but remained paralyzed.

"Selena?" he asked. He felt shame in hearing his voice crack with a fearful dissonance.

"Who the hell else would it be?" she answered, as she stood at his feet.

She stood, splendorous in her birthday suit, and sucked in a cloud of smoke through her nostrils from a cigarette. Even in his dreadful situation Donovan couldn't help but notice her ample curves. Long brown hair lay over her shoulders accentuating perky breast with milk chocolate nipples under her perfect neck. Selena dropped to the floor cachinnating.

"What's going on?" Donovan asked. "What did you give me?"

"You tell me. I gave you wine, fine wine at that, you handsome devil." A malicious smile formed slowly like a surgeon's laceration on her face. "You're going to experience something beautiful" His eyelids grew heavy. His vision blurred. He slept.

Ah! It hurts so much! Pull it out!

You're going to be fine. Just breathe.

Donovan found himself lying in the bed of a hospital room. The sharp pains had ceased. He threw his legs over the bed. He felt lightheaded as he came to his feet. There were no windows to look out, no noticeable hospital equipment, but there was the trace of a sanitary scent, like bleach in the air. The walls and floor were white. Sneakers squeaked in the hall. A doctor in a smock walked brusquely by the door.

Donovan called out, "Doctor! Excuse me doctor."

Ah! I can't do it! It hurts! It hurts so baaad!

Just hold on the doctor is coming.

The doctor continued on. Her hair bounced like a bale of hay being dropped from the tier of a barn. "Doctor," Donovan cried out.

She stopped, but didn't turn and face him. "How may I help you, sir?"

"I don't know how I got here, or even where here is."

She didn't respond.

"Can you tell me what is going on?"

"I have a baby to deliver. Go to the information desk if you want information," she said.

Donovan marched out of his room toward the doctor. His frustration mounted not knowing where he was and the doctor's attitude did not help. "Wait a minute. I . . ."

The doctor whipped around, and stopped Donovan in his tracks. Her face was puffed and bruised;

ecchymosed with a column of lacerations under each eye. Eyes so blood shot they were purple with no trace of white in them. Only the bruised blood that appeared to have spilled into what were once brown pupils, now the color of dark sludge likened to that of over used cooking oil.

"What happened to you?" Donovan asked. His eyes bugged at the sight. Her eyes twitched, but not from nervous reactions. Maggots spilled from her lids. They made a slight popping sound, like toothpaste being squeezed from its tube. Donovan wanted to turn and scramble for the nearest exit, but fear cemented his feet to the floor. The woman in labor screamed again in agony. The doctor turned and stepped purposefully in the direction of the woman's cries.

"Please!" he beckoned. "How do I get out of here?"

The doctor stopped, turned, and opened her mouth wide, as if to scream. Her stomach rumbled. Chunky black sludge spilled from her mouth. A steady stream of it snaked toward him. Filthy hands emerged and withdrew like dorsal fins in the ocean. The sludge spread over the walls and floor; eclipsing all light. He ran, but in vain. Every direction he went led him right back where he started. The room he'd come out of was filled with the black substance. Voices emanated with malicious lisp talking amongst themselves from the room.

She has found a mate.

His soul is ripe for harvest.

He must breed first, and then we will feast.

His fear is savory on my tongue.

Donovan had nowhere to go. The sludge covered all routes. It took hold of him. Vile fingers explored every inch of his flesh. He attempted to scream, but only gurgles seeped from his throat, the dark substance filled his mouth. The panic of not being able to breathe kicked in, but it was strange not being able to hear his own heartbeat, like he'd be able to underwater. No, this was a more terrifying way to drown. Donovan was immersed in darkness, not water, in lascivious mire permeating with creatures devouring his essence. The world turned into a starless midnight with a hidden moon. Only susurrus sounds and mischievous whispers resonated in the muck. The chatter of God's forsaken. He recoiled from the fight to survive. A sea of calm rolled over him. The voices ceased. The drowning sensation eased into a euphoric rest.

Beep! Beep! Beep!

The sounding of his alarm clock roused him to sit up quickly. Donovan snatched the sweat soaked covers back and got out of bed. He shuffled to the bathroom and looked in the mirror. Donovan ran his fingers through his sweaty hair. He seemed alright. "That was a terrible nightmare," he said aloud.

So, what did you do last night?

He whipped around and looked in the direction the question emanated from. He stared at the clock, realizing that he'd flipped the radio on instead of turning it off. The morning show host spoke to his co-host. Donovan sighed, turned to the medicine cabinet and grabbed his razor. He turned the hot water knob, and closed the cabinet. The doctor from his nightmare appeared in the mirror, maggots tumbling from the lacerations under her eyes. She reached for his shoulder. Unaware of her presence he turned to look behind him, feeling as if someone or something was present. She vanished. He shrugged and began lathering his face with shaving cream.

Ladies, did you find Mr. Right? Guys, did you get lucky last night? Call in with your stories of love, lust, and depravity! This is your host with the most, the man with the plan, Crazy Dan, here on 104.3 The Fox!

***

Donovan sat at his desk, staring at a memo. He didn't know what it said. His attention waned. It troubled him that he got so drunk that he couldn't remember how he got home. The image of the beautiful woman from the bar flashed onto his cerebral cortex. Was Selena laughing at him, because of his drunkenness, or did she slip him a Mickey?

"There he is," said his co-worker, Marvin.

"What's up, Marvin?" Donovan greeted half-heartedly.

"Has anyone ever told you that you were the man?"

Donovan looked up at him with exhausted raccoon eyes.

"Tired huh? Well, I bet a woman like that could wear down even the hardest of dudes, except me of course." Marvin slid his slim fingers down his silk red tie and flattened it against his shirt. "So?"

"So, what?"

"How was she, man? I mean, it looks like she drained you."

"I don't know." Donovan donned a confounded expression.

"Did you get the draws, or not?" Marvin smirked.

"No, I don't believe I did."

Marvin stood to leave. He waved a dismissive hand in the air and said, "And here I thought you were my hero." Donovan watched his co-worker frolic back to his cubicle and flirt with every female employee on his way back. Marvin had a slimy grin. He was the kind of guy you wouldn't introduce your sister to. He was half weasel, half wolf, in a stallion's clothing; a handsome bastard indeed.

"Get to work pretty boy," his boss said as he towered over him at his desk. "You're welcome to attend an AA meeting with me tonight. It's never too early to get help."

"…What?" Donovan gave him a sour face.

"You look like shit, son. You've got a hangover. I know. I've been there."

"Look, Mr. Samuelson . . ." His protest was stopped short when he looked at his computer screen and noticed he had an email from: s.mariposa@att.net. Mr. Samuelson was still speaking, but Donovan's attention had turned to the email. No subject. He pulled his eyes from his computer screen to give his boss the respect expected from a subordinate, but hadn't made out one word he was saying.

"…It took me two ex-wives, bankruptcy, and a year without my driver's license to come to grips with my problem. I'm still an alcoholic, but I've been sober for seven years."

"Congratulations, Mr. Samuelson."

"Whenever you need to talk I'll be in my office." Mr. Samuelson dropped a heavy hand on Donovan's shoulder.

Great now the boss thinks I'm a lush.

"I'll do that, thanks," he said through an appeasing smile.

***

Donovan tossed and turned in his bed. He sweated profusely. Another nightmare. He had nightmares since his encounter with Selena Mariposa. Raps on the door delivered him from his night terror. He sat up, and wiped his forehead. Another knock on the door. Donovan got out of bed and slipped his robe on.

"Who is it?" he asked.

"It's Selena."

He looked through the peep hole and froze.

"What do you want?"

"What?" She turned her nose up. "Can I come in?"

Man, she's gorgeous.

"How did you know where I lived?"

"I'm not going to keep talking to you through this door, Donovan."

He put the chain on and cracked the door. He sized her up. She wore pearl white high heeled shoes that accentuated her shapely brown legs, with the same colored sun dress that hugged her curves. He thought about that night he met her, and reasoned that he'd simply had a bad dream. It could've been reason, or the influence of the twins poking out at him. He let her in.

"Of course, come in, come in." He watched her backside as she strolled in the apartment dripping with sex appeal.

"I've been thinking about you," she said.

"How did you know where I lived?"

"Well," she paused pulling a cigarette from her purse. "When you were over my house that night I called you a cab. You were sloppy drunk. I pulled your I.D. out of your wallet so I could tell the driver where to drop you."

"I don't remember any of that."

She gave him a sly grin. "That's a good thing." She walked over to his stove, turned on the burner, and lit her cigarette.

"I do remember one thing about that night."

"Yeah, what's that?"

"You were naked."

"I was? I think you were hallucinating."

Donovan thought about that statement. He considered the nightmare, and not recalling how he'd made it home. He rubbed the stubble on his chin. "Did you lace my drink?"

"Do I look like a guy to you?"

"If you wanted to have your way with me you should've just asked."

"I don't ask for what I want. I take it." She seemed to float across the room. She took the belt in his robe and slid it through her fingers sensually, while piercing his eyes with her deep grey soul searchers. His robe opened. She looked at his member, rubbed his chiseled chest, and kissed his neck. She stepped back. Her skin glistened in the light, like a quiet lake in autumn's dawn.

Selena's lips made a faint popping sound as they parted slowly, allowing her tongue the privilege of tasting those supple lips. Donovan played cool, but nature's strongest inclination became increscent. He went in for a kiss.

"Wait," she demanded, pushing on his chest. She slipped her finger under the straps of her dress and let it fall to the ground. "Help me with my bra."

It was white lace with a thin nylon center that exposed her coco colored nipples. She was a curvy woman, with thick thighs, and child bearing hips. Donovan stroked her breast and back with his fingertips gently. He'd managed to transform his powerful hands into soft instruments of pleasure creating goose pimples on Selena's flesh. She turned to face him and ran her hands down his wide back, down to his rock-hard buttocks. Selena shivered with sexual angst. She whined, and he panted. Donovan disrobed, exposing the rest of his ripped physique.

Selena dropped to her knees, and grabbed his tree trunk thighs. His thick, elongated member inadvertently slapped her cheek. She took him in her mouth. Her lips expanded over him. Her mouth warm and tongue thick. She played with his tip. Her tongue flickered interminably as she kissed and sucked it. Spit fell from her chin onto her breast. Donovan closed his eyes and threw his head back. He grabbed a fist full of her hair and pumped into her mouth, like an oil well searching for black gold. Imprints of tormented men's faces formed in the flesh of Selena's back; surfacing and disappearing like they were caught in a vortex reaching for freedom He opened his eyes, cupped her chin and extracted himself from her mouth. Donovan lifted her in his arms and took her to his bedroom.

The sheets bunched and stuck to the perspiration on their skin. Selena dug her nails deep in his back. She bit his ear lobe. He penetrated deep and hard as he took hold of her legs. Selena's pussy creamed and dripped with every stroke Donovan delivered. The smacking sounds of their lovemaking resonated throughout the room with the fervency of a b-bop jazz trumpeter. Her eyes rolled to the back of her head. She pulled Donovan's head to hers.

"Yes, baby. Oh, yes fuck me, papi," she moaned. Her mouth opened wide. Darkness filled her gape. Slowly, deliberately a black snake followed by another slithered from her mouth and down Donovan's back. They eased past his buttocks and down to his hamstrings. They wrapped themselves around his legs and hers, binding them together in their copulation. Selena snatched the back of Donovan's head and gazed into his eyes.

A soul for a soul.

***

Donovan and Marvin sat at the bar downing draft specials, while watching sports on several flat screens. Marvin wiped suds from his mouth with the cuff of his shirt before saying, "So, you're out of the game?"

Donovan's lips pulled back into a forced smile; more surrendering than felicitous.

Marvin shook his head in disappointment. "I suppose that's a yes." He grabbed his mug and downed the rest of the cheap beer. "Can I get another, please?" He motioned to the bartender.

"Excuse me." A tall gorgeous blonde squeezed between Donovan and a large port bellied man sitting beside him. "Can I get a Pink Lady?" she asked the bartender, and then looked back at Donovan. "Hi." She had inviting cerulean eyes with a horny, liquor inspired glaze.

"Hello." He smiled.

"Here ya go," the bartender said, while passing the pretty woman her gin and pink lemonade drink.

"See ya," she said flirtatiously to Donovan before walking back to her table. He watched her shapely calves contract just below a flowing yellow skirt as she walked away.

Donovan peered over and realized Marvin was staring at him through slanted eyes.

"I'm committed now," Donovan said. "Besides, why didn't you talk to her?"

"Well, let me think." He sarcastically tilted his head back and scratched his chin. "Because she didn't throw her pussy in my face. She threw it in yours."

Donovan chuckled. "You know Selena is pregnant, right?"

"Man, please your pop has sixteen kids with three different women. What does it matter to you?"

Marvin's statement was true, but it was also a touchy subject for Donovan. He bit his tongue and conjured a neutral demeanor. His father's indiscretions were enough for his undaunted loyalty to the future mother of his child, besides he loved her. His days of promiscuity were over. The time had come to lead a new life with Selena.

Selena stood over the stove frying plantains and stirring the red beans with Andouille sausage into the saffron seasoned yellow rice. Her belly was huge now. Any day she'd have the baby. Donovan watched her cook. She smiled. Her skin was healthy, glowing, darkened from her daily afternoon walks in the park. He couldn't help the sensational feeling literally ruminating in his bones. A slight tremor traipsed along his nerve endings whenever he was in her presence.

Cynicism battled against his current feelings of love. Nobody fell in love. The emotions he experienced were infatuation. Weren't they? He only felt these things around her, because of some type of psychological flaw that he'd soon identify and realize that she'd played him. No! Yes. That was it! She caught him at a vulnerable point in his life. A point when he no longer needed to satisfy his ego, but his emotions that had been long neglected by his parents, siblings, friends. She smiled.

She's playing you for a fool!

"Wait, until you taste this Jerk chicken!" Selena pulled a casserole dish out of the oven filled with chicken pieces bubbling in Caribbean Jerk sauce. "I love cooking for my man."

"Do you?"

"Of course." She shrugged.

He realized his insecurities, and held back the inclination to question his complicated emotions. He held his tongue. They had a good thing, and he wasn't going to mess it up. The woman was having his child for Christ's sake. Selena had changed his life in a fantastic way. His days of impersonating Casanova were over. He wouldn't be like his father; the womanizing rake with little regard for his family, or families. No, he'd be there for his child and soon to be wife.

***

Donovan awoke in the same hospital room from his nightmare. He could hear the woman in labor screaming again. He got out of the bed, bracing himself for the terror that lay ahead. He remembered the ghastly doctor; her lacerated face spilling droves of maggots. With his body ague Donovan called up the courage to move toward the door.

My love.

"Selena?" he called.

It's time. The baby is coming.

"The baby is coming? The baby is coming!" He peered down the peristaltic hallway. He felt pushed by some invisible force toward the south corridor. The hall's fluorescent lights flickered. Voices emanated from the rooms; whispers, and whimpers pleading for mercy. The voices were malicious and cruel, in pain; tormented. A malodorous mixture of sulfur and sewage spilled from the rooms into the hall. A contradiction of sound extended from a room he neared.

Donovan stepped cautiously to the open doorway. A woman lay in bed clearly weary from child birth. Her husband sat motionless in the corner of the room. His face was stoic, unblinking, and seemingly comatose. Nurses crooned over a baby wrapped in a blood-stained blanket. The mother was beautiful. Selena came to mind. He smiled. For a moment, the nightmare took a backseat to the thought of his future family. One of the nurses turned in his direction. Her eyes were mint green with a rhombus shaped pupil. Those eyes were beautiful, dangerous, and seductive; reptilian. Her gaze stimulated a crawling sensation along his flesh.

The nurses turned their attention to the man in the chair. He remained still. The lights flickered rapidly now. An ice-cold gust of wind passed through Donovan into the room. Shadows leaped onto the walls moving about the room like hammerhead sharks hunting prey. The nurses surrounded the man. He stood. The nurse with the reptilian eyes pulled down on his jaw and opened his mouth. He grunted. His body shimmered. A blast of shadows thrust into his mouth. The nurses backed away, and bowed their heads. They slumped to their knees and raised their heads to the ceiling. They recited a mantra in an indecipherable language. Humanoid shapes shifted sinuously in the man's belly.

The recently possessed broke free from his mental imprisonment. His eyes bugged and met Donovan's. His hand shot toward him. "Please, help me!" The man attempted to step toward the door, but several scarred albino hands reached from the shadows, snatched him back, and slammed him against the wall. His eyes rolled into the back of his head. Black ooze drizzled from his nose, eyes, and ears. He collapsed to the floor.

Waves formed and moved through his belly. Fingers emerged from the man's throat. Guttural pleas screamed from inside the man. "No, please don't do this!" The man's body rocked like a ship passing through the eye of a hurricane. Shadows seeped from his mouth, and

The albino demons grabbed him. Their crushing grip began to transform his silvery color to the same tarnished one that Donovan saw on the other kidnapped victim. They whisked him away through the tunnel of blood. There was a moment of extreme darkness. Everything was silent, and then he heard something strange considering the setting, but familiar and peaceful; crickets.

"Honey, it's time," Selena hovered over him stroking his chest gently.

Donovan opened his eyes. The taste of metallic saline was prominent in his mouth. He wiped the corner of his mouth. Blood smeared his finger.

"Oh, baby," Selena said. "You must've bit your lip."

Either that or my soul was snatched out of my freaking throat.

As if reading his mind she said, "No more bad dreams for you, my love. The baby will be here soon, and you'll be at peace. I promise."

****

The nurse wheeled Selena upstairs to the delivery room. Donovan filled out the necessary paperwork, and headed upstairs. Anxiety gripped him. The sonogram had revealed that they'd be having a son. Bernard Letto, was to be his name. He'd decided to name the boy after his father. It was his way of forgiving the man that had been absent throughout his life; a second chance for Donovan and his father to become close. In fact, his dad had made plans to be in Donovan's and Selena's life prior to the delivery. He'd purchased diapers and clothes for the newborn. He'd sent flowers to Selena throughout her pregnancy. The senior Letto wanted to atone for his mistakes. Initially, Donovan was bitter and reluctant, but a heart to heart with his mother opened his mind to the possible future of a reunited family.

Still haunted by his nightmares Donovan looked around the hospital for shadows, disfigured doctors, and the other horrors that invaded his slumber in recent times. There were none. Doctors wore clean white coats. The nurses weren't beautiful with devilish serpent eyes. In fact, the nurse that had taken Selena upstairs wore orthopedic shoes to support the cankles above them. Her hair was frizzy from a bad perm, her teeth tobacco stained, and her eyes light red from too many night shifts.

He hurried to the gift shop to purchase flowers for Selena. A surprise waited for him inside.

"Hello, son," his father said. He stood by the register with a bundle of carnations in his fist. "I hope it's okay. Selena called me before she woke you. She thought I might want to see my grandson when he was born." His father paused for Donovan's reaction. He didn't offer one. "So, here I am!"

Donovan stood stunned. He didn't know how to react. The pace at which everything seemed to happen left him in a vertiginous state. He was going to be a father. The man he'd looked up to that was rarely present stood in his midst. Donovan's eyes swelled with tears. The prodigal father had returned. Donovan was advancing toward the matriculation from bachelor to family man. The two men embraced.

"I'm here for you, son," Donovan's father said, "I'm proud of you."

***

"He's coming!" Selena cried. Her legs were spread and supported by metal stirrups. The doctor was positioned at her feet encouraging Selena to push. Donovan held Selena's sweaty hand. Even in her agony she was gorgeous. With a long guttural grunt Selena pushed, and the crown appeared, followed by the body. There was brief silence. Selena sighed in relief, and then the high-pitched cries of the baby resonated throughout the room.

"Here's your son Mr. Letto." The nurse presented him with a healthy baby boy.

The nurse placed the baby in the incubator and wiped him down. His father burst into the room.

"I'm sorry. I couldn't wait. Where's my grandson?" he said excitedly.

The nurse motioned him to the incubator. They crooned over his whimpers. The nurse handed the baby to Selena. She was exhausted, but she found the strength to form an exasperated smile. "Take hold of our creation, baby." Selena extended her baby filled arms to Donovan. He moved toward her hesitant to take the frail child into his arms. He felt the splendid feeling of joy and accomplishment. There was no joy greater to a man than to witness the birth of a healthy heir; a son.

"I feel like I'm going to jump out of my skin!" his father shouted. "I'm going to bring your mother upstairs. If I'm correct, she's crying her eyes out right now."

"Calm down, pop," Donovan said.

His father held back tears. It'd been a while since he'd called him pop. Bernard's absenteeism in his son's life had previously stripped him of a father's title. The few times that they'd interacted over the years Donovan had called him Bernard. It was Donovan's way of punishing him for his lack of involvement. He handed little Bernard over to the nurse and shot out of the room.

The nurse chuckled. "I'll be taking him to the nursery now. You two get some rest," she said, before walking out of the room with the baby in tow; her hips delightfully swayed the way a woman's does when she's carrying precious cargo.

"I love you, baby," Donovan said gazing into Selena's eyes.

"Me too," she responded before falling into a deep sleep.

Donovan leaned back into a recliner in the corner of the room and dozed off with a smile plastered on his face.

Donovan woke up shivering. Arctic air chilled the room like a walk-in freezer. The air conditioning is ridiculous, he thought. Donovan rubbed his stiff neck He stood. Selena stared at him; her dark eyes shone like jewels in a display case.

"Hi," she said.

"Hi."

"Thank you for your sacrifice."

Her words seemed strange rolling off her tongue. Donovan squinted in confusion. He said, "My sacrifice? You were the one that endured all the pain. Thank you for your sacrifice."

"Endured the pain," she repeated his words in a whisper. "Yes, that was painful, but only for a spell; nothing like eternal torment."

A nervous laugh escaped Donovan. "What?" He thought he saw movement under the sheets between Selena's legs.

"I'm afraid some . . . after birth has spilled," she said.

Donovan stood slowly. Selena seemed different. Her demeanor changed from languid to energetic. Of course it changed. She'd gone through painful labor. She seemed easy. However, her mentioning of eternal torment troubled Donovan. She'd never been a religious person, not around him anyway. He shuffled to the bed and drew back the sheets.

Selena had a bowel movement. He motioned to call for the nurse. He stopped when he noticed something move between her legs. She hadn't had a bowel movement. What he first thought a pile of dung were a pile of small snakes atop each other; slithering up and tumbling down simultaneously. He jumped back.

"What the hell is going on?"

Selena had a sly grin on her face. She swung her legs off of the bed, knocking a pile of snakes onto the floor. They fell to the floor with a sickening thud. Donovan dry heaved.

"A soul for a soul, Donovan," she said, while walking toward him. He fell back into the recliner. Fear molested the nerve endings in his body and impregnated him with violent spasms. The shadows from his nightmares appeared on the walls. Those waves of albino skinned limbs and red eyes peeked from the blackness like gruesome dorsal fins in an ocean from Hell.

"What… what are you talking about? What are you?"

"I'm your fantasy, Donovan. Didn't I please you?"

Other than the trembles within his body, he couldn't move. Mangled, pale faces sneered at him as their fingers dug into his flesh while restraining him through the shadows. She stroked his cheek. He attempted to spit abhorring expletives her way, but only black goo spilled from his mouth.

"You know what that is, don't you baby? That's the void in your soul. It belongs to me now." Her words were venomous. "You're nothing more than a shell. From now on, I'll make the decisions for you. You'll help me raise little Bernard and then, oh I don't know.

Die in a car crash, heart attack, whatever pleases the gods!" A raucous laugh escaped her throat. She waved her hand to know one in particular in the room.

The shadows swarmed into his mouth. He let out a silent scream, and then he vomited. The snakes slithered quickly to the bile and licked it clean from the floor.

His soul is delicious.

Share him!

Let me taste his essence!

Ben Stevens' Shopping List

Any book by Neil or Neal, Gaiman and Stephenson
Suntory Hibiki Whiskey and a nice decanter
Gurkha Rogue Armageddon Cigars
Alan Moore's Providence Trade
SCUBA lessons
A classy globe
A leather Messenger Bag
More time off, less work

Breaking Ahab

Ben Stevens

His eyes were two gunshot wounds. Puffy, red and expressing a pain seldom felt by others. The pain of having your love ripped away, right in front of you, out of your very arms. His tormented eyes stared through a cold, small, double-pane plate of glass and watched three figures approach his wharf-cabin. Although the approaching figures visages were obscured by the fog of trapped moisture between the panes and darting rivulets of melting runoff, he could recognize the uniforms belonging to the Haines, Alaska Sheriff's Department, and knew the two folks that belonged to those uniforms. The third figure, the one in front, walking with some trepidation down his slippery driveway, the suit, that one was a stranger. Strangers were never welcome, even before the incident.

He watched the stranger, the Sheriff, and the Deputy (he had no doubt of their identity, any local worth his salt could recognize Deputy Laurie's rotund outline and Sheriff Robert's walrus mustache, their telltale uniforms besides) make their way onto his pier. The suit appeared to be relieved to be on stable ground once again, leaving behind the canyon like ruts of a driveway, unkempt, unplowed and driven through during daytime thaws and night time freezes.

The man behind the wounded eyes made no attempt to move, or call out. He watched the trio shuffle down his pier, wet with today's drizzle, yet free of the snow that still clung tenaciously to the land. He watched with as much disinterest as one possibly could, not even tracking them with his pained gaze when they moved off the pier proper and onto the deck that wrapped around his cabin.

Even the knocks, when they came, did not alarm him. But he did turn his head, as slow as the snow melted in Alaska's spring, to the audial intrusion.

"Tom! Tom, we know you're in there. Look, we need to talk. Open the door Tom." Tom did not rise, but his chest did as he inhaled deeply and sighed.

It was Sheriff Robert Wall speaking. Figures. Tom had grown up with Bob, even gone to school with him. His cohort, Deputy Laurie Jones was a transplant, but no cheechako. She had transferred into Haines from Fairbanks or some such place about nine or ten years ago. She wasn't local local, yet she was local.

"Come on Tom. We got a man here from Juneau. He needs to ask you some questions. Let's just do this the easy way, OK, bud?" The Sheriff sounded like he was trying to convince a toddler to stop throwing his food, more exhausted and depleted than angry. A year ago, hearing Robert sound so awkward would have made Tom smile. Not now. Not ever again. Another volley of knocks. No doubt Robert's meaty, hairy fist doing the dirty work. "Tom! Come on Tom!"

Tom slowly stood up and grunted, loud enough for the trio to hear and went to the door and unlatched its brass chain.

He opened the door and squinted at the diffused grey light of a melting morning. The three visitors stood under his wrap-around decks covered awning, their coats still dripping from the drizzle. Tom saw Sheriff Robert exhale a sigh of pained relief, but his eyes were fixed on the stranger. The one dumb enough to wear a suit in the slush of breakup and go without a hat. The man in the suit's ears were as crimson as the spider-webbed broken blood vessels in Tom's eyes and he shifted his weight back and forth, from one foot to the other, while vigorously rubbing his hands together. The overall result made him look like he had to use the little boys' room badly and yet appeared to be washing his hands as if he had already finished his business.

't ain't cold anymore. This city slicker would've died a few months back. Tom held the door between most of his body and the visitors, saying nothing.

"Tom, we need to talk." Sheriff Robert broke the uncomfortable silence. His voice was full of heartbreak, his eyes, sympathetic. He looked like a man who needed to put down a beloved dog. "Mind if we come in?"

Tom made no move to widen the passage.

"Who's the fucking suit?" His voice croaked.

Laurie Jones's (Deputy by day, Mom by night) eyes widened at the brazen display of hostility. Sheriff Robert however, turned his face down slightly, and closed his eyes, as if the question pained him. Robert raised his head and opened his mouth, along with his eyes and was about to answer when-

"My name, Mr. Moore," The 'suit' spoke up, matching Tom's piercing gaze with his own bright blue eyes, "is George Brister. Detective George Brister."

Tom saw in the detective's blue eyes a fierceness, a specific passion, often only seen in youth and true believers. He had no respect for such zealots, especially such young, ignorant zealots, but he knew enough to know what lengths this slicker would go to get his answers. Tom scowled and stepped back, disappearing into the shadowy hallows of his cabin and let the door slowly drift open behind him.

The officers stepped in, following Tom, their eyes adjusting to the dark.

The room they stood in nearly matched the outside footprint of the building. Only two small sections were cordoned off, presumably the bed and bath. The rest was open floor, living, dining, cooking, and storage all in one. Whereas the architecture of the square home was Spartan at best, the clutter inside the square would have put Tom in the semi-finals for a hoarding contest. Piles of papers avalanched off one side of the dining table, while small hand tools and fishing lures in various stages of assembly and disassembly covered the other half. One entire corner of the cabin was filled with a Gordian knot of fishing lines and nets, small floaty ovals interspersed throughout, like chunks of meat in a cheap, mostly rice stir-fry.

The kitchen, if it was in fact there, looked like a pile of wreckage from some post-apocalyptic nightmare. Tom's cooking and cleaning habits made even freshmen college boys look like OCD museum curators. The smell of stagnant water and old food mixed with the ever-present brine of the sea, creating a miasma that made Detective Brister dizzy and caused Laurie to stifle a gasp, covering her mouth and nose simultaneously.

"You want a drink?" Tom offered, wading out of the kitchen/dining area, weaving around piles of rubbish and boat supplies. He approached his visitors with a bottle of cheap rye, a quarter filled, no glasses.

"It's 10 am, Tom." Sheriff Robert said.

"And we are on duty, so it doesn't matter." Detective Brister frowned.

"Suit yourself." Tom gestured to two chairs and small couch. All but one were unusable, buried in what looked like dirty laundry. Tom uncapped the bottle of rye and said, "Just push that shit on the floor."

Detective Brister did just that, Sheriff Robert followed likewise, while Laurie hesitated, flustered.

"I'm sure worried about you, Tom." She said, holding her body awkwardly, looking around at the mess.

Say it. Tom thought, taking his first swig of the day. That it's gotten bad since Brenda died. I know. I don't care.

Once the chair was clear of laundry, Detective Brister scooted it across the floor, accidentally bunching up the carpet rug that helped to warm the old wooden planks of the wharf-cabin's floor. Ignoring the wrinkled rug, Detective Brister sat down in the chair, directly across from Tom and stared at him.

Sheriff Robert, now seated on the small couch, leaned forward, his hands clasped, in a sort of Buddhist Warrior-Monk prayer fashion, and spoke.

"Tom, I know we've been through this, but it has become far bigger than just you and me, OK? Detective Brister here has been sent by the big dogs in Juneau. I can't help you anymore unless you help us, OK? What I would like to see happen is-"

"Thank you, Sheriff. But I can handle it from here." The young Detective held up a hand. His eyes never left Tom and a slight grin was threatening to form on the edges of his thin mouth, like the first hints of a storm at sea, far off on the horizon.

"The Sheriff is right about one thing, Tom, can I call you Tom? Good. This situation has become 'big'. You see, we in the Field Office do not agree with Sheriff Wall's report of what happened the night of March 3rd. I have it on good authority, experts in the field from UAA all the way down the coast to San Francisco. They tell me that there are no giant squids in this part of the Pacific. None. No sightings ever. Ever." Tom listened, and took another sip of whiskey.

"So what does that tell you, Tom?" Detective Brister's threat of a grin had matured and was now showing. The winds had picked up, it was raining lightly.

Tom said nothing, only took another sip from the bottle. Laurie shifted uncomfortably.

"It tells me," The Detective continued, "that your story of the giant squid is just that, a story."

"Bullshit." Tom frowned, a dribble of booze ran down his chin in perfect imitation of the snow melt outside.

"Bullshit?" Detective Brister raised an eyebrow.

"What about all the sightings in Japan?"

"We're not in Japan, are we Tom?"

A heavy silence filled the room. They could hear their own hearts beating in rhythm with the lapping waves and the dripping snow outside.

"So why don't you tell me what really happened that night?" The young Detective leaned back in the chair, his grin triumphant, the storm now a squall, in full force and upon them.

Tom was still looking in the direction of the Detective, but his eyes were unfocused, adrift on the open sea of his wretched memories. He saw in his mind's eye his wife, his beautiful, beautiful wife. Her curly red hair being whipped by the wind, tangled. Her ruddy, burnt cheeks, dotted with as many freckles as there were waves upon the ocean. His boat bobbed up and down, yet stayed its course. She asked him to take her to their favorite harbor. What a silly girl. As if we weren't out on the water enough during the fishing season, she wanted me to take her out for fun. She loved it out there. She did, in fact love it out there, more than most anything. And every time, without fail, being upon the waves would make her green eyes shine with a brilliant delight. But that night, her emeralds had dimmed. She had said that she wanted to talk, that she needed to talk. Nothing good ever followed that statement. Ever. That night there was a sadness in her eyes. What was it dear? What was it you wanted to say?

"I... I shouldn't have let her talk me into going out at night. I'll give you that much. So if you want to charge me with something, charge me for being a damn fool."

"No one is talking about charging you with anything," Sheriff Robert tried to comfort, his voice soft.

"Actually, that is not true. I am very much looking to bring charges on Mr. Moore here." Detective Brister studied Tom. "And I will, as soon as I have the proof. I will get the proof. And you will get what is coming. Now you can make it easier on yourself and confess, tell us where you dumped the body, so we can send divers and give your poor wife a proper Christian burial, or-"

"You son of a bitch! Get the fuck out of my house!" Tom spat whiskey flecked saliva into the air. "If you had anything, I'd already be in jail! But you don't! And you won't! 'Cause I am telling the truth! That god-damned squid killed and ate my wife!" Tom's chin trembled like the Great Alaskan Quake of '64. Tears formed in the deep wells of his gunshot eyes and rolled out, bleeding down his wrinkled face and disappeared into his salt beard like streams into the sea.

In the silence that followed, the sound of the waves took center stage once again; this time sounding off beat, for everyone's hearts were pumping as fast as a marathon runners.

Detective Brister stood, his smirk only fading slightly.

"Tom, you don't know me, but let me tell you right now. I am very good at what I do. I will find the proof. Here," he paused and reached into the folds of his khaki long-coat and produced an envelope. He wiggled it back and forth for a moment and then dropped it into Tom's lap unceremoniously. "You didn't think I'd come unprepared now, did you?"

Tom ignored the envelope. Other than his still trembling chin, he made no move at all. Although far from weeping, hot streams of saltwater continued to bleed from his wounded eyes as he stared through the young Detective's legs. A frown tattooed his face.

"It's a warrant, Tom." Sheriff Robert too stood up and lay his giant paw of a hand on Tom's slouched shoulder. "I'm sorry. He wants to look at your boat, your shed, everything. You best just stay out of the way and let the man work."

"Can I... can I at least go get a drink?" He held up the bottle, showing them it was now empty.

"Sure pal. Go ahead." Robert nodded.

"Oh Tom?" Detective Brister added, as he systematically began to put on a pair of blue nitrile gloves, "Don't leave town."

***

Tom pulled his old Chevy into the only open spot, in between where the plow had pushed the year's accumulation and a newer model Dodge pickup with a bumper sticker that read "Haines, AK: A quaint little drinking town with a fishing problem." Yuk Yuk.

He shoved the rusty door of his truck open and stepped out into the dark of early evening and immediately discovered why this parking spot was empty.

"God dammit all." He cursed under his breath as he hustled and hopped to get his left boot out of the cold, ankle-deep slush it had found itself in and spare his right boot the same fate. A moment later and Tom was on high ground, teetering on the ridge of compacted snow and ice that had formed and grown over the long winter as sheets of fresh powder had fallen off the pubs slanted metal roof. Already a veritable mountain range, complete with peaks and saddles, the ridge now came with an added hazard; a layer of slick ice crusted and encased the berm, formed nightly from the dropping temps that caressed the days melt back to sleep.

Tom haphazardly made his way across the ridge of ice, reaching out and balancing himself on the hoods of the trucks that filled the lot of 'Pete's Watering Hole: Best place in town to get a burger and a drink.' Unless it were tourist season... It would be several more months before the ferries and cruise ships arrived, bring the double edge blade of tourism with them. The influx of strangers brought a much needed supplement to the otherwise poor fishing and logging community, but the tourists were often rude, and messy, and the clogged up the place. Turning my salty acre of paradise into the God-damned Vegas strip.

A moment later Tom was sliding down (still on his feet) the ice berm and pushing open the heavy wooden door, leaving his curmudgeonly reflections outside in the growing dark, and heading in to warmth, familiarity, and sweet, blissful liquid painkillers. Tom had been coming to Pete's since before it was called Pete's, since before Pete was even born. This was his Cheers, and yes, everyone did know his name. Up until now, that had always been a good thing.

The ambient noise in the establishment dropped decibels as quickly and wholly as the metal roof above shed its slabs of snow. Tom felt the eyes of his neighbors, fellow fishermen and even a few of the loggers who lived down the road a way, on him as he stood in the warm glow of the entrance. The music was still playing and now everyone could hear just how incongruous it was that a Taylor Swift song would be playing in a place like this. Anger boiled up inside him like acid reflux, but Tom just twisted his mouth as if it were a wet rag he was attempting to wring out and turned his back to them, making a bee-line straight to the bar and Pete, the man behind it.

Tom sloshed through the sawdust and peanut shells and pulled up a stool when he got to the counter. Pete watched him approach, drying a mason jar (that's all they served beer in) with a small towel.

"Whatcha doing in here, Tom?" Pete asked as he reached up and placed the jar out of sight.

Tom was stunned. He had always been welcome here.

"Etu, Brute?" Tom dripped the words out, like venom, falling from exposed fangs to the sawdust floor.

"What?" Pete squinted at Tom.

"You too? You believe I killed her?" Tom felt his nostrils flare out.

"Now Tom, I didn't-"

"How the HELL can you even think that? Huh? About me? About Brenda!?"

The Watering Holes' patrons again paused in their buzz when Tom raised his voice to Pete. Tom could feel their suspicious gazes, stabbing him in the back. That's what they are! All of 'em! Backstabbers!

"I don't, Tom." Pete swallowed hard and shifted his eyes. "It's just...It's just that having you in here right now isn't good for business. There's a lot of people talking right now. You know? Seeing you will just make them upset. Brenda was well loved-" Pete cut himself off and just stood there, as frozen as the berm outside, his mouth hanging open.

"I get it." Tom's shoulders dropped two inches. "Just let me at least get a god-damned bottle to take home with me."

***

The ruts cut by the day's traffic through the melt had completed their nightly re-freeze and now violently grabbed and pulled Tom's Chevy back and forth as it crept down his driveway. The beams of light bounced along with the truck, jostling all over the woods, the pier, the Wharf-Cabin and the dark granite colored sea beyond. It was Chaotic, but it proved to be enough for Tom to see that the cops had all left. Just for the night? Or for good?

He grabbed his brown bag and the elixir of forgetfulness inside it and got out, making his way down the bank. He was just about to step inside when he paused. The wind was warm tonight and it ruffled his beard, like Brenda's fingers often had, not long ago. He closed his eyes and listened to the night, to the wind, to the waves, not too choppy, lapping at the shore behind him and against the wharf-cabin and piers foundation posts. Something called him. The sea...

Tom had always felt a connection to the sea. He grew up on it. Working his father's boat since he could walk and talk. It wasn't so much a call to adventure, no, he had after all lived his entire life in little Haines, never leaving anywhere but the open waters, and had been happy. Oh, so happy. Brenda... No, it was more a connection type of call. A sense of belonging. Like having one's other half in the same room. She called to you with her presence alone. Asking nothing, offering everything.

But tonight's call was different. He wasn't quite sure how so, just that he knew it was. Without knowing or asking why, he turned from his front door and walked along the wrap-around deck.

He stopped when the kitchen window was at his back, and Chilkoot Inlet's narrow channel was at his face. The moon was only just past full, still offering enough light to see the rippled surface of the now black water and the dark navy hues of the partially snow-clad mountains beyond.

Tom... Tom, come to me. Come to me my love.

The sea pulled him as strongly as the moon ever pulled the sea. He felt ethereal strings reach from every wave that traveled across the obsidian surface attach themselves to his very heart and yank at it, ceaselessly, tirelessly, like the tide.

Tom stood there for what seemed like an hour, till his feet were as sore as his heart. Then,

"Fuck you, and fuck the sea. I want my wife back." Tom spat out into the water, frowned and turned to go inside and drink himself into oblivion.

***

Tom shut the door behind him, trying to put some distance between him and the sea, but his demons followed him inside anyway. Everything he saw, everything he looked at, reminded him of her, of it. He scowled at the pile of fishing nets and buoys in the corner, the ship in a bottle on the shelf above the fireplace, the slick orange overalls hanging on the peg behind the door and the rubber boots halfway hidden under them. There was no escape, save one.

He brushed past all his things, shrugging off the ghosts and crashed into his kitchen, flinging the dirty dishes around, breaking more than a few before finding what he was looking for. At last he held in his hand, the prize, an over-sized, square tumbler, made of thick glass.

A brush of his tumbler clutching fist and another haphazard pile of clutter was swept off the counter. He nearly slammed the tumbler down in the freshly made clear spot, such was his frenzy. He had reached emotional muscle fatigue and his spiritual legs were shaking, about to give out.

One quick twist and the top of the bottle was ripped free from its mooring and the sweet amber nectar inside was cascading down into its receptacle until it overflowed.

Tom...Tom, come to me. Come to me my love...

He grunted with effort as he set the bottle down and clutched the tumbler once more, lifting it as if it were as heavy as his heart. His lips parted, and he drank deep. He stopped only to catch his breath after the tumbler had been emptied. He gasped, less for air, more to coat the burn in his throat. A familiar warmth spread through his chest into his limbs and he closed his eyes in relief. His breathing slowed, his shaking settled. He calmly opened his eyes and went to repeat the ritual. He got as far as finishing the pour and raising the glass, this time with ease rather than effort, and saw her. He saw her and stopped dead in his destructive tracks.

There, in the burnt honey waters of the whiskey he saw the sea; in the sea he saw his wife, calling to him.

"No!" He screamed and flung the glass and its contents against the nearest wall. Surprisingly, the tumbler did not break, though the whiskey covered the wooden panels like arterial spray at a murder scene. Tom flew into a rage.

Tables (both kitchen and coffee) were overturned, objects were kicked and thrown, a tool of some kind was used in baseball-bat club fashion and Tom proceeded to attack and destroy two of the kitchen cabinets entirely before turning his blows against the mantle and the bottled ship upon it. His berserker rampage finally ended when he tried to wrestle the pile of net and buoys out the door and became tangled in it. Tiring himself out, just like a suffocating fish for which it was originally intended to hold.

He lay on the floor, wrapped in tangled mono-filament, gasping for breath, strong vapors rolling off his mouth like the night's fog outside, creeping over the waters of the inlet; until after a spell, he succumbed to exhaustion and passed out.

***

In his dream, he was with her. With Brenda. In his dream, he was at peace. For a while.

They were together. They were on his boat. They were on the sea. Everything was perfect. Fifty some odd years together and everything was still perfect.

In his dream, he was at peace.

For a while.

Then he noticed it. At first it was just on the edges, the outskirts, but it was there. Anxiety. Worry.

Something was wrong.

They were on the boat, and they were at sea, but it was night. Why are we out at night? He wondered. Brenda... Brenda wanted to and I said yes.

Something was wrong.

Brenda's eyes were normally so bright, but tonight they hid a sadness, a regret.

"I need to tell you something." She had said.

What was it my love? What did you need to tell me?

Something was wrong.

This was the night Brenda died. Must I relive it again? Every God-damned night?!

He slowed the boat and set about setting the anchor. They had at last come to Brenda's favorite spot. A small harbor, deep up the inlet, hidden away from the things of Haines and men. Tom watched his oblivious self work like he was Scrooge, visiting the past.

Pay attention, you old fool! Something is wrong! Can't you see?

"They're going to arrest you, Tom." Brenda smiled at him as he returned from the cabin with a lamp.

"That's great, hun." Tom smiled back at her and sat down across from her near the bow of the boat, placing the lamp next to him on the raised lip of the deck's walkway. He wondered where the wine was. It was cold. Really cold. "Why are we doing this, Brenda? It's freezing out. Let's take this inside the cabin, huh?"

"You're dreaming, love."

"Uh huh. That's great." Tom smiled.

You old fool! This isn't right! This is not how it happened!

Something was wrong.

"They are going to arrest you, unless you come to me. I'm waiting for you. Please."

What did you want to tell me baby? What was it?

The world shifted, but they stayed the same, only different.

"I have something to tell/show you." Tom heard her say 'tell' and 'show' at the same time.

The dream was wrong.

He stared into her sad (oh why were they sad?) green eyes. He returned her warm smile with his own, masking his confusion.

"What is it sweetheart?" He asked.

That's when it happened.

That's when Tom's world was ripped from him.

The boat lurched. The lamp fell.

Something was wrong.

Water splashed. It was dark. I can barely see! It was cold. He was wet. He heard something sliding over the deck. Brenda! Where is Brenda? Tom moved over the rocking and heaving boat to find the lamp.

"Tom!" Brenda's voice called out. More splashing, more heaving.

He caught his balance and turned, raising the lamp.

Brenda's green eyes. Water, black water everywhere, coming in, or was she going out? Oh my God! She's going overboard! But-

Something was wrong.

His face was white, stricken with horror.

In one horrific glimpse, delivered to him by the light of a pale lamp in the dark he beheld his world's end. He beheld that which broke his mind and his soul.

Brenda's green eyes, her beautiful, sad green eyes. Water, cold, black water. Flowing red hair, wet and tangled. Her outstretched hand, reaching to him. Her legs. NO! Her legs were gone, underwater perhaps, or...Tentacles. He saw the tentacles. Oh my god! No!

"Tom!" Brenda called to him. She reached for him, wanting him, needing him.

Frozen, like the winter world around them, Tom stood petrified in disbelief and watched his wife disappear into the sea.

"NOOOOOOOOOOOO!"

***

Images of the giant squid still burned into his vision like a retinal burn, Tom slowly opened his eyes. He was panting, exhausted, dehydrated and lying on the floor of his cabin, tangled in fishing nets.

Brenda. Oh God, Brenda.

He forced his heart rate down, and then slowly began to free himself from the webbing.

What time is it? He wondered to himself, and strained to see the clock on the wall from his prone position.

Midnight. Not that it matters anyway.

Once free, Tom stood and examined the damage.

"They are going to arrest you." The voice of his dream wife echoed in his mind. His eyes spied the bottle of whiskey, still half full. He strode to it, stepping over the mess of broken things and picked it up. He lifted it to his face and examined it like he had never seen a bottle before.

"Hmpfh." He grunted and proceeded to pour the rest of the bottle into the sink, filled with plates and bowls as it were.

They won't stop until I prove it to them. Everyone in this whole god-damned town. And-

He scanned the mess of his house once again and stopped when he caught the bitter, broken reflection of his leather face in a bronze platter Brenda had mounted on the wall. -and I will never have peace till I kill the beast that took you from me.

***

A pair of eyes, hiding behind binoculars watched Tom untie the rope from the pier, throttle up his boat and begin to sail off into to the moon-lit ocean. Glasses lowered, hands fished a cell-phone out from a pocket.

"Detective? Yes, I'm sorry, I know what time it is. Just thought you should know. Mr. Moore has left his home again. Yes. No sir. No, he left in his boat. Yes, yes sir. He is headed up the inlet, away from the mouth, yes. Yes, I think so too sir. Sir? He is armed. I saw him take a rifle with him. Yes. Yes. OK. Yes, I'll stand by. See you in a few. Yes, you're welcome, thank you Sir."

***

The midnight winds of March cut through Tom just as his boat cut through the icy waters and caused his eyes to water; each involuntary tear ran sideways to his temples, but never made it to their destination before freezing solid. Tom made no move to brush them away; his only focus was what lie ahead, and what he needed to do.

He maneuvered his boat up the inlet in blackout, with no running lights on. The light from the slightly waning moon was enough for him to see the coastlines on either side and besides, he knew the spot well.

Brenda's spot.

With all the determined acceptance of a dead man walking, Tom steered the boat on through the night, till only the softest hint of deep purplish-blue began to appear from behind the Eastern Mountains overlooking the water. Arriving at the secret harbor, snuggly tucked away under the bosom of the same mountains, now glowing faintly with proto-dawn, Tom cut the throttle and drifted silently.

Tom...Tom come to me...Come to me my love.

"No!" He shouted, forcing the voice from his mind. The pull was strong, incessant. "I can't take it! Come on out you spawn of hell!" Tears formed again, this time not from wind, but from grief and rage.

Tom...Sweetheart. I'm here. Come to me...

"Come on, god dammit!" Tom shrieked, shaking his fist at the wind over the waves. He turned from the wheel and dropped the anchor off the side, just as he did the other night, three weeks ago.

My love...

"Show yourself you son of a bitch! Come on!" He pulled his rifle out from under the bench and made his way to the bow of the ship, and waited, trembling.

The surface of the water was a mirror that had been painted black, smooth as liquid marble. Like the proverbial abyss, Tom stared into it and it did indeed, stare back. He felt he were losing his mind, what was left of it. It called to him. It called to him the way the spike calls to the junkie, the way the wind calls to the caged bird. Both the lure, the sweet song of the deep and the rippling obsidian surface of it hypnotized him; hypnotized his active mind, his drive for revenge and release, and for a moment, hidden things inside ruled him, they ran through the dusty corridors of his mind, opening every door they could find, letting bedlam out to play.

I could just jump in. I SHOULD just jump in. It won't hurt. I will be with my Brenda again that way, my sweet, sweet Brenda.

His grip on the rifle slacked, and the weapon slid down his lap and came to rest between his leg and the wall of the bow. Unknown minutes passed with Tom contemplating suicide, held fast in the grip of the sea's hypnosis. When suddenly new, different ripples appeared in the water, the black mirror reflection of the water's surface shattered into a million pieces and something appeared from behind it.

Tom, my love...Come to me...

So entranced was he that Tom failed to register even a hint of anger or rage at the sight before him once it had appeared. Where a second before there was a cold sheet of rippling black satin, there was now a writhing mass of sucker-dotted tentacles. In the center of this nest appeared a beak, the size of Tom's head, opening and closing slowly.

I could just jump in. Let the beast take me. And be with my wife.

Yes, Tom. That's it. Come to me.

Somewhere in the periphery of his thoughts, Tom registered the wet thump of one of the giant squid's massive club tipped feeding tentacles come over the bow of the ship and land inside. Yet, he did not snap out of his haunted reverie until the appendage made contact with him, wrapping itself around his thigh like the urgent caress from a lover in need.

The spell was broken and Tom issued a heaving gasp. The squid seemed not to notice Tom's change in demeanor, and continued to writhe seductively and reach out to him with its other tentacles. Tom jerked his head down and saw that the creature had a grip on his leg. In a white flash, Tom lurched forward and picked up the nearly forgotten rifle. The tentacle around his thigh relaxed and began to remove itself.

Tom, my love!

"NO! NO! NOOOO!" Tom cried and chambered a round in his old bolt-action.

Tom!

"Die, you fucker!" Tom leapt to his feet and pointed the rifle into the open mouth of the giant squid.

My love! Please!

A squeeze of the trigger. The crack of a gunshot echoing out over the icy dawn waters and mountains beyond.

It's longest tentacles still draped over the bow of the boat, the squid lulled and turned, floating on the surface of the water, next to the bow of the boat and did not sink.

The beast rolled over, its beak and the river of black blood issuing from it disappeared under the waves, while the oblong shape of the squid's body came up.

A single beautiful emerald eye, with sadness deep inside it stared up from the water into Tom's bleeding gunshots.

The call stopped. The voice stopped. But there was no peace to be found.

Like a deflated inner-tube, the strength went out of Tom's arms and the rifle lowered under its own weight and dropped to deck, spilling out of Tom's limp hands.

"No. Oh no. Oh god." His body trembling, his poor mind crumbling, Tom watched in disbelief as the Squid shifted and blurred. A wave washed over its carcass and when it had passed, only the pale, naked, and bleeding body of his wife remained.

"Oh my god! No!" Tom willed his arms, now nothing more than sacks of ice water, to reach over and pluck her from the sea before she sank. He struggled, grunting, whimpering and crying, racking sobs, as he pulled her into the boat and then collapsed. He held her dripping, limp and lolling head to his chest and squeezed her tightly.

His mind rebelled. It was Lucifer, everything else, God. Everything broke. And while he lay there, cradling his dead wife, free at last from the prison of illusion his mind had conjured, he remembered.

"Tom my love. Take me to the secret Harbor."

"Why? It's dark already, and cold."

"I have something I need to show you. Please. Let's hurry." Uncharacteristic sadness in those emeralds. Where did that come from?

"Hmmph. You're a funny girl. OK." A wry smile. The soft shake of a head.

"I love it when you call me a girl. Makes me feel...young again."

The slip of a boat through the water. She stared out over the bow the whole time.

"Here. Here is good. Now, come." A sad, apprehensive smile, the pat of small hands on her lap.

"I have to show you something...My time is up." Confusion.

"I want you to come with me. Come with me my love. Please." Confusion turning to fear. She stood, she jumped overboard.

Oh god. I see now. I couldn't see before! Faithless! You old fool! Grief. Grief unimaginable.

Her legs disappeared. Like a mermaid, No! Like a siren! her legs were gone, in their place, a web of tentacles.

"Come with me my love. Just jump in. We can be together forever."

I couldn't see it! I just couldn't see it! Oh god.

The sound of an approaching boat pulled him from the past to the present.

Tom opened his bleeding eyes and saw the light of a boat approaching. A spotlight was waving back and forth, bobbing in time with the coming boat. The light cast from the mighty lamp connected with Tom's boat and halted its scan.

"There he is!" Tom heard a voice call out.

It was the voice of Detective Brister.

Tom looked down at his poor wife's dead body in his lap.

"They're coming for me baby. No way out of this one." He looked up at watched the boat slow as it got nearer. He could see the multiple silhouettes moving about on its deck.

"I'm sorry. I'm so sorry. I wasn't strong enough to believe it. I screwed up babe. Please forgive me."

"That's him! He has the body! Holy shit!" Brister was shouting, the boat was close.

"Tom! Tom! Put your hands up where I can see them! Tom, Goddammit!" Sheriff Robert added to the shouting.

Tom rolled his wives body off him as gently as possible and reached out a hand to brush the tangles of wet red hair from her face. He then leaned down and kissed her forehead one last time.

"I'm sorry. I wasn't strong enough to join you in life. But we can still be together in death. I'm sorry my love."

"Tom! Hands up. NOW!" The police boat pulled up alongside Tom's and he heard the engine revering as whoever drove her slammed the engine in reverse to bring about a quick stop.

Never taking his eyes off his wife, Tom reached down to the deck and grabbed what lay there. The rifle needed to be re-chambered before it could be fired again, but they don't know that.

"Hands up! Now, Goddammit!"

"Sorry Bob." And with that last whispered statement, Tom stood up, and raised the bolt-action towards the blinding light.

Multiple echoes of gunshots echoed out and over the icy harbor. They could be heard as far away as Haines, which was just then waking up. Tom didn't even feel pain as the half dozen bullets ripped through his chest. He smiled, relieved, and collapsed on the deck. Although the sun was rising behind the nearby mountains, his vision was fading to black. He managed to crawl the foot or so necessary to lay next to his wife, side by side, with his arm over her, as they had so many times before. All the pain, the anguish and the questions faded with his last breath. He had at last, found a small peaceful harbor in which to anchor his boat.

I'll see you soon, love.

David F. Gray's Shopping List

1 Canister-Body Works Protein Powder
2 Cartons-Almond/Coconut Milk
8 Chobani Yogurt (single serving, 4 peach, 4 key lime)
2 boxes — LaCroix Carbonated water. (Lemon)
3 lbs — ground turkey
2 cans — tomato paste
1 can — angel hair pasta
Peanut Butter
8 chicken breasts — skinned
Bananas
Grapes
Blueberries
Romaine Lettuce

The Cypress Wood Terror

David F. Gray

The masked serial killer grabbed the lovely, half naked blonde from behind and jammed the serrated blade of the hunting knife deep into her back. The blood spewed from her mouth in an arc that covered at least five feet, splattering her stunned boyfriend from waist to shoulders.

I rubbed my eyes and groaned. While I had to give the director credit for chancing a practical gag over CGI, he really should have known better. The overall effect was cheesy at best and embarrassing at worst.

Fortunately, I was there to save the day.

I glanced at my watch and saw that it was a few minutes past midnight. A few years back, this would have been normal for me. I preferred working through the night. Fewer people meant fewer interruptions. More often than not, I would walk out of Cypress Wood Studios well past daylight, go home, crash, come back late in the afternoon and do it all over again.

Of course, at the time I had been single, carefree, and making way too much money. Cypress Wood may have been a smaller production house by Hollywood standards, but it maintained a healthy, well-funded clientele, and the owners were happy to share that wealth. I ran with a small group of friends who worked hard and played harder, oblivious to the fact that life changes.

For me, Jenny Mallon was that change. She started working at Cypress Wood a little over six years ago as an assistant editor. She was twenty-one, fresh out of film school, and eager to prove herself. She was also a stunning beauty. Barely five feet in height, she sported blonde hair that, unlike the unfortunate co-ed on my left screen, did not come out of a bottle. She was petite and perfectly proportioned, and I fell in love with her the instant I laid eyes on her.

I had competition, namely every single man (and two women) on the Cypress Wood staff. She made a pretense of playing the field, but it was mostly for show. We hit it off immediately. Don't ask me why, but she fell for me as hard as I did for her. We were married less than a year after we started dating. Five years later, we were still going strong.

Jenny discovered that she preferred production to post production and about a year after we were married managed to get hired as production assistant on a low budget indie flick. It was a modest hit and since the director liked surrounding himself with the same people from picture to picture, she was now firmly entrenched as his executive assistant. I was happy at Cypress Wood, she was happy shooting movies, and we were both happy with each other. We were making serious money and life was just about as good as it could get.

I froze the image of the hapless coed on the screen and picked up the shooting script, complete with the director's notes. That director, DeVonte Edwards, had already turned in his cut, so as far as the producers were concerned, his job was done. It was now my job to take his two hour and twenty minute opus and slash it down to a petite running time of one hour and forty five minutes.

I had worked with the producers on two other features so they trusted me to do what needed to be done. That meant I was alone in Edit Bay Three, and that suited me just fine. It was the smallest bay at Cypress Wood, maybe fifteen feet square and lit with five dim track lights set into the tiled ceiling. I sat at a wide desk that held two 30 inch screens, a keyboard, a mouse and a stylus. On the gray carpeted wall in front of the desk, about six away, was an ultra-high definition sixty-inch screen flanked by two large, high-end speakers. Two identical speakers hung on the wall behind me and one on each wall to my left and right. The amplifiers were racked mounted under the desk. EB-3 was soundproofed, which meant I could crank up the volume without disturbing anyone else who might be working late. All of the raw footage had been dumped onto one of Cypress Wood's many servers and was easily accessible. I had all the tools I needed at my fingertips.

I thumbed through the script until I found the scene that matched the one on my screen and chuckled when I read the DeVonte's notes. They were simple and to the point. Dean, for the love of God, save me! I laid the script on the wide desk, slid the frozen scene over to my right screen, and got to work.

Four hours later, I sat back and played the entire scene from start to finish on the big screen. I had chopped almost two minutes out of it, pairing it down to a lean three minutes and ten seconds. That was the easy part. Making all that fake blood disappear was much harder and far more time consuming. I had managed to get rid of the worst of it with a few well-placed cuts. The rest I replaced with millions of tiny, computer generated droplets of equally fake but now computer generated blood. True, I had never seen anyone stabbed, but the overall effect looked much more realistic. I still had at least another two days' worth of work to do on that scene, and at least three more weeks before I would hand in the finished product, but I was comfortably ahead of schedule. That should translate into a healthy bonus, and I was already envisioning a long weekend in the mountains with Jenny.

"That's good work." I jumped in my chair and swiveled to face the door. I had been so engrossed with my work that I had not heard it open. Ron Wibley, one of my counterparts, stood there, leaning against the frame and holding a cup of steaming coffee in a blue Cypress Wood mug. He knew better than to step into the bay. 'No food or beverages in technical areas' was a hard and fast rule that meant instant dismissal if broken. Liquid and electronics do not mix. Ron saw that he had startled me and waved his free hand in apology. "Sorry," he said.

"No problem," I replied. "In fact, I wouldn't mind a fresh set of eyes." Ron nodded and I played the scene again.

We got along okay, Ron and I... not great but okay. He had been at Cypress Wood a few years longer than me, and thus had seniority. He was a good editor, but the simple fact was, I was better. He had also been one of Jenny's suitors. It tended to make things awkward between us. He never admitted it...to me at least...but I think he had fallen for her as hard as I did. She had let him down as gently as she could, but I'm pretty sure the rejection had devastated him.

Physically he was fairly ordinary...maybe two or three inches shorter than me, with limp dark brown hair and a build that was at present stocky, but in a few years would probably translate to heavy. He wore thick, horned rimmed glassed that magnified his brown eyes just enough to give him a slightly creepy look. Still, he was nice enough. He even came to our wedding and when he wished us all the best, he seemed to mean it.

"I think you got it," he said when the scene ended. "You might consider trimming another few frames off that reaction shot, but once you clean up the rest of that blood, you're good."

"Thanks," I said. "That helps a lot. What are you working on?"

"That Honda commercial," said Ron. "You know, all the green screen stuff?" I nodded. Honda retained a much larger agency but a series of unfortunate events had forced them to farm out some of the work to smaller houses like Cypress Wood. It was an amazing opportunity. If they liked us, it would mean a lot more work and a lot more money. Did I say that I was a better editor than Ron? Maybe, but when it came to commercials, the man was a genius.

"I'm just finishing up the first cut," said Ron. "When you get a moment, maybe you could return the favor and give me a fresh set of eyes."

"Sure," I said. "Where are you?"

"A Control," said Ron. He saw my look of surprise and shrugged. A Control was a control room designed for live production. It could be used for editing, of course, but only when it wasn't being used for studio work. "The links to the servers for Bay One and Two went down a few hours ago, so I moved," he said. "The tech guys say they have to overnight a bunch of new modules, so they won't be back up until sometime late tomorrow morning."

"Got it," I said. I arched my back and raised both arms in a long stretch. "What else is going on?"

"Nothing," said Ron. "Other than you and me, it's just Billy in security and he's manning the front desk. Carl left about an hour ago. Said there's nothing he could do until those modules get here." I frowned at that. Carl was our chief engineer, and Cypress Wood was his baby. He was highly protective of each piece of equipment. For him to leave when something was off line, even when there was nothing he could do about it, was unusual. The man was obsessive. I shook off a sudden sense of unease and nodded.

"Give me twenty minutes," I said. "I'll wander over as soon as I make a few notes." Ron nodded and left, closing the door behind him. It took a little longer than twenty minutes, but finally I felt satisfied enough to take a short break. I made doubly sure that all my work was backed up and headed over to A Control.

Cypress Wood Studios is a full service production facility. We have two large studios equipped with ten top of the line HD cameras. There are two control rooms, 'A' and 'B', as well as three state of the art edit bays. The entire facility is housed in a converted rectangular warehouse. In the back is the prop room along with shipping and receiving. Studios A and B are parallel to each other, separated by a wide hall we call the Air Lock. Halls also run along the outer wall of each studio. Both halls and Air Lock end with a set of heavy double doors that lead directly into another hall that surrounds the entire the technical area. These doors are secured with high end locks that require both a card and a combination to open.

The technical area is laid out in a large square. The edit bays line the west side, while access to the two control rooms is from a hall on the east. The north side houses engineering as well as access to the servers. The south side, the side facing the studios, is a solid wall. It's a good arrangement. There's enough sound proofing and separation so that every area can be busy without anyone getting in anyone else's way.

I took my time walking down the north hall. I was stiff and my back was sore, so I tried to stretch as I walked. I passed the wide double doors on my right that led to the lobby, giving them a tug just to make sure they were locked. A few feet further allowed me to peek through the window into engineering on my left. It was an impressive room. The opposite wall boasted two 90 inch screens that could be divided into sectors as small as six inches and programmed to access any camera or the output of any bay or control room in the building. On the left and right were banks of instruments that not only monitored Cypress Wood's delicate systems but could be used to access any network on any satellite.

I continued on to the end of the hall, hung a left, went another ten feet to the entrance to A Control. I peeked through the waist high window set into the door, but Ron was nowhere in sight. I shrugged and stepped inside.

While not as large as Engineering, A Control was just as impressive. Facing me were two eighty inch screens that could be partitioned into smaller areas to show the outputs of any or all of our cameras as well as feeds from the servers. In the center of the left screen a large, forty inch sector was set aside for 'Preview', while an identical sector on the right screen was designated 'Program'. The 'Program' sector featured a beauty shot of one of Honda's latest models and the 'Preview' sector held a pair of actors standing in front of the large green screen that dominated one corner of Studio B.

A fifteen foot long control panel sat in the middle of A Control and boasted one of the best production switchers on the market. To the right of the switcher was an equally impressive audio board and to the left sat a powerful graphics unit. Next to the graphics unit was a smaller screen, and in front of that were ten rectangular control units that could be delegated to control the studio cameras. A smaller producer's desk sat about six feet behind the main control panel. At the moment it held a keyboard along with two thirty inch screens, the editing system Ron was using.

I figured that Ron had probably taken a potty break so I sat down in one of the two chairs in front of the editor and waited. I could have played the commercial myself, but that would have been inconsiderate. Instead I leaned back in the chair and tried to relax. The low lighting, the cool air and the comfortable chair all conspired to lead me into a light doze.

On the right screen, the Honda flickered. I blinked, wondering if I had imagined it. It flickered again, and an instant later, the entire sector went black. I groaned and sat up. If a server was crashing or another module was going bad, we were going to be in real trouble...as in missed deadlines, lost clients and no bonuses trouble. I started to get up and head back to EB-3 but suddenly the screen flared to life, only now, instead of the Honda, I could see Studio B, complete with green screen, staring back at me.

It took me a few seconds to understand that what I was seeing was impossible. The screens in A Control could only be programmed from the production switcher in front of me. There was no way that anyone could switch sources remotely, not even in engineering. I was still trying to process this when the Preview sector on the left blinked and went to black. When it came back up, it was showing a wide shot of Studio A.

"What the..." I slid out of my chair and stepped over to the production switcher. As I did, there was another flash and ten new, smaller squares appeared running along the bottom of both screens, five on each screen. I punched a few buttons on the switcher but it seemed to have crashed. The ten smaller squares flashed again, and now they each held a view from one of our studio cameras. Each camera was labeled with a number...cam 1, cam 2, cam 3 and so on. Cameras 1 through 5 were in Studio A, while 6 through 10 were in B. "No way," I muttered, still punching buttons. Only the fluorescents were on in both studios, so the pictures were dark but I could easily make out the various sets.

My first thought was that Ron was pulling some kind of stunt. With everyone else except for Billy gone, he was the only one with the technical savvy to pull it off, but I kept coming back to the simple fact that the screens could not be remotely programmed. I stared at them for another second or two and then decided to go over to engineering. It was possible that Carl or one of the other engineers had rewrote the software so that the screens could be accessed from there. Maybe...

On the left screen, the shot labeled Cam 1 started moving. I watched as it slid past an interview set that was scheduled to be torn down at the end of the week. A faux news set that was being used to tape an infomercial came into view and then disappeared just as quickly. The camera view swiveled right and started trucking along the outer hall toward the door that led to the technical area. I barely processed this when Cam 2 started to move, following Cam 1 past the two sets and toward the same door.

I had been feeling uneasy since my conversation with Ron, but now, as I stared at the moving cameras, that unease morphed into real fear. I stared at the shot on Cam 2. It was following close behind Cam 1, so I should have seen the camera, the dolly and whoever was pushing it, but all I could see was the door to the technical area. There was no camera, no dolly and no operator.

An instant later the rest of the camera shots started to move. Cams 3, 4 and 5 left Studio A and started trucking down the Air Lock toward the central entrance to the tech area. Cams 6 & 7 were heading through Studio B toward the opposite wall and the third entrance. 8, 9 and 10 seemed to be combing through the prop area. I could not see a single camera in any of the shots.

I was still trying to convince myself that I was the victim of some elaborate joke, but as I watched, Cam 1 reached the first set of doors to the technical area. It stopped for a moment and then tilted down to study the security lock bolted on the wall to the right. The lock consisted of a numerical key pad and a sensor that read our identity cards. On the top was a digital display. Cam 1 zoomed into a tight shot of the key pad and a moment later, I could see the buttons move. The display read the numbers as they were punched. It was a five digit sequence, and the instant the last number was entered the doors opened. The hall separating the tech area from the studios came into view. The shot panned right and started moving again. Seconds later Cam 2's shot followed Cam 1 into the hall.

I took a step back, fully intending to get out of A Control, but I could not tear my eyes from the screens. Cams 3 and 4 reached the doors at the end of the Air Lock. The sequence was repeated, much faster this time, and the camera shots passed through the open doors and turned right. An instant later Cams 5, 6 and 7 passed through the final set of doors. Cams 1 & 2 were now moving straight toward A Control, while Cams 3 and 4 were gliding past Edit Bay 3. When Cam 3 reached the door, it panned left. The bay came into view. I could see the final frame of the scene I had been working on displayed on the main screen, just as I had left it. The shot hovered there for a moment and then continued down the hall.

I suddenly realized that I was about to be surrounded. Never mind that what I was seeing was impossible to the point of absurdity. In a matter of minutes, the shots on Cams 1 through 7 would have me effectively trapped in A Control.

I realized something else. I needed to get out of the building...fast. I could not begin to imagine what force or intelligence was manipulating those shots, but I was absolutely certain that I did not want to find out. I backed away from the console, keeping my eyes on the screens. Again the screen flickered and now Cams 1 and 2 were displayed on the Preview and Program sectors.

I stumbled backward, but just as I made it to the door, Cam 1's shot swung around, revealing the hall that led directly to A Control. I could easily see the other side of the door that I was about to walk through. There was no other way out. I slid to the floor with a whimper and pressed hard against the door.

I could still see Cam 1's shot on the Preview sector, and as I watched, it drew even with the door. It hovered there for a second and then panned right. A Control slid into view. The shot hesitated and then zoomed into the switcher. It moved across the multicolored buttons and then zoomed out again, panning left until it was shooting straight through the door. Then it began to tilt down, drawing closer and closer to where I was crouching. I was trapped, but inches before my right foot would have been revealed, the shot stopped moving. It hovered there for several seconds, as if uncertain. Then it tilted up and panned the control room again.

The door shuddered, as if something very large and heavy leaned against it. I could feel it start to give way. The handle rattled and the frame creaked. I had a vision of the door shattering into thousands of tiny shards of wood and glass, shredding me in the process. A part of me actually welcomed the idea. I had a strong feeling that being flayed by an exploding door was infinitely better than being caught by the force responsible for the shattering.

The creaking stopped. The shot on the screens swung left, back to the hall and continued forward. When it reached the corner, it turned and headed toward Edit Bay 3. I stared at the screen, waiting for another view of A Control to appear, but for the moment, the hall outside was clear. I scrambled to my feet and staggered over to the switcher.

The camera shots were still active, but all of them were now on the other side of the technical area, blocking the entrance to the lobby. For the moment, a single path to the studios and prop room was clear.

I bolted through the door and ran down the hall to the entrance to Studio A. My only thought was to get out of the building, get to my car and get back to Jenny. I could use the loading dock that was just past the prop room. It meant setting off the alarm but that was the least of my worries. My hands were shaking, but I managed to punch in my security code. I started to pull the door open but sensed movement to my left. I glanced down the hall.

The next thing I remember I was running and screaming through the prop room to the loading dock. I have no memory of going through the door or running through Studio A. I also have no memory of what I may have seen or not seen coming toward me in that hall. I count that as a mercy, because I think that if I ever do remember, I will go insane.

The loading dock consisted of a large, wide entrance shuttered by a sturdy metal door that rolled down and locked in place. Next to that was a standard sized door that, although locked, opened easily from the inside. Outside was a retention ditch that bordered a wide field.

Just before I reached the door, something began to pound on it from the outside. At the same time the metal door covering the shipping entrance began to shudder. I pulled up, choking down a scream. Behind me I heard the double doors to the Airlock open.

There was nowhere to go, and I suddenly realized that the opening I had been given in A Control was no accident. I was in the prop room because that was where they wanted me. I started to back away from the loading dock, thinking that maybe there might be a place to hide among all the props, but before I could turn I was hit from behind. My vision exploded into millions of tiny, blazing points of light. I fell forward and hit the cold cement floor hard. I felt hands grab my feet and start to drag me across the floor. Then, like the end of so many movies I had edited, my mind faded to black.

***

I groaned as I fought my way back to consciousness. My head was on fire and my nose was throbbing. I could feel something wet trickling out of it.

I reached up to grab my head and the instant I touched my face my memory returned. My eyes snapped open and I sat up. My stomach heaved and I nearly lost my last meal, but a couple of deep breaths helped the nausea subside.

I was sitting on a couch in Studio B, on one of the generic interview sets we kept on hand. Directly in front of me were cameras six through ten. I nearly screamed until saw that they were powered down locked in place, exactly where they had been when I had reported for work.

I looked to my left and this time I did scream. Carl was there, sitting behind the interviewer's desk. At least, I think it was Carl. The body had the right build and I could see his employee security card clamped to his shirt pocket. That was where any similarities to the man I had known for years ended. The lower half of his body was missing, as was his head. The torso, complete with Carl's hairy arms, had been shoved into the chair like a child's broken doll and propped up by some of the cushions from the couch. There was blood everywhere, and I could see bits of his insides radiating out from the bottom of his torso like the roots of some obscene plant. I screamed again and rolled off the couch, landing on all fours.

"I didn't want him to suffer, but they like to play." The voice came from my right. I looked and saw Ron standing next to an announcer's podium, staring at me through those thick glasses.

"Ron?" It was all I could manage. My throat was dry and the instant I said his name I started to cough.

"He was in the way. If he had just left like he was supposed to, he would still be alive." Ron stepped around the podium and moved to the edge of the set, just a few feet away. "You, on the other hand," he snarled, "I want you to hurt...a lot. You took Jenny from me. I loved her and you took her from me." Somehow, I got my cough under control.

"Ron? What..."

"I made a deal," said Ron. He smiled and shook his head. "Not really. You don't make deals with them. You give them what they want, and if that makes them happy, then they might give you a little something in return. Scraps from the table, so to speak." He looked across the studio to the large green screen that dominated the entire north side. "I gave them a way in, and Jenny is my scrap. They're going to give her to me." My head was on fire and my thoughts were incoherent, but when Ron mentioned my wife, my adrenalin surged and my mind cleared. I focused on him, thinking of those floating shots that had herded me into the prop room.

"What have you done?" I said in a low voice. "And who the hell are they?" Ron's smile became a wide, cruel grin. The bastard actually laughed.

"They're old...beyond old, really, maybe older than the universe itself," he said. "But they've only recently become aware of us." He pointed to the row of cameras beside him. "It's the high definition tech," he said. "We're constantly trying to figure out ways to make our pictures clearer, brighter, and more vivid." He shrugged. "I think that coupled with all the WiFi, smart phones and other wireless tech, somehow our big, bright pictures became windows into our reality. They found those windows and turned them into doors."

"What, like something out of Poltergeist?" I gasped. "That's... insane."

"Maybe," he said. "But I don't think they use the signal. I think that they are the signal. When humanity first started using radio waves, we were somehow accessing the lowest part of their unconscious mind, but when we developed hi def and WiFi, we invaded their conscious thoughts. They're just returning the favor." He laughed again.

"If you stare at those screens long enough, they start to reach out to you, and not just places like Cypress Wood. Any HD TV or monitor is a portal for them." He pointed at my pants pocket. "They can even use that fancy I-phone you're so proud of." He looked down and for just an instant, I saw a look of pure terror cross his face.

"They found me," he said in a low voice. "And they talked to me. They told me that they can influence our thoughts. I get the feeling that a lot of people have seen them but have been made to forget." Behind him the green screen rippled and bulged. Whatever had herded me was behind it. In seconds, it would either be coming through it or around it. Ron started to back away.

"I don't really care," he said. "What I do know is that they like to...play...with us." He nodded at Carl's body. "You're next. Then they'll go to work on Jenny. They won't harm her body, just adjust her mind a little. In a few months, she'll have forgotten you and be in love with me. I could have just let them take you. But I wanted you to know, when you're slowly being ripped apart, that I'm going to have Jenny. I wanted..."

I sprang to my feet and charged. I took real satisfaction in wiping that smug look off his face as I ploughed into him. I wanted to beat the bastard to a pulp, but I wanted to get out of the building and back to my wife even more. I lowered my shoulders and hit him hard, grabbing him around his waist. He started to yell but I knocked the wind out of him. My legs kept churning and I forced him across the studio to the shuddering, bulging green screen.

My mind had cleared enough so that I understood two vital facts. One, whatever or whoever Ron was playing with, they were subject to physical barriers. They had been forced to open the doors to the technical area rather than just go through them. Two...

They liked to play.

And I had a feeling that they really didn't care with whom they played.

Desperation gave me the advantage. I could see the green screen fraying. More importantly, I could feel them leaking around the edges of screen, sloughing into Studio B like some kind of foul blob.

Now it was Ron's turn to scream. His feet scrambled against the concrete, but with a final, desperate surge, I shoved him through the green screen. It fluttered and ripped from top to bottom. Ron screamed again as he fell through the rip. He tried to pull back, but something grabbed him from the other side. I turned away as his scream became a high-pitched wail. Whatever had him, I did not want to see it.

I stumbled across the studio, praying to a God I never really believed in that the way was clear. Behind me, Ron's screams grew louder and then abruptly stopped. Seconds later they were replaced by high pitched, insane laughter. That laughter chased me as I ran through the prop room and the loading dock. I hit the door at full speed, the impact nearly dislocating my shoulder, and threw it open. The alarm sounded but I barely noticed.

I more than half expected to be devoured by something that had no right to exist in our safe little reality, but the only thing that greeted me as I stumbled through the door was the early morning sunlight. I ran around the building, got into my car and peeled out of the parking lot. As soon as I hit the main highway, I yanked my phone out of my pocket and threw it out of the window.

Twenty minutes later, I pulled into the driveway of the house Jenny and I had bought less than a year ago. The instant my feet hit the pavement, the front door opened and Jenny rushed out. I groaned in relief and grabbed her in a fierce hug. She fell into my arms, sobbing.

"I've been trying to call you for hours," she gasped, clinging to me as tightly as I was clinging to her. "Your phone kept going to voice mail." I pulled away and saw that she was trembling. I ignored the first five questions that ran through my mind and instead said the only thing that mattered.

"Get a bag packed," I said. "We're leaving." She stared at me for a few seconds. Then she asked me a short, simple question... a question that has haunted me every second of every day since.

"Is this about Ron?" I jerked back, as if she had slapped me.

"How did you..."

"Oh God," she sobbed. "I knew it!"

"Jenny?"

"I've been dreaming about him all night," said Jenny. "He came to me and said he killed you and that I belonged to him."

"It's okay," I lied.

"He takes me away and what he does to me..." She wrapped her arms around my waist held me tight. "But that's not the worst part. Dean, part of me wants to go with him. Do you understand? I want to go. What's happening to me?" I went cold inside.

"Just get packed," I said. "We're getting out of town and I don't think we're coming back."

***

That was six months ago. Police, responding to the alarm, found Carl's body in Studio B. They searched the rest of the building and discovered what was left of Billy, the security guard, stuffed between the servers. When they searched A Control, they found a video waiting for them on both screens. In it, Ron took credit for murders. The fact that he was cradling Carl's head in one arm convinced the police that he was telling the truth. Ron had already uploaded the video to YouTube, and within hours it had gone viral.

A state-wide manhunt was instituted, not only for him but for me and Jenny. When they could not find me at Cypress Wood they searched our home. They were not sure if we were accomplices or victims, but they wanted to talk to us. I would have gladly told them everything, but I had a bad feeling that Ron, or rather the thing he had become, would be hunting us. The last thing I wanted was to be stuck for hours at the local police station.

Jenny and I drove out of Los Angeles on Interstate 10, but as soon as we could we switched to the state routes. I made a single stop at our bank and emptied our savings account. It was risky, but we managed to get our money and get out of town.

For the past six months, we have kept moving. We left Jenny's phone and our pads at our house. I even disconnected the satellite radio and GPS in our Range Rover. Our latest stop is a cheap motel in a little Texas town. We have enough money to last another few months, but as of this morning, it doesn't matter.

Ron is following us. I can tell because wherever he stops, he kills. His body count is beyond staggering... seven towns and twenty-seven bodies... and every town is one where we have stayed. No matter how fast or far we travel, he's always behind us, and he's gaining ground. The statewide manhunt has become nationwide, but he always manages to escape the dragnets.

That's not the worst part. Jenny has become increasingly distant. I can feel her slipping away. They got into her mind and they won't let go. This morning, when I woke up, she was gone. I ran outside and saw that she had taken the Range Rover. I have no doubt that, even as I write this, she is with Ron, and the images that are playing themselves out in my mind are driving me to the edge of sanity.

I've got nowhere to go, and it really doesn't matter. I'm a loose end. Whatever is inside Ron won't let me live, which means that sooner or later they're going to come for me. So I'm going to stay right here and wait. Maybe there's still enough of Jenny's mind left to let me win her back, but I keep coming back to that one damnable thing Ron said about them.

They like to play.

***

To: Det. Latisha Barton, L.A.P.D.:
RE: File LA.M.18711:

Lattie:
I'm e-mailing you a copy of this manuscript. We found it at the crime scene, hidden between the mattresses. Forensics confirms that it was written by Dean Anderson. We're waiting on final confirmation, but we're fairly certain that, although it had been

dismembered and the head and hands were missing, the body found in the Melrose Motel belonged to him as well. We have intensified the search for Ron Wibley and his accomplice, now identified as Jennifer Anderson. Every resource the F.B.I. has available is being allocated to the manhunt.

As to the content of the attached manuscript, well, I think that it speaks volumes as to his state of mind, but I'll let you draw your own conclusions. My partner has been floating the idea that Anderson was also Wibley's accomplice and the two of them had a falling out, probably over Jenny Anderson. Frankly, I'm inclined to agree. Let me know what you think.

Give Bill my best.
Special Agent Leroy Edwards

Brandon Cracraft's Shopping List

Shopping List:
Orange
Strawberries
Grapes
Cookies
More Cookies
Milk

The Shine

Brandon Cracraft

My roommate, Carl Clutterbuck, called me a "tighty-whitey Christian." It's technically correct, but I still blushed whenever he says it out loud. My parents taught me old-fashioned conservative values. Even though I passed my eighteenth birthday three months ago, I still insisted on calling every adult "sir" or "ma'am," even the older students. I built my life on the bedrock of true Christian values: honor, dignity, self-respect, love, charity, and forgiveness.

"What's up?" Carl said, setting aside his comic book and looking over my shoulder. "Are you checking out that Christian Grindr again?" Ever since we became friends, Carl started wearing a silver cross around his neck. My parents would flip out if they discovered my roommate was gay, but I figured Jesus would be okay with it. He liked hanging out with harlots, tax collectors, and perverts.

I rolled my eyes. "It's not a dating app. The Shine allows us to track the good works done by other students. It inspires us to be our best person. Whenever I think that I don't have time to put in a little work at a homeless shelter, or should hoard a dollar rather than donate, I look at the selfless acts of my fellow students." I smiled as I showed him some of the good works being done around campus.

Carl's brow furled, and I gave him a quizzical look. "This all seems great, Jonah. I mean, I'm all for charity." I nodded. Carl taught me that gay people could be generous and moral. "The thing is, it seems like bragging."

I threw my arms up. "There you go again," I said. "Is this what public school does to you? Why do you always have to be so negative? I've posted on here a couple times. It's about inspiration, not acknowledgment."

It was time to ask. "You should go to church with me sometime."

"I don't ask you to go to the gay bar," he said, collapsing back on the iron-framed bunk. "Don't ask me to go to church." He looked away from me. The blood rushed out of his face, making his blue eyes appear sunken. "I met some evil people in a church once."

I turned back toward my phone, looking at some pictures that my family sent me of my baby brothers. They didn't send me pictures of my older sister, Mary, anymore. My parents wanted me to go to Christian College like she did, but I couldn't miss out on the chance to enter the best pre-med program in the state.

"God loves you," I reminded him. Carl nodded and returned to the adventures of Green Arrow.

***

The first time I had a wet dream, I was thirteen years old. I shared a room with Hosea and Malachi, both of which were chronic bedwetters. I barely knew what had happened, but I felt that my body had done something terribly wrong. I peed myself to hide the fact. When it happened again, I repeated the behavior.

Since I didn't have the guts to ask my parents, I decided to consult my pastor. I hoped he would keep it a secret.

"There's nothing wrong with that, Jonah," Pastor Jim said. "It's much better than masturbation." He blushed three shades of violet when I asked what that was. The grown man looked over his shoulder and joked that he feared my mother more than God.

It was my turn to blush. The truth was that I didn't understand half of what he said. I still don't. There was one thing that he made clear: "There's nothing wrong with it unless you think about men at the time."

From that moment on, I made sure to think about a woman right before the gunk shot out of me. If a girl was the last thing I thought about, I wasn't gay.

Mind you, I wouldn't mind being gay if it meant marrying Carl.

Of course, I wasn't just having wet dreams. I started playing with myself. I figured that it would be all right if I apologized to God afterward. Masturbation kept me out of trouble and it kept my boyhood from standing up at inappropriate times.

It wasn't like I was breaking one of the Ten Commandments. I looked over at Carl sleeping across from me, dark haired and pale skinned. A little of his blond roots started to show. Carl was so beautiful.

He once told me that I was pretty, but I know that was just gay talk. Carl told me that he didn't like blonds or skinny boys, so there was no way he found attractive.

I swallowed and thought about Jennifer Lawrence. Carl showed me The Hunger Games movies, and she was so hot that two guys were fighting over her. It only made sense that I use her as the last image.

The most important image.

When I was finished, I didn't feel the least bit guilty. I just wiped myself off and threw the tissue in the wastebasket.

My parents were right. College was changing me.

I grabbed my phone and checked my app. It was time for me to remember my responsibilities as a Christian and get my mind off my roommate's muscular chest and the cute little constellation of freckles on his lower back.

***

"Excuse me," I said after twenty minutes of psyching myself up. "Are you Sylvia McAfee?" I gave her my best smile, the one I practiced before going to help my parents mission in South America one summer. I hoped my braces wouldn't blind her.

The twenty-one-year-old college senior turned my direction. Sylvia McAfee wore earth tones, including a pair of bell bottoms made from hemp. "Do I know you?" She was the only black lady involved in Campus Crusade for Christ who kept her hair natural.

"Jonah Harris," I said pointing to myself. "I've been following you on The Shine."

Sylvia unclipped her phone from her faux-alligator belt and took a moment to search for my name. "Freshman, huh?" She returned her phone to its holster. "God bless you."

"God bless you, too," I said, unable to hide my glee. "I was wondering if there were any projects that I could help out with."

Sylvia raised an eyebrow. "Trying to increase your Shine profile?" I gave her a quizzical look. "I know

260

what you mean. John Adamson: unstoppable. I don't think the man sleeps. I'm never going to end up beating him."

I gave Sylvia McAfee my best church smile as I shoved the phone into the front pocket of my khakis. Far behind but I could catch up. There was a reason sloth was one of the Seven Deadly Sins. "It's not like it's a contest."

***

When I made it back to my dorm room, I crashed on my bed. I didn't have the strength to pull off my penny loafers, much less crawl under the afghan.

"You all right, Jonah?" Carl asked.

I opened my mouth to speak but all that escaped was an obnoxious yawn. After a few moments, I composed myself. "I met up with Sylvia McAfee." My roommate gave me a quizzical look, so I showed him her profile on The Shine. "I figured the two of us would volunteer for an hour or two at the homeless shelter." Another yawn. "Two homeless shelters and three battered women's shelters. Just when I thought we were done, we met up with John Adamson to pick up trash in the park."

"Did you get your homework done?"

My eyes shot open. My body was exhausted, but my mind was alert. "I can't believe that I forgot."

"The good news is that fourteen people swiped right on your profile." Carl showed me his phone. He downloaded The Shine. Probably to keep tabs on me.

I leaned on my elbows. "What are you talking about?"

"The Shine added a new feature. You can swipe right to commend a person on their charity work." He swiped, and a notice popped up on my phone. "I wonder what happens if you swipe left."

261

Carl's smile faded, and his gaze went from his phone to me. "Have you seen this, Jonah? It's pretty sick."

I checked The Shine app: SWIPE LEFT TO REPORT THEIR SINS.

***

The shirtless dude approached Carl and me while we were eating breakfast outside. I tried to retain eye contact and not stare at his trimmed and tanned chest. He had a boyish face but a man's torso. The boy shoved his hands nervously in his pockets, lowering his khaki shorts beneath the waistband of his boxer-briefs.

"Hey," he said, smiling and playing with the golden cross around his neck. "Aren't you Jonah Harris? I read about you on The Shine." I stood up, introduced myself, and shook his hand. "Name's Marcus Davenport."

He gushed at me for a few minutes, and my roommate kept looking at me sideways. When Marcus left, I asked Carl, "Do you think he's attractive?"

Carl gulped down his orange juice. "Not my type. You know I don't like blonds, especially California blonds." He smiled at me. "Do you think he's hot, Jonah?" He nudged me. "You don't secretly play for my team, do you?"

I looked around, making sure that no one else could hear. It took me a minute to find my courage. "I'm not going to date anyone until I'm finished with medical school. I see boys like Marcus Davenport as nothing but a temptation..."

"You're attracted to boys?!" Carl's voice was too loud. I begged him to calm down. "I had no idea."

"I'm attracted to some boys and some girls. Not that it matters. I'm not going to kiss anyone that I'm not going to marry, and I'm never going to marry a boy." I stopped myself before I said something stupid. Like admitting I found Carl more attractive than any other boy I met.

"Damn." I was so flustered that I didn't notice Carl taking out his phone. "It seems that Marcus is a bad boy."

I rolled my eyes. Carl was always telling dirty jokes that went over my head. "What are you talking about?"

Carl showed me Marcus Davenport's Shine profile. Someone had reported his sins. Marcus was a fraternity boy, and there were pictures of him with a bottle in his hands: UNDERAGE DRINKING. SEXUAL, TRIBAL UNDULATION. SECULAR, EXPLICIT HIP HOP MUSIC. POSSIBLE DRUG USE.

I turned away, unable to hide my anger. "I'm sure it's nothing, just some jerk being judgmental. A true Christian wouldn't take something like that seriously."

***

Sylvia McAfee called me that Saturday and asked if I wanted to help her make cookies for a residential facility for severely autistic children. I agreed, with the warning that I could only spare a couple hours. "Need to keep my GPA up if I'm going to make it into med school," I reminded her. "I'm sure fashion design is a fairly competitive..."

"See you then." Sylvia hung up, and I contemplated calling her back. She sounded desperate. I wondered if something was wrong.

I wore a periwinkle tie with my pink shirt, because I thought it made me look more whimsical. I reminded myself to wash them separately unless I wanted to be wearing "pinky tighties" for the rest of the semester.

Sylvia looked completely different. She reminded me of that old horror film from the seventies that Carl showed me: The Stepford Wives. The weirdest thing was that her beautiful, natural hair had been shaved and a long straight weave had been styled, similar to the way my grandmother wore her hair.

"What do you think?" Sylvia asked. Her smile was fake. I read terror and anguish in her eyes.

"I like it." It was a white lie, needing only a quick, silent prayer for forgiveness.

Sylvia checked her Shine profile several times, before letting out a sigh of frustration. "We should get going," she said. "I'll drive. If I remember right, you don't have a car."

On the way to the Kia, I checked her profile. Someone had reported a sin on Sylvia McAfee. When I was certain she wasn't looking, I checked it out. It was a close-up of her old natural hair and snapshots of the African and Middle Eastern inspired clothes that she had designed herself. The caption read: VANITY. VENERATION OF PAGAN AND HEATHEN CULTURE.

***

Carl Clutterbuck loved movies, so he was constantly showing me all the films that he felt I lost out on. Some of the modern films were all right, but I never got into cartoons and a lot of the live action ones were just too dirty for me. Watching people get naked and have sex made me uncomfortable. It felt as bad as watching porn.

I liked the older movies. Carl taught me about Katherine Hepburn, Carey Grant, Jimmy Stewart, Barbara Stanwyck, and a host of others in films both black-and-white and in Technicolor. At least one night a week, the two of us popped some popcorn and watch a movie together.

Heat in the dorm was terrible. The tile floor could cause frostbite, so slippers were a necessity. The two of us tried sleeping in pajamas, but we couldn't get comfortable. We sneaked in a small, space heater, which only helped if it was pointed directly at us.

"Don't take this the wrong way, Jonah," Carl suggested. I never saw him look so nervous. "Would you be uncomfortable if we pushed the bunks together and shared all the blankets and the heater?"

I swallowed, terrified that Carl might learn my dark secret. The only thing more sinful than being attracted to someone who would never feel that way back was having those thoughts about another man.

"Don't worry," Carl said. "I slept with lots of boys back at Bible retreats." He blushed. "Not slept with. Slept beside."

It was hard not to giggle. Carl seemed so worldly. My parents hunted, fished, and camped, but I always bought my clothes from the same store. I never even bought my own clothes until a couple weeks ago. Mother took care of that, because she said that boys had terrible taste. Not that it matters. I liked the collared shirts, ties, and khakis.

"I guess," I said, shivering as I stripped down to my jockeys and crawled into bed beside him. Carl positioned the heater perfectly, and I was warm. It felt like I was back in Phoenix. Carl stripped to his boxers, decorated with a superhero that I didn't recognize, and jumped into bed beside me.

The two of us watched Sayonara together, our bodies close. The near nakedness of being with a man that I was attracted to should have made me uncomfortable. It was quite the opposite. My body lost its tension. For the first time in weeks, Carl caused my penis to stiffen.

When I woke up, I asked if we could keep the beds like that.

***

The two of us burst out of bed when we heard a knocking on the door. It was a Friday night, so we were used to people getting rowdy and obnoxious. Fire alarms were pulled when there was still an hour before dawn. Boys walked to the bathroom even though the fronts of their pajamas were already stained with urine.

The room smelled like paint. Carl decided to expand his major. He wanted to teach chemistry, biology, art, and maybe even math to high schoolers instead of working in a lab. He joked that he was going to be in college longer than me.

"What do you want?" Carl said angrily as he threw the blankets off and winced as his feet touched the cold tile.

"It's Marcus Davenport." His voice was anguished. More than that, it was slurred. He was beyond drunk.

"I can't leave him out there," I explained opening the door without bothering to pull on some pants.

Marcus stumbled through the door. His sweat smelled of alcohol, not beer. Something nasty and hard that could damage a boy his size and age. "Thank you, Jesus." His eyes were bloodshot. I couldn't tell if he was stoned or had just finished crying.

"You all right, kid?" Carl said, moving him to the bed. He steadied Marcus with his arm while I got him some water. I also started the coffee pot, another vice I'd discovered since coming to college. Coffee was grown-up juice when I lived at home.

"They all hate me," Marcus said, pulling out his phone. I knew what he was about to do. There wasn't a move that Marcus Davenport made that wasn't reported.

His sins were drunkenness, dancing, flirting, eating nothing but junk food, and a lot of vanity. I wondered how they got a picture of him flexing in a locker room mirror.

"My dad told me that he expects kids to make mistakes when they go to college," I explained. My own parents experimented with premarital sex and had to drop out of school when they got pregnant with Mary. "God will forgive you. This is piddly stuff. Little things. There isn't even a commandment about underage drinking. Heck, Miriam led the Israelites in a dance when they escaped Egypt..."

"They won't forgive me, though." Carl showed me profiles for John Adamson and a now clean Sylvia McAfee. "They told me that I can't help out at the shelters anymore. They said that I'm too sinful."

"That's stupid," Carl interjected. "You two need to go to my church." While I went to the same church as the other Crusaders on campus, Carl rode his bike to a progressive church with a lesbian pastor.

Marcus collapsed into tears. "I'm a horrible person," he muttered before erupting into loud, braying sobs. Even though I couldn't make out a lot of what he said, I was certain that I heard Marcus say "I wish I was dead."

***

Marcus Davenport curled up under his makeshift bed and slept next to the heater like a dog. He had an accident in the middle of the night, and Carl mopped up the tile without judgment.

"You need to take better care of your body," Carl warned. "You don't want to ruin your kidneys before you turn twenty."

"I just had a couple beers," Marcus said. The younger boy couldn't look at us when he lied.

"I've never drank in my life," I admitted, "and I know the difference between beer sweat and whatever you smelled of."

Marcus fiddled with the belt buckle on his belt. "I'm sorry. You must think that I'm pretty terrible person."

I put my arm around him. "I would never think that. You've just got to show some self-control." He nodded. I never felt so grown up. Marcus Davenport was looking to me for advice. I was used to being "the kid."

Carl sneaked a bunch of washcloths into the shower so that Marcus could clean himself off in our room. While he was doing that, I tried to find something that I owned that would fit the shorter, stockier fraternity boy.

"How do you stand it?" Marcus asked. "I mean, he's obviously gay. I don't think I could live with a gay dude."

"Carl's my best friend." I felt anger rush through my blood, and I forced it down. Marcus needed understanding. "It's not bad. He doesn't hit on me or anything. We're best buddies."

Marcus nodded. "I was hoping that the two of us could become best friends. I need someone to help me stay on God's path."

"I'll help you however I can," I said.

"Can you talk to the others?" he asked. "Maybe get them to stop putting things on The Shine app?" He looked lost, younger than his almost eighteen years. "I just want people to like me, Jonah." He began to cry again. "I really do try to be a good boy."

***

Mother called me once a week, twice when my little brothers either did something great or terrible. It was time for me to ask the question. "How's Mary doing?" I

268

realized that my parents avoided saying anything about my older sister.

There was a long sigh. "Mary's quitting school." It sounded like Mother took it as a personal defeat. "That's not right, God bless it. Mary was kicked out of her Christian College. She's going to community college right now, might end up transferring to the same school as you next year."

"Why did she get kicked out of school?" I asked.

Silence. I checked my phone several times to make sure the call was still connected. "I love, Mary. The Devil himself can't change that. There are some things that I cannot approve of. That God does not approve of."

"Is Mary a lesbian?" I asked, covering my mouth. I wasn't surprised to see Carl raise an eyebrow at the mention of the L-word.

"Jonah Nahum Harris!" Mother said. "We don't use that word. It's foul."

"I'm sorry," I quickly replied. It didn't matter that I was eighteen-years-old. My mother's approval still meant everything to me.

"I'm sure that Mary will figure herself out and return to God." I started to say something, but my mother's next comment stunned me. "I don't want you to have anything to do with her, Jonah. I mean it."

***

I never heard Marcus Davenport sound so excited. For the last two weeks, he'd limited himself to no more than two beers a night. Any non-beer alcohol, including hard lemonade and wine, was forbidden. We hung out every Sunday after church and had lunch.

"Guess what," Marcus said, stuffing a strawberry waffle in his mouth. "John Adamson called me. He said that he noticed that I was doing better and wanted to talk to me about erasing some of my sins from Shine profile."

"You know that the only person..."

Marcus was too excited to let me remind him that his sins were between him and God (and the law, since underage drinking was illegal.) "He said that it could be wiped clean if I met him and the others for a simple act of contrition tonight."

"Act of contrition?" I said. "Is this the Dark Ages?"

"Will you come, Jonah?" he begged. "I need you to be there. It feels like I'm getting baptized again." Marcus grabbed my hand. "I feel like I'm being Born Again."

"Sure," I said, feeling uncomfortable. My parents didn't believe in speaking in tongues or begging God to forgive you. They were strict, but they told me that God was love, not some vengeful old man with a white beard.

The muscular boy threw his arms around me. "God bless you." As he left, Marcus said, "It must feel great to have a real best friend instead of a gay one."

***

Marcus Davenport didn't own a pair of long pants, so he wore his best shorts, white shirt, and school colored tie to the contrition. His tennis shoes were ratty. By his own admission, shoes didn't last more than a month with him with all the intermural sports that he was involved in.

Since John Adamson had the most right swipes on his profile, he took over as leader. People stopped think about us Campus Crusaders. We were too swept up in the Shine. John looked like a leader. He combed and dyed his hair to hide his Jewish heritage, and he stood taller than all of us at six and a half feet tall. All of his shirts and sweaters advertised the college except for one navy blue suit he wore to church and job interviews.

He wore the blue suit today. It made him look a lot older than his twenty-two years and a little frightening. His dark eyes were cold. I stood as far away from him as possible.

Sylvia McAfee acted as his accessory. She wore the same colors as him, all store bought. From what I understood, she'd changed her major to business like John Adamson.

"Do you remember what we talked about?" John Adamson asked Marcus. The younger boy nodded, stuffing his hands in his pocket. When his elder cleared his throat, Marcus took a more military stance.

"Yes sir," his voice was loud.

"You are a child, Marcus," John Adamson said. "You are far too young to be drinking. You shouldn't be hanging around those boys." His eyes narrowed. "Is that clear?" He spoke slowly to make his disapproval obvious.

"I will quit the fraternity, sir," Marcus said. I gasped. He loved fraternity life. "I have been spending time with Jonah Harris. He has been helping me live a more Christian lifestyle. I will give up drinking."

"You have been a naughty boy," John Adamson said. Several of the others nodded. I stared in disbelief, resisting the urge to run. "As my father used to say, 'you've got a little too big for your britches.'" A couple kids laughs. Marcus started to laugh, but John Adamson shook his head.

"I've been a sinner," Marcus said. "Please help me."

"It is obvious that you are not old enough to make your own decisions," John Adamson continued. "You don't even turn eighteen for another week. You are a little boy, and bad little boys get spankings."

My mouth dropped open. "You can't be serious."

"God's work is always serious," John Adamson said. I looked for sanity in anyone else, but I saw none.

"Should I take off my pants?" Marcus said.

John Adamson's belt buckle cracked against the floor like a scorpion's tale. "That won't be necessary. Jesus was scourged before going to the cross." He looked directly at me. "I think he can handle a spanking. Spare the rod and spoil the child."

The truth was that my parents believed in corporal punishment, but I had only been spanked three times in my life. Dad never used the belt. The worst part of a spanking was that Dad looked ready to cry when he was finished.

No one looked ready to cry. Carl told me that some gay guys get some weird sexual pleasure out of spanking. John Adamson made me wonder if straight guys had the same fetish. He couldn't stop grinning.

"Everyone must punish him," John Adamson said.

I wanted to run when I heard Marcus start to scream and bawl, but my feet refused to move. I was too scared that they would start attacking me.

"Maybe he's had enough," I suggested. There was little left of Marcus Davenport's new shorts. The agony made the boy throw up all over himself.

"Everyone must punish him," John Adamson repeated.

When John Adamson's belt finally came around me, there was blood and skin dripping from the buckle. I held it limply in my hand.

Marcus looked at me, his face wet with tears and sweat. "Please, Jonah, please." He wiped the mucus from his mouth. "Do this for me."

***

As soon as I got back, I slammed the door behind me and locked it. Tears burned behind my ears, but my tear ducts refused to release. My hands shook as I pulled off my shirt, tie, and tee-shirt. I ripped and ruined my khakis as I tried to kick them off without taking off my loafers first.

"What's wrong?" Carl asked. I jumped when he put his hand on my shoulder. I hugged him tightly, and he held me for a few minutes.

"Please don't ask me any questions." The two of us sat in silence for the rest of the evening. It was the nicest thing anyone had ever done for me.

***

Even though I felt better in the morning, I needed time away from the Shine app and the Campus Crusaders. I ignored any calls and responded to texts by telling them that was I too busy with school or just not feeling well.

When Sunday came around, I asked Carl if I could go to church with him. It was different. People in suits sat next to people in tee-shirts. A rock band covered some old church hymns and it was over in exactly one hour. Since the church wasn't just made up of students, some of them had to go to work as soon as it was done.

Carl and I ate breakfast at some hole-in-the-wall hipster café far away from the place on campus I used to fellowship at. Marcus Davenport sent me several texts. I never responded to him with longer than one word.

I managed to avoid Marcus Davenport for a month.

When he showed up at my door at five in the morning on a Sunday, Carl and I were still asleep. He wore long sleeves and trousers. I hoped that it was just a style thing. His scars had to have healed by now.

"What's going on?" Marcus said, crossing his arms. "Aren't you Christian anymore?" I opened my mouth to answer, but the fury in his eyes made me take a step back. "I don't get it. I thought the two of us were friends. Why are you treating me like dirt?"

I slumped down on the bed next to Carl Clutterbuck. I gave him a look to let him know that I needed to handle this. "I'm still Christian. I've just been going to another church, going to be doing a tee-shirt drive later this week if you want to contribute." Marcus remained silent. "This whole Shine thing got out of control."

"It's designed to help..." Marcus began.

"It was designed to make us judge each other," I said, feeling confident for the first time in my life. "It's terrible. John Adamson should take it down. You're supposed to do good deeds, because you want to help to the less fortunate. It's part of being a good Christian. Heck, it's because you're a good person. Jewish people. Buddhist. Hindus. It doesn't matter your religion. You're supposed to do this stuff because it's our duty to help people in need. Not to get into Heaven. Not so you can get more people to swipe right on your profile."

Marcus stared at us in silent. "I don't know you anymore." He stormed out. His last words were, "Not all churches are Christian, Jonah. I would remember that there were Sunday services during the days of the anti-Christ."

***

Even though I tried to avoid Shine, curiosity still compelled me to check it from time to time. I discovered that all of Marcus Davenport's sins were removed the night that we scourged him.

I got an urgent alert both on the app and in text. I shoved it back in my pocket without checking. There was still a ton of reading I needed to do for Biology 101. I made it through half of it before the suspense made it impossible.

Marcus took a picture of me sitting on the bed next to Carl Clutterbuck. We were both still in our underwear. The caption read HOMOSEXUALITY.

I told myself it was stupid. The picture was obviously taken out of context. It was just too guys in the early morning, sitting next to each other. The most embarrassing thing was how bad my bed head was.

My mother called me an hour later. I heard a shutter in your voice. "Jonah, what's going on." Her fear turned to anger. "What are you doing at that college? Your little brother, Hosea, he's been following you on this Shine app."

***

I sent a text to John Adamson: "Take it down!!!!!!" I followed it up with, "I'm not gay. Carl is just my roommate."

He answered immediately. "Why do you share a bed?"

"It's cold in my room. Take it down. Mother thinks I'm gay. I'm not gay. Carl is just my friend. Jesus hung out with sinners."

There was a long pause before John Adamson responded. "Do I need to add blasphemy to your sins? Did you just compare yourself to Jesus?"

"Just take it down!!!!" I demanded.

The next text posted as soon as I hit send. "If you want me to take it down, you must perform an act of contrition." He followed it with a prayer emoji.

I stared at my phone for a few seconds. My hands shook too badly to text back. I thought of them whipping me with John Adamson's belt.

"Please just take it down. I don't want to be part of this anymore."

John Adamson copy-pasted his message. "If you want me to take it down, you must perform an act of contrition."

I waited an hour before my response. "If I do this, I want you to leave me alone and let me live my life."

Two hours later. "See you at midnight at my place. Bring a change of clothes."

***

I found some pants at the bottom of my drawer that were an inch and half too short for me. For the first time in my life, I left a tie and jacket at home. I almost wore a tee-shirt, but I felt like I was walking around in my underwear. I packed up a better set of perfectly folded clothes, including freshly polished penny loafers.

Carl was at class, so I didn't have to worry about him trying to talk me out of it. He wouldn't understand. I didn't want my family to turn their backs on me like they had with Mary. They thought it would just be temporary, but it was possible that my parents would never speak to my older sister again.

Norman and Tabitha Adamson bought their son a house for his eighteenth birthday right next to campus. They thought that the dorms were full or nothing but drugs and sin. Their son agreed with them. He rented out rooms to five other Christian boys, making them sign a contract stating that he could throw them out if he caught them doing anything immoral.

The house was completely white. I wondered if John Adamson considered buying a brightly colored couch or a rug that didn't look like it belonged in an insane asylum was immoral. The bookshelves were empty except for an oversized ivory colored Bible.

"Maybe I should've worn all white," I said, surveying the circle of Christians. I smiled and nodded at Sylvia McAfee, but her eyes were glazed over.

"I don't think you are in any position to make jokes, Jonah," John Adamson said. He looked over at two of the younger boys, and they began laying down a plastic tarp. I tried to swallow my terror, but I couldn't stop shaking.

"Let's get this spanking over with." My voice broke, but I tried to sound brave.

John Adamson shook his head. "You're not some little kid pretending to be a grownup." He glared at Marcus Davenport, who lowered his gaze. "Your crime is homosexuality, and it must be dealt with."

"How?" I asked.

John Adamson raised an eyebrow, demanding silence and obedience. "In the Middle Ages, they devised something called the Pear of Anguish. It was inserted in the homosexual's rectum and then spread."

"You can't be serious," he said.

"We're not barbarians. I figured something more appropriate." He waited until some of the others nodded their approval. "To save you, Jonah Harris, some of us ventured into a disgusting shop. It was filled with pornography and the most disgusting mechanical devices." He made a face.

"I had to throw up," Sylvia McAfee added.

"We selected seven different items that homosexuals use to sodomize themselves with. When I was a little boy, I experimented with cigarettes. Daddy made me smoke an entire pack. I never smoked again."

"Praise Jesus," someone yelled, even though his statement had nothing to do with Jesus Christ.

"I am going to insert things inside of you, show you the pain of sodomy." John Adamson raised his hands and people grabbed. I saw scissors and knives, and my eyes widened. I didn't feel much better when I realized that they were slicing off my clothes and not my flesh. Marcus Davenport was the one who ripped off my underwear. "By the time I am through, Jonah Harris, you will never want to look at a man in such a manner. All you will be able to think about is this agony."

I screamed.

***

They left me in a widening pool of defecation, vomit, and blood. Since it was John Adamson's house, he remained. "You can use my shower if you want," he said, looking regretful. "There's plenty of hot water."

I didn't respond.

"You know that we did this for your own good," John Adamson said. He tried to help me up, but I pushed him away. "That was nothing like the actual Pear of Anguish---"

I wiped the blackened blood off my phone and deleted the Shine app.

M.S. Swift's Shopping List

Bottled ale - Blonde Witch
Bottled ale - Pendle Witch
Bottled ale - Black Wytch
Mother's Day card
Sage, bunch
Matches
Firelighters
Tea lights
Vegetarian sausages
Veggie burgers
Chilli
Chef's knife
Cat food
Crysanthemums, bunch

A Charm for the Shadows

M.S. Swift

Her breath sucks the night air from under the stars, summoning the scent of waves sifting around the sandbanks. She pauses, holding the taste of sand and of the sea's expanse in her mouth before exhaling into a shred of fabric cupped around her mouth.

She whistles softly, twisting the fabric into a ball. An answering whistle rises beyond the shadows as she secures the charm with twine. She steps back, smiling as the whistling rises and flutters around the swaying ornament.

***

The sun slipping behind the detached, post-war houses lacked the warmth of the train and Verity Saunders paused to wrap her coat around herself. The sunset over Liverpool bay and the Welsh hills would be magnificent and she was tempted to drop her shopping bags into the hallway of their home, pull on her boots and cross the road toward the sand-hills. However, her mother would be waiting for her dinner and besides, she told herself, such walks weren't the same without Dad.

Passing through the shadow of St Nic's church, she found her pace slowing. Light expanded through the open-plan upper floor of the derelict property opposite her home illuminating the cavernous space beyond the filthy net curtains; she had never seen so far into the place and casually she imagined what it would be like to move around that space in sight of the sand-hills and the sea.

The place had been empty before they moved in some thirty years ago. She and her school friends had been fascinated by it - they told stories about it involving witches and dead bodies. She found herself wondering why it had been empty for so long. Her dad had said something about legal time-frames in the absence of a will.

Several moments passed before she realised that she was watching movement behind the window. At first she thought it was dust stirred up by vermin. Then she wondered if it was people she was glimpsing, swaying and dancing through the sunlight until she detected what appeared to be thin ropes, snaking to and fro.

It was the break in that movement which set her scuttling toward her own house. She turned into the open porch where she retrieved her phone from her coat's inner pocket – no missed calls – and clicked onto the camera function. She paused a moment, wondering whether she might draw the attention of whoever was in the house, before she darted out and clicked a photo. A savage bunching of the nets - not a twitch but a violent snatch – echoed her own action and sent her back against her front door. Flustered, she fought for the keys and stumbled in.

Once inside she paused, waiting for the fear to subside. Her impressions were vague but she had the idea that a silhouette had lunged toward the window of the house. She put the bags down, glanced once at the phone before calling for her mother. She was relieved that there was no reply except for the kitchen radio burbling away and she got the kettle on before heading into the sitting room, phone in hand.

The sun filled their bay windows and as she stood, clasped in the warmth, a conviction took hold that an awareness was fixed upon her, was rooting within her, monitoring her.

Feeling exposed, she stole forward to the net curtains and stretched them to look across the street. The house opposite glared down, the upper floor windows sunset brazen. Another movement across the light saw her flinch away, dragging violently at the nets until their pull saw her release her grip.

"Hello... police, yes, police... please. There has been a break-in at the house across the road... there are people in there... I've just seen them... Bayswater Gardens, number one, oh no, it's an empty house... I think they may be squatters, or young people... oh, right, thank you... yes, of course...

After leaving her name and number, Verity went to the front door. She couldn't shake off the feeling that someone was staring at her; it prevented her from settling to anything and she even thought of locking herself in, deciding against it when she imagined mum forced to stand on the doorstep.

Back into the kitchen she found the note: 'at golf, don't wait up.'

Well how could she not wait up, with people across the road, in the twilight, watching their house? She looked at the photo of herself and Dad on the shelf, his tall form leaning down into her and shook her head as if in shared disbelief.

She checked her phone whilst tea was cooking. No message from mum. Remembering the photo she had taken, she forced herself to click onto it. She had captured only half of the house. The window was visible and although the sun flared across the image, a dusky streak smudged across it suggested a figure. Even above the familiar bubble of the pans, it was disconcerting to look at that image. Could a person really appear so insubstantial? She clicked the phone shut, telling herself that it was circling dust or a trick of the light.

***

"See ya Frank, God bless, love!"

Her mother's voice stirred her from slumber in front of the TV.

"You in, V? Well, where else would you be?" Mum's short, lean form rolled into the living room, refreshed from golf.

"Before you start, I've been having a drink with Frank, he dropped me off," she said.

"Was he driving?"

"Yeah, but we were only at the clubhouse and don't you worry, he's an ex-copper, if he gets stopped, he's right in there with them."

"Mum...I was worried."

"Well, you needn't have been," mum replied, slumping down in a chair with her coat still on.

Over tea in the living room, Verity broached the subject of the house across the street.

"What do you mean 'people in there'?" mum said, putting her tray down and heaving herself to her feet.

"Take care," Verity cautioned.

"Never mind take care, I'll call Frank!"

"What good would a drunk-driving geriatric do?"

Mum lunged into the nets and stood, peering across the street. Verity felt uncomfortable as her mum stood so brazenly in the window, framed against the dark house.

"Maybe we should get a dog," Verity said, thinking of the daily walks across the dunes and on to the water's edge, "it would be a guard dog."

"Your father never approved of dogs," mum replied, thrusting herself from the curtains, "I can't see anything now."

***

When cloud masked the stars, the dark that gathered over the shoulder of sand-dunes and spread of sea visible from her window was absolute, glowering where sky and sea and shore should have been.

She stood in the bedroom window in her dressing gown. She imagined that beyond her own reflection—mid-fifties, slim, plain at best—the windows of the empty house gaped like brackish pools. She was glad to snuggle into bed and think about the sand dunes tracking along the dark stretch of the Wirral coast.

There was a distinct whistle.

She knew that much as she lay awake. The night was still and there it was again, a piping answered by a plaintive, lonely wail. What birds were they, sandpipers perhaps?

A thud sounded. At least she thought it was a thud and not a dreamed translation of her pulse. It came again, a sudden savage thudding against the wall of the house. What was it? There was no wind. It might have been a wave, rearing and slapping against the wall.

Something of its sudden violence reminded her of the movement at the window of the abandoned house, no, told her it was the movement from that house, beating at the wall of hers.

"Don't come in, don't come in," she said, feeling herself constrict with fear until she half-believed that she was outside in the street, listening to the noises within the house opposite. To her relief, the sounds did not come again and only the call of the birds sounded once from the distance.

It was the phone that woke her a second time.

Its ring was so uncomfortably loud and shrill she started from her doze. She lay heart beating, as it chimed again. Even though it might have woken mum, she couldn't will herself out of bed to turn it off so after the fifth trill, the answer phone clicked in. She cringed at the sound of her own voice, hesitant and self-conscious, unable to assume possession of her own phone.

At first there was no message, only silence. As the moments passed, she became conscious of a faint, static hum suggesting a wide space. Several muffled bumps sounded followed by a drawn-out whistle which set her recoiling against the wall. There was a further sound suggestive of fabric moving and several more whistles before the guttural wail of a gull conveyed the empty expanse of the shore. She listened incredulously until a savage cracking sound sent her down under the bed clothes. The proximity of the sound suggested that it was in her room, or that she was across the street, inside the empty house.

She was wrenched from slumber by the dreaded sound of the phone issuing a curt beep. She curled back the covers, dreading what may be in the room with her but only the light of the phone and the stirring of dawn behind the blinds were visible. Horrid ideas flittered through her mind about who—or what—was contacting her in the night and it was only when the light grew outside the window and a milk-float sounded in the street that she was able to put her fears into perspective and relax again.

***

"We swung by late last night but couldn't find any sign of illegal access."

Verity stood alongside the officer on the driveway of the empty house. The young man knocked on the front door. The echoes reverberated around the place, prompting Verity to look to the upstairs window. There was no response from within. The suggestion that she had heard the police inspecting the area reassured her.

She didn't tell them about the call or the photo, it embarrassed her to think of how they might respond and she didn't want to talk about being in her bedroom alone.

A call on the radio drew the officer back to the car, disturbing her thoughts. He shouted reassurances as he sped off.

Mum was out golfing again, despite the rain that came in just before lunch so Verity spent the time rearranging her room, clearing out some of the old clothes, hanging the buys of the previous day. She found that she couldn't spend too long in there; it wasn't comfortable – it seemed cramped and dull and no matter where she was, she seemed always in view of the house opposite.

Later, with the breezy gusto of a US comedy show blaring from the telly, she checked her phone. A picture message had been sent at 3.23. Hesitantly, she clicked upon it. The image that greeted her was blurred – little more than a light behind smog. Was it a flash reflected from a window? There was the ghost of a structure suggested as well. She peered at it until something told that it was her own house, taken from that building opposite!

Stray thoughts were nagging her and she switched to the photo she had taken. It was possible to imagine something resembling a face contorted within the glare but it was reasonable to suppose that it was a reflection of the light across glass. Determined to reassure herself, she emailed the image to herself. As one-liners scattered around the living room, she listened to the message from the previous night.

The time registered was 2.15 and she wondered what time the police had called. There was silence, a slight crackling followed by a number of dull, faint raps. There was an echoing quality to those noises which was lost when the whistling began. There was a suggestion of the organic about those sounds but they did not seem like the calls of birds, certainly the echoing quality suggested they were indoors. It was as a sudden savage rap clattered from the phone that she realised that she was listening to the sounds inside the house as the police called.

Disturbed, she pushed the phone away from her so that it slid across the table and hit the wall. She paced to and fro in the living room, trying to lose herself in the comedy show but she found herself straightening the cushions, clearing away clutter, even kicking the footrest whose broken lid shoved to one side at the slightest touch. Surprised by her sudden anger, she sat down, nursing her left foot.

Through the blinds, she could see the house opposite, its windows blank under the clouds. No matter what she did, she found herself circling back into the radius of that building to check for any flicker of life.

The phone's ringtone sparked her fear again. Cautiously, she approached the kitchen where the thing shuddered to and fro on the table. She forced herself to pick the thing up, her skin crawling; number withheld.

"Hello?"

She winced as a serious of guttural noises echoed down the line.

"V?"

The voice surprised her.

"V? Is that you? Frank here love; your mother's taken a bit ill...are you ok? I'm on me way round with her..."

When the sound of a car reached her she rose from the kitchen chair and the comforting chatter of the radio to find a stocky, red-cheeked, bald man leading her mother into the house with a blanket around her head. She was unsure whether this was on account of the cold or to shield her mother's identity. Either way he supported her into the living room where she collapsed onto the sofa in a slur of profanities.

"Don't mind me, love," Frank boomed, "I won't be in your way, I'll just sort your mother out with a cup of the hot stuff."

Normally Verity would have been incredulous at his assumption that he could stay but she was rather pleased that he wasn't rushing off. Despite his assertion that he 'wasn't there' Frank managed to be everywhere at once. However, once he had tended her mother's needs, his talk turned to the house opposite.

"You called the boys about the place across the way? Did they show?"

More questions flew at her and she found herself telling him everything.

"Let's get those photos up on your computer shall we?" he said, "I'll just help meself to a quick glass of something..."

She set up her laptop whilst Frank clanked bottles in the kitchen.

"Here you go love," he said handing her a red wine and a glass of whiskey, "best thing for nerves."

"Shame that house is still empty," he said whilst she waited for the internet connection, "I found her, you know. I was first into that house."

"Found her?"

"Yeah, the woman, the one who, you know... ended it there," he added, his jolly face adopting a serious expression.

"I didn't know... I mean, I knew she died but I didn't know..."

"Oh yeah, strung herself up in the garage. She was an artist so they're always prone, like smack-'eads. She went mad after her son was lost at sea. He was grown up like, merchant navy, but she couldn't cope. Well, you know what it's like, losing yer dad, it's had a big impact on..."

"Yes, I know mum's taken it quite hard..."

Frank continued, "okay love. Now, let's put your mind at ease."

They sat on the sofa, manipulating the photos. The image from the early hours revealed little other than mist and bleared lights.

"Malfunction, love," Frank muttered when he clicked onto the image she had taken. Before their eyes patterns of dots formed like swirling sand; vague shapes - thin and gaunt like knotted rope or twisted trees - rose and vanished like waves.

"Have you dropped it, in the bath like?" Frank said, slapping her on the knee before downing his wine.

Verity shuffled out of his reach. She wasn't convinced, the patterns had awoken within her a sense of the space in the building and of its attendant loneliness; it was like a bleak landscape was zoning in and out of apprehension.

"I'll get on the phone, see if we can have a car down here through the night, don't you worry, my love!" He said after the whiskey. He slapped the sofa where she had been, stumbled over to mum and in a drawn-out motion that Verity found agonising, leant down and planted a kiss on the grey hairs protruding from under the blanket.

"Are you ok? Should I phone a taxi?" Verity called after his stumbling figure.

"It's alright love," he called as he fumbled about the car door, "used to be in the force, all the coppers know me!"

Once he had gone, Verity sat in the living room. Mum was snoring under the blanket. Although the curtains were now drawn over the blinds, she was aware of the house across the way; aware of its blank windows and the depths beyond the nets.

Serena Havers! The name of the woman who had lived there came back to her suddenly and that she wasn't an artist, she was a fashion designer! Googling the name, she soon found a site featuring the woman's work. The influence of the 1970s was evident – flowing dresses, warm colours, sun and wave images along with a use of nets and webbing.

Intending to take an early night, she left mum on the sofa. Twenty minutes after going up, she found herself still pottering about her room. By the stark electric light, it seemed crammed and cluttered.

Unable to read, she lay awake for an indeterminate time pondering whether she should try and move her mum, wondering if she had locked the front door, listening for the reassuring noise of a car outside. Yet all of these thoughts disguised an underlying urge to throw back the covers, rush to the window and reveal herself to the blank depths of the house opposite.

***

Sleep brought dreams of a woman weaving a net before a hulking shadow. When this lurched toward her, Verity started awake, smiling in recognition.

***

She woke mum carefully with fruit juice followed by coffee. She listened to much talk of dodgy salmon fillets and offered only sympathy. Eventually, she managed to direct the talk to the house opposite.

"Frank seems nice...he was telling me about some of his police work; he told me that he found the body of the woman opposite..."

"Terrible case; it was before we moved here," mum replied from the confines of her blankets, "she was on her own, that woman..."

"...like you..." was left unsaid; Verity had learnt to treat mum's observations with detachment but the latest strategy of pausing to indicate an unspoken criticism was wearing.

"She lost her son at sea; she was never the same after that, apparently went walking for hours at a time along the beach and across the dunes – like you and your father used to do. Apparently she was planning to move, even cleared everything out of the house and then..."

A silence fell save for the distant burble of the radio.

"Men are out there, you just have to net them and start enjoying the benefits," mum went on.

"What?" Verity didn't want to be drawn into another conversation about matrimony.

"Well, look at us, we're still living off your father's money. I knew what I was doing when I snared him."

"I'm not, I'm looking after you," Verity muttered.

"Nonsense, you're not looking after me, you're hanging round..."

"I left my job," Verity responded, "they have restructured since."

"You were bloody happy to get away and you're happy to stay away now! Find someone, V. Someone who will care for you. If you won't do it for yourself, at least do it for your father. He wouldn't want you hanging round here forever."

***

As Mum was propped on the sofa with a box of chocolate mints noted for their recuperative qualities and a DVD of a Catherine Cookson adaption, Verity was about to head out for a walk when Frank arrived.

"Alright, V," he boomed, "off out?"

"Just for a breath of fresh air on the sandhills."

"Cracking day for it," he said, his voice trailing behind him as he showed himself into the lounge, "hello there gorgeous…"

Verity winced at his words.

"You enjoy your walk," he called, "I'll look after your mother."

Verity was in two minds about going. She dreaded to think what the pair of them might get up to in the house but the day was glorious – an autumnal sun hung over the Welsh hills and she needed to escape.

"Eh, I asked an old mate about that house, he had nothing to tell me but it set me thinking," Frank had wandered into the kitchen after a bottle of red, "I was one of the detectives that found her. I remember thinking it odd how high up she was, all wrapped up in the net that strangled her… I can still see the face, you know, badly corrupted. Well they didn't find a ladder or any other way that she could have got up that high… where there's a will there's a way, you know…probably clambered up in the corner, limbs all out like a crab. Well, the whole place was empty, except for the mannequins, weird that, all those models up there…" he stood, looking into the distance.

Was that what she had seen, a mannequin? Had her imagination invested it with movement? Verity questioned herself as he spoke.

Mum's voice carried down the hallway, "were you talking about the woman across the way? Well, I've got my worries about our V. - she could end up like that…"

Verity could usually take such comments in her stride but she found herself angered by the casual, dismissive nature of the words. She flicked the radio on and did the washing up to Jerry and the Pacemakers.

She returned from putting the bin out to find her interest piqued by a guest on the show, "…the place-name 'Meols' actually means sand-hills…sand-dunes are one of the marginal places, between land and sea, a kind of twilight place where it was believed that the boundaries between the worlds, such as that between the living and the dead for example, could be breached…"

The presenter's rich tones interrupted his guest, "you've found evidence that witchcraft or black magic was practiced on the Wirral coast…"

"…yes," the guest replied, "seventeenth century church records contain accusations against wives of local fishermen, claiming they would consort with the devil in the lonely dunes or on the sands at low tide. It is said that these women could summon the souls of any who died at sea by whistling like sea-birds. Once such a spirit was present it would be bound into charms carved from the wood of wrecked ships or even the bones of those washed up on the shore. These 'witch-tokens' were left in the trees or hung from stakes driven into the sand as offerings to the devil who, in exchange for souls that had not received Christian burial, would keep their loved ones safe at sea..."

"Don't know why you're listening to that rubbish, you want to be out there, making a life for yourself," mum said as she tottered into the kitchen.

"I cook for you, clean up after you, worry about you..." Verity returned. She found herself looking again at the photo of dad - she didn't feel like a fight but her mother's ingratitude had been getting worse recently.

"Well that's the point? You need to find someone who needs that from you!"

"I promised dad I would look after you!"

"Keep an eye on me you mean..."

"I can't watch you throw yourself away on booze and flings with geriatric...lotharios!"

"Well what else have I got left?" Mum said.

"Plenty of fuel in your tank and mine," Frank saw fit to interject from the living room.

***

Light fell over the ribbons of water sweeping across the shore toward the horizon. The sky was unbound here and the sea seemed insignificant by comparison but Verity knew from experience that when the tide turned the waves would rise rebelliously and seize the gaze with their constant crash and leap. Across the shoreline, gulls' cries broke into indignant squawks or shrieking ululations that cast her back across the years to her walks with dad. The plaintive yearning of those cries had seemed sweet then. As the gulls drifted passed, she glimpsed the colours of the shifting sea and changing sky concentrated in their bodies.

She walked along the pedestrianised promenade that passed along the sea-wall above the shore; a lone cyclist was shooting into the distance along the cycle path, a team of elderly ramblers approached and a solitary couple walked a dog on the beach below. Perhaps it was the space which lifted her mood, or the un-intrusive reassurance that others were near which relaxed her, allowing her to half-believe that the dead lingered in such a lonely, elemental place. It seemed perfectly reasonable that back in the days when men were risking their lives out on the waves that their loved ones would want protective powers watching over them.

Her phone vibrated in her pocket before the ring sounded. Probably mum, checking on her; no, number withheld. The poor reception was doubtless responsible for the distortion, the hint of a voice, the thumping noise; she told herself that it wasn't an echo of a police man knocking on the front door or a mannequin falling in the deserted upper story; the whistle and faint shriek drifted from the sands rather than from the handset but she hung up and stashed the phone away, less comfortable than before.

It always cheered her to cut across into the sand dunes. Dad used to point out the extent of the sea's reach in the names of the vegetation - Isle of Mann Cabbage, Purple Sea Rocket, Sand Sedge – that grew among the furred marram grass. Remembering his delight in life's ability to hold on in such places, she watched the wind stroke the grass into perpetual motion; the ethereal movement was balanced by the sharp prick of the stalk's tip and the leathery texture that greeted a trailing hand. To look long enough, was to see a muted beauty emerge in those shifting green and yellow fronds.

The dunes sifted beneath her as she climbed into view of the sunset. The westward dunes were like mountain crags silhouetted against a sky the colour of candlelight. The last rays of light reached into temporary caves gaping in the sand, picking out unseen textures, tracing patterns of shadow; it enflamed too the fallen leaves snared in the grasses, an exhilarating array of colours glowing from their husks.

She thought a tall, lean figure waved but it was the upraised limbs of an alder. It was one of a clump that circled like dancers, limbs raised and writhing like celebrants' beneath the sky. Verity found herself thinking of the old lady who had walked here over those years, trailing her sorrow like a net, before she and dad would walk here. Another waving figure became paper fluttering from bare branches.

Verity wondered whether the woman who had walked here had called out to her son, whether she had heard the voices of spirits when the birds whistled. Did she know the tales of the witch-charms, binding lost spirits so that loved ones might be kept safe? Had she ever whistled into the sunset, hoping beyond hope that her loved one might return from the depths?

From within the dunes a high, shrill whistle started followed by an answering, plaintive croon from the deepening sky above. There was a quality to those sounds that saw her release herself, willing them to gather her so that she might remain in the dark and whistle up to the vast sky until the world unwound. Everything around her became unreal – the shifting dunes, the writhing vegetation and the deepening skies were all reflections webbing an endless, glassy surface whilst she soared away, free from everything into a welcoming darkness.

***

The house was empty once she returned. A pleasing sense of detachment had fallen over her and she was able to look at the silhouette of the Havers' house without fear.

Neither Mum nor Frank had returned by the time she went to bed however her calmness persisted and she was even able to sit in the dark, looking at the blank space across the road whilst the cries of the sea birds echoed through her mind.

When she awoke, the mood had gone. Instead, there was a panicked sensed that mum was trapped. She sat up. As nightmares slipped away, a conviction lingered that mum had cried out to her from the street. She listened awhile before stumbling from bed and dragged a dressing gown around her shoulders. Her phone's light gleamed with an eerie blue from the dressing table. One missed call.

It was her mother's voice on the message. Distorted and echoing, as if in a vast space. Her mum was afraid - she was talking quietly and when the whistling began, she whimpered...it was definitely her! Verity pulled back the curtains and lifted the blinds. Was that a light inside the house or was street lighting seeping into that cavernous space?

She slipped out of her front door and crossed the moonlit road into the radius of the other house. Its dark bulk swallowed her and she paused, hesitating until her mum's voice, far and faint, cried from within.

"Mum," she called out, tentatively pushing her hand at the door.

A whining came from the place – mum, now in pain or gagging in fear! She pushed at the door, banged it with her palm and cried out. Hearing her echo through the building, she stepped back to look at the impassive glass on the first floor. The echoes were answered by a frenzied knocking within. She hurried around the side of the house, fighting through weeds to a kitchen door. A side panel of glass had broken and it was possible to kneel and clamber through into a cold, dank space. Despite the panic bubbling inside, Verity could not leave, not whilst her mother was drunkenly sprawled in the gaping blankness above and she forced herself to step over broken glass and splintered shards of wood into the gut of the building.

When her eyes adjusted, she saw an open doorway ahead; movements, furtive but audible, sounded from the gloom. Verity advanced, whispering her mum's name.

The darkness hanging around her was tangible. Its silence and stillness clung to her, taut and tense, enveloping her in its depths. She passed from the corridor into a space where a soft light fell from the windows, illuminating a staircase and the upper floor opening above her. A low whistling from the downstairs room on her right drove her toward the stairs. Her mother's voice groaned from above and a sudden, violent thumping behind sent her scurrying up.

She was mindful of the missing balustrade as several whistles, shrill and loud like birds' warning cries, broke out from below. She reached the top of the stairs where the floor-length windows lessened the darkness.

"Verity!" Her mother's voice, "Verity. V, where are you?"

Her mother – she sounded like she was outside! She could hear the sound of a car and Frank's deeper voice as she stepped into the open space where the groan shuddered once more.

"It's not mum!" The thought froze her; it was neither panic, nor terror which took hold – instead, she felt a desire to fall still and blank out of existence when a sudden understanding rose:

"I know who is here. You spent hours here, grieving for him," the words flitted through her mind, "you cried out, you cast far the net of your sorrow and something responded. You offered yourself and he was given back to you."

Whistles sounded, echoing from the bare walls and the ceiling. Despite their volume, there was a strained quality to them, as if they were transmitted over a great distance.

"...and you called him back in...you whistled as you hung, but other spirits came too, into here...you bound them here, I don't know how but they wanted me to know they are all here...I will let them all go; I will release them, all of them, back to the power to which they were bound..."

Outside, there were raised voices; within, echoes of sounds once heard on the sands – the hush of the sea, the whistles and calls of the birds, the sough of the wind – all rose and fell around her. She sensed that the house enveloped her, tightening its grip on her as the waves of sound sifted around her, guiding her towards the front windows.

Perhaps the humped shape beneath the windows was one of the mannequins, forlorn in the dust.

"...you whistled him in...you whistled others in...I will return them, to their master, their father..."

A sharp knocking on the outside of the door made her jump. A sudden, lunged bang against the upper windows halted her; it was determination that moved her again - a determination that she would open up the windows, tear down the nets and let all that was trapped there escape!

More banging and shouting sounded outside; within, the whistles floated like birds on the wing - waves of shrill cries swelling and breaking, textures of sound twisting as tangibly as sand in the wind, urging her toward the corner of the room where now the hump was shifting and rising as if caught amongst the threads of sound. She too shivered at the power of those sounds; they vibrated through her, shaking loose feelings long buried until they broke out of her and she cried out in communion with them.

The shape against the window now hung from a knotted mass at the juncture of the wall and ceiling; through the darkness she sensed that it coiled and twisted, like sand caught by a driving wind. The front door shuddered at a heavy blow as she drew closer to the corner, close enough to reach out and touch the shadow.

There was more hammering on the door and voices raised outside again as her outstretched hand passed into the corner, where it was met; she stood among the whistling darkness and then she backed toward the stairs clutching a length of netting, knotted and crusted with sand, that unravelled from the shape in the corner.

As she reached the stairs, the material fell free from the corner and slithered after her as she descended. No trace of fear or doubt disturbed the excitement that shivered within her when she slipped back out through the open window and heard voices in the street. Lights blinked from a car whose motor was running. The whistling that had clustered around her within the house fell silent and she found herself calling some reassurance to her mother as she headed into the back garden.

She was fighting her way through weeds and long grasses when the shrill sounds started up again, far and faint, as if they had fled the house to range across the night sky or the reaches of the shore; she slowed and gathering in the coils of net, felt herself expand in the wake of those sweet notes until she might have been stretched thin between them. She continued in a daze, climbing a low wall, crossing the road beyond and on to the sand-dunes.

She arrived breathless, sensing something awakening behind the emptiness of the shore and the gentle sift and sigh of the sea on the horizon. She felt it too in the breeze threading the grass, among the piping that flurried near and far and in the passive immensity of the dunes that received her. From that reserve of silence and stillness, she contemplated the trees, imagining herself weaving around their trunks, fluttering through their highest branches until she was dispersed amongst stars that fluttered like candles.

She became aware that her right hand held her phone above her head, broadcasting the message from the house; each whistle and thud filtered from the handset into the gathering winds fired her exhilaration higher. The netting meanwhile slipped from her other hand and whipped through the sand to rise among the debris that hung from the branches of a tree.

It was Frank who drove her toward that tree.

His stout form approached against the headlights of a car left in the access road below the dunes. He advanced, hand outstretched as she backed away until under the netting swaying in the wind.

"...girl...lonely...your mother...enough...me..."

His words were lost in the wind but a joyless smile, just visible through the night, made his intentions clear and when he undid his belt and rummaged in his trousers, she felt herself laughing and slipped further back. Frank tried again before her laughter halted him. A flurry of whistling broke out and sand snaked around her before lunging toward Frank. The netting drew itself around her skin and whilst Frank struggled against the sand, she yielded to the material's insistent drag.

Shadows gathered around her, looming in the branches above, skirting the trunk below and moved through the surrounding grasses. The net twisted tighter against her neck, swinging her in broad circles. She glimpsed Frank, stumbling, reaching out but her mind roved through the branches above, danced with the shadows below and whistled across the dunes until a vast, stooping shadow appeared on the hills. As it approached, excitement and recognition reignited within a distant part of her and in the moment that figure fell across her, earth, sea and sky distorted into reflections across a blank pool.

She was summoned back to her body when the constriction around her neck loosened and she found herself on the ground. The whirr of the wind through the trees was accompanied by the medley of whistles and shrieks ringing near and far. Sand was cast around her and the netting lurched in the branches above. Although the skin of her neck burnt and one eye was closed, blinded by a poking twig, the pain was ephemeral. She felt herself immersed in a space that gaped behind the world. She registered more lights in the distance and the shapes of people approaching, their voices raised and at her feet, Frank lay, glassy-eyed and motionless.

An impulse from the darkness in which she was gathered prompted her body to kneel and tear at a corner of his shirt. A low whistling sprang through her mouth and in answer, another rose from Frank's body. She drew a deep breath, drawing in the scent of the sea and sand and as she exhaled into the cloth, she offered it, a charm to the shadows.

Kevin Holton's Shopping List

Fruit (Apples, oranges, bananas)
Bread (Gluten free and regular)
Vegetables (Broccoli, Boxed salad stuff, tomatoes)
(Zucchini?)
Sweet potatoes (Not the big ones! They lose their flavor)
Cold cuts + spicy mustard, misc sandwich stuff
Meat (Chicken legs, Pork chops + Sauerkraut) (Don't get
hamburger, we have enough)
Canned tuna! Don't forget this time!
Maybe anchovies? Bush's Baked Beans too.
Medium Salsa (NOT mild)
Yogurt (Yoplait Protein, not Chobani)
Mint Jelly, natural peanut butter
Jalapeño + shredded Mexican-style cheese
Eggs

The Cadenza

Kevin Holton

This was no place for classical music, yet as I lay in the begrimed bathtub, remembering Candice telling me that four people had all slit their wrists and bled out in this same room, I couldn't help myself. I reached over the edge, dried my hand on the spare towel I was using as a bath mat, and pulled my phone from the pocket of the jeans I'd kicked off a few minutes earlier.

Overhead, the lone lightbulb flickered, all twenty watts of its measly existence on the verge of going out. That's okay. My phone was brighter, and I prefer the darkness anyway.

The Samson Motel is no place for vivacious songs like the Ode to Joy, nor is it a place suited for complex pieces those like Flight of the Bumblebee. Perhaps a rock cover of those works could've sufficed, but not today. Today was for Rachmaninov's Prelude in C Sharp Minor, a dark, wild piece that declares its power from the first heavy chords. It's a song with the purple-tinged black of midnight and a dark, dark, bottomless blue rattling every note. Sitting in that old bathroom, in the waters of my own grime, surrounded by the ghosts of lonely tenants I'd never met, listening to the grief and chaos of a beautiful song crackling through my shitty iPhone speakers, I felt a twinge of peace. My head slowly angled back, resting against the curve of the porcelain, eyes shut.

As the Prelude wound to a close, I opened up my eyes again, resigning myself to another day. I had an interview for a consulting position, or something. Regina, from the unemployment agency, wasn't entirely clear. Or maybe she was, and I hadn't listened. That was more likely.

I hooked the drain cap with my right foot as I stepped out, yanking it away so the water would rush off, carrying my filth to a water treatment plant, where it would be cleaned, freshened up a bit, and sent back through the pipes to be used again. It might one day become someone else's bathwater, or perhaps even drinking water. The next person would never know the difference.

My towel sat on the toilet's tank, where I'd placed it. The stump of my right arm glistened. No matter how much time passed, I still saw fresh, red meat for that first instant. Then the vision would fade, replace itself with the healed mass I'd been left with. I'm not sure which was worse: the wound, or the scar.

Life with one hand isn't too hard. Living with just one is the real challenge. You can learn to brush your teeth, put on clothes, shuffle cards, all sorts of crap, but those are just passing details. Nuances. Before the accident, The New Yorker had called me "a revelation," had said I "was a gift," "a sign of classical music's resurgence in the modern era."

Now, I was "a pretty good pianist, for a guy with one hand," according to people who came to hear me play. Those crowds had dwindled by the day until my half-songs ceased to be profitable.

My room had no TV, which was fine, because I had a strong urge to be violent, and nothing scratches that itch like breakable objects. The more expensive, the better. Such as it was, the previous renter had broken it. All Candice had said was that it was destroyed in "a sex-related incident." She didn't clarify if the renter tried to have sex with the TV, or was just collateral damage in someone's tempestuous carnality. I didn't ask. Most of me didn't want to know, but I admit, part of me also enjoyed the mystery.

In days past, my morning routine was to get dressed slowly, savoring my time, the flow of fabric, the steady beat of my heart, a good cup of coffee, and my beautiful apartment in New York City, which had been spacious enough to fit at least eight of the room I was currently staying in. Now, I shoved my clothing on as quickly as possible. It's hard to appreciate your body when part of it is missing.

The resentment only got worse when I shoved my 'prosthetic' on. It was just a plastic hand, an obvious fake, but people tend to freak out when they see you're an amputee. Even if they know you are one, being able to pretend otherwise makes them like you more. They appreciate the illusion.

This room also didn't have a coffee pot, so I had avail myself of the burned swill in the lobby, or go to the gas station across the street, if I was going to get a caffeine boost. Studies show that caffeine can fight depression, so I'd increased my use from one cup a day to four. I'm not sure if it works. I'm not sure if I care.

Candice told me when I checked in that I'd never want to leave, but right now, I certainly didn't want to stick around. She and I could talk later, if at all.

The locks on my door never seemed to work right, and even the 205 placard didn't hand straight, but I had nothing worth stealing. Pretty much every decent worldly possession I had left came with me as I trudged down the hall, feet practically squelching into the stains on the diamond-patterned carpet. The design made me laugh—diamonds, as if this place would ever appear valuable or elegant, with its peeling yellow wallpaper that was once white, and cracked picture frames that didn't have pictures inside.

At the end of the hall, the elevator doors opened up to a whirlwind of graffiti, more than I'd ever seen in my time in New York. In one corner sat the clamps for a security camera that was forcibly removed long ago. A clever tagger had painted a bulging, bloodshot eye in its place. That one was amusing. It almost made me smile.

Between the motel and the gas station sat a fairly deserted road, which I crossed without looking for traffic. No one honked, hit the brakes, or hit me. I made it safely across. A prostitute leaned against one of the broken pumps, eyeing me with that Oh please don't let this weirdo talk to me stare. She had fading herpes sores around her mouth and hair falling out in clumps from her meth addiction. Not exactly shy about using either— she'd buy, then start on her next hit right there in the parking lot. Poor girl couldn't have been more than twenty.

Part of me envied her for that brazen attitude. She knew what she wanted and went for it. Nothing was going to hold her back. Me? I didn't have that option anymore. My dreams were beyond my grasp. Literally.

The gas station didn't appear to sell much gas, but it did have restrooms and a small convenience store, as most appear to have these days. This was no 7-11 though. Their coffee flavors were Regular, Decaf, and House Special. Today, I figured I'd risk the Special.

"Don't do that," said a raspy voice nearby as I placed my cup under its spigot. I turned to see Reggie, a man whose time was primarily spent pacing the motel's street. He had no eyelids, and a 3-D tattoo of a snake that started on his forehead and wound all the way down and around his right arm, where the head appeared be rising out of his palm. The trick about his tattoo was that the other end had a head as well, its shadow almost touching his eyebrows, tongue out, hissing at those who dared look him in the lidless eyes. It really took your gaze off his ratty old t-shirts and worn jeans, all of which spoke to more lively days. He'd clearly lost a lot of weight and a lot of years off his life expectancy since first buying them.

"Why not, Reg?" I asked.

"They put LSD in it," he whispered. "And some other things, you know? Dark stuff. Magic. Evil magic. It'll make you crazy."

Rumor had it that he'd sliced off his eyelids as part of an occult ritual, and now was damned to see demons everywhere he went. At the very least, they were perpetually bloodshot from drying out, despite the huge bottle of saline he carried in his front jeans' pocket. Still, if he really had removed them himself, it was hard to pity the guy. The second half was definitely true though. I had demons, sure, but everything about Reggie screamed "Haunted and Hunted."

"Damn, really?" I moved my cup under the regular spout.

"Good, good, that's good. You'd be better off leaving," he said. "The longer you spend around here, the more you get stuck. Trapped. A big old tree leaves big old roots, you know? This tree, so big." He looked out the dirty window at The Samson Motel. "Big old tree."

"And big trees leave big stumps, huh?" I growled, a little angrily, holding up my right arm.

Reggie's eyes nearly popped out and ran screaming from the building. "Sorry," he mumbled, shuffling off. Scowl set in place, I shoved my cup back under the House Special spigot and poured, got my coffee, paid, and left, all while surrounded in the red haze of my anger. I felt bad, but I was always angry. It's not like I was unusually cruel to him.

When it happened, the incident that cost me my arm and my career, I was told to see a therapist. The nurses recommended a few, the doctors a few more, and the head of the concert hall even knew a name or two. Fuck that. What did any of them know—what could any psychologist know—about what I was going through? A veteran, one injured in combat, might have an idea, but as sorry as I felt for myself, I still had boundaries. I don't compare to someone like that.

Outside, a large, angry man was yelling at the prostitute by the pump. I saw this often enough, but never learned either's name. Today, the man struck the woman across the face.

"Hey," I yelled, before I could stop myself. "Cut it out."

The pimp, who has scrawny, but still more than ready to take an amputee in a fight, glanced at me. "You wanna buy her? Fifty an hour. Forty if she mouths off and you gotta set her right." He had a look in his eye like he'd beat me down in broad daylight and knew he'd get away with it. I knew he could, and would.

I shook my head.

"Then shut the fuck up, stumpy." Bastard smacked her again. I almost intervened, but the girl looked at me, shook her head, and turned away from another blow.

There's no helping those who don't want help, so I left. I kept telling myself this as a breeze ruffled the flapping fabric around my stump. I sipped my coffee, which tasted exactly like the regular blend, and got in my car.

Driving with one hand is an act that should command full attention after a life of two-handed travels, but really, it was all a blur. Shades of green, gray, and brown flitted by my windows as I passed the abandoned structures all along the road. I didn't even bother to put music on, just made the trip in silence—an act that would've unthinkable a few months earlier. Even as I neared Wyatt, the city of my next interview, there was no point in paying attention. An empty, zen mind allowed me to ignore, momentarily, the life I now led.

I didn't get the job. The interviewer—some young prick and a half wearing an oversized suit his daddy probably bought him, who spent more time wiping sweat off his acne ridden brow than looking at me—said they'd be in touch, but I saw his eyes. They kept moving down to my prosthetic. Legally, the agency has to notify employers of my handicap (I could hear her suppress laughter while saying that, because—her words, not mine—she was a sucker for puns). Courtesy, and the ADA, says telling people about my limitation is necessary, but I know that's why I wasn't getting hired. They can't deny me employment because I'm missing a hand, but they can sure as hell use that as inspiration to find another reason. Usually "lack of relevant work experience." At least this was an honest one. A concert pianist doesn't know much about managing the floor at Macy's, does he?

These streets didn't seem real anymore. I stepped out onto the sidewalk, looking up at the clouded sky, wondering why it looked like a middle school play's backdrop. The clouds were too puffy, the gray hues all wrong. Perspective is everything on a convincing set, and here, I could swear each building touched its own corner of the sky. My car barely seemed right too. It stood out from the others, looming huge, drawing my eyes, appearing dirtier, darker than those I'd parked by—hardly saying much, since they were essentially shiny cardboard cut-outs.

I drove back along more fake roads, passing increasing amounts of make-believe plants, until I arrived at the motel. My world was becoming less real by the second, but it was mine. Anger usually faded into depression. This time, the fire wouldn't die, and I was ready to burn.

The pimp was still loitering in the gas station parking lot, and he reminded me that I'd forgotten to go to the store. Not that I ate much these days. Still, the rumble in my stomach demanded attention, so I got out of my car and walked across the street. The pimp glared at me, gave a little smirk too, but I ignored him. His girl was nowhere to be found.

Food these days consisted mostly of beef jerky and trail mix, which is what I walked out with. And a banana, just for a little health boost. I won't lie and say I'd ever been a healthy eater, but hey, I tried. Back across the street, I decided to stop by the motel office and say hi to Candice. True to form, she was right there behind the counter—the only nice feature in the whole lobby, if not the building. My shoes made a grungy sucking sound as I crossed the stained tiles.

"Hi Candice," I said. "How's things?"

Most times, you don't even bother saying hi to motel staff. I'd stayed in a few before, and everyone, even the owner, is pretty much an overweight, half-drunk slob in dirty clothes, or a disenchanted drug user trying to skirt the line between self-medication and self-destruction, taking just enough of their given poison to avoid dealing with reality without frying what's left of their brain.

Candice wasn't like that, at all. She was tall, really tall, a good five inches taller than my six feet, with hair shaved on both sides of her head, leaving the top to travel down her back in a thick, waist-length braid. I could never tell if she was wearing make-up, or was just very youthful. In fact, there was no way to know how old she was. Despite running of this motel, she could've passed for 18, and a model at that. Yet, here she was.

"Hello, Mr. Selissa," she said, voice subdued, lingering on the S sounds. Her breath was a fugue of cognac and smoke that reminded me of my mother, who died when I was fifteen. Not from cancer. She walked out in front of a bus when I told her I was gay. "How are you doing?"

With the motel's proprietor, you never got the full story. Something was hidden under every word, like she was waiting for them to slip in your ears and crack your head open from the inside so she could see what your brain was up to. "I'm okay. Job interview today." I crinkled my nose, thinking of that pudge-faced pud who'd interviewed me.

"Didn't go well?" she said with a sympathetic smile, a slight shake of her head that caused the ten or so piercings in along the outer curve of her ears to dazzle the wall with rainbow refractions. Her dark skin always glowed, luminous and vibrant.

I shrugged. "Kid was an idiot. Didn't like my… condition." My fake plastic hand shimmered in the grungy lobby light.

"It's a selfish world we live in, full of small, selfish people." She reached under the desk and pulled out a bundle of envelopes. "For you. Before I forget."

"Thanks. Can you, uh…?" I held up the bag from the gas station.

"Of course," she smiled, tucking the mail in with my horrible food choices. "You've been here nearly three weeks, and you spend every evening rotting away, alone in your room. Do you know why that is, Mr. Selissa?"

I shook my head.

"Because you feel your purpose has been taken away from you, when really, you haven't even discovered it." She wagged a finger, scolding me. "You're so miserable without your music, but music is a passing pleasure. It's fleeting. Shallow. Superficial. An auditory sunset. Brilliant, perhaps, but a memory that fades even faster than those final rays of light before the darkness sets in. The only acts that last in this world are those of service, destruction, or creation. Pick one," she smiled, showing off her pearlescent teeth, "and then you'll be happy again."

My eyebrows arched, broadcasting my bemusement. "And if I don't?"

Rather than be offended by my disbelief, she seemed even more delighted by my answer. "If you don't, one will choose you."

Yeah. Sure. "Well, thanks for the pep talk. I should open these," I said, holding up my mail and food, not sure which I was referring to.

"Of course," she nodded, eyes shutting on this world, though I got the feeling they opened on another. The look on her face suggested she was seeing something too beautiful for others to comprehend—or perhaps too terrible. Maybe they were the same.

"Before I forget, someone came looking for you. I'm afraid he didn't leave his name." Her ageless face remained smiling and peaceful.

"Oh," I shrugged. "Thanks anyway."

I got on the elevator at the end of the lobby. It was further from my room, but closer to my current position. As the doors shut, Candice whispered something, but couldn't catch what.

Back in my room, I emptied the bag onto my bed, grabbed the jerky, pinned the bag to my dresser with my elbow, and tore it open. Now happily munching on dried, over salted, low quality "beef," I sat cross-legged on the bed, alternating between shoving food in my mouth and opening the letters.

The first was from the IRS, saying I owed some ungodly amount in unpaid taxes due to me having filled out my last return incorrectly. The second was a check for my piano, which I'd sold to wealthy arts patron whose name I never learned by keeping in touch with her private accountant. Salty drool oozed from my lips as I sat slack-jawed at just how much she'd agreed to pay me. According to a handwritten note sent along with the check, she "was devastated to hear what I'd suffered through," and found "the whole affair to be absolutely abhorrent." It seemed the extra money was her way of helping make sure I got back on my feet without actually having to offer to help. Charity would've been too gauche. It was a good call though. I'd take a paycheck. I wouldn't take pity.

Upon reading the send for the third letter, I was nearly floored. It was from my father's attorney. I forgot all about my snacks as I scrambled to open it, heart in my stomach, boiling in acid and salt, knowing already what it said.

Dad was dead. We didn't exactly talk anymore, but he was my last living family member. That had meant something. We were all the other had. No brothers or sisters, no cousins, no grandparents, nothing. We were the last Selissas, together in a sea of everyone else.

Now I was alone.

The letter was pretty standard, at first. Untimely death, last will and testament, etc., until it said I was to receive absolutely nothing. Apparently, he had written me out after Mom's suicide. He blamed me.

His lawyer, Johnathan, was usually very formal, but offered one personal sentiment: "It is a sincere displeasure to offer so little in the wake of his passing, and I had urged him to reconcile with you, but he refused. I am, truly, sorry for how these events have transpired."

A wise and terrible man once said it only takes a single bad day to push a good, ordinary person off the deep end. Well, my life had been a thousand bad days, back to back, all punctuated, end stopped, by the period of my stump hand, a flesh stamp rammed onto the paperwork of my life reading, "Fuck you, sonny boy!"

I started to laugh. It wasn't easy, normal laughter, no, I felt it well up from deep in me, soon tearing its way out of my mouth, wild and alive, unending even as my jaw, sides, and lungs began to burn. The pain was nice, because I knew it wouldn't cripple me. I'd come back from this, stronger than before, better than before, because it's like they always say: if you don't laugh, you cry. And I was done feeling sorry for myself.

There were jobs to do and errands to run, so I went to piss before hitting the road. That's when I found her. The girl from the gas station, who the pimp had been beating up, dead in my tub, wrists sliced open. This must've been his way of sending a message: talk shit to me, I frame you for murder. No wonder this room was known for "suicides." Must be a hotspot for him, and setting me up was just convenience.

It was easy to factor her into my plan. I emptied my bladder, took the rest of the jerky, and left.

What's a former concert pianist to do when he's unemployed, rotting away in a motel hundreds of miles from anything he would've called home? Simple. He goes shopping, gets material to build a new life. That's exactly what I did. Don't even remember driving, just waved to Candice on the way out the door, waved with the stump, wound up at a local hardware store first, then buying cutlery at Bed, Bath, and Beyond.

When examining the knives, some idiot kid came up to ask if I needed help. I showed him the ghost of my right hand and said, "I think I know what I'm doing." The sight of his face was priceless, I tell you, YouTube gold. If I'd filmed it, I would've made enough to retire, but I had other things to do.

I laughed my way to the car, holding my sides, new cutlery rustling in hard plastic containers. The sun wasn't going to set soon but the business day was over. I pulled into an abandoned school's parking lot, circled behind the building, knowing the expanse of empty brick and boarded up windows would shield me from view, then made my preparations. When finished, it was the end of the business day. Perfect timing.

Finding that pimple-faced prick from the interview wasn't exactly hard. He was strolling to his car with the condescending confidence of someone who believes Death wouldn't dare to touch him. That shit is hard to hide. It's a crescendo when the horns miss their notes, shrieking instead of harmonizing. It broadcasts, smacks you in the face, makes people hate you even if they don't know you, because assholes stink no matter how clean they claim to be. Moron didn't even hear me coming. One quick whack to the head. Crumpled, a sack of flour. No, a carton of eggs knocked from the counter, all fall and splat and oh no I'm so fucking sorry.

Soon enough, he was in my car, and I was on my way. Back at the motel, I wrapped him in a tarp and dragged him along to the back elevators, not much caring who might've seen, not that anyone was around. There weren't exactly any cameras to catch me either.

Room 205, my temporary home, welcomed me back, welcomed my hostage, didn't seem to mind as I dumped him on my bed, tied him down, gagged him, rubbed some ammonia under his nose to wake him up. When he realized what was happening, he started to cry and whine, even shit himself like a little kid. I thought this would be more fun, but damn it, he ruined it with his runny nose and loose bowels.

In an effort to avoid my room stinking up with the rotten stench of whatever he shoveled down his throat that day, I cut his clothes off, not really caring how the knives scoured his flesh. The soiled garments went in the trash, which I covered with a scent-proof trash bag before returning to the bloody man on my bed.

Kneeling by his side, I said, "Do you wanna know why you're here?" and held up the biggest knife I'd been able to buy. It looked like he was about to scream, so I put the blade in his mouth, moron was smart enough not to get loud now, gag or no. "A few months back, some journalist, I don't even remember who, posed as a gay man on Grindr. Mind you, I'm gay, and I thought he sincerely wanted to meet up for drinks. When I got stood up, I figured, who cares. Some jerk, just like the rest of them. Then that asshole outs me, and a whole bunch of other people, in his paper, because in a twenty-four-hour news cycle, invading personal privacy and publicly airing out someone's… dirty laundry," I sneered, glancing at his pale, glistening body, "is just another reporting tactic." I removed the knife from his mouth and casually dragged the tip in circles around his left eye. "Want to know why that's such a huge problem?"

He snorted a wad of snot back into his lungs and nodded.

"Because," I said, slow and measured, feeling giddiness rampage inside me, a laughter virus threatening to spew out at any given moment, "even though we have marriage equality now, spectacle sells stories, so some people like to stir up bigotry for ratings. And sometimes, when those people do that, idiot citizens get the idea to hurt other people, to 'take back their country' from the elements they don't like. Elements like me."

I shifted and pressed my stump to his face. "Feel this? The soft meat, the scarring, the protrusion of bone that should be connected to more bones, but isn't? I was a concert pianist, a good one, and one night, as I'm walking along, a guy not much older than yourself pins me to a wall, knee driving into my back so I can't move, says, and I'm quoting here, 'Queerbone queeny bitches like you ain't takin' my tax dollars for your damn agenda!' Then he tapes a bunch of small explosives to my hand—fireworks, I think—sets it to blow, and runs off. I screamed for help, then came a bang, and blood, and I screamed more, for different reasons."

The tip of my knife dug into his forehead. I twirled it like a drill, drawing a pinpoint of blood. "So, see, when you kept looking at the plastic fake I wear just so squeamish little pricks like you don't get offended, and you didn't offer me the job anyway, because you don't like amputees, it made me angry. It reminded me of the guy who blew off my hand, ruined my life, walked all over me because he was so damn sure what he was doing was right." I looked at the stump and giggled. "Well, he did do something right. Now I've only got what's left!"

This made me cackle for a minute, only stopping when he asked, "I never meant to hurt you. Please, I'm innocent, just let me go!"

I took out my phone and set it to play something heavy, Chopin, opus 10, etude 12, known as a single word: Revolutionary. It's a beautiful, dark song full of energy, the unbridled thoughts of a madman swirling amongst the moonlight, the darkness of a thunderstorm in the dead of night. It masked a new song I was writing, a sinister piece, inscribed with crimson ink, with notes containing all of the composer's darkness. Perhaps I could not play music, but nothing would stop me from writing it.

Then I brought the knife to his lips. "You're just a sack of meat, but when I'm done, you'll be a symphony."

Thirty minutes later, I'd cleaned myself up, changed my clothes, and begun my walk down the hallway to the far elevators. The dirty diamond-patterned floor seemed precious to me now, and the flickering lights hinted at a darkness I could call home. Each piece of elevator graffiti was its own masterpiece, hung for my amusement.

Down at the desk, I approached Candice. "Hello there."

"Hello, Mr. Selissa," she beamed, creating little creases around her mouth. "How are you?"

"Well, I have a little bit of an issue," I said off-handedly, smiling, nice and casual. "Seems a man and his prostitute broke into my room for some activities and things got out of hand."

"Oh, no," the proprietor said, a hand to her mouth in mock surprise. "We do have a bit of a criminal element around here. I hope this doesn't discolor your opinion of The Samson Motel. Would you like me to call the police?"

"No, no, I'm sure none of us want that kind of attention," I waved dismissively. "It's just that, the two bodies in my room, well, it looks like the girl accidentally killed her john during some rough play. Bit out his tongue, it seems. Then she killed herself. I might need a new room. To let this one air out, you know. I'm sure you understand."

Candice nodded. "I'll make sure that room is cleaned as soon as possible. I take it you're interested in staying?"

"I don't think I could've ever really left," I said, a moment of clarity breaking through my jubilation.

"You're correct," she said, confirming what I already knew. "But we could use a new security expert around here, so long as you don't mind dealing with thieves, addicts, or tenants who just won't leave."

"How would you like me to deal with them?" I said, eyebrow curving from intrigue. My mind lingered on the thrill of removing his tongue, then gagging him again to watch him drown in the blood. I'd relished every slice and stab. The more I took from him, the more whole I became—and I had a lot of healing left to do. Starting with that pimp across the street.

"You may deal with them however you'd like." Her grin hinted at the same darkness that creeped in every time the lights flickered. "Does that sound okay to you?"

She didn't have to bother me with details about the pay, lodging, or benefits. I smiled. "It's music to my ears." She shook my left hand, and all the lights went out.

David Owain Hughes' Shopping List

BreadPens
Milk: x2Chicken
Various Preserves (for breakfast items)
Pasta: 1kg sackGloves
Weed KillerA mix of spices
Pasta Bakes: x4Cereal
SheersNacho Kit
Toiletries: body and hair spray, shampoo, etc...
RopeGravy Mix
New Tooth BrushChips
Lighter FluidRed/Brown Sauce
Tea Bags/CoffeePlastic Sheeting
CheeseSalt/Pepper
BiscuitsChocolate Ice Cream
Tinned PiesBeer 4pk x2
Paracetamol *take key to be cut
Nappies: x2*Pick up photos
Frozen/Fresh Vegetables*Go to Dry Cleaners
Baby Wipes: x4Frozen Meals x5
SoupsNote Pad
Pot NoodlesMince
Duct Tape
Tinned Foods: peas, sweet corn, etc...
Sandwich Paste
Spread Cheese
Light Bulbs
Bagels
Printing Paper/Ink

Blackout

David Owain Hughes

Slamming the door shut behind her, Jennifer closed out the cold October evening, with its slanting rain and blustering wind, but not before auburn-coloured leaves managed to whistle their way into her passageway, causing her to mutter under her breath.

"Oh, well. They can stay there until the morning," she huffed, slightly out of breath. The trek from her car to her house had been somewhat challenging, due to the strength of the wind.

Before removing her shoes, she swept stands of her hair out of her face, which had been blown into a raven-coloured shock. Free from the partial blindness, she sighed, and let her bag slip from her shoulder and hit the floor, before taking off her coat and locking the front door.

The heating clicked on, just as her second heel came off and crashed to the floor by the first. Staying bent over, she pulled a thick book out of her bag, and sighed again as she made her way down the short passageway, into her living room, where a lamp was aglow next to her reading chair.

As always, she left a light or two on in the house during the winter months, hating to return to a dark house after work. It was awfully lonely these days, ever since Daniel had left her.

"Stan," she called out. "Staaaan!" she tried again. Then listened.

Not a sound crept through the house. All she could hear was the whistle of the wind outside, which reminded her of a stranger's whisper in the night. She shivered.

"Hm," she said aloud, rerouting her thoughts. "He's probably still outside roaming around, the dirty Tom!" she tittered, which came with a tremble.

Moving into the kitchen, she flicked the light switch on and made for the kettle. Popping the button down on it, Jennifer went to the fridge and drew the milk out. After placing the plastic milk bottle by a mug, which she'd stuffed with a teabag, she went to the bathroom and used the toilet.

After urinating and wiping, she heard the kettle rumble to a boil, then click off, just before she flushed. Finishing using the toilet, she went back out to the kitchen, poured her tea and made her way back into the living room.

She put the hot mug on the table next to her lamp and reading chair, along with the book she'd been holding in her other hand. It hit the table with a loud thump. Cover up – In The Dark by Richard Laymon – her all-time favourite author.

This book had managed to avoid her for quite some time, and she was shocked to see it turn up at the library where she worked this evening. It was laying on a bank of benches close to one of the book aisle, with a note attached to it saying, "Read me".

Jennifer thought nothing of it, taking it to be one of those 'travelling books' you hear of, where someone leaves a book they have finished in a public place for someone else to pick up and read. The idea being that that person will then do the same.

"Oh well, it's my book now, and on to the shelf it will go with the rest of my Laymon collection."

She shrugged her shoulders and grinned stupidly, before dropping herself down onto her chair. She couldn't even be bothered to change out of her clothes and into her PJ's. She just wanted to read, to lose herself in fiction as she did so every Friday evening.

It took an empty mug and a crick her neck for Jen to realise she was two hundred pages into the book, and the best part of four hours had slipped by. Putting the open novel on the arm of the chair, she rubbed at her eyes, picked up her mug, and headed for the kitchen.

Laymon's at his best, she thought, smiling. Parts of the story had made her skin and scalp prickle. Her blood seeming to freeze in their tubes. As she passed the phone, it rang a seemingly angry ring, as it jangled in the cradle, startling Jennifer. Wiping the grin off her face.

"Who the heck would be ringing at this hour?" she said, scanning the clock on the wall, which read eleven forty-five. "If this is another bloody Indian order, I swear to God…Hello," she said, snatching the phone up.

Nothing.

Not even the sound of breathing.

Just static and dead air.

"Hello," she tried again, pricking her ears, thinking she could hear the screeching of a cat, or a small child, which seemed a great distance away, and was lost in the static sound.

She thought her heart was going to kick its way through her chest.

The line went dead.

"Damn it," she said, trying to sounds as courageous as she could, whilst slamming the phone down.

It rang again.

Instantly.

It jarred her, and she jumped back.

Delicately pick it up again, Jen whispered down the line. "Hello…"

"Hi," the voice said in a jovial tone, which made it sound sinister, more sinister than if the person had bellowed out a grotesque laugh.

"Who…" she started, but the line went dead for the second time, and the lights to the house went failed, casting her in darkness. Throwing the receiver to one side, she screamed, and screamed harder on hearing a thump from upstairs crash in her ears.

Jennifer searched in the darkness for something, anything, which could be used to defender herself with, but found nothing.

Making her way out to the hallway, hands out in front of her for aid, her breathing came in ragged ripping sounds. "Who the hell's up there?" she yelled up the stairs. "I have a knife, you bastard. Get out. Now!"

Tears began to slide down her face when she saw a pair of glowing eyes at the top of her stairs begin to descend towards her. She whimpered, and pressed her legs together. Before she could turn and bolt for the door, Stan leaped into her arms.

"Stan!" she said, her voice somewhat lost in the blackness of the hallway. "You scared the be-jiggered out me, you daft thing."

Letting go of a pinched breath, she let a nervous laugh escape her, as she felt the roughness of the Stan's small tongue lick her cheek. "Okay. I forgive you. Now scram," she told the cat, letting it go scuttling off into the dark house.

Maybe I should go outside, or go next door? she thought. What, over some silly phone call. What if he's in the house? Who? It was only someone saying hello, for Pete's sake. The storm knocked the phone out before they could say anything else. Yes, but that voice…"Tut," she said aloud. "This is not a horror movie."

But to the front door she went, double checking the lock. Whilst buy the door, a fat rumble of thunder rolled, and rattled the door in its frame, causing Jennifer to shrike, then giggle. Then she heard it, whilst standing there in the darkness – a faint scratching on the wall to her right, as though someone or something was trying to burrow its way through to her.

It was coming from the empty house next door.

Her flesh went Arctic cool. Her insides shrivelled and hid themselves.

Thunder crash again, but she was sure she heard a drawn out whispery screech of her name penetrate the walls – "Jeeeeeennnnniferrrr…"

My mind's playing tricks, she thought. What with the storm and…Her thoughts trailed off, and her hand went to the door handle.

The scratching continued. The noise reminded Jen of ripping wallpaper. She put her ear closer to the wall, still thinking she could hear her name being hissed out.

Flickers of lightening lit the house every so often, which was followed by grumbles of thunder.

Jennifer could hear nothing, but swearing she'd heard something coming from next door. Pulling away from the wall, she shook her head, and laughed at herself. "What silly Billy I'm being. That book sure has set me on edge," she said, letting out more laughter, as she made her way out to the kitchen with the aid of her hands. "I'm sure there are some candles under the sink, maybe even a flashlight."

Making it to the cabinets in the kitchen, Jen dug a torch out of the cupboard there, and used the beam to look for candles, but found none. "The torch will do," she said. Turning around, her beam caught movement out in the hallway. She stifled her scream, turned around, and tore the butcher's knife out of the wooden block on the counter.

Shining the light again in the direction of the hall again, she could see a figure in the gloom standing close to the door, blocking her escape route. "Shit."

Rain pelted the windows behind her with a deafening sound, as the thunder and lightening persisted.

The shadowy form remained still. Unmoving. She noticed a weapon of some sort, dangling from its right hand.

"I have a mobile. I'm calling the police right now, so you better get out."

Keeping the beam trained, she noticed the intruder still did move, didn't adhere to her warning.

He knows I'm bluffing, she thought.

Raising the knife, she moved forward. "Don't make me stab you," she said with a quiver, and holding the wicked blade up to be seen.

As she edged closer, the figure moved ever so slightly, and in that moment she could see coats and umbrellas hanging off her so-called 'intruder'.

"Ha-ha!" she blurted. "It's the bloody coat stand."

Jennifer got to the couch, sat down, and decided to try to get some sleep. It had gone midnight, and there was no point in trying to read now, and not by torch light. She hadn't done that since she was child.

Grabbing the wholly blanket from off the back of the settee, which she kept there for wintery snuggles on the sofa, she lay down, feeling Stan jump up and curl between her legs. Jennifer liked to sleep downstairs every so often since Daniel had left her. She found it somewhat comforting, not having to sleep in the bed they shared.

As she drifted off to sleep to the rhythmic sound of the rain, she startled at the feel, or so she thought, of someone gentle stroking her hair. She didn't jump, instead turned the torch on, scanned the room, and found no-one.

Waking the next morning to the sound of the TV blasting and the lights all on, Jen was thrown into confusion, as she raised from the sofa. She hadn't turned anything on. No lights, no TV. So how…

Her thoughts derailed as she spied the Polaroid on her mantelpiece. Stepping up close to it, she plucked it off the wooden shelf, and saw that it was a photo of her, asleep on the sofa.

Jennifer's blood turned to ice, as she flipped the snapshot over, and read what was written on the back in rough red lines, as though a three-year-old had done it.

"To a great blackout. Let's do it again some time."

Bertram Allan Mullin's Shopping List

Almond cheese
Bananas
Basil
Carbonated water
Chicken
Coffee
Edamame
Garlic
Ginger
Green onions
Green peppers
Lettuce
Mint
Nattō
Nori
Onigiri
Onsen eggs
Peanuts
Potatoes
Shiitake mushrooms
Soba noodles
Tea
Tofu
Tomatoes
Udon noodles

Zeitgeist

Bertram Allan Mullin

Nate sat up in a jail cell bunk, terrified when he observed a sticky reddish substance on his hands. Blood?

He'd been dressed in scrubs. His bare feet hit the frosty floor. There were fuzzy slip-on shoes next to him—an embarrassing bright pink. Nate had to force them on his westerner-sized feet.

The room was too dark to see beyond a few paces. With his eyes Nate traced long steel bars barricading him from freedom. A shadowy figure jingling keys walked his way, speaking speedy Japanese. When the man stepped in close enough, Nate noticed he was half his height and twice his age. An effulgent ray of light from the entrance door's tiny window revealed a silver badge.

He's a jailer.

It was an old guard approaching with a waddle. He had to lean downward from a hunched back. Nate knew about hard workers in Japan, yet this guard had been pushing four decades on the job at least... above and beyond. Similarly, Nate wasn't the type to retire at sixty-five. That was part of the reason he'd loved the idea of moving to the land of the Rising Sun. The country was brimming with dedicated individuals like this jailer. There was still one major issue with up and moving to a foreign land when communication became a necessity.

"I don't understand you," he said to the guard. Nate had only been in Osaka for three months. He had memorized a few survival words. None of which were terms the old man was using.

When the guard opened the squeaky cell door and pointed his nightstick onward, Nate took the hint. He followed the jailer into a room where he was directed to a backbreaking metal chair. Nate's chronic leg pain from a recent bicycle accident would definitely make a few appearances tonight. The jailer handcuffed him to chains attached to a bar on the table. As he leaned downward to brace himself for the future pain from that seat, his lips almost touched the microphone to a recording device.

"What's going on here?" Some of his hair was trapped in a tar-like splotch of blood on his forehead. Not his.

"Shosho omachi kudasai," said the guard with a blame-filled undertone.

"Please tell me what happened."

"Matte. Matte," the old man shouted, clenching his truncheon. It seemingly took all of his strength to lift that stick. The jailer stormed out of the room. An annoying light shined over Nate's head; then there was the sight and smell of the horrid blood. His neckline was sticky with dark red trails. He tried to rub his pain-ridden leg. The chains on the bar imprisoned him from the relief of a good rub.

"What'd I do?" Nate pleaded toward the thick glass mirror in front of him. In his reflection he saw there were blood trails covering his face. A ring of dark red formed around one of his bright blue eyes. A vermillion smear remained underneath his narrow chin.

He didn't know how long he'd been in the room alone, but he felt like at least thirty minutes had gone by. Then forty. His wrists began to chafe. He scratched at them nervously.

The question "why" kept him busy. Nothing made sense. Nate didn't drink. The likelihood of him getting wasted and hurting someone in a fight wasn't likely. He stared at the mirror, clearly one-way glass. Someone was watching him. Not a lot he could do to change that, so he focused on remembering what he did last.

After teaching four classes of forty high school students, Nate read through his lesson plans for the week. He said some polite goodbyes he'd memorized in Japanese to his co-workers. Mostly he had said: "Osaki ni shitsurei shimasu," which he couldn't remember the meaning of. But colleagues seemed pleased when he used the phrase. It had something to do with leaving earlier than another "hard worker" and telling them sorry he or she had to work. Formality was more important to professionals in Japan than knowing the language. That's why he always wore a suit to work. He loved the structure of life there, the rules of society everyone followed.

Never a black tie with a black suit and white shirt, because that attire was for funerals only.

Funerals.

The idea crossed his mind that someone had died. All the blood and the guard's hostility—did he . . .

No. No way. Not me.

Then it hit him. After leaving his school, he didn't know what had happened. Zilch came to mind. Blank. Nate closed his eyes to think. All he saw were patterns of red nothingness spinning in circles, distracting him from a sense of sanity. He blinked for clarity. Nate remembered walking down a stairway, passing an empty hall, and seeing the exit. He'd worked so long, the auspicious moon was visible, and a big red one it was—so gigantic it appeared reachable.

"The blood moon," an aloof voice from afar had called it.

A girl's voice.

What girl?

Then everything became as fuzzy as those uncomfortable slippers of his feet.

Nate squinted, rubbed his temples. The unwelcoming walls made the room feel as if they were about to crush him. As he turned toward the mirror—yearning for a reflection of stability, Nate instead saw a young girl with pigtails staring back at him from the glass. Not just any girl, a student from his school. He knew by her uniform, the blue and gray plaid skirt and navy jacket.

"Who—"

Too fast.

Too startled.

What he saw in that millisecond: bloodstains on her hands, a ring of dark red around her eye, a vermillion smear underneath her chin, red spots on her neckline.

No face, too dark.

Nate jolted back. Had it not been for the chains connecting him to the table, his head would've met the unforgiving cement floor.

The interrogation room door swung open. Nate shook off what he thought he saw.

"Mr. Gibson," a male detective in his fifties with a shabby suit and undone tie said with a pause. The man took a second to look at Nate's shoes. "Sorry about the color and size," he said. "My partner has an odd since of justice." The detective was holding two cups. He had recently spilled a little coffee on his white button-up shirt. His red and yellow striped tie blocked most of the brown discoloration. The detective kept a folder between his elbow and ribcage.

"Please, Nate's fine."

"Mr. Gibson," the detective put one cup next to Nate, "I address friends by their given names. I will never call a murderer a friend. Just the same, my name is Mr. Nakagawa."

"Did you just call me a mur—" So hard to fathom, the whole word wouldn't come. "Please, tell me what happened. Everything's a blur."

Nakagawa sat in his chair as he sipped his coffee. A drop fell onto his shirt collar. He didn't seem to care. The detective nudged his round glasses up his nose and stared Nate down. "Don't play the idiot. You know why you are here. Five witnesses know why. The whole precinct knows why." He pushed the s in knows forcefully. It came out like a z sound. "In a few hours, what you did will be on the national news, and all of Japan will know what you did. Your family back at home, everyone will know what you did."

Nate gazed at the steam escaping his drink. "Please," tears resisted falling from their ducts, "I've never been this terrified. If this is a prank, show the cameras. I'm ready to laugh."

"No one is laughing," Nakagawa said with a judge's gavel in his a tone. "Tell me something, Mr. Gibson. You are American, correct?"

"Yes, I'm from Panama Beach City. It's in Florida."

"Etto, really? So desu ne." The detective held a breath. "Do you know that television show with crime scene investigators in Miami? My wife is up to season three. I like the main character's sun-grasses . . ."

The mispronunciation caused Nate to hold back a gulp. He was used to correcting his students when they made similar mistakes. But the wise teacher within helped him to hold back, wait.

Nakagawa continued, "He tells those funny one-liners at the beginning of each episode." The detective laughed forcefully and grabbed his potbelly. "I have been thinking of getting a pair of sun-grasses like his." Nakagawa sounded less threatening. He showed a smile. "My Engrish is not so good. Did I say grasses correctly? Sometimes my l's sound like r's." The error made him appear to be less threatening, more human, trusting. Also, Nate thought, intentional.

The detective's newfound calm tone helped Nate relax slightly—he rested his palms on the table, nowhere else to put them due to the chains keeping him so close to the metal bar. He even forgot about the pain in his leg. "My students make the same blunder. You said 'glasses' just fine. And your English skills are awesome. I don't often get to speak with people as fluent as you."

Along with his lie and covert correction, Nate gave the detective a comforting glance. All the while, he longed for the coffee centimeters beyond his reach. His big eyes poked toward the drink. His throat was dry from hours without anything to quench his pallet. Nate reached. Then he gave up. "The show you're talking about is pretty famous. I saw a few episodes. But it's cancelled now."

"Etto, wakaru. I see. Tell me, Mr. Gibson, why did you move to Japan?"

"The culture." Plus, he'd never been anywhere. Nate spent his whole life in his small beach town. He'd watch the waves and long to follow them. One time he went to Walt Disney World—same state. He craved change in his life, a new adventure.

"All foreigners say 'the culture.' What is your real reason?" The detective slurped his coffee.

Nate scooted back, as if to escape the sound of sucking. The sudden movement caused his thigh muscle to spasm. He attempted to touch where it hurt, only for the chains to prevent his mobility.

Nakagawa reached for an old beaten timepiece in his front blazer pocket and then gazed into Nate's eyes as though gauging for some kind of reaction.

"But I really did," said Nate. "When I turned thirty, I needed a change." He had just enough bendability to move his arms over his head and push his dark blond hair behind his ear. He struggled, having to move his head down to complete the task. "I've always admired the way the Japanese language looked."

"So desu ka. Nan no hanashi desu ka?"

Nate gave Detective Nakagawa a blank stare.

The detective translated. "What do you mean?"

"I watched anime as a kid, in English, with Japanese subtitles on. Of course, I didn't know what any of the squiggly lines on the screen meant." He took a moment to chuckle as if he were ten years old again. "I'd focus on them for the art aspect—the beauty of the language. Later, in college I majored in philosophy and culture." Nate flexed a grim grin. "After graduation, I thought, there's no language quite as beautiful as Japanese. Hiragana, katakana, and kanji—it's so abstract." He let the aroma of the coffee wake his senses. "I realized after graduation I could help people here by teaching English, and at the same time study the influence behind the culture I've always been fond of. So here I am. The other day, I signed up for Japanese lessons so to learn more about my passion."

"I see. You're a zeitgeist."

"A what?" Nate brushed off the familiarity of the word. Perhaps something he'd heard in school. Never mind.

Nakagawa let his lined mouth help him form a knowing gaze. "When I am not busy being a world-class detective, I fill my time as a wordsmith. I have one of those calendars that give a new term each day. Zeitgeist . . . yes, I learned this one just yesterday as it turns out. It means you enjoy the spritualty of culture."

"I guess so. Yeah. I do."

"How long have you lived in Japan, Mr. Gibson?"

"Three months."

"Tell me, Mr. Gibson, are you injuring the culture of Japan?"

"Huh? Am I what?"

"Injury. Are you injuring the culture of Japan? The culture. The reason you say you came."

"Oh, enjoying." Nate rattled his cuffs and chains as he reached for his coffee cup. "Until I woke up here, yes, I was enjoying the culture of Japan."

The detective leaned over and loosened the chains to give Nate room to move his hands.

Nate gulped down some of his hot drink. Then he rubbed the epicenter of pain that was his right leg. He took a moment to stretch his foot, wiggle his toes.

"Tell me, Mr. Gibson, how did you hurt your leg?"

"I was in an accident."

"What kind of accident?"

Nate stopped massaging himself, realizing that everything he did was another way for the detective to figure him out—as if he had something to hide. Even relieving pain gave Nakagawa inspiration to the unknown questions ahead. Nate used his only form of defense. Truth. "I fell off my bike while riding home from school last Tuesday. No big deal."

"That's not all. I want the whole story." The detective rested in that wicked chair, as comfortable as Nate would be in a hammock.

"To be honest, it's a strange story."

"Oh. I love those kinds of stories."

"Fine. A car was speeding down the road by my school. I had to turn into a ditch to avoid getting hit. My bicycle fell on me, namely my leg."

"How's that strange?"

"Most drivers in Japan, in my experience, don't drive like maniacs."

"How long have you lived in Japan, Mr. Gibson?"

"I already told you." Nate paused. His fear of being interrogated, which he'd hoped to hide was now evident from his reluctance. He noticed the detective awaited his reply. "Three months."

"So desu ka." Nakagawa took a deep breath. "Tell me, Mr. Gibson, why did you kill Mr. Seto?"

When the question came, Nate was in mid-swig. He nearly gagged on his coffee. Instead, he spit his drink onto the ground and caught his breath. "What did you say?"

"Etto. You did not hear my words." Nakagawa raised his voice, "Why did you stab Mr. Seto with a red ballu pen in his groin, chest, neck, and eye?" The detective revealed the file under his arm. Although Nate didn't understand what a ballu pen was, he knew what the detective meant when a bloody ballpoint pen within an evidence bag fell from the file onto the table. The detective dropped some photos near Nate, who remained silenced from his utter shock.

"Mr. Gibson." Nakagawa lowered his opened hand toward a photo of a forty-something-year-old dead Japanese man: his crotch region bloody, his shirt with red spatter marks, his neck hacked open, his right eye unrecognizable due to a stab wound. "Why did you murder this teacher?"

Nate tried his best to look at the photos. He couldn't bear to, especially the close-ups of the specific wounds. His hand, as though possessed, shoved the images away. The pictures, all that blood; he wanted to hurl. So Nate did. The rest of what he'd drunk hit the concrete slabs and his slippers. "Please, take those away." His throat felt like sandpaper after all of that vomiting.

"That smell." Nakagawa left the room, waving his hand in the air.

Nate gagged. When he could breathe again, a flash entered his mind. He saw his hand plunging his pen into the teacher's neck. This was more like watching a movie from the killer's point of view, however. Someone else was controlling his movements.

"Did I really—k-kill this man?" Nate observed the lines of his palms with another human being's blood now stained to his flesh. He pointlessly preened away at his hands by wiping them together, to no avail. Nate reached the zenith of his horrors when he saw the girl in the mirror once more. He reached for her uncontrollably; she reached for him. The two nearly touched. But as Nate moved his head up to see her face, the girl was gone.

The detective swatted the door open and slumped into his chair. He picked up a photo of the body to force Nate to see reality. "Why is it so hard for you to look at your handiwork? We already know he is not your first victim. Stop pretending. We know you are used to bodies. Because you like doing this to people, do you not, Mr. Gibson?"

"That's—disgusting. I've never in my life . . . I can't even kill a cockroach." True. As a kid, they'd make him scream. His brother would do the dirty work for him.

"Please, I can't look at those anymore." He closed his eyes tight so that the comfort of darkness eased away the horrors before him. Nate tried to take his mind elsewhere. Think happy thoughts. A beagle he'd left at home entered his memory. The sanctuary of darkness didn't last. Soon he saw red spinning spirals, reminding him of all that blood. He couldn't keep his eyes closed any longer.

"We know Mr. Seto is not your first victim. My partner, Mr. Ehara, cannot speak good English. I have the highest level of the detectives at the station, so we are speaking now. My partner on the other side of the mirror tells me a sixteen-year-old girl's body was discovered early yesterday morning. We already know she was your victim as well. That's how you really hurt your leg, isn't it? My partner thinks you fell while you were chasing the poor girl. He's right, isn't he, Mr. Gibson? You even confessed to injuring your leg last Tuesday. The medical examiner placed her time of death the same day."

"I wouldn't. I couldn't. Never. There was a car. I swear." He pointed his index finger at the detective. "The light on my bike broke from the fall. There's probably still glass in the ditch. Check it out yourself."

"Convenient cover story, Mr. Gibson."

"I don't know anything about a sixteen-year-old girl." Yet the teenager he kept seeing in the mirror could've been about the same age. Still, he couldn't imagine harming anyone, let alone a child. Yet, why'd he keep seeing her in his reflection?

The detective went on, in a hurry to make his point. "What my partner and I have put together is you felt like they were going to catch you sooner or later in America, so you move over to Japan. You start killing here." He took a sip of coffee and slammed the cup down, spilling a little on the table as he stared Nate down. "That is, what my partner and I have put together is you are a serial killer, Mr. Gibson."

The hair's the on Nate's arms rose. His heart thumped so hard he felt like someone was knocking on his chest. His stomach sank. He was a small man in a big world with terrifying consequences, accusations, reactions, even for actions that had nothing to do with him.

"This is our theory at least. One part I do not understand is how you spoke fluent Japanese to the teacher while you stabbed him, yet you did not know what the jailer said or what I had said."

"I can't speak Japanese."

"You admitted to watching anime with Japanese subtitles, studying the squiggly lines, right? Furthermore, you had to have picked up some of the language after three months here."

"I can say 'thank you' and 'excuse me,' days and months. A few polite phrases, that's all."

"So desu ne." The detective hesitated. "Tell me, Mr. Gibson, why did you yell what you yelled to Mr. Seto?"

"What did I yell?"

"You know already, Mr. Gibson."

"Humor me."

"Hmm?" The detective clearly didn't understand the colloquialism.

"Just tell me, please."

Detective Nakagawa clammed his fingers together and rested them on the table behind his cup. "You yelled that he raped you. He did this to you. He deserved worse than death."

"This? I don't get it."

"How do you not understand your own words?"

"I never said them. All I remember is exiting my high school and looking at the big blood moon in the sky. Then nothing." Nate bit his bottom lip. He moved to his fingernails as he thought about the dream-like memory. The reflection of the girl in the mirror stained his mind, thick as the blood on his hands.

"Etto. Then you took your red ballu pen and stabbed Mr. Seto to death. Witnesses say you tackled him."

"I don't even watch football."

"A joke, now? So, you believe murder is funny?"

"Sorry, I spoke out of angst. Please, stop. I can't hear anymore."

Nakagawa flipped open the notepad that rested in his shirt pocket. "You stabbed his genitals five times," the detective read.

Nate rubbed his leg nervously.

"You turned to his chest. That was when you jammed your ballu pen into his body. About this time was when you yelled that he'd raped you, so on and so forth. You opened his neck and ended his life when you forced your red pen into his eye, which penetlated—etto—penetrated his brain. At least no children were present to see what you had done." He twirled the notepad closed.

Nate quivered in his seat.

Nakagawa opened the file again and surreptitiously laid one more picture on the table. "And as I pointed out a moment ago, last Tuesday you savagely murdered her." Silence and observation followed from the detective.

No blood, Nate noticed. Just a teenage girl's body chilled to the bone. Skin with a bluish hue. A bruise circled the front of her neckline. This was not just any girl. Nate recognized her as both his student and no doubt the girl he'd seen in his reflection. She had not been to class. Somehow, he feared she was dead. It was a feeling he couldn't make sense of in the pit of his stomach. He would've asked someone about her, but didn't know the procedure or if it was his place. Yet, he was unknowingly mourning her these past few days.

Nate had once heard a teacher's bond to a student could be as strong as a parent's to their child. Just then, he convinced himself that that was why he saw her in the mirror when he had. Something deep down had been warning him. Nothing more.

"You choked this innocent girl after you had your way with her, didn't you, Mr. Gibson?"

Nate closed his eyes. "You're wrong. I would never hurt her. She—she—she had the brightest, most beautiful smile."

"Her name was Miyuki Yamada. Say it."

"M—Miyuki Yamada was the kindest girl in all of Japan." Nate took deep breaths from his nostrils. "Whoever did this to her deserves worse than death." He sounded angry for the first time. Nate balled his fists.

"Yes, say that again, Mr. Gibson, exactly like you said to Mr. Seto. This time, try in Japanese, directly into the recorder's speakers." Nakagawa pushed the microphone near Nate's mouth.

Nate got as close to Nakagawa as his chains would allow. He felt as if he'd lost control of his body. "You don't understand. There was no one as sweet as this girl."

"That's why you killed her. She was too good for this world. Some sick game of yours."

"I didn't murder Miyuki."

Nakagawa gave a piteous glance out of sarcasm. "Tell me, Mr. Gibson, what made this girl so special to you?"

Nate pondered over how to answer the question. He knew he was being baited. In his mind there was nothing he did wrong. Nate believed the truth would set him free. "I could never be sad around her. She'd smile with every inch of her face, cheekbones and all. Like there was no reason to ever cry.

"We had the same birthday, as it turns out. Two weeks ago. I was down about getting older. She'd turned sixteen. Miyuki led the class as they sang 'Happy Birthday' in English to me. She taught the students how to sing the song in private as a surprise for me."

"Sweet story," said the detective. "Was that when you decided to strangle her to death, or was it just the moment you knew you were going to rape her?" Nakagawa edged intimidatingly toward Nate.

"Do I get a lawyer? A phone call? A . . . something, anything?"

"This is not America, Mr. Gibson. You get what I give you. Right now all you can have is that coffee. Wakarimasu ka?" Nakagawa squinted.

"What?" Nate grabbed the cup. "I told you, Mr. Nakagawa, I don't know Japanese."

A light bulb seemed to go off in Nakagawa's mind. "A few years ago I had a similar case. This man from America swore he was innocent. He told me he blacked out. The girl he'd hurt was the most gentle, innocent mind he'd ever known."

Nate drowned his misery into his coffee. Then he rested his head onto his palms to listen closely to the detective. Nakagawa's firm tone made Nate feel like this story was more important than anything else. "This man, Mr. Steven Myer, described his victim with a word I'd never forget. This was the case that got me into being a wordsmith."

"What was the word?"

"Pulchritudinous." Nakagawa jumped out of his seat to make himself seem taller, powerful, poignant. His grim glance told Nate this tale wouldn't end well. "Mr. Myer claimed he wouldn't have ever harmed someone so beautiful. He said she deserved the longest word in the dictionary for beautiful. Like you, Mr. Myer told me his victim had the brightest smile, yada, yada, on the planet. He was nauseous when I showed him the photos of his handiwork."

"What makes you so convinced he was guilty then?"

"The witnesses, the blood all over him. While he experienced some random blackout," the detective showed air quotes, "Mr. Myer strangled his pulchritudinous girl to death. He'd been laughing the whole time too."

"Sounds like a nut job."

The detective squinted at Nate. "At least we agree on something."

"So what happened?"

Nakagawa swallowed some coffee. "Mr. Myer had me believing in him. I bought his blackout story. So I persuaded the prosecutor to go easy on him. The young man was sentenced to a few years in prison. Then we sent him back home so they could deal with him. He was banned from returning to Japan. Six months ago, Mr. Myer was back at it, but in Korea this time. That is, he had a new blackout story. The crime was only attempted murder, however. You see, some locals stopped him from killing his new beauty. It didn't end there. This time when he was locked away, he didn't get out. Someone stabbed him. That was the end of Mr. Myer."

The detective had closed the case in his mind. Nate knew he was Steven Myer 2 in Nakagawa's view. But all the detective had solved in actuality was the reason he'd become so bitter toward foreigners who were suspected of horrible crimes.

"I get it," said Nate with an astute tone. "There's nothing I can say to change your mind about me. I don't care what you think though. I'd never harm Miyuki."

"Fine," Nakagawa said mockingly. "You are telling the truth. You do not know Japanese. You did not yell at anyone in Japanese. You are innocent of all crimes." He smirked. "Then who killed Ms. Yamada? Who killed Mr. Seto? What's the expression they say in America? Etto, mull it over." The detective stormed out, slamming the door shut.

A million thoughts spun around in Nate's mind: the blood, the moon, Miyuki appearing in the mirror. Then there was the part with him not being able to control his body in that surreal memory. His body? He gazed at the mirror for answers. How?

The detective came back in with a new cup of coffee for himself and dropped into his seat. "Any new ideas? Excuses? Or are you ready to confess?"

After having a moment of clarity, Nate felt as if he'd figured something out—not everything, yet he had one answer for the detective. "You say a bunch of people saw me stab this teacher, yet I held no ill will toward him. I swear I didn't even know his name until today.

"We'd wave to each other at the school's entrance. One time, I tried to say to him in the few words I knew, 'Sugoi kinyoubi ne.' Which I thought meant roughly: 'Awesome that it's Friday, right?' I was being friendly because we both greeted the students almost every morning together. He gave me a dirty look and said he didn't speak English. I never tried to talk to him again.

"In the mornings to come, as we'd wave the kids in at the front gate ignoring each other, and then I started to notice how he'd look up girls' skirts as they walked up the incline of the hill to get to the school. Other teachers do it too, so I heard. I never cared to look—the act grossed me out. They're just kids after all. This guy, Mr. Seto, he was rude and a pervert. Still, those aren't big enough reasons to conclude he did what he did. I know he did it though."

"Did what," Nakagawa asked.

Nate pictured his brother, the psychologist of the family, and thought about how he would question the meaning behind the blood moon that Nate kept picturing. The moon, it was completely circular. Circles often represented unity, bonds. Bonds!

Why did he keep thinking of this word? And why a blood moon? It's red. At first glance the color represented love. Red roses.

And those prickly spikes along the stem, sharp enough to make you bleed . . .

Thorns!

"The color of passion."

The detective fondled his cup with impatience.

Nate continued to conquer the riddles before him. Passion overload led to . . .

Yes, the hue was quite often associated with vengeance, anger. Red rage.

A child, an innocent little girl, someone's daughter, someone pure, someone he shared a special bond with . . . murdered and disposed of as if she were garbage.

"Red: the color defined as the energy that awakens something deep within.

"Red: the kind of force that ignites strength in the most docile of spirits.

"Red, the color of blood. The blood moon." Nate drummed the table with hammer fists. "Red. Bonds. Circles."

The detective's partner on the other side of the mirror tapped the glass loudly. Nakagawa ground his teeth. "You're rambling like a crazy person."

"Everything makes sense now. Don't you see?" His world stopped spinning, and the only thing he saw was the detective's confused gaze.

"What makes sense?"

Nate knew in his veins, although he couldn't fully explain. "Mr. Seto raped and killed Miyuki Yamada."

"Yatta." Nakagawa slapped the table. "Case closed." He clapped—held his hands out and slapped them together. "Thank you for doing my job for me." He shook Nate's hand. Then the detective smacked the file. "Just admit what you did so I can finish my paperwork and go home." The detective polished his timepiece.

Nate had an epiphany. One element was missing. But what was it?

What question wasn't he asking himself? Eureka.

When he saw Miyuki in the mirror, where was his reflection?

Not there.

He'd been seeing her instead. Almost as if . . .

Then a flash of familiarity leaped through his vocal cords and out of his mouth. "Zeitgeist." He aligned every bit of the puzzle into perfect cemetery. "That's the word you called me earlier. You said it had to do with philosophy and culture."

"I said many words. Why is this one so important, Mr. Gibson?"

The last thing he saw before everything went blurry, the giant red moon, illuminated within the confines of his mind. "I knew I'd heard the word somewhere. It was in an anime."

Nakagawa exhaled an exhausted breath and pressed his thumb to his temple. His gesture suggested he was half-listening.

"The story went that during an annual blood moon, a wronged soul, a zeitgeist they called it, was allowed to come back through someone they're connected to. Any bond—like the same birthday works, and they can use the host body to get justice for whatever wrong was done to them. When the blood moon's gone, they have to move on to the afterlife, justice served or not. And it's a known fact, lots of manga and anime derives from history." He soothed his leg's irking pain, moaned a bit. "Understand? The anime I saw must've come from a true story."

Nakagawa let out a loud laugh. Cackles were heard from the other side of the mirror.

"It's not so farfetched," Nate shouted. "Japan has Obon, and that's when the dead—"

"Yes, our ancestors come back. You don't have to educate me on my own cultural traditions." The detective rolled his eyes. "Frankly, all you have is an interesting story." Nakagawa nudged his forehead. "Nothing more." He gathered his photos and the bag with a bloody red pen, and closed his file. He got up from his chair and began to leave the room. "I shall let you sit in here a little longer to consider your confession."

"I'm actually proud of her," said Nate.

That stopped the detective before he could exit. "Nan de? Why do you say that?"

"Miyuki. In the end she wouldn't be a victim. She got him for what he had done. I'm happy for her. And I don't mind going to prison for killing that child-molesting sack of crap. Even though I didn't actually kill him—I wish I had. But I didn't. It's simply not in me to take a life. My body was taken by a zeitgeist: a vengeful spirit."

"Tell your story to the judge."

Nakagawa started to close the door behind him. He must have felt slight sympathy, because he turned back. "One thing I should mention before leaving you to your thoughts." The detective gripped his timepiece. "I know you were telling the truth about not killing Ms. Yamada."

"You do?"

"Because, when you lied about my English, your eyes averted mine. Yet you were staring dead at me when you denied killing Mr. Seto and Ms. Yamada. You killed the teacher, no doubt in my mind—there are many witnesses. We have your murder weapon. The student, however, perhaps you did not kill her. I do know you believe deep in your soul that you did not hurt anyone. You believe you are not a murderer."

"So you'll get me out of here?"

"No," was all that the detective said back.

"Mr. Nakagawa, you told me you and your wife watch those CSI shows. You know if I'd touched her there would be a trace of me somewhere on her. I wouldn't have hurt a hair on her pigtails. Take my blood sample. Anything. But I know—I just know you'll find something from that Seto guy on her body if you check." He gulped. "Check. Please."

Nakagawa stared blankly. He took a sip from his coffee. Nodded. Looked at the time. "Sun's up by now." The detective closed the door.

In the mirror, Nate imagined he was facing Miyuki's reflection. He wanted to see her smile once more—have a hint of his sadness taken away by her joy. "I'm proud of you, Miyuki," was what he whispered before he closed his eyes.

Jeff C. Stevenson's Shopping List

Fat Cat Natural Balance cat food
Fresh Step cat litter
Bananas
Salad fixings
Lite Blue Cheese dressing
Activia blueberry yogurt
Chubby Hubby Ben and Jerry ice cream

The Lights Unseen

Jeff C. Stevenson

I.

"It's not so much what the house on Levey Oaks Avenue does," Carly said over the phone. "It's what it doesn't do that makes people refer to it as being 'haunted'."

"I guess I'm confused," the man who had identified himself as Jack said. He had introduced himself as one of the team members of the Alameda Paranormal Research group, or APR. He told her he had received an email that suggested his organization "look into the odd house on Levey Oaks Avenue in Oakdale." When he had replied to the message, the email bounced back. Since there was no street address given, he simply typed "relator" and "Levey Oaks Avenue" into Google and Carly Harloson's name appeared, an agent at Sotheby's Realty.

"Jack, you do this type of investigation for a living, so I'm sure you've seen all the spooky stuff that they show in the movies and those true-life ghost shows on TV, right? To me, most haunted houses and stories about them sort of remind me of bratty kids or teenagers, desperate for attention, know what I mean? They act up, are loud, boisterous, with all the cliché nonsense we see in films and read in books."

Jack had to defend his profession. "It's not all nonsense. We think that most forms of paranormal activity are the attempts by entities to communicate with us the best they can."

Carly sighed. "Right. Sorry. That came out wrong. All I meant was that from what I've been told, this house is very quiet, very subtle in its…quirks. No cold spots, no banging or rapping or scratching sounds, no apparitions, no dragging people around or touching them. None of the usual stuff. Like I said, it's what it doesn't do…"

Curious about the property they had discussed over the phone, Jack had made an appointment for late the next afternoon so they could speak in person. Carly had offered him some water after showing him to her cubical. He looked around the office. Six desks faced the front, each with a computer on top. The place was pristine, all white and very efficient-looking. But vacant, very quiet; it was just the two of them. The sun was setting, leaving a butterscotch coating of light over the immaculate space. Carly returned and they twisted off the tops of their drinks. She was attractive in a plain, Midwestern fashion; late twenties, short with thick legs, dark blond hair, an earnest, wide open face with large eyes, straightforward in conversation and appearance.

Jack was still unclear about the questionable paranormal status of the house. "We've never heard of this property," he said. "There are only two homes in Oakdale that have had confirmed activity, and APR has investigated both of them. That's why I'm so curious, especially after getting the weird email and the few things you told me over the phone. There's really nothing about it online, which is strange."

Carly shrugged. "It's not for sale—the city owns it—so there's no need to list it anywhere. And, with the help of the state, we have scrubbed the internet pretty clean as to its history and exact location."

"Why go to all that effort?"

Carly's chair squeaked as she leaned forward. "This property has an… unusual history. Everything connected to it is a bit strange; that's what's given it its reputation I suppose. You see, no one has ever claimed to own it. It's really more like an orphaned property."

Jack looked at her, puzzled.

Carly cleared her throat. "Supposedly, the house just…appeared one day."

When Jack started to say something, Carly gestured him to silence. "Let me save you some time. I'll tell you what I know, then you can ask your questions. But this is all going to sound a bit off-the-wall so bear with me…"

Jack said, "Don't worry about how it sounds; remember what I do for a living." He liked her, could see she was struggling in what she was holding back and was about to say. He smiled, encouraging her to begin.

She relaxed, appreciated his receptive attitude. "Like I was saying, it was reported that this house just appeared—poof!—out of nowhere. One day it was just a vacant lot, part of the faming community, and the next, this property—fully landscaped—was there. Local residents are quoted as saying that the place was literally birthed out of the earth; it just plowed its way upward, shaken loose by the massive earthquake."

"What earthquake?"

"The best historians could discern was that it first appeared in April of

1906, right after the San Francisco earthquake. Since no ownership was determined, the town eventually took control of the house. To tell you the truth, they really just wanted to forget about it, but they had to list it with some real estate agency, and it was passed along from firm to firm and we've had it for decades."

"So it's more than a hundred years old?" Jack asked, fascinated by what she was saying.

"No one knows exactly. Any documents that might have established its date of construction were destroyed in the earthquake."

"But there must be some chain of possession, a deed or building contract, right?"

Carly shook her head. "No, it was all lost, and they've never found a deed for the house, no one knows where it came from, or who legally owns it, or even exactly when it was built. You said you've been to Oakdale?"

Jack nodded. It was about twenty miles away.

Carly said, "Well, back in 1906, that town became a place of refuge for those who had survived the earthquake. More than 150,000 fled there for shelter. It sustained a lot of damage, but nowhere near as much as the city. Since the house is somewhat isolated, no one discovered it for several weeks. None of the surrounding area maps even indicated it existed. No insurance companies had an account for it, and no photos have ever surfaced of the house before that disaster. Even now it's considered 'camera shy'."

"Meaning?"

"I've been told that photos and videos always turn out blurry or under or overexposed. But I have no record of anyone being there since 1994; things were getting out of hand, and stories were starting to get out—"

Jack put his palms up to stop her. "Whoa! Slow down. Back up. All you've told me is this house mysteriously appeared after the San Francisco earthquake. What happened after that, what stories were getting 'out of hand'?"

Carly looked at him, wondered what he thought about her. He was a nice looking guy, early-thirties, black hair, trim, wearing a windbreaker over a black APR t-shirt. She liked his eyes, deep green, and he seemed to really listen to what she was saying. She was glad they had agreed to meet in person.

She resettled herself, took a breath, couldn't help rolling her eyes. "You're going to think it's all a bit too much, I suppose, even for what you do for a living. First off, it's not pleasant. The history is not something the city really wants people to know, so keep this to yourself; you won't find it on the internet."

He nodded soberly, very serious, then grinned.

Carly added, "You might say the house…embarrasses the town officials, I guess. That, or maybe they are just a little afraid of it."

She took a sip of her water. Jack settled back into his chair, ready to listen.

"At first, according to all I've been told and have read, the city originally tried to sell it in the early years but with no success," Carly said. "Each potential buyer had a tragic story that contributed to its disturbing legacy, so they gave up and pulled it off the market before things got too crazy with rumors."

Jack waited, noticed his heart rate was increasing as it always did when he was about to hear a ghost story. Maybe this time it would be true…

"Seventeen people have tried to purchase the house," Carly continued. "Exactly seventeen, but no one ever succeeded."

"What does that mean, tried to purchase it?"

Carly excused herself, went to another part of the office, then returned with a thick, heavy binder. She sat down, began to flip through the pages as she spoke.

"Over the years, people have applied and many of them were qualified to buy the property, but before it got to escrow, something always happened." She found what she was looking for, read from a paragraph, her finger pointing out the sections as she spoke.

"Back in 1908, Roger Hestess died of a stroke immediately after being approved for a loan. A year later, Daniel Forthright had his entire fortune wiped out after investing in a crooked investment scheme, so he was forced to withdraw his offer. A banker and his wife, the J. Roger Samuelsons, drowned in a riverboat accident in 1912, a day before he was scheduled to sign the ownership papers."

She glanced up at Jack to be certain he was following. His eyes were wide with attention.

Carly found her place, resumed narrating. "Marvin and Nancy Gilmore committed suicide together by holding hands and jumping off a cliff while hiking the Devil's Postpile in 1919, a week after their offer was accepted. The Jordon brothers, Peter and Alex, were each shot in a freak hunting accident in 1921. Earlier that morning, they had told a cousin about their intent to purchase the property. In 1933, Trisha Pearson died of a heart attack on the porch of the house immediately after telling the estate agent she'd take it."

Carly looked back up at Jack. "Those are the first six we have records of. It continued that way for many decades. It got a nickname as the Death House. Over the years, fewer and fewer offers were made."

"This is incredible! Isn't this all in the public record? I still don't understand why I've never heard about it."

"We—the estate agents—kept it as quiet as we could, for obvious reasons," Carly said, her eyes drifting to the sunset, which was now cooling just outside the far window. She turned on her desk lamp, pushed back the shadows. "Of course, it was much easier to hide this information before the internet. The town would have loved to have someone take it off their hands, but it simply became impossible to sell once it was saddled with its nickname. They even tried to bulldoze it down several times but equipment failures, attacks by insects—"

Jack's mouth was open, preparing a question.

"Wasps," she answered. "In the winter, which isn't possible, but it happened. Three times. They swarmed the crew, chased them away. During the spring and summer, it was the same thing. The insects drove the workers off. No one would get near the house after that, no matter how much was offered to get the job done, and a lot of money was on the table."

She glanced back down at the binder.

"There are eleven more incidents, the most recent occurred in 1989. Driving home after viewing the house, Eden Longmire accelerated, then steered into a tree. Her ten-year-old daughter was in the car at the time; she survived, Eden did not. In 1994, the city of Oakland Landmarks Board put an end to all the self-destruction; they took it permanently off the market. It was designated a Heritage Property, which means it received a survey rating of A or 'highest importance' due to its historical significance, which is dubious, of course since no one knows the history of the house or its origins. Anyway, it can't be touched or altered in any way, but at the same time there's no need to protect it since no one wants to go near it. It's a house that wants to be left alone, ignored or forgotten. It…pushes people away is probably the best way to say it."

Her throat dry after reading so much aloud, Carly took a swig of her water. Jack seemed to be lost in thought, his mind absorbing all she had told him.

Not wanting the conversation to end, she casually tossed out, "Oh, and the house doesn't appear to age. At all." She sat back, her smile easy and satisfied as if she had just delivered the perfect punch line to a difficult joke.

Jack took the bait. "Really?" His grinned was wide with delight, as if he was happily losing to Carly in a game of Can You Top This?

She nodded. "Over the years, relators who have been there to confirm all is well say that the windows are all intact, the floors are solid with no warping and the roof is as strong as whatever year it was installed. The paint never peels, the grass is always a perfect two inches in height and all the shrubs and landscaping are pruned to perfection." She paused. "At least, that's what I've been told since the property became my listing. I've never been there and it's rare that I get a query about the place." She added, "You're the first I've met in person."

"But people have reported things, correct?" Jack asked. "That email I got said it was an odd house. You said it was called the Death House because of what happened to the people who wanted to purchase it, but was there any paranormal activity that took place?"

"Nothing too dramatic," Carly answered. "I do know I read somewhere that the furniture doesn't like to be moved or rearranged. It was reported that chairs and others objects reposition themselves when people leave the room."

Jack nodded. "That's cool."

After a moment, she nonchalantly added, "Oh, and there is something about the dust."

He waited.

"It's a bit silly, I guess. But there's a story that a realtor back in the 1960s wrote 'Wash me' on the dining room table as a joke. The dust was apparently all over the house, almost like a preservative. When this agent and the potential buyers departed, the words were gone, the grime had returned and covered it. It was like nothing had ever been written."

She closed the binder, end of story. While she excused herself to return it, Jack was left to ponder all Carly had told him. All of his life, he had yearned for an encounter with a true supernatural force, an intelligence that could prove the existence of another realm, life after death or something even bigger. He wanted to believe in something greater than himself, but so far, he had encountered no evidence. Zilch. Things went unexplained all the time; the APR had file cabinets jammed with EVPs, blurry photos of supposedly otherworldly creatures, signed statements of personal encounters with ghosts, demons and UFOs, videos of objects apparently moving on their own, but none of the thousands of pages provided any irrefutable proof of an actual paranormal intelligence trying to communicate. So what if a chair scooted across the floor, a door slammed, a disembodied voice spoke some random phrases, or an apparition appeared as someone was falling asleep or jolted them awake from a bad dream? It was meaningless, the gibberish of a newborn.

In the company of the APR group, Jack had placed himself into hundreds of situations in hopes that whatever was out there would reveal itself to him, but it had never happened. Still, he pursued every lead, always hoping that maybe this time…

He came out of his reflections to see Carly once again seated across from him.

"Sorry," he said. "Lost in thought. Many thoughts."

She returned his smile.

He said, "Somebody sent us an email about this house, someone wants us to investigate it. So I have two questions. Can I get a key to the house, and when do you get off work? Can I take you to dinner?"

Carly said, "That's actually three questions."

II.

The entire story was fascinating. Jack was hooked. The concept of a haunted house that didn't want any attention, didn't want to be investigated was unheard of in his experience. He wanted to invite the research team with him, but thought he'd better check it out on his own first, just to confirm it really existed.

After a quick dinner, they returned to the Sotheby's office. Carly had given him a photocopied map that was clearly marked to get him to the area around Levey Oaks Avenue. Once he was there, he'd have to go, "Off map," as Carly said. "Just keep driving, keep going. Realtors have said you'll eventually find your way there." He had been pleased she had been so willing to let him see the house on his own. He had assumed she would insist on accompanying him, which he wouldn't have minded at all. But when he asked, she had recoiled as if she had smelled something foul.

"Ugh! Visit that creepy place? No way! It's bad enough I had to study up on it and represent it." He told her he'd call the next day after his visit to tell her how it went.

363

"You'd better call," she said, her eyes holding his for a moment. He moved in for the kiss.

***

Jack left the next morning at eight, was off map forty-five minutes later. It was a rural area with very few homes clustered together. Soon the distance between them became wider and wider. Carly told him to just keep driving until he came into an overgrown area where the road narrowed. It became almost impassible, like driving into a tunnel that tightened the deeper you went. Overhead, the broad tree branches joined hands to block out the sun while shrubs and wild grass edged out his peripheral vision. The area was growing thicker and darker and heavier the further he went. By 9:30, he sensed he was lost, but recalled what Carly had said: "Just keep driving, keep going," so he did. He smiled, thinking of her.

A little before ten, he approached an abrupt turn in the road. He rotated the steering wheel to the right, braked gently. The tires crunched over the rocky, uneven terrain. The car crept through the shadowy, vine-strewn area. The green canopy of dull light surrounded him as he slowed the car. He finally stopped in front of a row of random-sized shrubs. The vaguely human silhouettes were creepy in the dusky morning shade, standing before him like guards or lookouts. The road appeared to end at the wall of foliage.

Just keep driving, keep going.

He turned off the car, climbed out, his tennis shoes slipping a bit over the pebbly, crooked road. He steadied himself against the side of the Honda as he made his way toward the shrubs. Keep going... He pushed through the greeneries, which were two or three deep and six to fifteen feet in height. Their roots went deep, their tough, muscular branches resisted him but he fought against them until he stumbled into a clearing.

Before him was the house.

Carpenter gothic in style, it gleamed harshly in the morning sunshine, freshly scrubbed and polished. After the deep emerald gloom he had driven and struggled through, he had to shield his eyes from the fresh burst of sunlight. It was like he was in a whole new world of light and clarity, transported from Kansas to Oz.

A perfectly manicured lawn led grandly to the front door with all the importance of a red carpet. The house was painted pale gray with a white trim, red roof, and he counted six sharp gables that rose up to scratch against the clear blue sky. He remembered what Carly had said about the home, that it had been birthed out of the earth, had plowed its way upward. The half-dozen pointed canopies that arched over each second-floor window resembled garden trowels; he could imagine them digging their way out from the soil, pulling the house to the surface, settling it on the land. The image was fascinating and horrifying; it lingered in his mind.

Each of the six windows resembled arched eyebrows while the small front porch opened out like a mouth in mid-yawn. A flowerbed in full bloom exhibited a palate of gold, yellow and purple. Hedges stood tall and proud, nuzzling the sides of the house. A lavish forest enfolded the rear of the estate, with mighty tree branches peeking out from behind the property. It was all breath taking in its flawlessness.

"Picture perfect," Jack said. He pulled out his phone, clicked off several shots, glanced at them. He grinned. Each image was terribly overexposed, unreadable white-yellow squares. Just like Carly had said. He used the edit feature to change the contrast, but it was no use. He spent another few minutes taking fresh photos and video but without success.

"Picture perfect, but camera shy," he said, pocketing his phone, marveling at the experience he was having. Maybe this time…

Jack stood there, taking it all in, trying to hold in his mind what the camera was unable to capture. The view confirmed all that Carly had said, from its isolation to its ideal appearance. It was hard to believe that the place was more than one hundred years old. It would take a small team of landscapers to maintain the property to this level of perfection, but there was no access for any crews or equipment, nor were there any tire marks indicating anyone had been in the location recently.

The grass was thick and plush as he tromped across it, the sky was summer blue with a shy breeze; it was a perfect day. He was excited, like he was in a roller coaster starting up a hill. He stepped on the front porch, the sound bold, hollow, announcing that a trespasser was on the land. He reached into his pocket but suddenly wondered why there would even be the need for a key? Carly had given him one of course; it was the first time their hands had touched. Somehow he knew the door would not be locked. The paint on the porch looked new, like it had been recently applied. He sniffed, but didn't smell the fresh oily scent. There was no dirt or dust or evidence that anyone had ever been there. The brass doorknob glittered dully, even in the shade of the porch. He grasped it. It felt cool and secure in his hand, like holding a weapon. It turned easily. With a soft click, he stepped into the house.

***

In front of him to the left a staircase disappeared into the shadows, a dim hallway tucked under it. A dining room with a doorway leading to the kitchen was on his right. The floors gleamed with polish. The air had no scent to it, but it wasn't stale, didn't have the shut-in smell a never-visited home would harbor.

He listened. Not a sound. A large window to his right allowed for a square patch of sunlight. He turned and opened the front door wider, allowing in more of the golden rays. The door wavered a bit in the breeze. Jack dragged over one of the dining room chairs to prop it open.

He noticed then how sparsely furnished the house was. The dining room had a table with eight chairs. That was all. He looked into the kitchen. A stove and refrigerator from decades ago were in place, appeared to be brand new, but there were no kitchen cabinets, no sink, no decorations. The items were in place as if to simply indicate what the various room were to be used for, a casual blueprint.

Although the house appeared to be spotless, he noticed on the dining
room tabletop a thin layer of dust, very fine particles that had a very subtle shimmer to them. He leaned in closer. Each speck had a glow or sheen. He couldn't help himself. With his finger, he wrote Wash Me!

Jack first noticed the reverberation as soon as he put his foot on the step leading to the second floor. A very low-grade hum, like a washing machine at work in the basement. It was a busy, whirring activity, continuous with no modulation. He lifted his shoe but the sound continued.

He shrugged, clumped up the stairs, his tennis shoes shushing a bit on the freshly polished wood. There were no pictures on the walls, nothing at all to personalize the space. The banister had a coat of dust on it. It collected in his hand as he worked his way up. There was a faint oily texture to it that was tingling, pleasant to his skin. On the second floor a bedroom was to his left, a bathroom just in front, and a larger bedroom on the right. Each of the rooms had a bed; the larger one also had a dresser. The bathroom had a toilet propped against the wall. Like the rooms downstairs, these were furnished with just the basics.

Jack rubbed his hands together, freeing them from the dust. He paused, straining to hear. He heard the distant, machine-like drone, but that was all. It was peculiar that the house seemed so much larger when viewed from the outside. Hadn't he seen six windows on the second floor? He looked again in the bedrooms, each of which had one window facing the front of the house. The bathroom had no window. Shouldn't there be several more rooms; he wished the photos from outside had turned out so he could view them, confirm the window count.

Jack pulled out his iPhone, took a picture of the small bedroom. He glanced at the image, expecting it to be over or under exposed.

He almost dropped the phone.

The photograph was sharp and clear, and almost entirely covered and obscured by hundreds of circular orbs that resembled particles of dust. They hadn't been there when he'd clicked the image. He had never seen so many spheres in one picture. His heart pounding with excitement, he immediately took more snapshots of the bedroom. It was as if an image of the Milky Way, with its billions of stars, had been overlaid on the photos he was taking. He hurried into the bathroom and master bedroom. The images all came back infested with countless balls of transparent light.

Astonished, he stood in the master bedroom, thumbing through the pictures on his phone, astounded at what he was seeing. He knew he was looking at what were referred to as ghost or spirit orbs, often thought to be the souls of people. No one knew of their origins, purpose or why they appeared in photographs but rarely to the naked eye. Their presence had been reported and verified for decades, but it was unclear why they chose to manifest themselves.

He zoomed in on the images, enlarging the orbs. He knew that close to eighty percent of them were nothing more than air born contaminates, dust particles that were thin, wispy, mostly transparent, often with a ring around them. The difference between them was that real spirit orbs were much more opaque and appeared to be three-dimensional. They were bright and sometimes had tiny, comet-like tails.

What he was looking at was the real thing. Hundreds, maybe thousands of orbs in each photo. Even as he stared at the camera, reviewing the pictures, he knew they were actually swarming around him, unseen, at that very moment. He marveled at the idea. Maybe this time…

He decided to video both rooms since there was so much apparent activity. He slowly panned the master bedroom seeing nothing out of the ordinary. But when he checked what he had recorded, a mass of orbs were fluttering and twisting about the room. They were so densely packed together it was like a fog had settled in.

He had just started to film the smaller bedroom when from downstairs he heard a sharp, loud bang. Startled, he wondered if Carly had shown up to surprise him.

Jack kept recording, called out "Hello?" as he started carefully down the stairs, looking through the lens to find his way. When the entry area came into view, the front door was closed. He panned left to locate where the chair was that he had used to prop open the door. Moving into the dining room, he saw that it was back where he had taken it from, tucked securely under the table.

He pushed in closer until he saw the tabletop. The words he had etched in the dust were gone. The table was once again covered with a thin layer of undisturbed tiny particles.

"Incredible," he whispered into the silent house. He stopped recording, looked around the room, his smile so wide it began to hurt. The house had not disappointed him after all. He replayed the video, shaking his head in wonder at what he had captured; never before had he ever seen such amazing footage. Usually there were only a handful of orbs in photos or caught on video. Nothing like this. He forwarded the content to his home computer, emailed his team that they needed to schedule a meeting as soon as possible, then hurried out of the house.

He couldn't help but do a little shimmy dance of delight once he was out on the vast front yard, couldn't wait to share the amazing news with Carly. Jack turned, blew a kiss at the house. "Thank you!" he shouted. "See you soon!"

***

He left a message on Carly's voice mail, hoped he had reached her number. The greeting was one of those robots.

During the drive home, he had wondered about the house, begun to form a hypothesis. It was just conjecture, but if one house rose up after a natural disaster, wouldn't it be possible that there would be others? Could a cataclysmic event somehow spawn these homes, create them or "birth them" as Carly had said? And what if each dwelling was filled with orbs?

He began researching to support his theory, knowing it would be tough, slow going since these homes—or whatever they were—didn't seem to want to be discovered or explored. He limited his search to natural disasters that occurred in the United State beginning in 1900.

Two hours later, he slumped in his chair, his back stiff and tense, eyes smarting from staring so intently at the screen. But he was encouraged, knew he was on to something. He had come across a few websites that were also curious about what were being called "hidden houses." Each site had little information, just a few paragraphs, with no comments, no links, no photos. Most hadn't been active for years.

"They post their theory, and then they are never heard from again,"

Jack mumbled, then gave out an exaggerated, ghoulish laugh. He stood, stretched, opened a beer, drank half of it, grabbed some chips, then settled down to eat and drink. He checked his phone, surprised Carly hadn't returned his call.

Four hours later, he had printed out a pile of material. His thoughts were buzzing with information. He was wired and when it was time to sleep, he took an Ambien in hopes it would quiet his mind, pull him into dreamland. He needed to give his brain a rest. If what he suspected was true, if he could prove it—and he thought he could—then the next meeting of the Alameda Paranormal Research group would be a very lively one.

III.

It was Tuesday evening and Jack and several team members from the APR group had finished their Taco Bell dinners and were noisily slurping the dregs of their soft drinks.

Alexandra, who had founded the group, finished her soda with relish. "So, tell us everything." Her hair was yellow and green and she wore black-framed glasses because she thought they contrasted nicely with her pale skin. She was always thirty pounds overweight, but insisted on wearing tight fitting black t-shirts because she believed they helped to make her look slimmer.

Jack had printouts of his research, which he handed out as he spoke.

"The first thing I was able to confirm is that this house did not exist before the San Francisco earthquake of 1906. I was able to locate maps before that disaster but there was no evidence any structure was on that location."

"So it just appeared sometime that year?" Alexandra asked.

"Specifically, it was 'discovered' the end of April 1906," Jack said. "The earthquake occurred the morning of April 18. Hundreds of thousands of people fled to the town of Oakdale after the city was destroyed, and that's where the house was found."

"Who discovered it?" Chad asked. He headed up IT for the small group and managed their website. Small, skinny and with what he himself admitted was a freakishly overlarge head, he resembled Woody Allen but without the glasses; he wore contacts and enjoyed changing the colors based on the season.

Jack shuffled through the papers until he came to a printout from the San Francisco Chronicle. He read from the two-inch column article:

Mystery House Baffles Neighbors

The discovery of a two-story home on Levey

Oaks Avenue has perplexed neighbors in the rural farm area of Oakdale. Mr. William Bixabee says the home wasn't there a week ago. "I get to town a couple times a month and frequently pass this way," he said, referring to Levey Oaks Avenue, "so I was shocked to see this brand new house, plus the fancy yard, all in place like it had been here for years. Where did it come from?"

Photos of the home were taken but the negatives were damaged in development. As this issue went to press, there was no indication that the home was occupied. The city is understandably overwhelmed with caring for the influx of those souls who miraculously survived the Great Earthquake, so locating the owners of this home and solving its "mystery" is not a priority at the time.

Jack cleared his throat; this was where it was going to get interesting. "So, as you know, I visited this house, and I'll share with you the results of the activity I experienced."

"You experienced something?" Chad asked, his mouth open in mock surprise.

Jack smiled, "Yes. I really think I did."

"Finally," Alexandra said dryly under her breath. "Thank God."

"But I also came away with a theory about this house and its connection with the San Francisco earthquake. I think there may be many more of these properties, these hidden homes that spring up after massive destruction occurs. What I'm thinking is that each horrible event—an earthquake or tornado—is actually used as sort of a distraction, allowing these houses to go unnoticed for a bit, giving them time to take root..."

"'Take root?'" Alexandra asked.

Jack nodded. "I have a hunch that these properties are like…newborns and they need a couple days to 'settle' before they reach their full potential."

People began murmuring, kidding him, making little jokes, hands were raised. "Wait!" Jack said, laughing. "Hear me out, see what you think. I'm still trying to figure it out myself. Let me show you what I've found."

He handed out a sheet of paper with a heading at the top that read Natural Disasters in the United States since 1900.

"You can see that there have been more than nine hundred catastrophes from 1900 to today. Storms, floods, earthquakes, heat waves, tropical cyclones, tornadoes, wildfires, droughts, cold waves, and so on.

"The deadliest natural disaster in North American history was the Texas hurricane in Galveston. Up to eight thousand people were thought to have been killed when the cyclone hit on September 8, 1900. But get this, two weeks later, on September 22, you can see the tiny item in the Galveston Daily News that reads, 'Where did a pristine home come from in the midst of such destruction?' The article stated that no photo was available. Members of the Central Relief Committee discovered the house while they were out looking for structures that had managed to withstand the storm. Of course, all the property records were lost in the storm so no ownership information was available."

Jack waited until they caught up with him, then had them turn the pages as he recounted the 1910 avalanche in Wellington, Washington that killed almost a hundred;

the Great Lakes Storm of 1913 where 250 perished, and the Dayton, Ohio flood of the same year that swept away almost four hundred. In each case, a mysterious, fully formed and well-landscaped home appeared days or weeks after the catastrophe. Court records were always lost or destroyed as a result of the disaster, and the city eventually took possession of the property since no one claimed ownership.

"These are not what we would typically consider to be haunted houses," Jack finished. "Other than the bizarre way in which they suddenly materialize, they otherwise seem to want be left alone, remain in solitude to do what they were created to do."

"Which is?" Chad asked.

"I'll show you."

Jack had uploaded his photos into the large computer monitor that was positioned at the head of the table. He showed the first picture. Everyone gasped. He switched to the next image, then the next, and the next, then switched to the video. The orbs swirled and danced about the monitor like high-speed fireflies encased in glass crystals. The video lasted more than two minutes and for those gathered in the research office, it was like the Fourth of July and they were gazing at the unfolding of an astonishing fireworks display.

Once the computer screen was dark, Jack said, "I think that these houses are generating or giving birth somehow to thousands, if not millions, of orbs. I believe there is a connection between each catastrophe and the emergence of one of these properties."

"Wait. What?" Alexandra said. Her chair rattled loudly. "You think these houses are used as sort of…paranormal safe houses or….incubators?"

"Yes! Yes! Exactly!" Jack said, pointing at her.

Everyone began to talk at the same time, with new theories and explanations and questions tossed about and shouted down. It was like a conversation traffic jam, much noise and gesturing as they tried to build on the foundation Jack had presented to them. When everyone had finally taken a moment to ponder the significance of what they were discussing, the room hushed. Chad asked, "So, what do we do with this theory of yours, Jack?"

"Well, like any revelation or discovered knowledge, we explore it," Jack said. "We study it, test it, stretch it to the breaking point to ensure it's valid. That's why I presented all of this to you. We're a research team, so let's research. Let's visit the house on Levey Oaks Avenue."

IV.

Jack didn't bother contacting Carly for permission to visit the property again. She hadn't returned the calls or texts he'd sent her and he was hurt and angry. His last message had been one of concern, hoping she was all right, but he told himself they had only just met and if she didn't want to see him again, that was her choice.

The house, however, that was not something he was going to let go of so easily. Jack considered it his discovery, his passion, and saw no need to involve Carly. He, Alexandra and Chad left Saturday morning. They arrived at the house by noon. This time, Jack hadn't hesitated at all as the car made its way through the overgrowth or under the familiar canopy of dark green foliage. He thought of Carly only once, remembering her refrain of Just keep driving, keep going. He ignored the weird, isolated hush that greeted them after they had walked a bit, then pushed hard through the guardsman-like shrubs.

The house gleamed, inviting, friendly, welcoming. Alexandra and Chad held back, didn't immediately begin the short hike up to the front porch. Jack turned to them.

"What?" he asked, puffing slightly. They each were carrying heavy backpacks loaded with investigative equipment. The sun was warm overhead.

"It's…just a lot to take in," Chad finally said. He looked dazed.

Alexandra nodded. She could only stare at the house. "After all you said and showed us, it's a bit overwhelming to see it in person."

Jack looked at the property with fresh eyes. Yes, it was overwhelming, a lot to take in. He was excited to be there, desired to be inside as soon as possible, wanted to feel that peculiar hum that had vibrated through his body. "Come on," he said eagerly, proceeding forward, not looking back this time. They were foolish if they didn't follow. Everything they had ever wanted or wondered about was now in front of them, theirs for the taking.

It was all oddly familiar: The hollow tromp of his footsteps on the porch as he strode over the floorboards, the fresh oily scent of paint…. So it had been freshly touched up! He stood there. Waiting. He could almost feel the house was embracing him, welcoming him back. The distant vibration under his feet began, huge machinery hard at work somewhere deep in the house. It constantly murmured, rattling gently against the floorboards, a lullaby of industry. The recognizable hum returned, too, like a long-forgotten song suddenly known again. Last time, he hadn't felt or heard anything until he was inside the house on the second floor. Now the pulsations and sounds were reaching out to him sooner than expected, drawing him in.

The doorknob seemed to reach for his right hand, met him halfway, a shake of friendship, of renewed acquaintance. He felt the door gently pull him into the house.

Jack turned to close the door, but it was already shut. Where were

Alexandra and Chad? He peered out of the dining room window but the sun's glare against the sparkling clean glass made it impossible to see outside. Oh well, their loss.

The tabletop was alive with the sparkling dust. He was quickly mesmerized as he watched it sway in motion like it was the waves of the ocean seen from hundreds of feet above. It glittered, shifted about in constant movement. Wash me, he suddenly thought, desiring to plunge in like a diver seeks his spot in the waters below. His hand reached forward. He felt the surface of the table. It was firm, but also cushiony; there was a give to it. He pushed down, felt his shoulders sag. He stumbled forward and was immediately elbow deep in the swirling mass. He treaded further, now up to his waist in the churning tide.

Wash me.

Jack closed his eyes, waited. For this visit, he felt more like a guest than an investigator. So he would wait for the host to determine where to go, when to venture further into the residence. The constant vibration and drone lulled him to a relaxed state. He stood there in the dining room, swaying in the push and pull of the whirlpool of particles, all them joining, thickening in the marvelous current.

A yawn stretched his jaw out long and hard. He desired to lie down. It seemed perfectly appropriate to rest on one of the upstairs beds.

Before that thought had fully formed, Jack was astonished to find himself at the top of the stairs. Was I transported? he wondered. He rocked forward as if in sudden stop. He stumbled. And where was his backpack? The weight was gone from his shoulders; he felt so much lighter. The hallway was dark, the bedroom doors both closed. Which one to enter, he pondered.

The low-grade rumble was louder on the second floor. Was the cause of the noise coming from one of the rooms? He went left, toward the smaller of the two bedrooms. His arms and legs felt buoyant. They tingled and throbbed in time with the steady murmur that permeated the house. He pitched himself toward the door, his ear bobbing against the smooth paneled wood. No, that wasn't the source of the sound, not that room…

He moved back lightly, feeling almost weightless. Now, like a dancer, he pirouetted soundlessly to the master bedroom door. He pressed his ear to it, listened. It rattled against its frame as it tried to contain whatever amazing activity was behind it. He had to get in there. It was Christmas morning and this was a present with Jack's name on it.

"Jack?" Downstairs, Alexandra called out.

Footsteps approaching, scuffling on the wood. Jack backed away into the darker recess of the landing to give them room once they arrived, didn't want them to come into contact with him. He saw Alexandra, growing larger as she approached, filling up the space. Behind her, Chad loomed into view, his body mass expanding, clogging up the area. Jack pressed himself backward until he was squeezed in tight against the master bedroom door.

"I thought I heard him up here," Alexandra said.

"Jack, where are you?" Chad's voice, so loud, so unforgiving in the tight confines where the three of them found themselves.

"Are there lights anywhere?"

Jack heard their hands reaching across the walls, dirtying them as they sought out a switch.

"There's a door here," Alexandra said, pushing it open. Light spilled into the landing. She called out Jack's name again.

"Let's try the other one," Chad said. His face lunged so close that Jack cried out in surprise, a mere flicker of a sound that barely registered. Jack found himself in the master bedroom where he immediately swooped back to the far corner. He hovered above the four-poster bed; the brass columns were shimmering and luminous, aglow as they reflected the afternoon sun.

He blinked. What was he seeing? And then suddenly the room was ablaze with clarity and movement. Astounded, it was as if he had just been given sight without ever realizing he was blind. The orbs dashed and veered and jostled as they all magnificently and effortlessly made room for one another. They never collided, always holding their own in their timeless space. It was a glorious choreography.

He joined in, desired to be lost in their midst, at one with them. Instead, they aligned behind him, trailed him as he soared, plunged, spun and illuminated his way throughout the master bedroom. Giddy with the swiftness, the light, the awareness that he was their leader, Jack delightedly led the mass of spheres. He was astounded at their brilliance—at his brilliance—never having expected any of it to be so exhilarating. He marveled at their speed and dexterity and their sheer volume. Countless, countless, was the only notion he could summon.

And then, within the span of a thought, as one they abruptly left the room. Behind them for an instant echoed the calling voices of Alexandra and Chad, but then they were silent, swallowed up in the distance. Over his shoulder, Jack stole a glance as he and the others soared. The gleaming house was now so very small, a square, a sparkling speck, then it vanished, lost in the woods, covered, hidden, and then gone.

He ascended and they sped along with him. Then, with no signal or warning, they abruptly dispersed like slivers of light gone into every possible direction, shattered pieces of the finest crystal.

***

Inside the house, Alexandra and Chad gave up calling for Jack, distracted by the strange, sparkling dust that clung to them. There was a faint oily texture to it that was tingling and pleasant to their skin.

***

Seven miles away, animals had already begun to vocalize their dread, aware and unsettled that the ground was preparing to split in a profound schism. Spitfire rain had collected, about to fall, scorching and scarring the earth.

The lights unseen gathered, prepared to be a part of it all.

***

381

    She crossed APR off her list. She typed in the address for the Supernatural Research Society in San Antonio, Texas. She composed an email on her alias postmaster account: "Look into the odd house on West Laurel Avenue in the town of Kirby."
    Carly hit send.

-For Pete and Dale Levey

Sebastian Crow's Shopping List

BananasPaper Towels
ApplesGreek Yoghurt
Potatoes (Red)Butter (Unsalted)
CeleryDiet Soda
Cucumbers6 pack Newcastle Beer
Sweet OnionsToilet Paper
Garlic
Bell Peppers (red and green)
Boneless chicken breasts
Italian sausage
Spaghetti
2 cans Italian Tomato Paste
Pork Chops
Pork Ribs
Barbecue Sauce
6 Frozen Dinners
Wheat Bread
Smoked Ham
Oven Roasted Turkey Breast
Banana Nut Oatmeal
Strawberry Pop-Tarts
Pepper Jack Cheese
8 Cans of Green Beans
8 Cans of Corn
Chicken Noodle Soup
Tomato Soup
Dog Food
Cat Food
Skim Milk
Eggs

Carnaval Macabro

Sebastian Crow

In a season of plague, I fled north along the coast, escaping the stifling claustrophobia of the city and rancid perfume of its filthy, diseased air. So, on a crisp, golden Spring morning I found myself driving along the coast highway in my eco-friendly hybrid sedan, my mind and body at ease for the first time in years, taking in the small, postcard perfect villages that peppered the eastern seaboard and dining on local cuisine at quaint mom and pop diners. At night, I stayed in pleasant, bucolic bed and breakfasts, sat on porch in the cool evening air and watched the fishing boats sail into the sun while sea gulls glided across the sky, swooping and diving the water like acrobatic kites.

Wherever I stopped for food or gas, I chatted with the locals about the area, getting a feel for the area and its people. I was continuously amazed by their unassuming kindness. Again and again, I was assured there was no place nicer to live than Buxton, no better town than Reeveston, nowhere would you find more decent folk than in Murphysburg. After the stench of the city, with its streets filled with the odor of putrescence from the forgotten dead, the freshness of the country was invigorating. There was no sign of the plague ravaging the city, as if the air itself repelled the disease.

As I sipped my coffee on the porch of "The Reeveston Inn," breathing in the petrichor rising from the dewy, morning grass I contemplated never returning to the haven of madness that was the city. It really was no place to live anymore.

After all, I was quite well off enough now to live wherever I chose. The royalties from my last two novels were sufficient to provide a comfortable lifestyle anyplace I decided to set down roots. It wasn't like I needed to live in the city. I had no family, and with few friends to speak of, there was little holding me to the city. All that was left was to arrange the sale of my apartment and a call to my agent, Sal would suffice in that department. He could take care of arranging the transfer of my meager belongings, mostly boxes of books, a computer and a few portable drives, to whatever address I requested.

Now as I continued my voyage north, I began to observe my surroundings with an eye towards settling down but approaching the border, the towns came further and further apart. The countryside became more populated with isolated farms and lone homesteads. Acres of coniferous forests arose on the west while rocky cliffs and pebbled beaches gave way on the east. Darkness stole quickly upon these northern lands and when the trees cast their long shadows over the gloomy road I pulled into a small roadside motel and took a room for the night.

Following a quick supper at the attached diner, I settled into my cramped room, stomach full and contented, happy to find the room clean and tidy despite its diminutive size. I eschewed the television and instead pored over the roadside atlas I had picked up at a gas station earlier in my journey and contemplated which of the towns I had passed through would be my new home. I really wanted someplace that was quiet, close to the ocean and would excite my imagination. I thought I might turn from the horror novels that had made me reasonably wealthy and turn instead to writing "The Great American Novel," whatever that might be. I saw myself becoming a J.D. Salinger type recluse, cordoned off from the world at large while quietly pursuing the life of a lonely scholar.

Finally, I decided upon Buxton. It was a hundred miles south of my present location, but I remembered how picturesque the village was with its quiet, town common and pleasant elm lined streets. The houses facing the ocean were all trim, well-maintained Cape Cod's, probably over-priced but surely not in the same range as what I paid for my apartment in the city. I pulled my laptop out of my bag, connected to the motel Wi-Fi and did a search for Buxton real estate. I clicked on the website of a local real estate agent and began browsing properties. Several hours later I had narrowed it down to three properties; all reasonably priced cottages that either faced the ocean or were a quick walk away to the lovely town beach. Rubbing my eyes, I vowed to call the real estate agent first thing in the morning and arrange tours of the properties. I only hoped I would have no problem selling my apartment. Luckily, I lived in a desirable, upscale neighborhood, even if the apartment itself was nothing fancy. I figured I would have no problem unloading it at a fair price.

Over the phone the next morning, my agent was quick to agree to my requests and immediately set about putting the apartment on the market. The sum he quoted, even minus his commission, was still sufficient to cover the cost of the cottages I was considering with a little cash left over for any improvements that might be needed. After hanging up, I called the Buxton real estate agent.

A woman, answering to the name Ellen Ripley picked up the phone. She spoke with a pleasant, nasal New England drawl. She assured me both properties were still on the market. Would Thursday, say around one o'clock be acceptable?

I replied this was fine and hung up feeling excited and a little sick to my stomach. The move I was about to undertake was the biggest of my life. Not since I gave up my position as junior editor at a large publishing house in order to devote myself entirely to my writing had I embarked on anything so grand. Luckily, that had worked out well enough.

Still, this left me with several days to kill and the thought of just hanging around the motel until Thursday was simply inconceivable.

Grabbing up my laptop I did a search for local sites of interest, looking for something to keep me entertained and my mind occupied.

There were a few historical monuments; the home of a famous Revolutionary War general, a 17th century courthouse that had been the site of a notorious series of witchcraft trials that oversaw the executions of half a dozen "witches" and a museum dedicated to local artists. But nothing really attracted my interest and I had decided upon a hike down to the ocean when I caught an odd, Wiki listing about a local town and its unique May Day celebrations. The town, Carnavale, was home to its very own amusement park called Clowne Towne. The park operated full time between April and October but in the last week of April leading up to May 1st, the town really went all out with parades, concerts and special events. Citizens dressed as clowns and other circus folk flooded the streets, entertaining the tourists that flocked the town in droves for the festivities. According to the Wiki post, Carnavale was also the year-round home of a number of sideshow freaks who were employed as performers at Clowne Towne.

A quick web search and I was delighted to find Carnavale was a mere thirty miles to the north. Although, it was located on a small island just off the coast, ferries made regular trips between the island and the mainland. If I left now I could just make the next ferry. Packing up my few clothes, personal sundries and computer I was on the road in a matter of minutes.

The trip took me longer than I expected, as I became lost several times, once requiring me to backtrack some ten miles before finding the right turn. The road to Carnavale was down a winding, hazardous two-lane highway filled with hairpin curves and steep hills. I found it strange that such a popular tourist destination wasn't better marked, but once on the proper road finding the ferry was relatively easy. Even from the shore I could see the large Ferris wheel on the island, like a giant flying saucer lying on its side, turning on its axle.

I paid to park my car on a small lot as the island's website had informed me everything was within walking distance and with the crowded, festival streets, a car was more trouble than it was worth. I bought a ticket for the ferry and shared the short ride with several other excited tourists.

The sound of carnival rides, carousel music and laughter could be heard even before the ferry docked. The odor of cotton candy and popcorn wafted over the air, mixing with the scent of sea and salt.

The little village of Carnavale, where I disembarked, did not appear all that different from any other secluded, coastal community. It was perhaps a bit larger than average, but per the brochure I nabbed at the island's visitor center, the year-round population was only 235 souls. Everyone else were just visitors, here to visit the amusement park, which by the sounds coming from down the boardwalk was already doing healthy business.

The island itself, again referring to the brochure, was approximately twelve miles long and five miles at its widest. The village itself only occupied a few square miles and the rest of the island's length was devoted to Clowne Towne and a line of shops and diners. The remainer of the island was forest, although there were some spectacular views on the eastern part of the island looking out across The Atlantic.

I had scarcely stepped foot out of the visitor's center when I saw my first clowns. There were two of them, one dressed in a silver and blue costume that ballooned around him until he looked like a giant, under inflated ball, his face was painted a traditional white but his sanguinary grin was sharp and pointed, a bit like a jack-o-lantern's, and with the gaudy orange hair, it lent him a rather sinister appearance. The other clown was dressed in hobo rags with grease paint around the eyes and a wide, friendly smile painted around his lips. Both were handing out balloons to the new arrivals.

The hobo clown waddled up to me, his comical walk exaggerated by his size 24 shoes. With a flourish, he pulled several uninflated balloons from the hip pocket of his ragged jacket, then amused me by quickly inflating the balloons and twisting them into a passable imitation of a wiener dog. With a deep bow, he offered me the balloon dog. Laughing, I accepted, returning his bow with one of my own.

"You know of any hotels or inns that might have a room available?" I asked the lachrymose clown.

The clown glanced upwards, tapping his chin with one, white gloved finger as if deep in thought. Then he lifted his finger and eyebrows in a eureka moment. He patted his jacket and turned out his pants as he searched his pockets, spilling out scarves, water pistols, balloons and stuffed animals before presenting me with a small card that read; Barstow Inn, 3604 Harlequin Street. Fine Wines and Dining, Rooms; Let By The Night or The Week.

I thanked the clown and headed off in the direction he pointed me, making my way through the bustling crowd. There were a astonishing number of clowns roaming the streets, I nearly walked into one jolly fellow whizzing by on a unicycle and juggling three bowling pins. The near accident was entirely my fault as I was so absorbed in the antics of another clown crossing the middle of the street on a pair of stilts that must have raised him ten feet above the ground. The clown on the unicycle did a little expert bob and turn to avoid a most embarrassing collision and went on his merry way, juggling and peddling as if such incidents were routine. I imagine for him they were.

I had expected most of the entertainers to be confined to the park itself but, referring to the brochure, I discovered most were themselves tourists. During the Festival of Harlequin, visitors were encouraged to dress up to better assure their experience was the most enjoyable. There were even several shops along the promenade that rented costumes and sold make-up kits and props for would be clowns and acrobats. I found the idea of dressing up amusing but since I was only going to be here for one night, I decided against renting a costume, opting instead to purchase a t-shirt from a street vendor that showed a clown standing astride an elephant. Above the clown, the caption read "Festival of Harlequin" and under the picture it read, "Carnavale City."

Locating the Barstow Inn was just a matter of following Harlequin Street and keeping an eye on the building numbers. There really wasn't much to the town of Carnavale, a half dozen or so streets, the primary being Harlequin Street which ran the length of the town and consisted mainly of souvenir shops, motels, a few bars and a diner called The Joker's Wild. The Barstow Inn was near the end of the street, close to Clowne Towne itself. I hoped they would have a room left, the proximity to the amusement park would be a convenience.

The Inn itself was lodged in between the diner and a tee-shirt shop. I found myself immediately charmed by the rustic looking building which reminded me of an Old West style saloon or one of those vintage hotels from black and white noir films. Stepping into the cool, air conditioned lobby was like stepping back into another age. Several Queen Anne sofas, their leather cracked and worn, faced each other in the center of the room. On the left was a stained-glass entry way that led into a dining room which a sign informed me was called "The Mahogany Diner." Against the right wall was a long lobby desk made of rich, red wood. Behind the desk, letter box cubicles covered the back wall. Near an enormous, antiquated cash register, a bored, balding gentleman sat perched on a stool reading a paperback and smoking a cigarette. Otherwise, the place seemed empty. Probably, everyone was down to the amusement park, I thought.

I approached the clerk who barely glanced up from his book when I entered. "Wouldn't happen to have any rooms available perchance?" I inquired.

The clerk lowered his book to his generous belly and looked at me over his thick, horn-rimmed glasses. "Ayup, got two left. One ona second floor and another on the third."

I nodded, relieved. "Which do you recommend?"

"Well, the third floor has a nice view of the ocean and the park but it's hotter than blue blazes, air's on the fritz. Room on the second is a lot cooler but it looks out over the street. It can get a mite noisy, especially when the parades start."

I thought for a moment before deciding on the third floor room. I didn't mind the heat and I liked the idea of being able to look out at the amusement park.

The clerk fished around under the counter until he found an ancient, leather bound ledger. He plopped the heavy volume onto the desk, opened it near the middle and asked me to fill in my name and address. My eyes were drawn to his hands, which were so deformed they resembled claws more than hands.

One of the freaks, I thought, then felt ashamed of myself. It was obvious he suffered from ectrodactyly, a birth defect that caused the fingers and toes to be fused together. Although, the condition was rare, it hardly made him freak. And he appeared to be quite deft and agile despite the defect.

"Haven't seen one of these in forever? I thought everyone kept their records on computers these days."

"Service is too spotty out here and I like do things the old-fashioned way." The clerk scratched his whiskery face and stubbed out his cigarette in a chipped, ceramic ashtray overflowing with butts.

While I filled in my name and address, the clerk reached behind him, grabbed a key out of one of the mail cubicles and placed it on the table in front of me. I picked the key up by its red, plastic keychain.

"How many nights?" The clerk asked.

"Just one for now."

The clerk went to the antique cash register and rang me up. "That'll be ninety-four dollars even. Will this be cash or charge?"

I handed him my Visa and waited while he ran the card through an ancient phone charge machine.

"What time does your restaurant open?" I asked, realizing that I had not eaten anything except a couple hotel donuts since this morning.

"Not until four. My wife, Linda runs the dining room but she only does dinner from four until eight, then it becomes a bar until closing. But if you're hungry, you can call down from your room and order something from the kitchen and they'll deliver. This time of day it's a limited menu, but the sammitches are pretty good."

"So this your place?"

"Ayup, John Barstow, third generation owner of the Barstow Inn. My granddaddy was one of the first to settle on the island year round. He was the lobster boy with the Original Sorum and Dark Traveling Carnival, until Mr. Sorum and Mr. Dark tired of the road and came up with the idea of one year-round spot for the carnival. They turned the whole island over to the attraction and gave my grands the concession for the Inn. We Barstow's been here ever since."

I reached across the lobby desk and offered Barstow my hand before I could stop myself. "Pleased to meet you, Mr. Barstow. My name is Jeff Cones."

Barstow took my hand in his claw-like mitts and gave it a shake. "And pleased to meet you to Mr. Cones.

And don't fret about staring. We island freaks are used to it. Hell, it's what we get paid for and the money is damned good."

A flush crept up my face as I nodded and thanked him. I felt the burn in my cheeks as I climbed the steps all the way to the third floor.

The room was hot, but not as unpleasant as I feared. Once I opened the window and let the breeze from the ocean circulate in the room, it was barely warm at all.

I was quite pleased with the room itself. It was a good size for such a small inn. The walls were finished in French country wallpaper above white wainscoting and I was delighted to find, upon closer inspection, the wallpaper continued the festival theme with images of clowns and magicians and acrobats. Against one wall was a heavy, oak armoire where I deposited my overnight bag, computer and a light jacket I had brought along in case it became too cool, as it was apt to do in the evening this far north. Beside the armoire was a door that led to a small, prim bathroom. Against the interior wall was a desk with a microwave and coffeepot, beside the coffeepot was a basket of complimentary coffee, filters and plastic-wear. The only other furniture was the queen bed that took up much of the room, a comfortable looking wingback chair and a nightstand with an old-fashioned rotary phone. I was a bit surprised to find there was no television. Not that I minded, I had a few books in my bag as well as my computer for entertainment if I became bored, but considering the noxious presence the glass demon had insinuated into our lives I found the lack somewhat odd.

I sat down on the bed and gave a little bounce. The springs squeaked a bit, but the bed felt soft and sturdy. Thinking I'd just stretch my bones out for a few minutes before calling down to the kitchen for a sandwich, I kicked off my shoes and lay down, feeling the warm press of the mattress against my tired muscles. Then there was only darkness… and dreams.

Laughter - shrill, hysterical. The frenetic hurdy-gurdy jazz beat of a calliope, far and wee.

I woke from my nap, disorientated in the dark, unfamiliar room. For several frightening moments, I was not sure where I was or how I came to be here. Then as the fog lifted my brain, I remembered 'Carnavale, off the coast, Barstow Inn.'

I lay quietly in the bed, listening to the sound of the amusement park drift through my window. Now that I was fully awake, I could hear the calliope quite clearly. A melancholic nostalgia settled over my heart, memories of the county fairs of my youth filled my mind with a wistful ache that was unlike my usual self. It occurred to me that I should remain in bed, forgo the lure of the calliope, the enticing scents of a thousand savory delicacies; cotton candy, popcorn, hot dogs and elephant ears.

Stay in bed, I warned myself, stay in bed, then in the morning, check out and catch the first ferry back to the mainland. Let those old memories remain, pure and true. Surely, the reality of the amusement park would be a let down from the fantasies of youth. Nothing is ever as good as you remember.

But in the end, the siren song of the calliope was too much to resist. So, I climbed out of bed and plodded on bare feet across the carpeted floor to the opened window, my naked body cool from the night air.

Outside my window, a pair of clowns, mouths painted in malevolent, sanguinary grins, beckoned me to join them, waggling their fat, red-gloved fingers in slow motion. In the distance, the Ferris wheel spun round and round its axis like a wheel of fortune casting lots for wayward souls. The gaudy, flashing neon lights of the amusement park reflecting off the surface of the water. The carnival looked alive tonight. I could see throngs of tourists and locals jamming the beach and boardwalk, jostling in line for ride on The Zipper and The Tilt-a-Whirl. Most of the loudest shrieks seemed to be coming from the direction of the roller coaster, its cars careening recklessly fast through 360 degree loops and sphincter puckering descents. The spook house also looked to be drawing long lines. It had been years since I'd been in one. I had fond memories of the cheap plastic skeletons and papier-mâché monsters, the cheesy jump scares like a bad B-movie. I thought how nice it would be to go down to the boardwalk, climb into one of the small, uncomfortable box cars with the sticky, vinyl seats and lose myself in the funhouse's nostalgic darkness.

I looked back at the clowns who were doing cartwheels and handstands to regain my attention. I smiled and waved as they clapped and danced, doing a little, comical jig for my amusement. I could hear their voices inside my head, crooning, "Come on down, Jeffrey. The fun never stops at the carnival." "We love you Jeffrey, you're one of us."

Yes, this could be fun. I snatched my jacket from the oak wardrobe and headed out the door. The lobby was mostly empty. A white-faced mime in a striped shirt, red trousers and suspenders pretended to be trapped in a box while a bearded young lady lounged on the lobby sofa, applauding and encouraging the mime. I gave a quick wave to Mr. Barstow who was leaning over the long, lobby desk reading a newspaper, one hand on a coffee stained mug, a lit cigarette smoldering in the ashtray beside him.

"Good evening, Mr. Cones."

"Evening, Mr. Barstow. Just headed to check out the carnival."

He glanced towards the window and took a sip from his mug. "It's a nice night for it. Just be careful around the clowns. They nibble."

I assured him I would indeed take care around the clowns, no need for any nasty bites, then I was outside, feeling the crisp, sweet autumn air, surrounded by the carnival sounds that were so muted inside the hotel. With an expectant air and feeling of childlike excitement, I followed the smells and sounds towards the boardwalk. Keeping my word to beware the clowns who looked much larger and more ominous in the dark, I hastily made my way along the sidewalk, hugging the side of the buildings that lined the street all the way to the entrance of Clowne Towne.

An outlandish, automated, ten-foot high electronic clown greeted visitors, turning side to side and up and down, one huge, gloved hand pointing up towards an arched sign that proclaimed the park's name in garish, neon lettering.

Here the alluring smells of fried foods was much stronger, setting my mouth to slaver like Pavlov's mutt. But underneath all those delicious odors lay another scent, this one sour and rancid - like meat that had been left too long in the sun.

At the gate, a chunky girl with frizzled, auburn hair, wearing a pink tube top that showed off her ample bosom and too much makeup sat reading a celebrity magazine, her jaw gnawing at a wad of bubblegum with all the intensity of a cow chewing its cud. I passed her a couple bills, which disappeared in a flash into the cash drawer before she stamped my hand and waved me through.

The crowd was a lively bunch, mostly tourists from the southlands, thirty-somethings with young children in tow and middle-aged couples on holiday. A smattering of teenagers, who might have been locals, loitered in front of a penny arcade, smoking cigarettes and sucking on Icee's. Here in the park proper, I could no longer make out the calliope. Instead, current and old pop tunes blared from an overhead speaker system, competing with the pitchmen calling from their game booths; Heya, heya feeling lucky? Step right up, two spins for a dollar, five for two, pitch 'til you win, never a loser, win your best girl a Kewpie.

I didn't have a best girl and no use for a kewpie, what I really wanted was to take a ride on that Ferris wheel. So, I passed up the games but did stop to watch a muscular youth try his strength at Ring the Bell. In an interesting twist to the familiar game, instead of a puck or ball rising to ring the bell, what appeared to be a genuine human skull had been substituted. The boy swung the heavy mallet like a railroad worker driving a spike, delivering a winning strike that sent the skull screaming to the top where the bell not only rang but glass eyes hidden inside the skull rolled over in comical fashion while steam shot out its side. For his effort, the boy was awarded a large, stuffed elephant which he passed off to his doe-eyed companion - his best girl, I presumed - who hugged the stuffed toy and jumped up and down in excitement. His buddies slapped him on the back and punched him in the arm in typical adolescent bravado. I scooted away before the huge, tank sized operator could turn his pitch to me. I doubt if I could even have lifted the mallet with my scrawny arms. Besides I really wanted to get to the Ferris wheel. Something inside was insisting it was imperative I ride to the top of that wheel.

Outside an especially large tent, a tophatted huckster in coat and tails with a silver, handlebar moustache assured the crowd of men gathered around, that inside was the most amazing thing they would ever lay their eyes upon. A bright, painted billboard read Rosalito the Snake Woman and featured a scantily clad woman with a snake wrapped around her torso. Burlesque show, I thought and moved on. My attention so focused on my destination that not even the lure of naked flesh could dissuade me.

Outside the spook house which had so fascinated me earlier, the sinister clown whom I had seen this afternoon upon my arrival was performing a juggling act with a trio of severed human heads.

Got too close, I thought and shook my head. The clowns nibble.

I moved along quickly before my head became part of the act. A car screamed out of the spook house, but the car's occupant days of screaming were over. The couple still sat side by side, their hands clutching the safety bar, their faces contorted forever in their deathmasks.

All around me scenes of murder and mayhem were taking place, children giggled as their parents were flayed alive in front of them by a demonic looking clown dressed in harlequin black and white, a pair of hircine horns growing from his forehead. Young lovers strolled past, smiling and holding hands, their faces smeared in blood as they feasted on raw bits of human flesh, offering each other bites of the tastiest morsels. A creature with the head and body of a man scurried by on eight human legs erupting from its side. Its face, painted in clown greasepaint, twisted in a hungry leer.

Blood ran down the boardwalk like a sticky river, making footing slick and treacherous. I saw more than one person go down and not get up as clowns descended on the unfortunate, tearing and ripping with their savage, razor teeth. I slowed my pace to avoid suffering the same fate, but strangely none of the clowns paid any particular attention to me. In fact, they went out of their way to be courteous towards me and gave way as I passed.

After what seemed hours, I came to the Ferris Wheel. I was not surprised to find Mr. Barstow at the gate waiting for me. He was dressed in a rumpled white shirt and black vest. He had painted a grin on his face with silver greasepaint.

"Ah, Mr. Cones, come for a spin on the old wheel?"

"Nothing I would enjoy more." I reached for my wallet only to stopped by Barstow.

"Your money's no good here. Your one of us."

Then, for the first time since I stepped on the island, I became frightened. The skin of my dream-world peeled back and I was abruptly aware of reality unfolding around me. I heard the screams of those being slaughtered, the gnawing and chewing of the clowns that feasted. Madness was my only escape from the horror that I was witnessing.

Barstow looked at me curiously, his eyes squinting in concern. "Mr. Cones, are you okay?"

My eyes dashed wildly from one scene of extreme violence to another. Was that really a little girl ripping the flesh from a baby? Am I really seeing that old man bash his wife's head in with his cane?

"Mr. Cones? Sir, are you ready for your ride?"

Suddenly, everything came back into focus. "Of course, excuse me Mr. Barstow. Must be this ocean air. Been away in the city you know?"

Barstow threw back his head and laughed, "And the plague? It ripens the population?"

"Thousands are dead. Soon it will be ready for harvesting. The Old Ones will feed well."

"Excellent, excellent. You have done well for yourself."

'Thank you. I live only to serve. But it is strange. Away from the island, the memory seems to suffer. Have I been gone long? I don't remember"

Mr. Barstow led me to car, as I climbed inside, he locked the safety bar. "Why no. You were only gone as long as needed."

I nodded. "When I get to the top, just leave me there for a bit. I love the view from the top."

"Don't I always?" He replied, before releasing the brake.

Up, up I went, flying towards the moon which had risen full and white overhead. The ground became small and wee, the people like ants, scampering about in fun and panic. As he promised, Barstow stopped the ride just as I reached the top.

I looked out over the vast emptiness of the ocean. In the distance, I could see Mr. Sorum and Mr. Dark, their gargantuan bodies rising from the sea, wading towards their island for their feeding. It was good to be home.

S.E. Rise's Shopping List

French dip Au Ju
Buns
Ketchup
Shrimp
Italian Roast Beef
Provolone
Pads and pons
Socks
Coffee creamer
Soda
Gatorade
Smokes
Velcro
Saran Wrap
Sharpening Stone

Daddy, I'm So Hungry

S.E. Rise

I need to eat. There is no use resisting them if I end up starving to death.

Smoked Salmon is on the menu today. I have plenty of that. During the summer the water is thick with them, it's one of the reasons we bought this place. I also have a butchered bear in the freezer, a moose and two sides of beef. There's only so much gamey meat you can eat before you need some nice fat rib eye, or burgers...

Where is a good place to begin? Here's a good spot...

This house is bigger than I had initially wanted.

Last summer I had a trail cut and installed electricity in the house. Now, I am smart enough to know I am not an electrician. That being said, I also know that during the winter the lines need to be cleared every week or they get too heavy with the snow. The cold makes them brittle and the weight of the snow can snap the line. It's a cold, thankless job but somebody needed to do it.

"Hey, buddy, want to give me a hand clearing the lines?" I asked Brandon, my fourteen-year-old son. I wasn't really surprised when he turned down the invitation. It sucks when they get to the point where they don't really want to do things with you. To be fair, he still liked hanging out with his old man from time to time. Just growing up, is all. And, it was the weekend. Nobody likes to work on the weekend, especially not on their Christmas Break.

Before I can respond with a "That's okay, Bran," my eleven year old baby girl volunteers to go with me instead.

"That's okay, Kelly, honey," I say. "It's twenty three below out today and there is a bit of a wind. I don't want that pretty little face of yours getting frostbite." She grimaced a bit, thinking to object before rethinking the idea. The idea of frost bite was serious, not something to be taken lightly.

"Yeah…maybe I'll pass this time," she said.

"Oh, but it's okay if I freeze my face off? The babes like my face," Brandon cut in, his fourteen-year-old priorities obvious to see. His sister saw, and was quick with her chiding response.

"Babes like Mindy Calhoun? Or maybe Gertrude McGuire, I hear she has the hots for you?" she taunted, as only a little sister can. I waited for the war to begin. I happened to know what Gertrude McGuire looks like and it ain't pretty. In fact, Gertrude was downright fugly.

"Shut it…" was all Bran said. I could hear the man he was becoming surface, and so did Kelly. She didn't back down though. She never did.

"You shut it… Dog." She said it with such snotty venom that it made me double take at her. Her expression told that she knew she had gone too far.

"What?" Brandon responded, voice low with challenge.

I didn't need this to escalate. It was bad enough that we were all cooped up inside and weren't going out anytime soon.

"Sorry… It's what I say to the idiot boys at school. They are so stupid sometimes…" Kelly began to apologize, but not for long. "…but you do smell like one," she finished, chortling as she took off down the hall towards her bedroom. She stopped and ran back to give me a hug and kiss. That's my girl.

"He kind of does smell like a dog doesn't he?" I whispered to her, conspiratorially. She covered her laugh and then fanned the air in front of her nose.

"And farts." She started to giggle again.

"Heard that!" My son said and I could hear the humor in his voice. "I do kind of smell like dog farts…Wait, what the…?"

All three of us burst out laughing.

It felt good. It felt like it was supposed to feel. Like a loving family.

"Tell Mom, if she gets up, that I went to clear the lines." I said and felt a moment of apprehension. I wondered if she was suffering from depression.

No, she's just tired and the lack of sunlight is draining her. Not everyone adjusts well to the eighteen or more hours of darkness up here. That much darkness messes with your biological clock. Your circadian sleep cycle. Mess with that for too long and it has been known to drive people bat-shit crazy.

I was one of the few people to be immune to that. I have always only ever slept for a total of four hours a night. Not sure why, it's just who I am. At least, all my adult life.

It took an hour and a half to clear half a mile of line, what with a couple of minor quakes swaying the lines;

not an unusual occurrence up here on top of the Ring of Fire.

Darkness had come by the time I finished and I knew the kids would be worried. The snow machine cut through the new snow on the road as I rounded the corner to home. The sight of the house caused a sudden dread to sink into place.

The house lay still and cold. The totality of the darkness sent a shiver through me and set me on edge. "Son of a bitch." I said to the crisp air, my breath showing in the light of the full moon, words frozen in a plume of crystal moisture. I guess I broke the damn line anyway. Or maybe the quake did it.

Something feel wrong.

Weird.

Why?

I should be seeing flashlights. Where are the flashlights?

They're probably worried sick. Two tremors, the power out and Dad's not home yet. Hell yeah, they're going to be worried!

Shit, I need to get the generator up and running.

Why wasn't the generator up and running? The implications hit me. At 20 degrees below, the house would freeze solid within an hour; water pipes… wife… children.

How long has the power been out?

Then I saw the long black crack that ran diagonally across the frozen river. The ground too had been split apart. It led up the bank and across part of the lawn.

Oh shit! The goddamn ice broke.

"Kids!" I shouted, "hey is everybody okay?"

Fuck. No. Fuck.

"Where are you? This isn't funny." My voice sounded alone.

How long did I search? I don't know. Hours, days, months… I searched and I screamed and I cried. I raged at the world. Pain, fear and dread exist outside time. When you are experiencing such emotions it can be as an eternity.

They were simply gone. I ran through every scenario, every possibility. Gone…how could they just be gone?

I even checked the big fucking crack in the yard and river ice.

And now…The dismal, dismal now.

God help me, I found them.

They only come with the darkness. Unfortunately, during the winter it's almost always dark and cold up here.

The Yankee candle is burning low and they crouch in expectation just at the edge of its light. Waiting. Waiting for it to flicker out, because they can't come into the light.

It's so damn cold in here. With each breath, a plume of frozen moisture escapes me—my heat ever escaping, bringing me closer to death.

"You should go to sleep," says the five-year-old version of Kelly. She is sitting crisscross-apple-sauce with her hands clasped together in her lap. Such a good little kindergartener.

Her voice is high like most children at that age. I could almost believe it was her…if not for the six-year-old version of her sitting right alongside.

"Yeah, Dad. Just go to sleep already. We don't care if you snore." The ten year old version of Brandon says. He laughs from the shadows. The other versions of him begin laughing as well and the discordant cacophony pushes at the edges of my sanity.

It hasn't escaped me that their laughs aren't accompanied by a moisture plume of breath.

"Stop it. You're just keeping him awake." The eight-year-old version of my son says. The black ribbons slither and undulate across the perfect skin of his face.

Those black, slippery, eel-like ribbons… It's the only thing I can compare them to. Long, thin and flat. I hate the fucking things. Outside my ring of light the shadows shine and ripple. I can see the thick fat ones further back, in the shadows. Making more copies of my children.

When they are eating or reproducing, or whatever they are doing, they are like long, shiny, black eggplants. But I never forget that they are quick. I don't know what they are or how they're doing it. But I make no mistake…they are not my children.

They are parasites. They grow, they are born, and they taunt me with my love for them.

"Daddy, we're hungry," a nine-year-old version of my daughter says, and begins to devour a two-year-old version of my son.

They must be memories because they wear the clothes I remember them in.

"You're not my children," I whisper, and all of them turn their heads in my direction. They either don't like that statement or they don't like the sound of my voice.

Or maybe they do like sound of my voice.

A few of the little ones start crying when I say that and it makes me want to jam sharpened pencils into my ears.

"We are the only children you have left," says the ten-year-old Bran. The pain of those words tears through me and I want to lash out at him, but before I can a voice chimes in from the other side.

"Come on, Dad, give your children hugs and kisses." Kelly laughs and stretches her preadolescent hands into the edge of the light. Her fingertips begin to burn and peel. A pitiful, wailing cry escapes her as the hands move closer to me.

"Daddy, please hold me."

Its eyes are shiny with the inky darkness. Then they shift back into that familiar shade of blue that I can't help but love. Tears roll down her cheeks and the face of my daughter's doppelganger contorts with the pain. But the eyes don't fool me. There is no true emotion within them. If they ever learn that, if they ever adapt, I will be lost.

As her burning flesh comes closer, the smell of it makes my stomach growl. I am starving, as well as losing my mind, and I imagine one does not help against the other.

The tips of her fingers become ash and crumble as she slides further into the candlelight. Her wailing is picked up by the younger ones surrounding her and it tears at my core.

I remember those cries. They are written upon my soul. They were etched into the very fabric of my being as I soothed and loved them.

This entity, whatever it is, does not play fair.

Suddenly the wailing stops and this Kelly is yanked from my sight, into the shifting shadows of the brood. The ripping, crunching sounds of her being torn apart, fed upon, destroys me.

The other ones will not allow for weakness.

"Do you miss us Daddy? Do you miss me?"

Please stop, for God's sake, just stop.

I rest my head against the wall. Wherever there is darkness; they are there. The black, liquid ribbons. I don't need to look. I know they cover the entire walls around me. The ceiling above me is dark with them.

I only need to hold out for three hours and twenty-seven minutes. I have to move slowly, or remain absolutely still. I cannot afford to cast a shadow that connects to the outer ring of darkness.

"I'm cold, Daddy…" Her little voice whispers and my eyes slam open. Oh, Jesus! I almost fell asleep. The voice is so close I have to use everything I've got left in me not to give in to my startled reaction.

"Stop calling me that," I mumble.

"But you're my Daddy," she says and I slowly turn my face to her. Her voice is killing me. I can see its face at the edge of my vision. That's not the face of my little girl, with the circle of razor sharp teeth, the black, shiny eyes. Yet now it's morphing into the face I cherish. Except the eyes aren't the right color. Her eyes were— Jesus! Were. Her eyes were—cornflower blue, with flecks of gray.

"You've got the color wrong," I say to its face and slowly bring the lighter up in front of me and spin my Zippo. The reaction is instantaneous. The lovely face of my daughter peels away and the monster is once again revealed. It screeches and throws itself back into the collective shadow.

"That wasn't very nice, Dad," one of the Brans says.

Please stop calling me that.

Fuck it's cold.

Rubbing my hands together only makes them hurt but at least the pain keeps me awake. Outside the frosted window, I can see dawn slowly approaching. The bay windows face the east and I can see the sky lightening on the horizon.

There are at least a hundred of them now, all standing in the shadow, watching me, measuring me. As one, their faces turn to the lightening sky. The five-year-old Kelly turns her head to face me instead, looking at the candle and then up to my face. I see the intent just before she makes her move.

Shit.

She takes a few running steps and leaps. Her little body floats through the air, tuning to ash and cinder as it crosses into the candle light. I can't stop myself and I reach for her little, hurdling body. It's a father's instinct to catch his little girl if she jumps towards him. I do what any father would have…

I catch her and her little body explodes in my grasp. The light of the sun spears through the glass and the chaos of their withdrawal is instantaneous. They are gone. The ash of my little girl douses the flame of the candle— No! Not my little girl. The creature, the doppelganger…the parasite.

"That's good to know." The voice of Brandon comes from the left of me, out of the remaining shadow. It means the doused candle. I can see it's wearing that wry smile he always wore when he thought he'd outsmarted me. We make eye contact and he holds it for a long second.

"See you tonight, Dad," he says and the physical structure of my fourteen-year-old boy collapses into the black bulging ribbon behind him and just like that it has withdrawn into the dark places of the house—between the walls and under the floors—spaces that the light cannot reach.

They are testing their limits and they are learning.

I sit and wait. I luxuriate in the sunlight as it slowly creeps down from the ceiling, washing down towards me.

All houses have shadows, though. I can feel them hiding in the deep corners.

It's time to get my ass in gear. There's only going to be around 6 hours of daylight today and I have a lot to do.

As the sun drops below the horizon I check and double check my interventions. I have a feeling they are going to up their game. Let them. My heart died when they took my family. I don't know the moment I gave up hope that they were still alive, but I have seen these things in action. They are unforgiving, they are vicious. They pull no punches.

The problem with using multiple candles and light sources is this: They create multiple shadows. Shadows that you need to keep track of because that's all they need...

I have LED lanterns set up in designated spots in the living room. The chance for overlapping shadows is still there but I am aware of the areas.

I searched the house earlier today during the daylight hours. I used the lights even though the house was bright enough as it was. Or, at least, I thought it was. It started simply enough, with a bump and a giggle. It came from the kids' rooms and I told myself not to go. But the heart will lie to itself even when it knows the truth. My son was fourteen and my daughter was eleven...they haven't made giggling, kiddy noises for quite a few years. I knew better but...maybe I just missed seeing my kids.

Even though they are not my kids.

Fuck...

I am not going to win this.

I paused outside Bran's room and took a slow deep breath. The door was slightly ajar and I could see light filling the room. Reassured, I pushed the door open and entered. Seeing his stuff lying as he left it hurts, so goddamn bad, but I grab onto that hurt and turn it into anger.

There that's better… Anger, I can use…

"Come on out, you little shits, it's time to die."

The giggling comes from the closet. Of course it came from the closet. Where else would it come from, right?

As I said before, the house was bigger than I had wanted. One of the benefits that came with it were the walk in closets. Not actually a benefit at the moment.

Hehehe

Hehehe

That giggle I knew so well, that sounded like they were up to something they weren't supposed to be doing.

What are you guys doing…? Shit! Please don't be playing with the gun!

Wait…

They are not your fucking children!

I flipped the light switch. They had gotten to the bulb already. No problem, I turned on the million candle flashlight and enjoyed watching the shadows evaporate. I made the light beam travel slowly across the floor and let it stop short of their feet. I wanted to see what they were doing.

I knew they were not my kids, but my throat still constricted when I saw my revolvers in their hands. Both Brandon and Kelly sat on the old flip-top toy chest. They wore the summer clothes we had gotten them years ago. Though this time it was wrong because my son never wore that outfit.

Its adapting…

It wasn't the outfits that made my heart stop and throat constrict. It was what they were doing with the revolvers. Their little hands held the guns in small, shaky hands. Both giggled at the game they were playing. The barrels were pointed each at the other's face, index fingers pulling at the trigger. The hammer…

"These are fun, Daddy." Bran said. My daughter nodded in agreement.

"Bang!" Bran started.

Bang Bang…

"Bang!" Kelly finished and the thunderous roar was enormous, as both their heads exploded from their shoulders. My mind rebelled and my body hit the floor as I stumbled backwards. I was on the floor in the doorway of the closet.

Oh fuck! When did I fucking go inside?

I started scrambling backwards even as the black ribbons wrapped themselves around my boots and yanked me further into the darkness. My hand fumbled at the flash light even as the headless, mangled bodies of my kids slumped to the floor towards me. The beam of light blazed across the black tendrils around my boots. Smoke turned to ash and ash gave me my freedom. The sliding, humping, headless bodies of my children stopped moving and were yanked away into the shadow.

I was still three feet inside the door. I blazed the beam of my million lumen flashlight like a lightsaber. I swung the light upwards.

My two year old little girl, sitting on the top shelf. She went peek-a-boo and made a leap towards my face. It was too fast for me to put the beam on it so I smashed the flashlight into it like a club, pitching it up and over my head, into the light. It screamed as it caught fire.

I wasted no time and clumsily got up into a fighting stance. I threw my head around in a wild scan of my surroundings.

Holy shit. That was close.

My eyes returned to the doorway of the closet. My soul cried out in despair. She stood there in the shadow, wearing the lingerie she had bought for me so long ago, for our wedding night.

"Oh God... No." I spoke aloud. Despair and happiness warred within me. The love of my life stood before me in perfect health, perfect shape. Perfect youth.

"What's the matter, baby, don't you like it?" she asked. I could see the swell of her breasts and the points of her nipples just under the white lace.

"Of course I do," I said. I was telling the truth. She looked gorgeous.

I was now three feet from the door.

I took a deep breath and let it out with a shudder.

"You're not her..." I said and started to bring the beam around to destroy her.

"No but I could be," she said and her long, black tongue slithered out to lick her luscious, inviting lips.

Whoa! That's new.

"You mean we could bang away on each other... Right next to our dead, headless children." Her head tilted as if she didn't understand me. She looked towards the back of the closet and smiled.

"What's wrong with you? Our children are just fine, silly." She reached out and set her hands on the two headless corpses, shuffling them forward to stand next to her. "See." Their black-splattered hands waved in confirmation. "Show Daddy your pretty smiles."

I brought the beam around and incinerated my wife's doppelganger, plus our two headless children. She laughed as her structure collapsed and I slammed the door of the closet closed.

Bang Bang.

Fuck this.

"Soon honey...soon," her voice came from within the closet. I shut the door to my son's room.

It's going to be a long night.

I throw on the parka and snow gear, just in case they shut off the heat again. I leave the overhead light on in the kitchen and stand in my sanctuary of light. I have one of the fueled lanterns and one of the battery operated ones. The huge Yankee candles burn as if they are at war with the shadows. I check both of my million-or-so-lumen flashlights.

Good to go.

A wall separates the living room from the kitchen, wrapping around to the dining room. I leave the dining room dark. Light spills into it from the kitchen entrance. On the opposite side of the room, bright light spills into the living room and into the darkened hallway to the bedrooms.

I am a little more prepared tonight. I have two battle fronts. The dining room and the hallway.

That should work.

But to what end?

I sit in the rolling office chair. The center of the room is shadow free. I feel the night weighing upon my biological clock. Though I normally only sleep around four hours a night, I still get tired when I am supposed to. So far, the night has been quiet. I stifle a yawn. I need to move around. I get up and slowly cross the room to the fireplace. I let my gaze slide down the darkened hallway and hear my daughter singing. I throw a few logs on the fire, feeling the heat even through my parka.

I return to my chair. It is starting.

My light sanctuary illuminates some of the hallway. I see Kelly step out of her room, singing a nursery rhyme in her sweet little voice.

"Ring-a-round the rosie..." The melody is beautiful, but I know the history of that little tune and it is a dark one. She starts skipping.

"...A pocket full of posies..."

Her speed increases.

"Ashes! Ashes…"

She skips towards the light as if it is no problem.

"We all fall…down!" she finishes, as her body explodes in the glare. Ashes and dust floats in the light, drifting into the kitchen.

What the hell was that about?

A young version of Brandon steps into the hallway and begins singing a rhyme as well.

"Engine, engine, number nine, going down Chicago line…"

He shakes his head from side to side as if to pop his neck. Odd, that's very familiar. I lean forward to watch. He's probably six years old…

"…If the train should jump the track…" He begins running. My God, he was even fast at that age. He barrels on towards the light. Balls-to-the-wall and gaining speed.

"…Do you want your money back?" He shouts the last words just before he hits the light. He jumps, as if doing a long jump and his body explodes. I turn my eyes away and hear the loud thump as it hits the ground. My head whips around at the sound. The upper portion of his torso lies on the floor, in my sanctuary of light. Smoke smolders from the underside of his rib cage. His head comes up and his face contorts with pain. The light has burned through him diagonally.

It's not him.

"Please Daddy, help me. Help me please." It cries, and my instinct as a father almost overwhelms. It uses its one good arm to start pulling itself towards the shadowed edge of the living room.

"Oh for fuck's sakes." I swear, getting up to do something. Anything. The display is pitiful, wrenching.

I should be happy to see this thing suffer. What is wrong with me?

I get behind it. I need to put this thing out of its misery. I raise my foot to stomp its head and it looks at me. It wears Bran's face and it smiles. It smiles with my son's precious, fucking smile. I try to look away and reposition my foot, giving it a nudge towards the darkness of the dining room. As its good hand stretches into the shadow, my wife reaches down to take hold of it. It looks back at me, strangely. I didn't like the look...

It was...

I turn from both and go to the fire place. I toss another log onto the fire and feel the heat of it begin to make me sweat under the parka.

I have lost.

And it knows it has won.

"Why?" I ask, without turning to the figure of my wife.

"I could ask you the same thing."

I turn and face her. She wears a conservative blouse and slacks. Her blond hair is brushed and shining. Her blue eyes twinkle at the corners. She knows she has won.

"Because I am done seeing my family suffer. Do they suffer within you? Do they feel the pain happening to them?" I ask in resignation. Isn't this how it always plays out in the movies? At the end there is always a revelation, a confession...and understanding. A coming to terms.

"Why are you so strong?" it asks.

The question confuses me. "What?"

"Why are you so strong?"

"Fuck you. My family was strong too and you slaughtered them." I say. I feel the anger growing within me.

My wife tilts her head in consideration. As if searching for an answer.

"Did we?" It asks, simply, and I want to slam an axe into her doppelganger face. I grip the flashlight tighter and position my thumb on the engage button.

"What? What the hell do you mean, 'did we?'"

It faces me and waits for me to comprehend the question. I step away from her, towards my plan of last resort. As I am about to lay my hand on the handle of the gas can, it speaks and I hesitate.

Damn me to hell for hesitating.

"Did we slaughter your family? How do you know this? Have you seen their dead, mutilated bodies?" she asks. I pick up the can of gasoline and pop the top. I begin pouring the fuel onto the carpet as I walk back across the room toward her.

"I am tired of this game. These games… I am done. I am going to burn this motherfucker to the ground and you with it."

"So strong. You would rather die than become one with us." My Dopple-wife says. Gas splashes across the line between light and shadow.

"You killed my family. The reason I lived in the first place! I am done with this and I am taking you with me." I say, walking towards the hallway and the stairs that lead to the door.

"If we killed your family then; who are they?" she asks.

I hear the thud against the glass pane of the bay window. I turn towards the sound and drop the empty plastic can to the floor.

No…oh, God no…

The, black, tuberous tentacles press their battered, abused flesh against the outside of the bay window. My Bran. My Kelly. My…

It can't be them.

But I knew it was.

"Are they alive?"

I hear something strange, then. Something the doppelgangers have never done before. It sighs in resignation and says the word "Yes."

I glance towards the window and see the moisture frosting on the glass near their mouths.

"What do you want?" I ask, thumbing the lid of my Zippo open.

"Good, straight to the point," it says and I notice that the Dopple-wife has changed her clothes into a slim, flattering, black, business suit. "We want you. Simple as that. They were fun but you are strong."

Fuck… of course it did. Of course it wanted me. With me, they would eventually have them as well.

"How do I know you won't just take them as well, after you have me?"

"You don't…but then, where would be the fun in that?" It teases. I can see it waiting for an answer. "Better hurry, I'm not sure how much longer they've got, out there in the cold. It is cold, isn't it? So bitterly cold."

It's right. How long can they last out there without their winter gear?

I keep the flashlight in the ready position, walking across to the kitchen and grabbing the keys from the hook. "Deal. But let me go start the truck for them. You can put them in there."

"If you try to trick us, I will tear them to pieces and you can live with that memory as you drive away." It says. I see the tension on my Dopple-wife's face. It would do it.

"I won't trick you. Search my wife's memories if you doubt me."

I head out to the garage without waiting for an answer. I start the four wheel drive SUV and back it out of the garage, turning the heat on and opening the door. I pull the light out and turn it on.

It pauses, still in the shape of my beloved. I reach out and take the hand of my Dopple-daughter. There are at least ten different versions of her lined up, but I choose an eleven-year-old Kelly. I turn the light on and point it towards the ground. I'm not going to break the deal. The warmness of my Dopple-daughter's flesh surprises me and I feel her hand grip mine tighter.

The Dopples take my unconscious wife and kids from the strong, black, tentacle ribbons that nearly engulf them and place them gently into the SUV. They put my wife in the passenger side, which I make a mental note of. I hear the heater pumping out warm air. I can see my wife starting to regain consciousness, her cold-pinched face gaining color.

When the doors shut, I turn and follow my new Dopple-family back into the house. They should have attacked me then, but what was the point? They had me. I let loose of my Dopple-daughter's hand, feeling her reluctance to release me.

Odd.

I stumble into my light sanctuary and turn to face her.

I pull out a cigarette. It's been at least a day since I enjoyed a smoke and I sure as hell wasn't going to die without having at least one more.

I flip open my Zippo and light the cigarette.

"Better enjoy that. It's going to be your last," my Dopple-wife says. I blow smoke into her face. She is not amused.

She still isn't amused when I drop the still lit Zippo onto the floor. The flame hits the gasoline soaked carpet and quickly goes up with a loud whoomph.

My Dopple-wife smiles. For a second, I doubt my plan.

"Do you think you've won?" she, asks.

"No, but I am making damn sure that you don't." I grab the second can from where I had hidden it near the fireplace.

"Are you sure about that?" she challenges. The hall suddenly fills with a hundred or so Dopples. Perfect and imperfect copies of my wife and kids block my egress. That's fine. I am kind of winging it now, anyway. I don't actually have a plan of escape, only a plan for how to free my family. I pop the top off the second gas can and start splashing it across the lit flames and onto my Dopple-family. The effect is instantaneous. Wherever the burning fuel touches, bursts into flames. They leap higher, such an intense heat. The Dopples are in a chaotic, spasmodic frenzy, in the fire and the light it casts. I turn to my Dopple-wife.

"You can either save yourself or you can try to stop me and kill my family. Your choice." I say, but I don't wait for a response. I rush forward into the burning wall of bodies. They explode on impact. I feel my hair catch fire, cover my face with my hands, and stumble down the stairs and towards the door. I pull a hand away from my face and tug the door open. I don't stop until I dive into the cool, refreshing snow. I scoop up handfuls of it and quickly chill my singed, burned flesh.

I see them, lined up against the window, in agony.

I roll over and crawl towards the SUV. My eyes water and my flesh screams from the cold and heat.

The hard-packed ice cuts at my hands but I keep crawling. I have to get to my family. I have to get them out of here. I have to…

The rear passenger door opens and I see the white high tops Kelly always wears, stepping across the snow and ice. "Oh my God, Daddy!" I hear my daughter say. At this moment there is not a lovelier voice in all existence. But I don't want her outside of the SUV. I want her safe. I am going to be there to drive them away. In just a minute…

Of course, she doesn't listen to my attempts to stop her; she runs to me. "Oh my God, Daddy!" That's the only thing it seems she can say and I am fine with it. I lift my head and she helps me to a kneeling position. I look up into her beautiful, loving face…

And noticed something odd.

She stands before me and smiles. Her hands grasp my neck, cradling my head.

"You stupid man. Of course your family is dead. I love to win this way," my Kelly-Dopple-daughter says. Her breath plumes in the air realistically.

They adapted.

"The eyes are still the wrong color," I say and watch as they turn liquid black.

I even watch as they turn the same color as mine.

So cold now… so very, very cold.

Kathy Dinisi's Shopping List

Hot dogs
Hamburger buns
Skittles
Sour Patch Extreme
Apple Pie
Blackberry Pie
Chocolate Pie
M/Maid orange
White Flour
Cereal
Taco shells
Carne Asada
Ice cream
Vegetable oil
Homo milk
Bags
Imperial Spread

The Stranger

Kathy Dinisi

Chapter 1
From the devil, who is the ape of God
-Latin Proverb

"I'm driving as fast as I can mom." I manage to say without giving my mother too much of an attitude. I hate that I can't depend on her for help. She's my mother, I should always be able to ask for help, especially when it's work related.

"Well, when will you be home, April? I leave for my cruise in two days." I can already see the red vein on my mother's head burst with anger as she scolds me.

I pull the car over to the shoulder, the wheels running over clumpy rocks. Shoving the gear handle into park, "Mom, I told you this was at least a three to four-day trip. It's far from a pleasure cruise, but my job requires that I travel a lot and Daniel bailed on me." I was twenty-two years old when I met Daniel in college. He was the sweetest, sexiest, strongest, and most intelligent man I'd ever met. He was every girl's dream. I fell for his charm quickly and got pregnant even quicker. Once I told Daniel I was two months pregnant, he blew a fuse and decided he wanted nothing to do with me. He accused me of trying to trap him and make him marry him. Which was far from the truth.

We used protection every time we were together. But sometimes you can be careful and do everything to prevent a pregnancy and still get pregnant. And just because he didn't want to be with me anymore, that didn't seem to stop him from trying to tell me how to raise our daughter. It's a constant battle between us. He hates the fact that I travel a lot for my work and I hate the fact he bitches about me traveling a lot. I work to provide for my daughter. I was never one to want to live off another man.

My mother exhales on the other side of the receiver, "I told you not to go out with that boy. I knew he was nothing but trouble. If you would have just listened to me, you wouldn't be in this mess." My mother hated Daniel from the first moment she met him and told me every day since my daughter was born that I should have listened to her. Four years later she is still reminding me.

My hand clenches the steering wheel, "Yeah, I know mom. I made a big mistake and now Rose and I are suffering, but this job is my lively hood and I can't always take her with me." My boss, Aden is amazing. He hired me right away even though he knew I had a baby girl. He said he was judging me for my talented eye and not for my mistakes. Even though my daughter isn't a mistake, I understood where he was coming from and was eternally grateful. As she grew older, he would let me take her on certain photoshoots. Mostly the local ones. The out of state photoshoots, I would leave Rose with her dad for those couple of days.

"Fine, April, but you better be here by the time me and Josh leave on our vacation." Josh is my mother's new boyfriend who is five years older than her and owns his own furniture business. He spoils her rotten, which is why my mother is with him. Unlike my mother, he loves having Rose around. He never had kids of his own, so he just adores Rose and spoils her every chance he gets. He begs my mother to have Rose over more often, but my mother prefers just them two.

"I am leaving Nevada now mom. I will be back in Oregon in just over ten hours. I would have finished my photoshoot sooner, but we were rained out and had to wait for the sun to come out." I was lucky to land a job working for a fashion magazine right out of college. It's an easy job and I have always loved taking pictures. Being a photographer had always been my childhood dream. It's a wonderful job and pays for my small condo that I share with my baby girl, Rose. But at times, my boss demands I travel to get certain pictures. I hardly ask my mom to babysit for this reason alone. She doesn't want to deal with my mess even if that mess up is her own flesh and blood. "I promise I am going as fast as I can."

"I hope so, April. I really do." She says with a warning. My mother would never just leave Rose with anyone, but if I'm a minute late, she will make my life a living hell and I, for one, don't feel like hearing her bitch.

"Can I please talk to Rose?" I ask my mother.

"Yes, dear. Rose, sweetheart, your momma is on the phone." I can hear toys falling to the carpet and the little pitter patter of feet running.

"Momma?" Rose's sweet voice echoes through the receiver, out of breath from whatever she was doing.

"Yes, baby, it's me. I'll be home real soon. Have you been a good girl for grams?"

"Oh, yes momma, I have. Grams is playing Barbie with me." Her sweet voice puts a smile on my face. "And grandpa Josh is Ken!" She explains.

The thought of Josh playing with Barbie dolls makes me giggle. "Are they now? Well, I'm glad to hear that. I love you, Rosy baby. I'll see you soon, okay? Momma's got to get on the road."

"Are you coming to pick me up, momma?"

"Yes, sweetheart, and then we will spend two whole days together."

"Just you and me?" Her voice growing excited.

"Just you and me, baby."

"I wub you momma."

My heart breaks when I hear her say that to me. I just hate leaving her behind like this, but I have no choice. I work to provide a better life for us. "I love you, sweetpea." I swipe my finger along my phone ending our conversation, put my small Prius in drive and get back on the road. If I drive all the way through Nevada without stopping, I'll be able to make it by tomorrow evening. I can't wait to get home and lay in my own bed with my sweet girl next to me. Maybe I should surprise her with a puppy? She would like that. Or even a kitty?

This is going to be a very long and boring car ride back home. My boss told me to take Highway 18 all the way home. Aden said it would be the fastest way to go without any traffic delaying my trip home. I hope he is right, because I enjoy taking the back roads because of all the wonderful and unique pictures I can get.

Thirty minutes later, my bladder is angry that I drank so much Pepsi that it's begging me to empty it. I pull into a small gas station and quickly jump out of my car, grabbing my purse before I close the door. I click the button on my rental car and briskly walk towards the gas station. A man with a black hoodie draped over his head sits at a picnic table in front of the entrance of the gas station. His body is hunched over with his hands folded in front of him. It's ninety-nine degrees at ten am and he is wearing a thick hoodie? Is he crazy? I'm burning up in my shorts and tank top. I can just imagine how hot he is in a thick hoodie and jeans. He barely lifts his head as I walk by, tilting his head to the side. Like something caught his interest.

Instantly I get a creepy feeling from this stranger in the bottom of my gut. I try to ignore the feeling as I quickly open the glass door and rush inside. "Bathroom, please?" I ask the receptionist with such urgency. I try to restrain myself from doing the potty dance.

"In the back, second door on the right." I nod my head, practically jogging to the back. The whole three second walk to the bathroom, I feel a set of eyes following me. The tiny hairs on my arms stand on end. After coming out of the bathroom I decide to grab some snacks. Going down each aisle one by one I get that awkward creepy feeling that someone is watching my every move. I look around, but I'm alone. I stand on my tiptoes to see if I can see any heads over the aisle but it's empty. I look throughout the store and only see the lady behind the register. She is staring at a magazine, reading.

I brush off the creepy feeling and grab a couple Twinkies, a bottle of water and a Coke. I put my items on the counter and look around the store again. I still feel like someone is staring at me, but I can't see where they are. The lady behind the register slowly scans my items. I can't help it, but I keep looking around to locate the eyes. The girl can't scan my items fast enough. One item, two- eyes staring holes in the back of my head. I look to my left, nothing. I look to my right, nothing. I quickly swipe my debit card in the machine, punch in my four-digit code and grab the bag from the lady. I leave my receipt behind and rush outside.

The creepy man with the black hoodie is gone. I quickly walk to my car, unlocking it with a beep. I throw my bag in the passenger seat and start up the car. The engine quietly roars to life. The radio blares through the speakers. *"Run little girl. Run!"* Giving me the creeps. A black truck pulls out of the gas station parking lot. I can swear my car was the only one in the parking lot. But I didn't get a clear look around at my surroundings because of my state of urgency.

I ignore my gut instinct even though I know you should never do that and keep going. I look in the rearview mirror and notice the truck had stopped. I press on the gas and pick up speed to fifty miles per hour. Driving several miles down the road I look in the rearview mirror but don't see the truck anymore. Taking in a deep breath I feel silly for thinking someone was following me. I pass a small town called Hope, but I don't bother to stop because I still have almost a full tank of gas and this car gets excellent mileage. I pass a sign that says no gas station for the next seventy miles.

The road turns curvy, with nothing but a long, boring empty road- nothing on either side of me. I roll down my windows, letting the breeze roll in, but it's a hot breeze that doesn't do anything to cool down my sweaty body. I wipe the sweat off my forehead. I come up to an abandoned building on my right, deciding to pull over and take some snapshots. It could make a good cover for a Halloween article. Sometimes my boss will let me make some extra money by submitting pictures for small articles here and there. I'm about to pull out the key to the ignition when a song comes on the radio, "I'm coming for you."

"Creepy song." I say out loud as I turn the ignition off and take out the keys. I grab my black camera bag from the back seat. Unzipping the bag and screwing on the lens, I get out and start snapping pictures of the old building from every angle. The black truck I saw from the gas station speeds down the highway only slowing down as he drives by me. Instantly I get that creepy feeling like someone is watching me. His radio blares the same song that came on the radio in my car. "I'm coming for you, I'm coming for you." My body shivers as he races by.

I jump inside my car only to see the big truck make a U-turn and rush back towards me. I get on the road when the truck quickly approaches behind me. I accelerate to sixty-five but the truck picks up speed until he is inches from my bumper. He slows down, then picks up speed. Again and again he does this- toying with me.

I stick my hand out the window and motion for him to pass me but he doesn't move. Instead, he backs off ever so slightly and then picks up speed again until he is inches from my bumper. I motion with my hand again for him to pass, but he doesn't. "Oh my gosh," I say out loud to no one. "What does he want?"

I swerve over to the shoulder to let him pass. The truck honks his horn several times before he passes me. *Asshole*. I watch him dip down the hill. I wait impatiently for him to come up the other side of the hill but he never does. "Where did he go?" I stare at the empty road for another couple of minutes but I never see him. *Is he waiting for me?*

I get my heart beat under control before I continue. I maneuver the car onto the main road again, hoping to God that I don't see the truck again, waiting for me at the bottom of the hill. My heart beats frantically against my chest as I drive down the hill. I look around and see that the truck is nowhere to be found. My arms feel like jelly. I shake my body trying to dispel the jitters.

An hour later the sun is directly over the car. The heat is unbearable. The dashboard says one hundred degrees outside, but it feels more like one hundred and fifty degrees. My whole body is burning with sweat. I often have to rub the palms of my hands on my pants just to keep them dry. A big Joshua Tree stands awkwardly alone on the side of the road. The weight of the top of the tree making it hunch over in a sad pathetic way.

I push the button on the radio hoping to find something other than static. After several scans through the stations, I find nothing and turn down the volume, leaning my head back against the head rest. I have at least five and a half hours until I make it home. I haven't seen one single car since the crazy black truck. The radio crackles to life, a woman's voice flows through the speakers. "Sweet girl, just jun." I tilt my head and stare at the radio, repeating the words in my head. Trying to understand the meaning. If there is a meaning?

I pass by the Joshua Tree when the black truck quickly pulls behind me picking up dust and rocks around him. *"Where did he come from? Didn't he pass me up?"* I think to myself.

He fishtails back and forth. My heart beats faster, my palms start to sweat. The truck quickly picks up speed coming inches from my bumper again. With how big his truck is, he would do so much damage to my little car that it alarms me.

Chapter 2
Tis no sin to cheat the devil
-Daniel Defoe

Panicking, I accelerate my speed, my speedometer reaches higher and higher, fifty-five, sixty, sixty-five, seventy. The more speed the car picks up the more my stomach starts to turn. The red arrow rises and rises to a very uncomfortable number. The Prius threatens to lose control with the tires trying desperately not to lose their traction on the road. My grip around the steering wheel tightens, causing my palms to sweat. "What does he want?" The truck catches up to me in half of the time it took me to pick up speed. He honks his horn making me jump in my seat.

The sweet song on the radio ends. A man's deep voice takes her place, "Death is around the corner." My breath hitches in my throat. It's like the man's voice is speaking to me. Warning me that evil is near. The truck behind me honks his horn repeatedly, each time making me jump and yelp. With my right hand, I reach down towards the middle counsel looking for my cell phone. I start feeling around for it while trying to concentrate on the road. It takes me several seconds until my hand lands on the square figure.

I pick it up and dial 911. My phone beeps in my ear telling me my phone call won't go through. I dial 911 again in hopes that I'll get a signal, but it beeps again. I throw my phone down in frustration. It lands on the passenger seat and then bounces to the floor with a clunk.

The stranger behind me speeds up until he is practically on my bumper. I wait for the impact of his truck, but it never comes. "What do you want!!!" I scream in fear even though I know he can't hear me.

The truck swerves to the left, driving on the wrong side of the road. I look over as the truck pulls up next to me.

My pulse ramped up as I look over at the driver. The man from the gas station with the black hoodie stares at me. My jaw practically hits the floor. His hoodie lies so far over his face shielding it from me that I can't get a good clear look at his face. He lifts his hand at me, and that's when my eyes grow big with fear. His fingers are long and wrinkled. His nails are as sharp as a razor. This can't be real. It just can't be real. No, it's a figment of my imagination. I close my eyes begging the scene to not be real. When I open them, his fingers are normal, like mine.

I should be keeping an eye on the road, but I can't steer my eyes away from him. *Why is he following me? Did I make him upset somehow? What does he want?* All these questions run through my head

He points his finger towards the road. I cock my head to the side and then quickly turn towards the road. Inches in front of me is a slow-moving car. I grip the steering wheel as I slam on my brakes. But it's too late and I'm too close. I swerve my Prius to the right, so I don't hit the car in front of me. I drive on the dirt shoulder trying to get a handle on my car. Dirt and rocks fly all around me in a thick fog covering my view of the truck. Pebbles hit the side of the Prius with a click, click, click. The small car swerves left then right before I finally get a handle on it.

I finally come to a stop, sending my body forward then back, against my seat with a thump. My palms are sweating as they continue to grip the steering wheel so tight my knuckles are turning white. My heart is racing frantically. I stare straight ahead trying to get my thoughts in order. I was so close to hitting that other car at eighty miles per hour. I could have done so much damage to whomever was driving.

My breathing is so ragged I feel like I'm hyperventilating. I close my eyes and put my hand over my heart and concentrate on slowing down my breathing. Once that's back to normal, I look around for the black truck. I don't see him or the other car anywhere. I push the black button on my arm rest. The doors click unlock. I open the driver's side door and step out into the dry heat. My legs feel like jelly as I stand on them. I brace myself against my car until I'm sure my legs can hold the weight of my body up.

I put my hand to my forehead to shield the sun from my eyes. Turning completely around I'm alone, no truck in sight. The desert covers the land to my left and to my right. Just the lonely trees and tumble weeds. Reaching into my car over the middle console I pull out the map and lay it against the hood of my car. I stare at the blue and red lines like they are foreign to me. "Where the Hell am I? I came from here." I lay my finger down at the location of the gas station where I met the crazy man in the black truck. I run it down to where I think I am. There should be a tiny town about five or six miles from here. I'll stop there and grab a bite to eat and call my mother and tell her I might be late. She isn't going to like it. But I still should have plenty of time to make it back home to pick up my little angel so my mother can be off on her vacation with her boyfriend.

I fold the map in four even squares and reach over through the driver door and set it down on the passenger seat. I reach between the seat and the glove compartment until I find my phone." No signal, of course." I say in frustration.

Chapter 3
The soul that has conceived one wickedness
can nurse no good thereafter
Sophocles

A loud rumbling sound startles me out of my thoughts. I turn towards the road and see a big truck going fast on the opposite side of the road. A cry breaks from my lips. I jump in my car throwing my phone on the passenger seat, slamming the car door shut. I look up to see the truck coming closer and closer. I turn the key, but the car doesn't start. "No!" I scream in terror.

I stare at the key then at the oncoming vehicle, fearing the black truck is coming back to finish me off. I silently pray that the car will turn on. I turn the key and press on the gas at the same time. The car finally rumbles to life just when a big dark blue truck passes by. I watch it as it drives off out of sight, hauling ass down the road. I lean back, against the headrest as the adrenaline wears off. I laugh out loud at how stupid I must look. I feel stupid. I'm imagining a crazy stalker in a black truck with long sharp fingernails like Freddy Krueger. "I need to get out of here."

I pull onto the road and continue driving, hoping to find the town on the map and hoping I don't see the black truck again. I look down at the gas gauge, I still have more than half a tank. I hate small cars because there is no leg room, but right now I'm thankful for such a small, good fuel efficient vehicle. I would have had to stop to get gas already if I would have used my own vehicle.

A wooden sign on the left-hand side of the highway reads, "Woody's Dinner, open 24 hours." I decide to pull in to use the restroom and to make sure I'm still on the right highway to get home. Plus, they may have a phone so I can call my mother and hear the wealth of her evil voice screaming at me to hurry home.

I make a sharp left into Woody's Dinner, finding the closest parking spot to the front door. I put the car in park, grab my purse and jump out. I push the lock button on the keyless entry. The car beeps and the lights flash. I throw my purse over my right shoulder and pick up my head. I stop in my tracks when I see the black truck pull into Woody's Diner. I can't breathe- it feels like someone is choking me. This can't be a coincidence. No, it can't be. I take a step back towards my car about to jump in and drive far away from here when I think better of it. I need to call my mom, I need to call the police. I need help. This has gotten way out of hand.

I quickly pull out my phone and take several pictures of the truck's license plates. I run into the diner and look around my surroundings. "Would you like to be seated?" An older woman with sandy white hair asks me.

I turn around, pressing my face to the glass when I hear a truck door slam shut. With my nose and mouth smashed against the glass I look around for the black truck- I don't see him- but every muscle in my body knows it's him. It has to be him.

With a huff the woman asks me again," Can I help you?"

I turn around to face her, but my lips can't seem to form the words. It takes me several tries before I'm coherent enough to answer. "Yes, I need to use your phone please. It's an emergency. I'm being followed."

"Followed? By whom, young lady?" She asks, tilting her head to the side.

"Please, where's your phone?" I ask, my voice rising with every passing second I stand here. I feel vulnerable standing out here in the open. I can feel eyes watching me- his eyes, his evil eyes. My body trembles at the thought.

"Calm down, missy. The phone is in the back by the kitchen. It's fifty cents."

"Thank you," I start walking back towards the kitchen when the hostess whispers to herself shaking her head, "Damn city folks always stirring up trouble."

Ignoring her, I practically jog to the kitchen. I spot the pay phone next to the kitchen door. I rummage through my purse looking for fifty cents. Finding it, I pull the receiver off the hook. I try to shove quarters in the change slot but I miss and the change falls to the ground. I drop the receiver and fall to my knees searching for the quarters. I quickly find them and try once again to shove them in the machine. My hands shake so bad that I can barely manage to hold the phone. It takes both hands for me to place the quarters in the slot.

It rings twice before a young lady's voice answers, "911 please state your emergency."

"Hello, I'm on Highway 18 on the outskirts of Nevada and there's a black truck following me. He ran me off the road." I stumble out so fast I can barely understand my own words.

"Slow down, miss. You said you are off Highway 18 in Nevada?" She asks as she clicks away on her keyboard.

"Yes, there's a black truck following me," I repeat.

"Are you somewhere safe right now? Near people?"

"Yes, I'm inside of a diner off the main road. I'm not sure if he followed me inside or not." I take deep breaths. My nerves are a bundle of jitters. The phone receiver clings and clangs against my head, and I grab onto it with both hands to try to steady it.

"Good. Stay inside. But, ma'am, where did you say you were at?"

"I'm on Highway 18 on the outskirts of Nevada on my way to Oregon. This highway connects to Oregon."

"Ma'am There is no Highway 18."

"What? Yes, there is! It says so on my map." I squeal in fear.

"Ma'am, I need you to ask a waiter or waitress what highway you are on and where it leads." The operator says slowly.

"Okay, I'm going to put the phone down."

"Yes, go ahead, I'll be waiting for you." I set the receiver down on the edge of the pay phone and take a step out of the hallway.

I look around for the nearest waiter or waitress or even a cook. I don't want to walk too far from the pay phone in fear that someone may hang up the receiver. "Excuse me?" I call out to a waiter that came out of the kitchen door.

"Yes?" He answers me, trying to concentrate on not tipping over the plate of orders he is balancing on the palm of his hands.

"What highway is that?" I point towards the road.

"Highway 18, ma'am." He says, shifting from foot to foot.

"Does it run into Oregon?"

"Yes, in about five hours you will be in Oregon. Is there anything else I can help you with?" He asks a little rushed.

"No, that's it. Thank you." He nods his head and quickly walks by me heading towards whomever the food belongs to. I walk back to the receiver and pick it up. Confused on why the operator can't find my location. "Excuse me?"

"I'm watching you." The women on the receiver disappeared and now it's a deep hoarse voice.

"Exxcusse me, ma'am?" I ask my voice shivers full of fear.

"I'm watching you." The whispery voice says sending a chill down to the very marrow of my spine.

My hand shakes, my teeth clatter together, "Who are you?"

"I'm watching you." His deep, emotionless voice repeats.

"What do you want?" I cry into the receiver almost pleading. Several tormenting seconds go by before his hoarse voice answers me.

"YOU!" I let out a loud scream with his hard-disturbing words and slam the receiver down hard, hanging up on him. The phone bounces off the hook and falls, dangling off its cord from side to side. I stare at it blankly like it bit me on my ear. I take a step back away from the phone until my body is flushed against the wall. I hold the wall for dear life, like it's my life support.

"Ma'am, can I help you with something?" The hostess from earlier asks me. "Ma'am, can you hear me?"

"No, I'm okay." I lie not taking my eyes off the phone. If the police can't help me then no one can. She shakes her head at me as she walks into the kitchen. I must look like some crazy city girl to her. Someone who is making up a tragic event for the attention. If I were her, I am not so sure if I wouldn't think the same. I wish I was making this up. I really do, I've never been so scared in my entire life as I am now.

What do I do? The police don't know where I am and I have five hours until I reach Oregon. I have no weapon and I sure in Hell can't stay in this diner. I need to call my mother. She needs to know what's going on. Maybe she can help me. Maybe her boyfriend can help me. Maybe they can call the police and explain to them where I am. Or maybe I should call my boss. He is the one who told me to take this highway to begin with.

I nervously take a step closer to the receiver and pick up the phone. Putting it to my ear ever so slowly. I wait for a ringtone but it never comes. "Hello? Is there anyone there?" I whisper into the receiver.

"I'm still watching you. I'll follow you and I will kill you." His chilling voice laughs a deep horrific laugh. Making my skin crawl with every threat he spits out.

"Why? Why me?" I ask even though the answer won't make me feel any better. But a part of me needs to know why he is doing this. Why he is chasing me and tormenting me?

He smacks his lips together and then makes a licking sound. Like he is slowing savoring whatever it is on his lips. "I can smell your blood. Your sweet, sweet blood and I want it." He slurps something, the sound moist and wet. Like he's drinking through a straw. I'm in tears as he keeps speaking. Slowly torturing me with his words and actions. "You can't run from me, my sweet pet, no matter how fast you go in your small car. I'll catch up to you. And once I do, I won't kill you right away. No, I'm going to lick every single bone you have dry of your sweet delicious blood. Hmmm. I can just imagine you staring at me, crying for help." He moans loudly in the receiver making his point very clear. "I can practically taste your delicious blood." He smacks his lips together as if he sucked something off his fingers.

"What are you?" I cry into the receiver.

"A monster that is going to enjoy playing cat and mouse with you. Now run so I can chase you," he coos playfully.

"Fuck you!" I scream into the receiver and turn to head out of the diner, not bothering to look around for the man in the black truck. I know he is here, I feel his eyes on my back, watching my every move.

I push past the same waiter who helped me earlier, making him drop a plate full of food all over the floor. The dishes clatter together. Everyone turns to look at the loud disturbing commotion. "Hey, watch it!" He barks at me.

"I'm sorry, so sorry." I cry as I run out of the diner crying hysterically. I click the keyless entry, but it doesn't unlock the car. I click it several more times as hard as I can until it finally beeps and the lights flash. I open the door and jump in, throwing my purse across the car, the contents inside scattering. My lipstick rolls off the seat onto the floor.

I jab the key into the ignition and start the car. Shoving the car into reverse I high-tail it out of the parking lot. Before I know it, I'm doing eighty down the highway. I look in the rearview mirror and my side mirrors waiting for the black truck to pull out behind me. No matter what, I don't want to believe that I know he wants to kill me. But why did he mention my blood? Why did he say my blood smells good? What is he, a vampire? Do vampires even exist? It's an urban legend. All I know is nowhere is safe and I need to get the hell out of here and hope to God I can lose him along the way.

Before I know it, the diner is far behind me and out of sight. I look down at the speedometer and realize I've picked up speed to ninety-five miles per hour. I take my foot of the gas and slow my speed back to eighty, where

I'm more comfortable. If I can keep one eye watching behind me and one eye on the road I would. I don't see the truck. Maybe it was a sick joke. Maybe I'm tired from all the traveling and work these past couple days, and I'm hallucinating. Maybe I need to see a specialist because I'm slowly going crazy.

An hour goes by and I still don't see the truck. The gas gauge says I'm at a half of a tank. I'm still good on gas, but once I find another gas station I'm filling up. I don't want to be stranded out here in the middle of nowhere. Especially after all of this. A white car cruises behind me. The car's appearance makes me feel more comfortable, letting me know that I'm not alone, that somehow I am safer, as long as he is behind me.

Two miles later the car pulls off to a side road with no name. Once again, I'm alone on this lonely highway with nothing but my mind and my heart running wild with fear. The radio instantly starts scanning the radio stations on its own. My eyes grow big and the hair on the back of my neck sticks up. I haven't had the radio on since my last stop. This has happened before, but only when the truck was near.

It scans until it finds the station it wants. AM 103, and instead of a song this time, it's a deep haunting voice. The familiar voice that makes every bone in my body tremble, the man in the black hoodie, the man in the black truck. The man who wants to watch me suffer while he drinks my blood. "The smell of fresh young blood. I can taste it on my tongue. I can feel the thick contents run through my fingertips. If you think that you can drive away and out run me, you better think twice. It's not my car that's fast, it's me, little girl. Me, me, me, I will drink every ounce of blood from your veins, and lick every drop off of your bones. I'm coming for you and there is nowhere to hide, my sweet frightened meal." His words haunt me like a bad dream.

Tears drench my face, "Why me?" I whisper to no one.

"Because I love the smell of pure fear in your veins!" The radio comes back on just for one quick sentence. One quick sentence that sends my heart into overdrive. A simple sentence that clarifies that if I don't get to civilization soon I'm going to die a horrible agonizing death. I push my foot on the gas pedal and this time I don't let off until I reach one hundred miles per hour.

An hour later and less than a half of a tank of gas left, I decide to pull off to the side of the road and look at the map. I need to figure out where the nearest gas station is. I pull to the soft shoulder. The car struggling in the loose dirt. I quickly rummage the floor of the car looking for the map. I find it and my phone and pull it out. Of course, my phone has no signal. Tossing the worthless piece of plastic to the side, I unfold the very winkled map across the steering wheel.

I'm not too far from the Oregon border. About another three hours. "I can make it! And I'll look back at this whole thing and laugh. Or will I?

Chapter 4
A dimple on the chin,
the Devil within.
-Gaelic Proverb

Two hours until I reach the Oregon border. *I can make it, I can make it, I can make it.* I repeat to myself over and over again. But it doesn't make it anymore truer. There's no doubt in my mind that this is really happening to me. The man in the black hoodie is after one thing and that is to kill me. He wants my blood, my bones, my heart- but why? What is it? And why does he want me? How long has he been hunting innocent people for? Years? Either way, I'm in danger and I need to get home. I need to reach my baby girl. She needs me and I need her. I refuse to leave her an orphan. I will get through this for her. I will make it back to my daughter and one day when she is grown up I'll tell her about this nightmare of a road and protect her. Maybe she will stay clear of the back roads in fear of seeing the Devil. Yes, that's what he is, the Devil. That's the only thing that will describe someone who would hunt humans for food. The Devil.

There's only one way home and that is straight down this highway to Hell. The dashboard lights on my car flicker off and on several times. The blue light on the radio flickers before his voice comes on the radio. My heart stops when I hear his deep horrendous voice, "I'm getting closer to you, my pet. So much closer. I can barely wait to taste you. The thought of your sweet, thick blood makes my mouth water. Mmmm." He moans.

A sudden pop makes me jump and lose control over the car. I slap both hands over the steering wheel and try to maneuver the car to the dirt shoulder. "This is my road, my pet. I own this highway. I hope you have a spare tire?" He laughs a deep throaty laugh. "You better hurry. I'm near."

Once the car is at a full stop I quickly take his advice and jump out of the car to see which tire it was that blew. The front driver side tire is blown to pieces. The rubber on the rim is torn to shreds. I pop the trunk of the small car and tear through it as fast as I can, throwing my suitcase on the dirt, the suitcase snaps open spilling my clothes all over the place. Ignoring it, I quickly get to work with the tire. My life depends on this car. Grabbing the spare tire, the jack and the hook that goes into the jack, I quickly throw it down by the side of the car. I've only ever changed a tire once before and I had Daniel's help. I just hope I can remember how to do it.

I jack up my car and start taking off the bolts to the rim. I'm all alone out here- stranded; the black truck could be watching me right now. Waiting for his moment to kill me. Or in his words, suck my bones dry. It takes me several turns to get all five lug nuts off the rim, but I manage to do it. I manage to slide off what is left of the tire and put the donut on. I quickly grab the lug nuts from the ground and start tightening them one by one. I was down to the last nut when my heart stops beating as I fear the worse. My car radio turns on full blast, "I told you pet, I'm coming for you."

I quickly turn towards my car and twist and turn the bolt as tight as I can get it. The rumble of the truck's engine is getting closer. I start to lower the jack- up and down, up and down- turning it over and over again. All the way around, but I can only go so fast. The car descends slowly to the ground, but the truck is getting closer and closer. My eyes grow wide as if someone were coming to deliver a fatal blow to my gut.

"What happened, my pet? Car trouble?" His voice rumbles through the car speakers with laughter.

"Fuck," I cry as I turn the jack faster. Sweat trickled down my forehead dripping down my chin. My hands are full of sweat, making it hard to keep a grip on the metal lever.

"I see you." He laughs again, sending goose bumps up my arm.

"Ahhh," I scream as the car reaches the ground and I pull the lever out of the jack and kick the it out of the way. I jump into the car, chucking the lever in the back seat, leaving the jack in the dirt.

"You managed to put the tire on, I see." His voice is more of a whisper. "Hello, my pet, I see you." His voice growing deeper and anxious.

The engine starts with a rumble just when the truck shows its ugly face in my rearview mirror. He is still an ant in my mirror, but too close for comfort. I slam my foot on the gas, but the car doesn't move. The tires squeal under me. The truck is closer now- so close. I can make out his license plate number. The numbers read 666. I shove the car into reverse and press on the gas. The car doesn't move, dirt flies in the sky. The truck is even closer now. I shove the car in drive and press on the gas. The tires squeal as they finally find something to grip on. I quickly get on the main road when the truck is about five feet behind me. I press my foot all the way down on the gas pedal, the little car picking up speed, but not fast enough.

The truck rams my bumper, knocking me around in the front seat and making me scream. I swerve the car to the left and then the right. He rams my bumper almost making me lose control of the car. "I told you, you can't out run me. Yumm, the smell of fear running through your veins. You're a tease, my little pet. I can't wait to enjoy my next meal."

"No!" I scream as I swerve when the truck is about to ram my car again- to the left, then the right again. Trying to make it hard for him to hit me. About three miles ahead of me, a small gas station comes into view. I keep swerving back and forth making it hard for the truck to hit me. If I can just make it to that gas station I might have a chance at surviving. The check engine light comes on my dashboard. "No, no, not now! Please not now!" I scream at my car as I slam my fist against the steering wheel.

"I don't know how much longer your little vehicle will last." He chuckles. "Then what are you going to do?"

"How do you know?" I say towards the radio. My heart beats frantically against my chest, threatening to break through my rib cage.

He chews on something as he speaks through my speakers, "Like I said, this is my highway and I know and see everything. And when I want to eat and drink something living and breathing, I'll do it. And that something is you."

He manages to ram my car, the bumper dragging on the cement road behind me, causing sparks to fly around the car. One mile until I reach the small gas station. *Just one mile, I can make it. I know I can. So close!! Yet so far. Too far. God, help me*

The truck speeds up just when I swerve to the left-hand side of the road in oncoming traffic. Thankfully, there's no one coming. He pulls up beside to my car and we drive next to each other- he is toying with me. Waiting to see my next move. He swerves to the left to ram me on the passenger side.

I squeal as he manages to make me lose control and I swerve to the left, in the shoulder, the bumper on my car dragging along the dirt. I pull back on the road just when he rams me again. "Please stop!" I cry frightened, my cries making him laugh. He's feeding off of my screams and fears. I slam on my brakes just when he is about to ram me from the side again. I'm now behind him and just a few more feet to go to reach the gas station. I quickly swerve the car to the right and drive right into the gas station's parking lot, barely missing the gas pumps.

The car comes to a stop next to one of two gas pumps. Dirt flies everywhere, causing a cloud of dust to block my view of the truck. I breathe in and out but I can't seem to get enough air into my lungs. Starved for air, my heart is racing at a tremendous speed. Once the dust settles, I quickly jump out of the car. I don't see the truck anywhere, he must have kept going. I reach back in and grab my wallet off of the floor, not bothering to clean up the mess of makeup and nail polish that is scattered all over the passenger seat and the floor mat, my pink nail polish bottle broken open from all the bouncing around I was doing- pink contents leaving a trail all over the mat.

With shaky hands, I go to swipe my Visa card in the card reader- but nothing happens. I try two more times when I finally give up and run inside of the store. I throw my debit card along the counter, "I need twenty dollars on pump one, please!" I rush out, my words stumbling over each other. Twenty dollars should be enough. I'm not far from salvation, just a little more.

The lady behind the register cocks her head to the side and eyes my body up and down. Her big green eyes grow wide as she stares at me in disgust. I look down at myself, seeing perspiration soaking through my shirt staining underneath my arms, my chest and my back. My hair sticks to my neck and the side of my face. I must look like I haven't had a shower in days. I must smell just as bad as a dead animal my face is flushed, "Please?" I ask nicely.

Her nose wrinkles in disgust, "Ahhh yeah,sure." She swipes my card through the ATM machine. As she hands it to me she tells me, "We do sell soap if you're interested." She points with the end of my debit card towards an aisle on the far left. My face follows her hand in that direction and for one split second I would love nothing more than to grab a bar of soap and wash myself and change my clothes.

I bite my tongue, ignoring her rude comment. After all, if I saw someone who looked as horrible as I do come barging into my store I would probably say the same thing. I would probably think she is a crazy alcoholic drug user or something. I snatch the card from her and run out of the door. I can care less about my appearance- my life is more important right now. Pulling the handle of the gas pump out, I shove it in the gas tank. It starts pumping as soon as I hit the cheapest price option. I watch impatiently around me, waiting for the man in the hoodie to jump out and snatch me. After all, I am practically alone here. I doubt that would stop him from killing me or the clerk. Should I warn her about the man on the radio? Or will I sound insane? The right thing to do is tell her about him. I know I should, but I can't seem to push myself to go back in there. I just want to leave this place and never come back. Ever!

The gas pump clicks as it finishes pumping the last drop of gas in the car. I shove the handle back into its rightful place then jump in the car. The car struggles to turn on but finally it does. I speed off towards the highway not caring about my speed or the fact my car is hanging on by a very thin thread. The engine light is still on, my bumper is smashed to pieces and hanging on to the back of the car by a small metal piece. And now the engine is making a loud clicking noise- it does not sound good. I don't know if this car can make it another two miles, let alone another hour until the Oregon state border.

If I make it out of here alive I have no clue how I'm going to give this car back to the rental company. They would probably make me pay for all the damages, or worse- make the company I work for pay for all the damages. God, I hope I don't get fired. How do I explain this whole big ordeal to them? Will they believe me or send me to a mental hospital for evaluation? After all, how do I explain that I've been followed since Nevada, hunted by some guy? No, creature- who says he is going to lick and suck out my blood from my bones? How do I explain his truck is beyond fast and somehow, he always ends up finding me no matter how far I get? He knows exactly where I am and he knows exactly what's going on with my car and me. How do I explain he can interrupt my phone call with the police and he can even talk to me through my radio? Or he can even hear me talk to him as well? Hell, I'm living through it and I don't believe it. My car is completely damaged and I still don't believe it.

I don't know what I'm going to do if I make it out of here alive. All I know is I'll be thankful that I did and I will never take another back road again. From now on I vow to stick to freeways that are surrounded by houses and businesses. My hands grip the steering wheel- my heart is beating fast. Too fast, I may just have a heart attack.

One hour later and there's still no sign of the black truck. He hasn't tried speaking to me either. For that I'm thankful- his voice is creepy. I've never heard anything like it before. His voice crackles when he talks, and is loud and petrifying. Maybe he decided to leave me alone? Sadly, maybe he found another poor soul to hunt. Is it wrong of me to wish that that is what has indeed happened and he'd leave me alone? I wipe the sweat off my forehead. *God, that's sad that I would wish this nightmare on someone else. What kind of person am I? I'm a horrible one, is what I am. I'm a monster too.*

"Oh, my pet, you thought you could get away from me, but you were wrong. You know I'm always near. You can feel my eyes on you as you walk. You can feel my need for you, my want."

How does he know? How does he know where I'll be at? How does he know what I'm thinking? He is always a step ahead of me. A step ahead of my every move, my every thought.

"I can feel your heart race every time you look around for me. I can feel your blood start to race. You sense me just as much as I sense you."

I reach behind me with one arm on the steering wheel and the other feels for the jack handle I know I threw back here. Once I find it, I'll use it as a weapon. Anything is better than nothing. I wish I carried a gun in my purse the way many other men and women do- if only. But for now, the jack handle will have to do. I come across it on the floor in the back, wedged in between the seat and the cup holder. I pull and pull until it finally comes loose. I lay it on my lap and keep driving.

Chapter 5
And the great dragon was cast out,
that old serpent, called the Devil, and Satan which
deceiveth the whole world
-Revelation 12:9

I pass a green sign saying I'm about forty miles from Oregon. My heart skips a beat, I'm so close to home and I haven't seen the black truck. I just may make it out of this alive!!

"What? Did you think you were safe?"

I don't bother to answer his taunting voice on the radio. He already knows that answer. For a split second, I did think I was safe and home free. I should have known better. I should have known he would be back for me. The black truck speeds up to me going so fast it's not possible. I scream not knowing what to do. I'm going as fast as I can. My foot is pressed as far as it will go on the gas pedal. I'm so close to Oregon I want to cry. I can see my baby's face. I must get home to her. The truck rams me from what's left of the back of the car.

"Ahhh," I scream as my body is jerked forward against the steering wheel with the force of the impact.

There's nowhere for me to go, nowhere for me to hide. My car is too damaged and there's no place around here for me to pull into and hide. I'm live bait. He rams me from behind again making me lose control, making the car swerve from side to side. "Leave me alone! Leave me alone!" I scream out loud.

The radio crackles to life and his horrifying crackled voice laughs. Slow and soft at first, then louder and deeper. Then he rams me hard with such force I lose full control over the small car. I twist and turn, then the car rolls and rolls. I'm sure my screams can be heard for miles. I hold onto the steering wheel for dear life as I'm flipping upside down then right side up. Everything in the car flies around me. The car finally comes to a stop upside down. I'm dangling there, the only thing keeping me in place is the seatbelt that protected me from crashing around in the car. My head hurts so bad I can barely open my eyes. Blood trickles down my temple. I lay my hand against the top of my head. Blood soaks through, slipping between my fingers. My face stings and throbs.

"Ahhhh," I cry when I unbuckle my seat belt. I fall upside down in the front seat." Ouch," I lay at a very uncomfortable angle. I quickly start to crawl out of the car, my hands and knees scratching against the broken glass. The sun shines directly on me, burning my skin. I quickly stand up on wobbly legs. My head spins, causing me to have trouble looking around. The black truck waits several feet behind the car. He stands outside of the vehicle with his hands inside of his hoodie pocket. "Oh, my god!" I cry as I try to run away, but my head is spinning so bad I can't see straight. I put my hand to my head.

He slowly starts walking towards me. Every step I take is equivalent to three of his. I'm so frightened that these might be the last seconds of my life. My knees and palms burn as shattered glass pricks and pokes through my skin. I'm so close to the Oregon border. So close. I start running but it's more of a fast walk. I can hear him behind me. "Help!" I scream as loud as I can. My voice echoes through the desert. "Please someone help me! Please." I cry.

A dark green sign with white letters reads: "Welcome to Oregon." The world around me spins and spins- causing me to stumble and fall. I immediately get to my feet but the pain in my head flashes hard and hot causing my eyes to lose focus. Black flashes across my vision. I reach my hand out towards the sign but fall short just inches from it. My body slams against the hard, hot dirt. The cuts on my palms and knees burn with fury.

Through my hooded eyes, I can see his big black boots come towards me. I start to crawl back trying to get away from him, but it's no use. He reaches me. "I told you I would find you, my pet." I slowly make my way up his body, starting with his black scuffed up boots, his blood stained blue jeans, to his black hoodie that looks wet in certain spots. My heart is beating so fast I can hear it go thump, thump, thump. My teeth clatter against each other. I lay my eyes on his face which is still covered by the black hood. "What do you want?" I cry, crawling behind me on my cut palms. Pain shoots up and down my arms, making me groan. "Why me?" My head pounds against my skull.

"Because your blood is so sweet," he says as he takes out his hands from the front pocket of his hoodie. My eyes go down from his face to the pocket. His hands are wrinkled like an older working man, the nails long and razor sharp. There's blood caked underneath them.

He brings his sharp fingertip to my chin, forcing me to raise my head to meet his face. He smears someone else's cold wet blood along my chin. "Before I kill you, my pet, I want you to see why I hide behind this dark hood. Why I am so very hungry for your blood." He keeps his one finger on my chin, while his other hand starts to uncover his face.

My heart hitches in my throat as he reveals himself to me. His face is as white as a ghost and just as wrinkled as his hands. His eyes are as red as the Devil's and slanted like an oval, making him look evil and unreal. Like some horrible creature out of a bad dream. "What do you think I am?"

"The Devil," I cry as I stare at his face in disbelief.

His lips smirk with my answer, "Maybe I am. Maybe I'm not. But I'm from Hell and I am living in Hell every day that I'm here." He slowly circles me like a lion would circle his prey before a meal. He keeps his finger on my chin the whole time. "Your blood runs thick through your veins." He drags the tip of his fingernail across my neck. Blood oozes out of the gaping hole. He swipes his finger across my warm blood.

He comes back around in front of me, sticking his bloody finger into his mouth and sucking it dry. With his eyes closed he throws his head back and savors the taste of my blood on his cracked lips. He snaps his head back toward me revealing the hunger in his dark, cold evil eyes. Something that only Hell can create; a demon from the darkest depths of Hell. "Oh my God." I whisper knowing what's coming. Knowing no one can save me. No one can hear my cries.

"God can't help you." His mouth opens wide. So, wide it can fit my whole head into his filthy foulness. His brown rotten teeth slowly drop down from his gums revealing long sharp fangs. I watch as some poor soul's blood drips from the tip of them, dropping to the tip of his tongue. I close my eyes as he draws closer to my face. I picture my sweet baby girl's beautiful smile. The last thing I remember is my strangled cry- a cry so loud that even the animals run scared. A scream of one in mortal terror. One that knows real pain. One that knows her life has come to a fatal and horrible end.

The End

Other HellBound Books
For You To Enjoy

**All available now in paperback and eBook
from Amazon, iBooks, Barnes & Noble, Kobo etc.
For full details, visit our official website
www.hellboundbookspublishing.com**

**Or
Download our App from iTunes / Google Play
– or scan the QR Code below**

The Big Book of Bootleg Horror

Twenty tales of terror, darkness, the truly macabre and things most unpleasant from a delectably eclectic bunch of the very best independent horror authors on the scene today:

S.E. Rise, Kevin Wetmore, Paul Stansfield, Craig Stwewart, Shaun Avery, Jeff Myers, Marc DeWit, Timothy Wilkie, Quinn Cunningham, Melanie Waghorne, Marc E. Fitch, Stanley B. Webb, Tim J. Finn, Ken Goldman, Ralph Greco Jr, Roger Leatherwood, Vincent Treewell, David Owain Hughes, J.J. Smith and the inimitable James H. Longmore

In this superlative tome, HellBound Books have embraced the taboo, gone all-out to horrify and have broken the flimsy boundaries of good taste to make The Big Book of Bootleg Horror the perfect anthology for those who take their horror like we take our coffee - insidiously dark and most definitely unsweetened

Depraved Desires

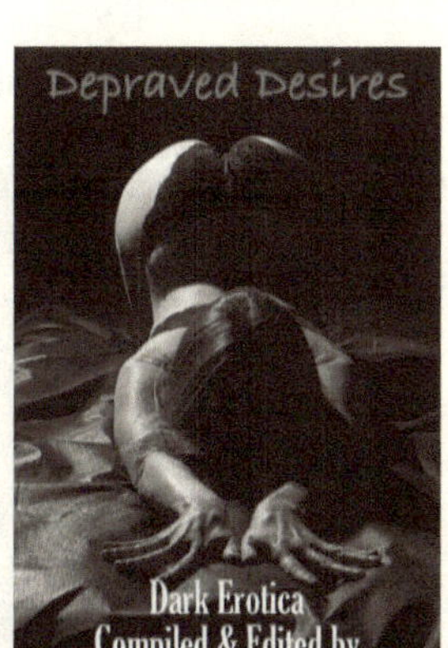

A mind-blowing collection of the very darkest erotica from the very best minds in the business!

Desires - we all have them, even if we won't admit it. Some are considered normal, and probably healthy. But what about the others?

Those haunting stirrings within that rail against societal norms and the bounds of decency?

Depraved Desires delves into the writhing depths of carnal appetites and sin, peeling back the veneer to reveal tales of wanton lust and supernatural depravity...

The terrifying prospect of knife play; a cosmic liaison; a

classy party that turned out to be more than a hired call girl ever expected; or when a sinister fantasy becomes reality - all will shock you.

Whether your desires drive you mad or your madness drives your desires, delving within these pages will take you to places where those itches live, the ones that demand to be scratched.

Sángre: The Color of Dying
By
Carlos Colón

Carlos Colón's first published novel is this story of Nicky Negrón, a Puerto Rican salesman in New York City who is turned into foul-mouthed, urban vampire with a taste for the undesirables of society such as sexual predators, domestic abusers and drug dealers.

A tragic anti-hero, Nicky is haunted by profound loss. When his life is cut short due to an unforeseen event at the Ritz-Carlton, it results in a public sex scandal for his surviving family. He then rises from the dead to become a night stalker with a genetic resistance that enables him to retain his humanity, still valuing his family whilst also struggling to somehow maintain a sense of normalcy.

Simultaneously described as haunting, hilarious, horrifying and heartbreaking, Sángre: The Color of Dying is a breathtakingly fun read.

Nightly Visits
By
Stephen Helmes

When you close your eyes, where do you go? What do you see? The moment you drift off into that world of the unknown, you are on a rollercoaster ride, speeding down a track that takes you anywhere it wants to take you.

Often it takes us to places that we would never voluntarily go when we're awake, into a world of darkness, tragedy, and fear. In this virtual reality world, you do things that you would never do when you're awake, such as jumping from a plane without a chute, or opening the door to a room when you know there is something behind it waiting for you to enter.

But dreams can also tell you stories of love, wit, and treasures. You may wake laughing, crying, or screaming, because your dreams know your weaknesses. They know your every thought, and they know how to attack.

That's not what Nightly Visits is *about*. THAT'S WHAT *NIGHTLY VISITS* IS!

**A HellBound Books LLC
Publication**

www.hellboundbookspublishing.com

Printed in the United States of America

www.ingramcontent.com/pod-product-compliance
Lightning Source LLC
Chambersburg PA
CBHW030645120726
47905CB00001B/65